A WORLD OF HER OWN CREATION...

RENEE DUBOIS—She rose from the poverty of a small French farm to dazzle the golden salons of Paris with couture fashion that would become known throughout the world. But she'd never escape the torment of one woman's vengeance or the memory of one man's love.

VIRGENIE RUILLE—The aristocratic *grande dame* of Parisian society who destroyed her own son rather than allow him to marry Renee Dubois—she devoted the rest of her life to trying to ruin Renee, her family, and her business empire.

GASTON—Renee's handsome and ambitious son was adored by his mother and by every woman he encountered. Determined to equal Renee's success, he blazed new trails in American fashion—but New York and Hollywood almost destroyed him.

JULIETTE—Renee's beautiful golden-haired love child—she idealized the man she believed to be her father, and never stopped looking for a man who would equal him.

GRANT MORGAN—Renee Dubois was the love of his life, but pride and ambition tore them apart ... until he saw his giant Hollywood success was all an empty dream without Renee at his side.

Other Avon Books by
Catherine Lanigan

ADMIT DESIRE
BOUND BY LOVE

and writing as Joan Wilder

THE JEWEL OF THE NILE
ROMANCING THE STONE

Avon Books are available at special quantity discounts for bulk purchases for sales promotions, premiums, fund raising or educational use. Special books, or book excerpts, can also be created to fit specific needs.

For details write or telephone the office of the Director of Special Markets, Avon Books, Dept. FP, 1790 Broadway, New York, New York 10019, 212-399-1357.

SINS OF OMISSION

CATHERINE LANIGAN

AVON
PUBLISHERS OF BARD, CAMELOT, DISCUS AND FLARE BOOKS

SINS OF OMISSION is an original publication of Avon Books. This work has never before appeared in book form.

AVON BOOKS
A division of
The Hearst Corporation
1790 Broadway
New York, New York 10019

Copyright © 1986 by Catherine Lanigan
Published by arrangement with the author
Library of Congress Catalog Card Number: 86-90799
ISBN: 0-380-89582-X

All rights reserved, which includes the right to reproduce this book or portions thereof in any form whatsoever except as provided by the U.S. Copyright Law. For information address The Robbins Office, Inc., 2 Dag Hammarskjold Plaza, Suite 403, New York, New York 10017.

First Avon Printing: October 1986

AVON TRADEMARK REG. U. S. PAT. OFF. AND IN OTHER COUNTRIES. MARCA REGISTRADA. HECHO EN U.S.A.

Printed in the U.S.A.

K-R 10 9 8 7 6 5 4 3 2 1

For their faith, courage and strength;
For being the bond that holds our family;
This book is dedicated to the three
generations of Lanigan women.

First generation: Dorothy Lanigan

Second generation: Nancy Jean Lanigan
Mary Vail Lanigan
Deborah Hayes Lanigan

Third generation: Karen Lanigan
Elizabeth Lanigan
Elaine Dorothy Lanigan
Meghan Lanigan

SINS OF OMISSION

Prologue

New York
1972

Lacy epaulets of snow capped the grand shoulders of St. Patrick's Cathedral as the Yuletide congregation streamed in. The thundering applause to the Rockettes' rendition of "The March of the Wooden Soldiers" at Radio City Music Hall could be heard by those outside. None of the holiday crowd admiring the mammoth lighted tree in the middle of Rockefeller Center noticed the screaming siren or flashing lights coming from the speeding ambulance as it darted and twisted its way through traffic down Fifth Avenue. The motorized dolls and puppets that filled the windows of B. Altman's stared blankly at the ambulance as it sped past Thirty-fourth Street, careened around a corner, skidded on a patch of ice, and braked to a stop at the emergency room doors of New York University Hospital.

Two blasts on the horn summoned a nurse and two orderlies who hussled into the frosty night with a gurney. A tall paramedic jumped from the back of the ambulance holding an IV bag as the patient was moved onto the gurney and rushed inside.

Christmas Eve in emergency saw only a skeleton staff of nurses, orderlies, and one intern. Alec Grantham, an aging orderly, peered down at the woman's bloodied face as he and his young counterpart, John, lifted her onto the examining table. She winced and rolled her head to one side as if to avoid the painfully bright fluorescent lights. She moaned again, then gasped for air and began choking.

Rapidly, Alec and John stripped away the woman's clothing. "Nice threads . . . expensive," Alec said as he quickly discarded them in a bloody heap.

The woman's chest was badly bruised and her lungs gave every sign they were filling with fluid.

Nurse Anderson stepped in front of John and took the woman's blood pressure and pulse while Alec covered the patient with a clean sheet.

"BP is 80 over 60. Pulse is 140," she said aloud as Alec quickly jotted the numbers down on the chart. "Pupils dilated. Patient appears shocky. Get blankets!" she shouted to John.

Suddenly, the woman's gasps became shorter and more rapid. Nurse Anderson did not think the larynx was crushed, which would require a tracheotomy. The throat was extremely bruised. She could not be certain of anything more than the fact that the bronchial tubes were closing.

"I'll go for Doctor Nelson. It looks as if we'll have to intubate her."

Alec arranged the equipment and intubator the doctor would need and then stared down at the woman gasping for air.

"She doesn't look too good to me." He glanced at John. "Five to one says she doesn't make it."

"You're on," John said.

The intern was jerked away by a frantic Nurse Anderson.

"Doctor Nelson, please wake up!" She shook his shoulder again. "You're needed in ER Four immediately!"

Groggily he focused on her and then looked at his watch. Ten-forty. "Shit. I've only slept two hours! I've been on call for a fucking thirty-nine hours! Get someone else!" He rolled over with his face to the wall and yanked the wool blanket over his head.

"Brandon is at Christmas Mass and won't be back for over an hour yet, and Hurvitz skipped on me. You're all I've got." She poked him in the back with a stethoscope. "It's a Jane Doe and she may need a trach."

Angrily, he threw off the blanket, stood quickly, and tightened the drawstring on his surgical greens. He splashed cold water on his face, roughly dried it, and stalked out of the room.

Alec was securing the gurney straps when Dr. Nelson dashed into the room. The woman was thrashing about as she choked and gasped. Alec thrust the intubator tube at Dr. Nelson, who immediately went to work on the woman. Nurse Anderson brought a tray of sterilized instruments, cleaning solutions, gauze, and dressings. Nelson ordered Alec to hold the patient's head while he inserted the tube.

Slowly, the woman's breathing normalized. A relieved smile flickered momentarily in Dr. Nelson's eyes before he began a careful scrutiny of the other injuries. "Internal damage does not seem severe but X ray will tell us more," he mumbled as he continued with his probing.

Nurse Anderson began cleaning the facial wounds. Both eyes were badly bruised and the mouth was swollen on the bottom and sides, giving her an eerie waxen smile. Dr. Nelson sutured a long gash that ran from the jawline to her earlobe.

"Seems the lady is no stranger to plastic surgery," Dr. Nelson said and pointed out a thin silver crescent of scar tissue behind each ear.

While Dr. Nelson was completing his examination and ordering X rays, an obese, middle-aged policeman lumbered into the room. He was not one of New York's modern fleet of cops who looked more like addicts, pimps, and murderers than the criminals themselves. He was as antiquated as the Hollywood ideal of the Irish beat cop who patrolled with a smile and a wooden stick, never a gun. He removed his cap with a childlike sense of respect and hugged it to his enormous belly. He positioned himself in a corner lest he disturb the sanctity of the medical domain.

Nelson glanced toward the policeman. "Have we found any identification yet? I'd like to notify the family."

The patrolman stepped a foot closer and spoke in a gruff whisper. "I was on the scene, Doc, and I was hoping you'd be able to tell me who she is." He glanced at the woman and realized she was still unconscious. "I guess not."

Dr. Nelson finished the stitches and crossed over to where the patrolman was standing. "Officer . . ."

"Burns."

"Officer Burns, all I can tell you is that the woman is five feet eight inches tall, weighs about one hundred thirty pounds, and is in excellent physical condition. I would guess she's over fifty, but anything else would be conjecture."

"I have a little to add to that," Burns said. "We found the car was registered to Maeve Dunning, the Broadway actress, but she's in Connecticut for the holidays and we can't reach her. We'll keep trying."

"Any idea what caused the accident?" Nelson asked.

"Witnesses said it was a hit-and-run. I would guess a Christmas drunk behind the wheel."

Nelson nodded. "That would be the fifth tonight. It's not surprising."

Burns looked over at the woman. "She gonna make it?"

Nelson's bushy eyebrows crinkled, shadowing his blue eyes. "I don't know. I wish to hell I knew who she was. I have this feeling that someone like her won't be missed for long."

The next morning brought little new information. Found in the car were a full-length Russian sable coat, a maroon alligator bag with designer insignia, and a white silk scarf. The lady had excellent taste in clothes, celebrity friends, and no identification.

At the nurses' station, Patrolman Burns questioned Nurse Anderson, who shed no light on the mystery, but who did allow him to examine the woman's jewelry. Included in the group were a gold Florentine wedding band, amethyst earrings—at least two carats each—and a plain but unusual signet ring. "Something about the ring and the woman are familiar," he mumbled as he handed the jewelry back to Nurse Anderson. He then asked for Dr. Nelson so he could get clearance to question the lady, but he hadn't arrived yet. Burns decided to wait in the staff lounge, which was empty.

He poured himself a cup of coffee and turned on the television to the local news.

"That's it from here, Dan," the interviewer said and the scene switched back to the station.

"There you have it. If anyone has seen Renée Dubois please contact this station. The numbers are flashing on the bottom of the screen." A black and white photograph of an astonishingly beautiful woman remained on the set for a full ten seconds before a commercial came on.

Burns's mind raced ahead of itself puzzling the pieces together and it all fit: the celebrity friends, the expensive clothes; the signet ring, he remembered, was the Maison Dubois logo. In the past year alone, Renée Dubois had been on the cover of *Vogue*, *Newsweek*, *Town and Country*, and *Forbes*. For over thirty years her name had been linked with some of the most influential and wealthy men in the world, from Aly Khan and Cary Grant to Aristotle Onassis. In the midfifties, photos in *Life* and *Paris Match* of Renée sunning herself nude on the Riviera had shocked the world. The battle still raged over the identity of the man in the photos with her. Some claimed it was Jack Kennedy; others said it was Grant Morgan, the film producer. Renée Dubois was undoubtedly the most famous designer France had given the world. She and her son and daughter had kept the paparazzi globe-hopping for years. Their lives, loves, and careers were constantly under public scrutiny.

The *Today* show had recently interviewed via satellite the second generation of Dubois: Gaston, Juliette, and Désirée, a trio of financially successful trendsetters.

Gaston was the founder of a network of glittering boutiques located on both the West and East coasts and for years he'd been dubbed "dressmaker to the stars." After twenty years there were still double-entendre jokes about Gaston insinuating he spent more time undressing the stars than he did dressing them.

Juliette was the darling of the French modeling industry and the "ugly duckling" story of her life continued to win her new fans despite the scandals in her love life.

Finally, there was Désirée, the niece who reportedly bungled a million-dollar deal and was booted out of the business by Renée herself. The young lady was very bitter; so much so that she made disparaging comments to Barbara Walters about her aunt's questionable worthiness in receiving the STYLE award, more coveted than the Coty.

Burns remembered reading in the newspapers that Dubois was to receive the STYLE award tomorrow in Paris, so what, he wondered, was she doing in New York?

Twenty-three years on the force had taught Burns to be wary of celebrities. They were always trouble. Half of them craved publicity and then raised hell when they didn't get it; the other half sued the city when they did. Taken as a group, he wanted nothing to do with them. As he rose and headed down the corridor toward Renée Dubois's room, he could only consider it his very bad luck to be assigned her case.

Book One

The Twenties

Chapter One

Paris
1928

That August, Paris experienced the most intense heat wave in ten years. The heat rose from the cobblestone streets like swaying banshees and drove Parisians to more tolerable climates. The city's pace was lethargic. Nowhere could escape from the heat be found.

As if to defy nature, Renée Dubois wore a fiery russet linen chemise as she walked past Hermès on the rue du Faubourg-St.-Honoré. Just four doors east was Lanvin and a few steps away on the rue Cambon was Chanel.

Along this corridor, discriminating women from the world over flocked to purchase the finest fashions. Paris couture was the epitome, the pinnacle. It was the end of the rainbow.

Renée had dreamed all her life of being one of the Paris fashion dictators. As a child growing up in Lyon, Renée assisted her mother, Hélène, a *petite couturière*. Hélène had worked at home, sometimes until late into the night, her expert fingers stitching delicate silks for the wealthy women of Lyon. Hélène copied patterns from fashion magazines, for she readily admitted she had no designing talent. But when Renée, at the age of six, showed interest in making clothes from her own sketches, Hélène encouraged her daughter to experiment. "You will never know unless you try," she told Renée.

Renée learned everything she knew about fashion from her mother. The "lay of the cloth" as it rolled from the bolt; the skill to cut the most temperamental panné velvet; beadwork; appliqué; how to balance a hem and set a sleeve. Hélène was a strict taskmaster, for if every stitch was not precise, she would make Renée rip out the seam and do it again. By the time Renée was thirteen, she was as skilled a seamstress as any in Paris.

The Duboises were not poor, but it took every centime Antoine earned as a dyer at the silk manufacturing plant plus Hélène's income to keep the family going. Renée loved her parents and appreciated everything they did for her. Somehow, she knew that someday she would be rich and famous and give them everything they deserved. She wanted to see her mother dressed in the kind of fabulous clothes Hélène made for her clients. She wanted to give her father a life free from long hours and worry over bills. She wanted to send them on an ocean cruise—to America, perhaps. She wanted the best for them.

With her arms crossed beneath her head, she would lie in bed, staring at the pink painted ceiling of the room she shared with her younger brother, Pierre—and soon a new brother or sister. The moonlight would turn the pink into a warm glow and she would dream of her shop—the only thing that would insure happiness for her family.

Today, as she peered through the sparkling glass window at Lanvin, her competitor, she knew her girlhood dream was a reality. But sometimes she wondered if her dream had not cost her more than she should have been willing to pay.

Six months ago, Maison Dubois opened its doors to songs of praise and congratulatory wishes from her friends, her brother, and aunt. But the whispers of outrage from the more venerable fashion and social circles had distorted the earlier melody. Those who had known Renée these past four years she'd been in Paris, felt she was far too young and inexperienced to take on such pressures. Often, she'd listened patiently while her friends droned on about the risk she was taking and how she'd be better off saving her money.

"You're a beautiful young woman," they would say. "All that chestnut hair, those high cheekbones and huge violet eyes. You should use what God gave you—make some man happy."

She could see their ruby lips clamp down on ivory cigarette

holders as they continued their crusade. "Honestly, Renée, enterprise is perilously difficult for a woman. Why are you so opposed to an easier life?"

Renée waved an indifferent hand. She was only twenty but most of them thought her much older. She had lied about many things in her quest for her shop. She'd told them she'd graduated from high school, that she'd had formal couture training, and that she was not at all worried about the fate of her shop. Her lies had been necessary for survival.

Renée turned away from Lanvin's and, with a more determined pace, headed for Maison Dubois. She pulled the narrow brim of her cloche hat over her eyes ostensibly to shield them from the morning sun. She hoped no one could see the doubts that surely shone there.

Renée had always believed her best defense was an attack. She'd heard others say she was "determined" and "courageous." Renée wasn't so sure. She sometimes thought she was more frightened than anything else. She knew what she wanted and she felt she couldn't pass up any chances to attain it. She could only hope her decisions were the right ones.

She knew her designs were not revolutionary like Chanel's nor did she have the flamboyance of Schiaparelli. And she knew she had embarked on a venture that from all aspects was destined to fail.

But Renée believed in herself. She had to, for no one else did.

Often, her mother had told her that God had given her a sense of style, and that it was a talent to be used and developed like that of any artist. Today, Renée could spot fashion trends before the *grande couturières* had breathed life into their sketches. She had succeeded in putting her talent to good use.

In the 1928 fall collection, Chanel had presented a black fringed dress, a red chenille dress, and a beige crepe de chine that stopped all of Paris dead in their tracks. Two weeks before the showing, Renée filled her display cases with exquisite accessories to match. In less than a month, they'd sold out completely. It was enough to convince Renée that she'd been right to limit her line to accessories. She was still too inexperienced to pit herself against the couturiers. Later, when she was more sure of herself she would expand into clothing.

Renée knew that not everyone in Paris could afford couture

clothes, but even a shop girl could splurge once or twice a year on a Renée handbag or an extravagant article of lingerie. The prices for her accessories were far from inexpensive, but her quality was superior to anything on the Continent. Her customers ranged from the wives of American investors and millionaires to duchesses and maharanis and mistresses of dukes and kings to secretaries and actresses. Renée was the only designer to put her label, a discreet monogram, on the outside of the article, usually in a concealed place.

Renée had worked hard to achieve the small measure of success she enjoyed but this was only the beginning—and a precarious one at that. For the first months after the opening, sales were brisk, but this was August and half her clientele was in Cap d'Antibes, Nice, and Cannes, not placing orders for her merchandise.

As she approached the shop, she tried to find her smile, the one that masked her fears and inspired confidence in her employees. They all looked to her as their leader, their rock. Little did they know she often felt as if she were sinking.

"Good morning," Renée said to her head *vendeuse*, Marie.

"Good morning, Mademoiselle," she replied cheerfully.

"Is Monsieur Larousse in yet?"

"Yes, he is. He's in your office. Mademoiselle, the shipment of silk just arrived from Lyon. The men are unloading it in the workrooms now. Here's the invoice. Monsieur Moreau telephoned to say that the trims and laces Monsieur Larousse ordered will be delivered tomorrow but only if he has payment in full. In the mail was the notice that the beadings and sequins won't be here until next week. That, too, is cash on delivery. I told Monsieur Moreau you would return his call."

Renée's eyes filled with distress. "Thank you, Marie."

"Is there something wrong?"

Renée shook her head. "Nothing that robbing a bank wouldn't cure." She chuckled nervously. "I'll take care of it, Marie."

"Yes, Mademoiselle." Marie went back to her station.

Renée glanced around the showroom making certain everything was in readiness for the day's business. Three enormous chandeliers of long crystal cylinders bathed the room in light and the plum velvet-lined display cases were illuminated, displaying hand-beaded scarves, shawls, and evening bags; there were leather purses, belts, and gloves. The mirrored walls had been cleaned recently and the brass cornices polished to a high gleam. As she walked to the back of the shop the gray wool carpeting changed to a soft salmon color, the mirrors disappeared and were replaced by salmon suede-covered walls. The lighting was more subtle and the Louis XVI chairs and settees in the fitting rooms were upholstered in pale blue watered silk. Here the patrons were fitted for the most luxurious lingerie in Paris.

Before she turned down the corridor that led to her office she was stopped by Angélique, the head fitter. Angélique was over fifty and had lived in the world of couture since she was ten. Years of bending and crouching on the floor to mark hems, align sleeves, and place darts had caused her shoulders to hunch and her head to cock curiously to one side. Her gray hair, usually in a neat knot on top of her head, had come partially undone. Gray wires of long hair hung down her neck.

"Mademoiselle, do you know if the Countess d'Itagnio is expected today? I must finish these alterations . . ."

Renée immediately brightened at the mention of the countess. "Not yet. Let me speak with Jean first."

As Renée headed to her office she mumbled: "Thank God for the countess!" Renée hoped the fee from the countess would save her shop.

She opened the door to her office and found Jean Larousse sitting at her desk, his feet propped on a low bookshelf to his right with his sketch pad in his lap.

She walked over to him and put her hand on his shoulder.

"I didn't hear you come in," he said without looking up.

She looked at his disheveled hair and rumpled clothing. "You were here all night?"

He made a few more strokes on the sketch. "I know how important this gown is to you." Finally he looked up at her with soft brown eyes. "How could I disappoint my best friend?"

She smiled. "You never could."

Jean Larousse had been with Renée since her darkest days in Paris and every day she prayed he would never leave her. Not only was he an accomplished artist, though he'd never sold much of anything, but he was an excellent designer and together they were artistically attuned. His ambition was nearly as strong as hers. When the pressure was the greatest and the hours the longest, he pulled from an inner reserve and pushed them both to their mutual goals.

"Perhaps if I cut the neckline a bit lower," he said impishly, drawing extra cleavage into the sketch.

Renée tousled his soft brown hair. "Honestly, Jean. Pay attention to the gown!"

"But what's in the gown is far more fascinating."

More than any man she'd ever met, Jean categorically loved women. Women were his business, his religion, his life. He adored everything about them.

He held the pad up in the air, turning it this way and that in the morning light. "I think it's grand, don't you?" She snatched the drawing out of his hands, scrutinizing every line. "Jean, you've outdone yourself on this one. The countess will be pleased."

"It's been a bitch working for her."

Renée smiled. "You mean she has challenged you more than anyone else. It isn't every day of the week that we are commissioned to design an entire trousseau of lingerie for one of the most influential women in Paris."

Renée gazed at the sketch again. The countess *had* been a bitch about this negligee, but then it was the one she was to wear on her wedding night. She had refused five designs and had nearly driven them all crazy with her demands. The rest of the trousseau she had accepted instantly. The list was endless. There was the apricot crepe de chine peignoir with cream ostrich-feather trim; the geranium silk teddy with hand-embroidered straps and beaded scalloped hem; and a fuchsia satin nightgown and peignoir to match with a two-carat diamond fastener, especially designed by Cartier for the countess.

There were twenty-four negligees and peignoirs, thirteen teddies in assorted silks and satins; six half slips, six full slips; one dozen pairs of pajamas all in satin but assorted colors; one hand-made lace dressing gown in white (at a cost of ten thousand francs); twenty-four pairs of panties, each with lace trim and monogram; a dozen corselettes and *soutiens-gorge* to match the panties. Lastly, there were three dozen pairs of silk stockings.

The countess was marrying a wealthy American industrialist and since this was her third and, she declared, her *last* marriage, she was pulling out all the stops. Maison Dubois was the only shop in Paris at full throttle. Some of Renée's seamstresses had been working fourteen- to sixteen-hour days. Jean had been equal to the challenges the countess had given him, except for this most important gown.

Jean had been trying to bestow a virginal quality on the white satin negligee and each time the countess had rejected it. She said she wanted "something Victorian, gay, romantic, and innocent." When Jean's dilemma finally came to Renée's attention she realized that what the countess thought she wanted and what she truly wanted were two different things.

Renée suggested that this time Jean design something scandalously low cut in front and back. Jean took Renée's suggestion a bit further and in the back where the V of the gown would show the crack in the countess's derrière, he placed a four-carat "faux" square-cut ruby which was detachable.

"A playful incentive for the groom," he said to Renée, who laughed mischievously.

"I want to get her in here today to see this. If she approves it then I might stand a chance of asking her for another payment."

"It's that bad?"

"All we have is her money to pull us through until September. The wedding is on the twenty-sixth of October and I'm sure every shop in Paris will be inundated with work, fitting the wedding guests. Once all that starts we should have plenty of orders in addition to the normal fall buying. Which reminds me. Check on the delivery of the felt for the cloches. I want those displayed in three weeks. Two if possible."

Jean gave her an exasperated look.

"God," she exclaimed, "whoever invented this idiotic custom of summer holidays?"

"The same wealthy Frenchman who thought of preposterously priced women's clothing." Jean laughed.

The glare she gave him vanished as a smile conquered her face. "You look like you could use a bath and some rest. Why don't you go home while I tend the shop?"

"I think I should be here if the countess comes in. With this design and my charming ways I can talk her into anything. There's nothing I like better than bending a woman to my will," he said, and then looked down at his shirt. "You're right, though, I don't stand a chance looking like this. But before I go, I was wondering if you've thought any more about going to the countess's wedding. If it doesn't turn out to be the most extravagant event of the decade it most certainly is the most publicized. The exposure would be good for business. Besides, the countess is more than just a client to you and you know it."

"I've heard your litany of pros for my attending the wedding for weeks now, Jean, and I still refuse to set foot on the same piece of earth as *that woman!*"

Jean leaned over the desk with his face almost touching Renée's.

"Look, chérie, just because Virginie Ruille is giving the wedding reception doesn't mean you can't go. Stand up to her and show her what you're made of. She can't hurt you anymore. You've accomplished a hell of a lot since the old days. Your relationship with the countess should be proof. I know for a fact that Virginie, in her cold, indomitable manner, let the countess know that she was none too pleased that she hired you; nor did she like the fact that the countess had invited you to the wedding. But the countess is no jellyfish and chose to ignore Virginie's imperial command. You owe her for that."

Renée put up her hands. "All right, you win. If it will stop your badgering me, it will be worth it to go and get it over with so we can all return to normal around here."

Jean kissed her on the forehead and as he started to leave, she spied two-and-a-half-year-old Gaston hiding behind the half-opened door.

Gaston was a bright, energetic child who was almost too beautiful for his own good. Many times strangers had stopped Renée on the streets or in the shop to comment on her son's good looks. Physically, he looked like a Pre-Raphaelite cherub unless one delved into his eyes. They were of a brown so dark they were almost black and behind them was an inner fire that even at this young age Renée said could frighten her when it surfaced. Gaston needed a great deal of attention, and Renée wondered if she would ever be able to give him all he demanded.

She loved him, sometimes too much, she thought. He was the world to her. She had fought many battles over him and she knew there were more to come. Because she loved him, she kept him close to her, wanting him to share her time at Maison Dubois.

Some of Renée's friends told her she was isolating him too much and that he didn't have enough contact with other chilren.

Renée countered with the fact that when he started school he would be with other children more than with her. She knew she was protective and possibly too possessive, but she didn't care. What was the fun of being a mother if she couldn't be a bit overbearing at times?

For the most part Gaston reveled in his mother's attention, but when she was forced to choose work obligations over time with him, the dark side of his personality rose. Gaston could be very moody and often he was given to fits of temper. But he tried to control his anger because he wanted to please his mother. Most of all, he never wanted her to know he feared losing her love.

Renée beamed and walked over to him. She bent down and peered into Gaston's dark brown eyes. "How long have you been here, you little rascal?"

"Not very." He pouted. "Pierre won't play games with me anymore. He brought me here to stay with you."

Renée gathered him up in her arms. "And was it Uncle Pierre's idea that you come down here or yours?" She smiled at him, already knowing the answer.

"It was mine!" Gaston said, his curly locks bouncing as he clapped his hands together. Then he flung his arms around his mother's neck. "I wanted to be with you."

"I'm glad you're here. Now we can have lunch together!"

"Could we have ice cream too?"

"Certainly."

Just then, Jean cleared his throat and Renée looked up. "I hate to spoil this impromptu luncheon of yours, but you're forgetting your lunch meeting with Madame Paquin. Twice you've had to reschedule. You'll lose a close ally and a friend if you don't make it this time."

Renée's smile vanished upon seeing Gaston's disappointment. She hugged him tightly. "I'm sorry, chéri. I wish I didn't have to go. But Madame Paquin will be very angry with me if I don't see her."

Gaston's eyes were huge hopeful pools. "Tomorrow?"

"Better still, tonight. We'll make our evening together extra special."

Gaston picked up a pencil and began drawing circles on Jean's sketchpad.

"Gaston, I'll make it up to you."

He kept his head down and nodded but he wouldn't answer.

Renée's heart went out to him. She felt just as cheated as he did. It wasn't easy being mother and father, protector and provider. She wished it could be different somehow. But she knew it never would.

Chapter Two

In the decade of the twenties while Paris was giving its splashiest parties, Virginie Ruille established herself as the reigning monarch of Parisian society. It was a position she believed to be hers not only by merit but by birthright.

Virginie's father, Louis de Montespan, was a descendant of the notorious, intelligent, and scheming Marquise de Montespan who bore King Louis XIV eight children but who fell from grace during the "poison scandal" in 1680. Some said it was not the toxic poisons she gave the king that caused her downfall, but the fact that she had a total lack of maternal feeling for her children.

Virginie had heard the story a hundred times before her tenth birthday and to her young mind, her ancestor was a shining example of a stimulating and witty woman who had held on to a king's attention for twelve years. Virginie believed that her ancestor was a victim of the backward minds of the times. She admired women who had the wit to aspire to being something more than a decorous object. Virginie knew that the royal blood in her veins would never allow her to be satisfied with only a role as someone's wife. She was just as ambitious as her father, who had successfully increased the earnings of the family bank—originally won by her grandfather in a card game in 1840—into a profitable concern.

Virginie's mother died when she was only six months old, so her formative years were dominated by her father. On Saturday mornings they would ride in his black lacquered carriage to the bank, where he would teach her about the business. Virginie was a quick and apt pupil. To many a thirteen-year-old, interest rates, amortization, dividend statements, and stocks were like a foreign language. To Virginie, they were music.

Louis de Montespan had given his life to banking and he expected Virginie to do the same. It was a point they agreed on for seventeen years. Not once in all those years did Virginie ever question her father about *his* interpretation of that statement until she met Denis de Vallière.

Denis met Virginie at a family dinner when he was six years old, just prior to his family's move to Ceylon. When they returned twelve years later, Virginie stated she did not remember the initial meeting. Surely, she thought, she would remember feeling these odd sensations whenever she was near Denis.

Virginie did not have many suitors since most of the young men of Paris were put off by her formidable father and, too, Virginie was not considered "pretty," though she was attractive in a haughty way. Virginie learned quickly that Denis responded to the new softness in her emerald eyes and she took special care with her raven dark hair. Small in stature and bone structure, Virginie commissioned the bottier to fashion her boots a full three inches high so that she could look more closely into Denis's eyes. She frequented a frightfully expensive Swiss cosmetician on the rue des Capucines and she slathered her body in scented lotions.

Virginie was not at all surprised when she realized that Denis was falling in love with her. After all, she was a Montespan. For the first time, Virginie doubted, but only momentarily, that money wielded the greatest power.

For months Virginie lived in a romantic world as Denis escorted her to balls and parties. She dreamed of how, when, and where he would propose. Because his family background was similar to hers, she was convinced her father would be overjoyed with the union. She was certain she and Denis would have a lavish wedding and that scores of parties would be given in their honor. It was a bright future she planned.

On a rainy May morning Louis de Montespan looked up from

his three-minute egg nestled in a pink Haviland china cup and said, "I have wonderful news, Virginie."

Brightening and, as always, hanging on his every word, Virginie replied: "I can't imagine what—unless it's the trip to Rome you've been promising."

"Better still. I spoke with Paul Ruille last evening and your marriage to Claude will be announced at a ball in your honor next month."

Virginie dropped her fork and it clattered on her plate. It was the first time in her life she'd ever known utter surprise. Louis frowned and she instantly realized her mistake. She had lost her composure—a grievous error in her father's eyes. In seconds she was her controlled self again.

"I thought you knew how I felt about Denis."

"Those feelings are simply youthful exuberance. Everyone experiences them at your age, but they have nothing to do with marriage."

"But I—"

Louis held up his hand. "Denis is a fine young man, but his interests are not ours. Claude's family is willing to merge all their holdings with ours the day of the wedding. Your future will be secure."

Virginie remained calm, knowing only cool logic would sway her father. "For as long as I can remember, you have done nothing but teach me the business. You have said yourself I was more adept at handling major decisions than you. Father, I have been groomed to run a bank. Have some faith in me and my ability. I don't need Claude Ruille. I can expand our bank myself."

"You are still a woman . . . no one but myself and a few friends would listen to you."

"Father," she said, struggling with her frustration, "then please explain why you have spent seventeen years teaching me to be a banker when all along you knew no one would respect my decisions."

"With the proper husband you will have enormous power."

"Only through a man?"

"Precisely."

"All right. Until I am able to establish a reputation for myself, I grant that my gender would hinder me. But . . . Claude Ruille?

His family isn't interested in banking. All they want is our royal blood!"

"That suits me fine!"

"Father, Claude Ruille is a dimwit with no talent and he'd have the first year's earnings bet in a game of cards! I can see that a merger would greatly benefit us but to include me as part of the package is an insult. I'm afraid I can't do it."

Louis's patience vanished. "Damn it, Virginie! You have no choice. My mind is made up. I've given my word and I won't go back on it. If you would just think about all this with an open mind, you would see that the merger must take place!"

Virginie was speechless. What affection she had for her father died at that instant. She realized he'd played her for a fool. All her life he'd told her she was special—bright, talented, and intelligent. He'd taught her not to be pushed around, how to think fast and get what she wanted. Now he was showing her she was no better than all the rest of her girlfriends who were trained and molded for the ultimate experience in their lives—marriage.

Virginie knew she would never forget her father's indifference to her pleas. She vowed she would never again place herself in a position of being vulnerable. She would use everything he taught her against him. Clever as she was, she could easily manipulate Claude and ultimately exact revenge on her father and anyone else who dared to stand in her way. She would teach him that she could have built his banking empire on her own wits with Denis at her side. Never again would anyone underestimate her because of her gender.

Edouard was a combination of both his parents. He inherited Virginie's dark hair and bone structure and Claude's dark eyes, height, and tawny skin, which made him look like a miniature South Seas pirate. He was an exceptionally bright child and Virginie found that when she rewarded him for good marks, well-mannered behavior, or thoughtfulness, Edouard was inclined to try to please her even more.

It was a pattern that was to continue throughout his formative years. But by the time Edouard was sixteen, he'd learned how to charm and manipulate his mother in order to get his own way. Edouard was aware that his mother felt no emotional affection for anyone, but there was a bond between them that he could not explain. Because he had never been taught to love, he believed this bond existed for him to utilize as a wedge against her.

Because Edouard showed an interest and talent for banking and chose willingly to study finance in school, Virginie rewarded him with more freedoms, privileges, and material things than she otherwise would have. By his early twenties, Edouard was spoiled to the point of depravity. He came and went as he pleased and he developed a love for fast cars which Virginie indulged for him. He flattered her friends, kept his drinking just short of embarrassing, and never disclosed his addiction to cocaine.

Because he handled banking matters with expediency and ingenuity, and shared his mother's desire for an international bank, Virginie made no secret of her plans to bestow the presidency upon him. Edouard was the future of Crédit de Paris. Edouard made certain he got everything he wanted—one way or another.

Edouard had never known a woman he could not have. Young or old, married, titled, or commoner, women fell prey to his good looks and charm. Love was a game he played where everyone knew the rules and played for the fun of the moment. When the affair ended, Edouard paid off his mistresses handsomely. Virginie knew of Edouard's affairs and she indulged him in his pastimes because she knew these women were of no consequence. When she felt Edouard was ready for marriage, she would discuss her plans with him at that time.

When Edouard was three, Lucienne was born. If it were possible, Lucienne was even more beautiful than Edouard, with Virginie's emerald eyes and Claude's height. Virginie was far stricter with her daughter, and she groomed her for the explicit purpose of marrying well. Invitations from the wealthy parents of her girlfriends for fox hunting in the English Cotswolds or skiing in Saint Moritz came frequently to Lucienne, and Virginie welcomed them. To date, however, she had not found an acceptable candidate in the group of suitors who called on Lucienne. Background and wealth were essential, but more importantly, Virginie wanted a man who would augment the business. However, Lucienne was very young and there was plenty of time.

Virginie's third child, Emile, was the result of one of Claude's drunken nights, and during the hour of his groping and probing of his wife, he called her "Marie" five times, a fact Virginie filed in her memory vault with full intentions of utilizing against him when it suited her.

Emile inherited all that was deficient in his father's character, none of Claude's good looks, and worst of all, his mother's height, making him a short, slow-witted child whose only joy was petit fours, *tartines,* and *glaces.* Emile could be molded, Virginie thought, but it would take more patience than she had.

Virginie sent Emile to a private school in England whose strict rules and highly competitive scholastics were certain to shape the boy. It had cost Virginie twice the normal tuition since Emile's entrance grades had been near to failing. Only through promises of further endowments was she able to keep him there. Emile was her son, nonetheless, and she was committed to do all she could for him. Fortunately for Emile, he possessed an overabundance of compelling charm that saw him through many a skirmish with the headmaster and his teachers. What he lacked in forbearance, he made up with eloquent discourse that disarmed the most stalwart of his detractors.

In 1927 tragedy struck the Ruille family when Edouard died in an automobile accident; and, in Virginie's mind, one which had been caused by Renée Dubois as surely as if Renée had severed the brake linings.

She had underestimated the young harlot from Lyon and now Renée was to be a guest in her own home.

Reluctantly, she had agreed only because Countess Cécile d'Itagnio, who came as close as anyone on earth to being a friend, had insisted. Why Cécile had befriended the murderous tramp, Virginie could only take as a slip, a crack in Cécile's better judgment. Possibly it was the heady state in which this wedding had put Cécile, so that now she was beyond all hopes of reason. Virginie chose to humor the countess rather than argue. She had not seen Renée in over two years and it was time she reassessed her enemy.

Renée alighted from the dark red Renault taxi that deposited her at the bricked entrance to the Ruille château where the reception was being held, the ceremony having been a private, civil ceremony. Wearing her own design, an ice blue crepe-back satin bias-cut dress with draped surplice line at the back ending in bow and streamers, she fit easily into the crowd of Vionnet,

Paquin, and Lanvin gowns. Her lustrous brown hair shone in the coach-lamp light while her violet eyes glistened with guarded anticipation. As she entered the château and was announced, heads turned and mouths gaped.

It had taken her three days to build the courage to come here. Twice she'd backed down completely, but Jean's reprimands and the guilt she felt over disappointing Cécile outweighed her earlier panic.

She regarded herself in the vestibule mirror as she entered the château. Her face revealed none of her tension. She was becoming an expert actress, she thought as she moved forward into the crowd of upturned faces.

She could see it in their eyes. They were waiting for her to blunder; to trip on the marble steps. They were all poised for the moment when her background would betray her; when she would cause her own downfall.

Though she wanted to turn and run, she didn't. She was there for Cécile, she told herself. And she could never disappoint her friend who had so willingly and often supported her.

When Renée reached the fabulously bejeweled and gowned bride, the countess welcomed her with open arms. Cécile's eyes spilled with affection as she kissed her friend and took her hand. Cécile's embrace had never felt so warm and protective, nor was it ever so welcome.

"I'm so pleased you're here. I want you to meet my husband." Cécile turned toward the tall, solidly built man with the open smile.

"I'm Alvin Thorpe and you can be none other than Renée. I'm glad to know you after all these weeks of hearing your name. It's my regret that I had to spend so much time in New York and missed meeting you sooner."

Renée turned to Cécile. "Shame on you for not telling me just how charming and handsome he was! I'm envious, but so happy for you." She hugged Cécile, thinking how much she would miss her when she sailed with Alvin for America.

"Once I finish greeting my guests, I want to spend some time with you this evening."

"I'll be here, Countess."

"Not 'Countess' anymore," she corrected. "Just Cécile . . . happy Cécile."

Renée left them, accepted a glass of champagne from a waiter and spoke to a few old acquaintances. It had been over three years since she'd seen these people. It was as if she'd locked herself away from those memories and the emotions they could stir. The past held few joys for Renée. It was easier to keep herself in check—easier to nullify living. Her life was better now; not many joys, but there was no great pain, either. It frightened her to delve into herself—her past—but as she stood at the entrance to the gardens listening to the orchestra play a Chopin piece, she found it impossible not to think of those days.

Chapter Three

Paris
1925–1928

Renée's first impression of Paris was one of confusion. On June 15, 1925, when she arrived at Gare de Lyon train station with her ten-year-old brother, Pierre, and holding a squealing eighteen-month-old brother, Michel, she thought she'd never seen so many people in her life.

Conductors yelled directions to each other, passengers pressed against her in their mad shuffle to meet loved ones and check luggage. Young boys raced about, hoping to earn a few centimes from overburdened travelers. Clouds of steam bellowed out from the train, obscuring Renée's vision.

Pierre followed behind her lugging their battered old suitcase and a cardboard box. Twice he lost sight of his sister in the crowd, but she stopped and waited for him.

"Down! I want down!" Michel screamed in Renée's ear.

"No. You'll get lost." Renée hoisted him to her left hip and repositioned the large satchel she carried.

Renée scanned the oncoming wave of faces. "I don't see her anywhere," she said to Pierre as she stood on tiptoes.

"Maybe she won't know us. It's been six years since she saw us."

Renée shook her head impatiently. "But I'll know her! There's only one Aunt Céleste." Renée looked again for the tall, auburn-haired woman whom she remembered always smelled of lilies of the valley whenever she hugged Renée to her huge bosom.

This should have been a happy reunion for them—a holiday. But since the death of both her parents from the influenza epidemic that swept southern France in late winter, Renée had found little happiness.

She often wondered if it showed—that she was an orphan. A penniless orphan being forced upon her aunt by order of the Lyon courts. Was there anything in her face, her manner, that betrayed her? She knew there must be grief in her eyes for she felt it every moment. She missed her mother tremendously and at the same time she was angry at Hélène and Antoine for leaving her to care for Pierre and Michel alone. She was only fifteen, and though she loved them, she was afraid she might not do the right things for them. She felt she wasn't enough.

Renée knew they would be a burden to Aunt Céleste and she felt guilty and ashamed about it. Worse, she felt helpless.

Céleste worked at Chanel, and Renée knew the thousand francs her parents' estate had brought was not enough to compensate her aunt for their care. Renée hoped her aunt would not hate them too much.

"Let me down!" Michel cried as he pushed against Renée's shoulder with his hands.

"In a minute," Renée replied impatiently as she suddenly spied Céleste.

From a distance a smartly dressed, tall, middle-aged woman approached them with an uncertain smile.

At forty years of age, Céleste was still a handsome woman, her voluptuous proportions reminiscent of an age long since past. Renée remembered the stories her mother had told, often with an envious strain in her voice, about Céleste and the influential and wealthy men who had showered her with luxurious apartments, clothes, and oftentimes, jewels. Céleste had traveled extensively with these men and had lived lavishly during the affair. The affair over, Céleste was forced to sell her jewels to pay her bills, though she declared she wanted no sentimental reminders. In truth it had been four years since she had last been the recipient of magnanimous presents from a man. Her bank account had dwindled away with her youth. But as she approached them, waving her arm, Renée could not see any remorse or regret in her aunt's eyes, only joy.

Perhaps she wouldn't hate them after all.

"*Mes enfants!* Welcome to Paris!"

"Hello," Pierre mumbled sadly and kept his distance. His jaw was tightly set and it was evident he kept his emotions fiercely under control.

Renée leaned close to her aunt. "Pierre is still grieving for Papa and Maman. He isn't always this cold."

"We have all the time in the world to get acquainted," Céleste said and kissed Renée's cheek.

"I'm so happy to see you, Aunt Céleste. I'm glad we have you to come to when—" Renée's words caught in a sob. She had promised herself she would cry only in private, but Céleste reminded her of her mother and she found her earlier conviction dissolving.

"So am I, chérie." She sighed and took Renée's chin in her hand. "You're so grown up! I was expecting the little girl I last saw in Lyon. And so very beautiful—just like Hélène. Those same huge violet eyes I'll always remember." Céleste reached for Michel. "And this one I haven't met. What a beautiful child! Come, I have a taxi waiting," she said, taking a cooing Michel in her arms. "Now that you are finally here, we'll have a grand time!"

Céleste lived in a ninety-five-franc-a-month apartment on the Left Bank which barely had enough room for a single person much less three children. They made do the best they could with Renée and Céleste sharing the only bedroom and Pierre and Michel sleeping in the living room.

Those first days, Céleste went to work every morning while Renée cleaned the apartment and prepared their small but filling meals. Pierre busied himself with reading and taking Michel to the Jardin du Luxembourg in the early evenings when the sun filtered through the tall trees and skimmed across the pond where other little boys raced homemade sailboats. As the days passed, Renée felt hope renew itself. Céleste was much like Hélène. They talked about fashions and Céleste's work at Chanel. The intonation of Céleste's voice, the gleam in her eye, and the particular crook of her head were familiar to her, and that void in Renée's life seemed slightly less terrifying.

Once Michel was asleep at night and Mme. Poitier, who lived across the hall, could watch him, Céleste would take Renée and Pierre around to her favorite cafés and introduce her new family to her friends, and soon Renée learned that Céleste had a new man in her life, Herbert Simcox. He was British, short, a bit overweight, and in his fifties. Of all the people she'd met in Paris, Renée liked Herbert the most. He owned an antique shop in London, and loved to tell her and Pierre stories of his world travels.

One night after dinner when Céleste and Renée were alone, Renée felt her curiosity about Herbert had to be satisfied.

"Aunt Céleste, you love Mr. Simcox, don't you?"

"I didn't think it showed so much," Céleste admitted.

"Why have you tried to hide it?"

"Because I know you are still grieving for your parents. Herbert hasn't *exactly* proposed as yet."

"But you're hoping."

"Yes, always."

"Oh, Aunt Céleste! It's all so romantic!" Renée gushed. "I think he loves you."

"You do? He's never said so, though I believe he does."

Suddenly Renée realized what Céleste's decision could mean to her, Pierre, and Michel. "You want to marry him, don't you?"

"Very much. I don't want to be alone anymore. I've had too many years already with no one truly caring for me. I have no regrets over the past. If I had to live it over, I doubt I would do anything differently. But I'm older now and I want to be needed and loved. I know I need Herbert."

"Herbert's business is in London and he often talks of moving back. If you were to marry, what would happen to us?"

Céleste put down her mending. "Why, you would come to London with us, of course! I certainly wouldn't leave you here!"

"We don't know anything about London."

"You don't know anything about Paris, but you're here."

"Yes, I guess that's true. Do you think Herbert will mind?"

Céleste's face knitted with concern. "I don't know how he could refuse."

Renée thought that Céleste didn't sound quite as positive about the situation as she would like. Renée feared Herbert would take their aunt away just when she and her brothers needed her most.

When Herbert came to call, the three children slept in Céleste's bedroom: Pierre and Renée on the bed and Michel snuggled in an upholstered chair in the corner near the window. The room was very still as Pierre and Renée strained their ears to hear the conversation in the next room.

"I think Herbert just said something about moving to London."

"No he didn't. He said he wanted to *show* London to her. There's a big difference," Renée answered.

"What will happen to us if she leaves Paris?" Pierre asked.

"She told me we would move with them. She knows we love her and need her. Why, it's almost as if . . . as if . . . Maman were still alive . . . Céleste is so much like her." Renée knew she must be strong for Pierre and tried not to show her grief.

Pierre frowned. "But Herbert is nothing like Papa."

Renée turned her head on the pillow and strained her eyes in the darkness trying to see Pierre. "I like Herbert. He's very nice. He doesn't tease us and hug us the way Papa did, but then we aren't related to him. Besides, he's English."

"Oh," Pierre replied, deferring to his sister's observation and superior knowledge of the world.

"I know Aunt Céleste loves him. I hope they do get married."

"Who cares?"

"I do! And you should too!" But she understood Pierre's fear. "Perhaps we should make a special friend of Herbert. Maybe he would like us more . . . enough to never want to move to London. And then we could stay in Paris! If we asked him to teach us to speak English . . . he would be flattered."

"Yes, and then we could know everything he's saying to Aunt Céleste. Not just bits and pieces."

Renée's brows rose in shock. "You sound as if he were the enemy!"

Pierre rolled onto his side so that Renée couldn't see his tears. "I didn't mean it like that . . . but, he's not family, either."

* * *

Herbert accepted the children's proposal. Renée's knowledge of Italian and German facilitated her studies. She took the books he gave her and read them while Michel slept. Her energy and earnestness impressed him. What he did not know was that Renée had heard from Mme. Poitier and the children in the park that Parisian schools were extremely difficult, and coming from a provincial school, she was sure to fail in their more aggressive academic system. That the children had been teasing her, never entered Renée's mind.

As fall approached, Céleste seemed preoccupied and tense.

"Aunt Céleste, are you ill?" Renée asked one night after dinner.

"No, chérie."

"Something is wrong. I can tell. What is it?"

Céleste squeezed Renée's hand and called Pierre to her. "I'm afraid it's our finances that are in bad health. The money from the estate is gone. I had no idea it would cost so much to feed us all."

"I think I should look for a job," Renée said as she swallowed the lump in her throat. She had wanted to study languages this year at school, but she knew Céleste would not have said anything if the situation were not desperate.

"Chérie, this is too great a sacrifice for you."

"With two salaries you wouldn't have to worry so much. I'm not afraid of the work."

"I know you could do it too. I wish there was some other way, but I don't know what it would be." Céleste wrung her hands. "I hate doing this!"

Renée hugged Céleste. "So do I. But I can do it."

"What about me?" Pierre asked. "I could find something and help out."

"Absolutely not! You will go to school just as Papa wanted! Besides, you're too young to find work."

"You'll be needed here after school to watch Michel," Céleste explained. "We'll find someone to watch him during the day until you get home."

"Pierre, I'm relying on you to learn everything you can and then you must teach me. We have to stick together. Except for my English lessons with Herbert, you're my only chance."

"I won't let you down."

* * *

Céleste procured employment for Renée as a vendeuse at Worth where she herself had started so many years ago. Renée could not believe her good fortune. She remembered the whisper of reverence in her mother's voice when she spoke of Worth. It was like a dream come true.

Renée was totally unprepared for the luxury and opulence at Worth. The ivory satin drapes, crystal chandeliers, and gilt-framed mirrors made her reel with heady delight.

She was employed to attend customers in the showroom, and spent the majority of her day noting the patrons' wishes with regard to alterations, fetching completed ensembles from the cabine, and running errands in the workrooms. She was thrilled to be at the great house of Worth, and in trying to please her employer, she accepted menial tasks in the workroom, unaware of the caste system that governed the lives of the couture workers.

Finally, a particularly pretty vendeuse by the name of Lorraine took Renée aside.

"Renée, you simply cannot continue as you are, sweeping floors and helping seamstresses and cutters."

"Why not?" Renée asked naïvely. "I thought I was helping."

"It's not done! I know this is new to you, but 'shop work' is beneath your station. If you don't comply with etiquette, the other vendeuses will make certain you lose your job."

"I didn't know."

Lorraine patted her hand. "I like you, Renée, and so do the customers. But there are workers here who want what you have and you must guard against their jealousy. In couture there is no other world beyond these walls. Maybe all you are concerned with is your paycheck, but it is more than that to me. This is my life—my only religion."

Renée was surprised by Lorraine's earnestness. Renée had only known her mother's little business. Lorraine was right. There were certain age-old ways of doing things that made couture what it was. Deviations and shortcuts were not tolerated, nor were those who promoted them. More than ever, she realized that Paris and Lyon were planets apart.

Sometimes, she thought her head would burst with all the things she was learning. Everything was different in Paris. She moved faster, met more people, and smiled more than she ever had in her life. Though the boundaries of her life were the walls of Worth and Céleste's apartment, she believed she could not assimilate any more than this.

As the weeks passed, Renée's respect for the system increased as did her awe for the artistic talent of the designers, the fitters, and the seamstresses. It was a world where ideals of beauty and perfection were not easily tarnished by corruption. Preservation of the old ways was paramount.

Renée learned everything about haute couture her quick mind could absorb. Her tasks as vendeuse were minimal and she found dealing with the customers pleasant and fun. She listened to their gossip and chatter and quickly learned the pecking order of the most influential women in Paris. Everything she heard and saw was important to her.

One day she was instructed to wait on a young girl, Lucienne Ruille, who was to receive her last fitting for a party dress her mother had ordered. It was an unscheduled visit and Renée told the *directrice* that she had previously confirmed a three-o'clock appointment with Mme. Devereaux who could be quite unmanageable when kept waiting. The directrice assured Renée that "the Ruille child" would not take more than half an hour.

When she found Lucienne Ruille standing in front of the huge gilt mirror clad in a cream-colored teddy impatiently tapping her foot, Renée realized that this was no child. She had the body of a fully mature woman and she inspected herself in the mirror with scrupulous and not-too-innocent eyes. She ran her hands over her breasts, flat stomach, and narrow hips, reveling in the sensuous delight she felt. However, she was quick to criticize her shortcomings.

As Renée walked forward with the pumpkin-colored taffeta dress, Lucienne tossed a dark curl over her shoulder and asked: "Don't you think I should flatten my breasts more? All my friends have chic small bosoms. It just doesn't seem fair!" She pouted as Renée lifted the dress and pulled it down over Lucienne's head.

"My mother doesn't know it, but before the party I'm having my hair bobbed. How do you think it will look?"

"I think your hair is much too beautiful to cut," Renée answered honestly, but Lucienne's eyes narrowed suspiciously.

"You needn't pay me compliments! It won't get your salary

raised. Besides, I will be beautiful no matter what the length of my hair."

The fitter was called in to make two minor adjustments to the tightly fitted sleeves. Renée assisted Lucienne in dressing once again, charged the dress to her mother's account, and followed her to the main salon where a tall, exceedingly handsome man was waiting for her.

"Edouard!" Lucienne called to him, embraced him quickly, and turned back to Renée, who was holding the tissue-wrapped dress. "Wait till you see what I've chosen! It was such fun not to have Mother breathing down my neck making all my decisions for me."

He smiled at Lucienne and then gazed at Renée. "Has my little sister done well?"

"Yes, monsieur. She has," was all Renée could say, for he stared at her so intently she thought he was inspecting her every pore. Renée did not blush as she usually did, but instead kept her eyes defiantly riveted on his. At first, she was incensed at his boldness. Renée had never been aware of masculine gazes and she was unsure what exactly should be her response. Suddenly, she became all too conscious of a turbulence inside her. The longer he looked at her, the more unsteady she became. Vehemently, she wished he would go away so she could return to normal.

"I'll take the dress for her," Edouard said and she gave it to him.

When their hands touched, a charge went off in Renée's head and she could tell from the look in his eyes that he'd felt it too.

For a long moment they gazed at each other. Renée's mind was blank, not thinking anything, only feeling her peculiar reaction to this man. She wondered why he said nothing, though she could almost hear his words with her eyes. He liked her, she knew, but she didn't know why.

"Will there be anything else?" she finally asked. Suddenly, she didn't want him to leave.

"I don't believe so," he replied, but made no move to leave.

"Edouard, we must be going. Mother will scold me if I'm late for my music lesson," Lucienne pleaded.

"What? Oh, yes, she will." He started to leave. "Thank you for helping my sister, Mademoiselle . . ."

"Dubois," she said a bit too quickly.

Edouard walked Lucienne to the door. Renée stared after him, unable to move from the spot. Just as he reached the door, he glanced back, and when he saw Renée boldly watching him, he smiled, then he left.

Renée felt suspended in time, as if everything had stopped or she had moved forward some infinitesimal second and was now placed in a new sphere. Something had changed, though she wasn't sure what. Whatever she had been before, was never to be again. And if anyone were to ask her how this happened, she knew she could never explain it. Not even to herself.

Pondering her reaction to Edouard, she did not see the directrice approach her from behind.

"Mademoiselle Dubois! I trust you have work to do!"

"Yes, madame," she said quickly and scurried back to her duties.

Renée finished out her day in a fog, unable to concentrate on anything but Edouard Ruille. As she rode the bus across the Seine to go home, she wondered what precisely had happened to her to make her think that her life had changed that day. The more she thought about it, the more absurd it seemed. She was only a working girl. She knew nothing of fancy balls, parties, and teas. Edouard was a wealthy man from a fine family. Hadn't she heard just yesterday from the Marchesa di Dricoli that the Ruilles were one of the most influential families in France? He must know beautiful women from all over the world—cultured, elegant women like the Worth patrons. She knew she was unsophisticated and unworldly. Edouard could never be interested in her.

The next day near noon Renée came back from the fitting rooms to find Edouard waiting for her.

Her smile was immediate. "May I help you with something?"

"I could pretend I was here to pick up my mother's order. But I'm not."

"You . . . aren't?"

"No. I'd like to know if you would have lunch with me."

"You would?" She felt warm standing this close to him.

He chuckled at her surprise. "I would."

"I'd like that very much," she replied, embarrassed by the blush that enveloped her.

They drove to the Café de la Paix. Renée could not remember what she ate except that it was good and the wine not nearly as heady as the excitement he caused. She was afraid to ask him why he wasted his most valuable time with her. She sensed that as wonderful as this was, he would never see her again. For him, this must surely be a lark.

"I have three cars," he was saying. "A Bugatti, an Isotta, and a Mercedes-Benz. I've raced several times and won first place twice. I work at my family's bank, I have a brother and a sister, two normal parents, and I think you are astonishingly beautiful."

He spoke so quickly that Renée had the odd sensation he was trying to tell her everything about himself in one sitting.

"I have two brothers—" she began and he interrupted.

"I don't much care for mine, actually. He's a bit slow . . . but then since he's so much younger than I, we couldn't possibly have the same interests, now could we? Would you care for more wine?"

"No, thank you."

"Perhaps a ride through the park? It's lovely this time of day." He paused but only briefly. "Did I tell you that your eyes are the loveliest I've ever seen? Would you have lunch with me tomorrow?" He flashed a charming and inviting smile.

"Yes, I will," she responded so quickly she hadn't thought whether she should or shouldn't go. She thought it a miracle she was to see him again. There would be one more chance to feel this way again. To hear his voice and look into his eyes.

She knew there were only twenty-four hours to live through between now and then. It might as well have been an eternity.

Renée floated through her days, awakening early to take extra care with her hair and to iron her uniform. Worth did not allow her to wear accessories, but she stole early morning hours to make belts and scarves that would augment her wardrobe. She polished her shoes to a high gleam. She wanted to be prepared should Edouard want to see her on her free time.

It didn't take Céleste long to realize there was something behind Renée's altered routine.

"If you buff your nails any more, you'll wear them away."

Renée chuckled and looked longingly out the window at the rooftops.

"Where did you meet him?"
"At Worth's," Renée replied without thinking.
"What's his name?"
"Edouard Ruille."

Upon hearing the name of one of Paris's more notorious bachelors, Céleste's nerves jumped. Carefully, she continued her questioning. She wanted to extract information, not reprimand the girl if it wasn't necessary.

"Do you see him often?"

"Only twice . . . for lunch. And he stops by the shop almost every day. He's taking me to lunch tomorrow."

"I think you are a bit young to be seeing anyone, don't you?"

"The other girls at work all have someone, why can't I?"

"You may have forgotten that I lied to the directrice and told her you were eighteen not fifteen. You may look older, but fact is fact. I'm sure your young man doesn't know the truth, does he?"

"No . . ."

"You see! I'm certain if he did, it would make a difference."

Renée's defenses rose swiftly. "What are you telling me? That I can't see Edouard?"

"I am only saying that I would prefer that you did not. I would also like it if you told him your real age. But the decison is yours to make," she said and left the room.

Céleste was counting on the fact that Edouard had only escorted daughters of prominent families, and all Paris knew that his mother arranged the majority of his social life.

All she could do now was guide Renée and hope that the innocent affair would remain just that and burn itself out.

Renée said nothing to Edouard or anyone about her age and concentrated on her work. She paid particular attention to the clothes and what the fitter and the vendeuses discussed regarding the newest styles for fall. She became more assertive in her suggestions to her customers and offered advice on accessories, the correct furs, and additions to their wardrobes that would augment their original purchases.

She learned everything she could about the latest in hair adornments and jewelry, both costume and real. Renée began to view her job at Worth as a bridge between her world and Edouard's.

On the days when he did not take her to lunch, she talked to the assistant designers, the cutters, fitters, and second sewing hands; even the *midinettes*. She observed the organization and the fine-honed management required to run a business of this magnitude.

Renée pulled from every scrap of information her mother had ever taught her about dressmaking and poked even further into Céleste's mind.

"The most important part of the gown is the fit," Céleste told her. "I should know. Did you know that if the lining doesn't fit properly, the line of the skirt will never be right? Executing a perfectly straight hem is probably the most difficult task. Chanel places tiny chains in the hems to achieve proper balance. In couture no step can be overlooked, from the original design to the cutting of the cloth, the making of the toile, the stitching of seams, and finally to the selection of trims, buttons, and fasteners. Perfection must be achieved in everything."

Renée had known her mother's work to be very good, but what she observed in Paris was unequaled excellence. The more she investigated couture, the more insatiable her appetite for it became. She found to her delight that she was a quick study. She could see a dress for only five minutes and remember every last detail down to the exact millimeter spacing of the buttons. She saw design changes evolving in the workrooms and anticipated the finished product before the designer himself knew the outcome. She found she was able to judge the correct fabric for a particular design according to weight, drape, and balance. She could spot even the most precise Poiret copy on a customer and quickly eliminate them as a Worth patron. Most importantly, she learned that fashion must have a sense of recklessness; without it, boredom and practicality enter and destroy creativity.

Through it all, she continued to see Edouard Ruille.

Sometimes he would merely stop by for a quick chat that was difficult to conceal from the directrice, but Edouard, being who he was, knew his family's influence would keep Renée from serious reprimand. Other times he walked her to the bus stop.

When he held her hand, Renée felt goosebumps rise.

"Let me drive you home."

"I couldn't do that, Edouard. My aunt would be furious."

"I just wanted to be with you a while longer."

He smiled at her and every time he did, Renée thought she would sink through the pavement.

"I don't know why you spend your time with me. I'm not all that interesting. I haven't been to all the places you have."

"You needn't fish for compliments from me, but to amuse you, I'll say it again—I think you're gorgeous and you do something to me . . ."

But before he could finish, the bus pulled up and Renée dashed on.

"Goodbye, Edouard."

"See you tomorrow?" he called.

"Yes!" She smiled to herself as she watched him wave to her and then fade from sight when the bus rode away.

She felt light-headed and gay when she was with Edouard, and sad when they were apart. She counted the minutes until she saw him again. When he talked of his travels and the people he knew, she was awestruck at his knowledge of the world, business, and people.

She learned to relate the gossip she heard in the fitting rooms, which pleased Edouard. She copied the latest designs and wore her ensembles with new confidence. She utilized every bit of her newly acquired knowledge to refine herself and make herself pleasing in Edouard's eyes. She thought she had successfully hidden the provincial side of her background, never knowing it was that freshness, that artlessness that drew Edouard to her.

Renée's greatest regret at this time was that she felt she had to lie to Céleste about the number of times she saw Edouard. She didn't want her aunt to worry about her needlessly. Renée knew that Céleste's fears were unfounded because she believed Edouard to be a good man, honest and sincere. Once Céleste got used to the idea of Edouard and, perhaps, met him and learned to like him as she did, perhaps then she could be truthful with her aunt again. Above all, Renée wanted to believe in the magic of love, not in ominous warnings.

Chapter Four

It was not until Edouard invited Renée for dinner that Pierre began to regard this man's intrusion in his sister's life as a threat. Now, as she sat at the kitchen table finishing the hem on the silk fabric she'd bought on sale at Bon Marché, Pierre came to the conclusion that he hated Edouard Ruille.

"What if I get sick tomorrow night while you are gone?" he asked.

"Aunt Céleste will be here."

"No she won't. She's having dinner with Mr. Simcox."

"Then Madame Poitier will look out for you and Michel. Honestly, Pierre, you act as if I'm leaving you forever."

Pierre's anger flared and he answered her with a scathing look. "I never get to see you anymore! You work all day and when you come home you must cook, then I must finish my studies, and then we must sleep. The only time we do things together is weekends. I hate it!"

"I can't help it if we aren't rich and I have to work! I'm doing the best I can!" She slammed her scissors down on the table and instantly regretted her outburst. She walked over to Pierre and put her arms around him.

"It's hard for you without Papa, isn't it, Pierre? I don't play the games with you that he did, or whittle sailboats and trucks out of wood. I wish you would make more friends at school, then perhaps you would be happier."

"It's just that we don't seem like a family anymore."

Renée took Pierre's face in her hands and looked at him with an intensity that made him tremble.

"Listen to me, Pierre. We are still a family and there is nothing more important to me than the three of us. Aunt Céleste is our mother's sister and part of our family too."

Pierre flung his arms around his sister. "I miss Maman and Papa so much. No matter how much I pray, I know they won't be coming back."

Renée didn't answer but only held him tighter. Pierre had always held his feelings in check, but now the grief and hopelessness he felt overpowered him. "I promise that we'll make better use of our time together from now on. You'll have to help me and I'll help you." But even as she spoke she thought of Edouard and instantly she felt guilty for wanting time with him too. She was torn between her feelings for Edouard and her responsibility to her family.

"I don't have to go out tonight. I'd rather be here with you and Michel anyway. We could play cards or read that new book you got at the library."

Pierre's eyes brightened and when she saw his trusting smile, she knew she had made the right decision.

Edouard took the news of his canceled evening with Renée good-naturedly, but extracted a promise from her to accompany him three days later for a ride in the Bois.

"A country girl like you? I don't believe it," he said, giving her a leg up into the saddle.

"It's true! I've never been on horseback," she said quietly, hoping the horse could not sense her trepidation. Her hands trembled as she took the reins.

"Then I don't think you should ride this horse. The mare is more even-tempered."

"No, Edouard. This white stallion is so beautiful and you said yourself he is your favorite."

"Shadow is a good steed, but he's used to experienced riders."

"I'll be fine," she said as she waited for Edouard to mount the chestnut mare.

Together they trotted down the path that led to a grove of trees.

"We'll go through here," Edouard said. "It's quite lovely and my favorite part of the Bois."

With Edouard's instruction, Renée learned to hold the reins with more confidence.

Edouard picked up speed and Renée followed suit until she was galloping alongside him. She smiled and was about to surpass him when suddenly, just ahead, three dogs burst across the path barking at each other and then went crashing into the thicket on the other side.

Shadow whinnied and reared up on his hind legs, jabbing his forelegs into the air. Renée screamed.

"Hold on!" Edouard shouted as he dismounted.

Shadow again reared up and then landed his forelegs on the ground with a thud. This time, Renée lost her grip and went tumbling to the ground.

Fearing she was hurt, Edouard dashed over to her. He was met with an angry glare.

"He can't do that to me!" she said angrily and scrambled to her feet as she dusted off her jodhpurs.

Before Edouard could stop her, she'd grabbed Shadow's reins and was trying to remount. She turned to Edouard. "Well? Are you going to help me or not?"

"Why don't you ride Lady instead?"

"Not on your life! This horse is going to find out he can't get rid of me so easily!"

"The horse is more determined than you are, believe me," he warned.

"Never!"

Edouard shrugged and boosted her into the seat. As soon as she was astride the horse, he reared up and Renée fell off again.

This time she landed in a pile of muddy leaves, her eyes blazing with resolution.

Edouard could not stifle his laughter. "That's really enough, chérie. The horse has made his point."

Renée got to her feet once again and snatched the reins out of Edouard's hands. She stared Shadow straight in the eye. "I am the rider. You are the beast and you *will* allow me to sit on your back!"

This time when she put her foot in the stirrup, she bounced herself off the ground with her other foot and managed to mount Shadow without Edouard's help. She took the reins, pressed her thighs into the horse's flanks, and trotted away from Edouard. Not once did Shadow flinch or display any sign he would rear again.

It seemed that with their every meeting, Edouard found Renée more fascinating than before. She was without a doubt the most beautiful girl he'd ever seen. She had the polish and sophistication of the society women he'd known for years. And yet there was something he could not describe. She was honest and genuine in a way he was only beginning to understand. He didn't know what it was, but it appealed to him enormously.

Edouard had reacted physically to many beautiful women but never with this intensity. He felt a strange need to protect her that was at odds with her obvious independence. As he stared openmouthed while Renée mastered the stallion, Edouard was more determined than ever to win Renée.

One Saturday afternoon Edouard took her to the steeplechase races at Auteuil and introduced her to Carrie and Joseph Baldwin. They sat in the boxes, shared Martinique rum out of a silver flask, and were joined by Ursula and Harry Ames.

Though the race was exciting and Renée felt a rush of adrenaline when she placed her first bet, she couldn't enjoy the outing as much as the others. Renée was keenly aware of Céleste's harsh glares and anxious tones whenever she left the apartment to see Edouard. She didn't lie outright to Céleste, she simply avoided speaking of Edouard at all. Selfishly, Renée wanted to be with Edouard more than she wanted to please Céleste.

She felt so alive in his presence, so wanted and needed. She liked the protective gestures he made. For the first time, she came to expect the compliments, the little gifts of a nosegay or chocolates he gave her. Most of all, she realized that he was happy and that she was responsible for the joyous gleam in his eyes. She was aware that when she left the room, he became fidgety and nervous. Once she returned to his side, he seemed to relax and his smile was again warm and assured. She was becoming necessary to him. She wondered if he knew it.

Renée peered through the binoculars, her mind more on her guilt over deceiving Céleste than the race. When she looked up she noticed for the third time that Ursula was staring at her. Finally, she boldly asked, "Is there something wrong?"

Flustered at her own impoliteness, Ursula sheepishly replied, "Forgive me for staring, but I've never seen a jacket cut quite like that. I've been trying to place the designer all afternoon, but I can't."

Renée glanced down at the double-breasted, narrow-lapeled green wool jacket trimmed in camel to match her skirt and said: "I'm the designer. I made it myself."

Ursula's eyes flew open, as did Carrie's, who had been wondering the same thing. "It's gorgeous!" Carrie said.

"With clothes like that you could open your own shop."

"I intend to," Renée replied confidently and picked up her binoculars in time to watch her horse place first.

As the weeks passed, they dined at Le Grand Véfour and Maxim's, and Edouard introduced her to the Marquis de Chandeley, Lord and Lady Wellesley, and Denis and Marguerite Corbeil, all friends of the Ruille family.

They were brief encounters and Renée thought it strange that Edouard did not discuss plans to go to the races or dancing as he did with his other friends. However, these people were polite to her and Edouard acted no differently and so Renée was unaware of any tension.

Renée did not understand that Edouard, like many young men of the aristocracy, led two lives. His after-dark life was one inhabited by flashy Americans and titled Parisians escorting their mistresses and whores. It was an underworld where young men of society unleashed their passions. She knew nothing of orgies, homosexuals, sadism, and the twisted appetites that drugs induced. She did not know that her name was whispered or sputtered in anger and disgust because she was associated with this underworld. Renée believed her love for Edouard was clean, good, and pure. Renée did not know that Edouard and his society friends assumed she knew the boundaries of the two worlds.

* * *

At the end of October, Edouard and Renée drove through southern France to his villa at Saint-Jean-Cap-Ferrat. It was a warm day, the sky filled with voluminous white clouds as a salty breeze wafted over the picturesque coastal village. Edouard had never been as relaxed as he was that day.

He delighted in showing her the four-bedroom house with its high ceilings, large rooms, and spectacular view of the ocean. There was only one servant on duty since his trip had been impromptu. Edouard loved helping Renée prepare their lunch in the rustic kitchen with its hand-painted tile walls and copper-covered work counters.

"You make the simplest things seem like fun. I've adored being with you."

Then he held her so tightly she thought he would crush her ribs. It was times like this that she sensed he needed her in a way no one ever had before. She wondered if this was how Céleste felt about Herbert.

"I want you to share the rest of your life with me, Renée. I love you and I don't know what I would do if you weren't there for me."

Renée folded herself into his arms. "I don't ever want to be without you, Edouard. I always feel safe and so very loved with you."

"Renée . . ." He moaned and kissed her again. "Say yes, Renée."

She looked into his handsome face, knowing his dark eyes could impel her to do anything he asked.

"Yes, Edouard. A thousand times, yes." She smiled, thinking of how full her life would be with him. They were going to be a family now. Nothing else was as important to her as that.

When Céleste heard of Edouard's "proposal," she calmly looked her niece in the eye and said: "I'll lock you in a closet for the rest of your life if you think I'll ever let that beast near you again!"

Renée stammered in shock, not understanding her aunt's tirade.

"I'm getting married! Girls do it every day. And I love him, what can be wrong with that?"

Céleste quickly poured herself a glass of wine, gulped it down, and then poured another.

"I think it is about time I told you the facts of life I'm sure your mother knew nothing about. Chérie, Edouard did not propose marriage to you. I see no ring on your finger. He has not said anything to you about meeting his family. What he *is* proposing is that you become his mistress."

Renée listened attentively as her aunt droned on.

"Edouard can't marry you, Renée."

"Of course he can. He loves me. What else is there?"

"Family . . . class . . . society. I know you don't understand all this, since you've only lived in Lyon, where there is no aristocracy."

"Lyon has wealthy people like the du Fauvres."

Céleste shook her head. "The du Fauvres are bourgeois. It's not the same thing. They have no royal ancestors. From the day Edouard was born, his parents have had his entire future laid out for him. He can do as he pleases to a certain extent. When I was just a little older than you I fell in love with a young man like Edouard who could give me anything . . . except his name."

"The situations aren't the same at all. Edouard has asked me to marry him."

Céleste looked into Renée's imperturbable eyes. The girl hadn't understood a thing. "I don't want your heart to be broken as mine was."

"You just don't know him the way I do," Renée said and walked away, thinking it impossible for someone Céleste's age to understand the kind of all-encompassing love she felt for Edouard.

When Céleste spoke to Herbert about Renée she was truly distraught. "What is there about love that causes intelligent people to act as if they'd had a lobotomy?"

Herbert was too much in love himself to belittle another's intentions when his were most honorable. "I know you feel responsible. I wish I could offer some solutions."

"Renée is too young to be this involved. She is naïve and impressionable. I have no idea how to protect her from him and when I do try to make her see reality, it's *me* she rejects."

She sighed dejectedly. "She doesn't understand that men of Edouard's class don't marry common girls." She reflected for a moment. "I must think of some way to wrestle her out of Edouard's grasp. She's a sensible girl and quite responsible.

She's done well at her job, even earning favorable comments from the directrice. She has handled her grief well, in fact, I feel she has recovered more than Pierre. Perhaps if I finally took a strong stand on the matter of Edouard—forced her to stay home . . .''

"Perhaps if you concentrated more on yourself and less on your niece, everything would fall into place," he said, taking her hand.

There was a fire in his eyes that made Céleste's heart swell. As he touched her cheek, thoughts of Edouard stealing her niece faded.

He pulled her close and kissed her and at the same time kept fidgeting with her hand. It wasn't until she pulled away that she realized what he'd done.

"Herbert?" Céleste was confused as she looked at the exquisite diamond and coral ring on her finger.

"It once belonged to the czarina of Russia. It's yours but only if you say you'll marry me."

At forty-plus Céleste thought she was impervious to surprise. "Yes! Yes!" she said as the threw her arms around him and showered him with kisses. "You make me feel like a schoolgirl again."

"You are a schoolgirl to me," he said. "And we're going to have a wonderful life together."

When Céleste announced her wedding plans to Renée and Pierre, she noted that Renée's initial excitement evaporated quickly. The girl was thinking of Edouard, she thought.

"All of us will be moving to London very soon," she said.

Renée's eyes were wide. She started to protest, but Céleste's face was stern. Suddenly, Renée's future looked bleak. She could not fathom a life without Edouard, not when she had such hopes, such dreams. She couldn't think of moving to London without becoming ill. There had to be another way.

With Céleste engulfed in a whirlwind of wedding preparations, Renée saw Edouard without Céleste's knowledge.

"Aunt Céleste will be marrying soon and all of us will be moving to London," she told Edouard. "I'll never see you again," she cried.

"Over my dead body!" he declared. "You can't leave me, not when I've just found you!"

"What are you going to do?"

"I'll think of something."

Two days later he called for Renée. "I have a surprise for you."

"What?"

"Come," he said, leading her to his car. "You'll see."

He drove her to a tree-lined street just off the rue du Faubourg-St.-Honoré. He handed her a key to the front door. "Open it."

Gingerly she opened the door and entered a spacious marble-floored vestibule. The intimate salon was draped in rose damask with matching settees facing each other before the black marble fireplace. He ushered her into the large dining room, where a bay window overlooked a lushly planted garden in back. Edouard delighted in her pleasure and then he took her up the wide staircase to the bedrooms. On the second floor a large room had been outfitted with two beds and two dressers and was decorated in the masculine colors of forest green and camel.

"This is for Pierre and Michel," Edouard said, beaming down at her surprised face.

"I can't believe it! This is where we will all live? Together?"

"If I had to bed down half of Paris to keep you here, I would do it. I don't want you going to London."

"Oh, Edouard. You *are* good to us."

When Renée returned to tell Céleste that she, Pierre, and Michel would all be living in the beautiful house on the Right Bank, Céleste said: "That means nothing."

"What can I say or do that will convince you Edouard means to marry me?"

Céleste felt her heart crumbling. "I *want* it to be true, chérie. For your sake . . . your happiness. I can tell you love him. It's just that I don't trust him."

Three days later, Renée came home from work and stated: "Edouard told me today he's taking me to meet his parents at their château."

"He said that?"

"Yes."

Céleste peered at Renée. "I've given this a great deal of

thought, Renée. When did he say he was going to move you to the town house?"

"The day after you leave."

"Hmm. Well, I'm not sure if I believe that either. But I have decided that you, Pierre, and Michel can remain here in Paris. I won't force you to come to London if you don't want to."

"Aunt Céleste! You've made me so happy!"

"Don't be too thrilled just yet. I also think it best to test Edouard."

"How?"

"I'm not going to send you any money, Renée. That way he will have to make good his promises. However," she said sternly, "if he doesn't, you must promise me that you will pack immediately for London. I'll come for you myself if necessary. Do you understand?"

"Yes! I promise. But that won't happen. You'll see. Edouard and I will be married as soon as I meet his parents."

"London is not that far, Renée. I'm very close if you need me. And you *will* contact me if there is any trouble . . . of any kind? I'm relying on your good sense."

"Yes, I will."

Céleste didn't tell Renée her true motive behind her scheme. Céleste was certain Edouard had no intention of marrying Renée. She also believed that less than a month of juggling her job at Worth, caring for Michel and Pierre, household chores, laundry and cooking would send the girl straight to Céleste's doorstep. The realities of being mother, father, and provider were the surest cure for Renée's infatuation with Edouard Ruille. Neither did Edouard impress her as the domestic kind of husband. It would not be long before Edouard was a memory and Renée was safe with her and Herbert in London.

After the civil ceremony in which Céleste became Mrs. Herbert Simcox, they all stood at the train station saying goodbye. Renée felt her heart sink when Céleste embraced her for the last time.

"I'm going to miss you so much, Aunt Céleste."

"If you need me for anything—if anything happens—you come straight to London." She wagged her finger at Renée.

"I will," she said, fighting tears.

"Goodbye, Aunt Céleste," Pierre said and hugged her close. "I love you."

"Pierre," Céleste sobbed and bent down to his face. "Take care of Renée and Michel. I'm depending on you."

"I will."

Céleste held Michel, who squealed happily when she bounced him in her arms.

"Tante Ciel," he sputtered and flung his arms round her neck.

"My baby . . ." She handed him back to Renée.

"All aboard!" the conductor shouted as steam bellowed out from the train.

"Goodbye, children." Herbert waved as he and Céleste stepped aboard the train.

The train pulled out slowly. "You write to me, Renée!"

"Of course!"

"If anything happens . . ." Céleste's tears were streaming down her cheeks.

"It won't. I love you, Aunt Céleste!"

The train picked up speed. Céleste kept waving until long after the children had disappeared from sight. Her decision to leave them had been a painful one, but she was convinced it was the only way to rid themselves of Edouard. She wanted Renée to come to her willingly. She prayed she was doing the right thing.

True to his word, Edouard moved Renée and her brothers into the apartment the very next day. He hired a cook, a maid, and a housekeeper whose duties included caring for Michel.

That first night, Edouard arranged for an elaborate dinner for them after Michel was conveniently in bed. Edouard rightly guessed that Pierre's friendship could be quite valuable to him, and so after the meal they retired to the salon where a blazing fire crackled in the fireplace. On the tea table were two brightly wrapped packages.

"These are for you, Pierre."

"Why?"

"I want to be your friend."

Still skeptical, Pierre said nothing more and unwrapped the first box, which contained a complete set of the works of Rousseau. The second package contained a pair of binoculars.

"Thank you, Edouard. These are the nicest gifts I've ever received. But I didn't do anything to earn them."

"I just wanted you to have them. I hope that you will come to trust me."

Pierre looked at his sister. "I want whatever makes Renée happy."

Though Renée smiled, she did not understand Pierre's misgivings. Perhaps things were moving too quickly for Pierre. His grief was still evident in his manner, and just when he'd begun to replace their parents with Céleste and Herbert, they, too, had left him. She wondered if Pierre was reluctant to form a bond with Edouard for fear he would leave too. She knew she could not convince Pierre. Only time and love could do that.

Pierre went up to bed and the minute he was gone Edouard took Renée in his arms and kissed her more hungrily than ever before. She was surprised at his forcefulness. She tried to draw away, but he held her firmly.

"Edouard, now that we are settled in, I was hoping we could talk about our plans."

He pulled her back to him and buried his head in her shoulder, placing maddeningly hot kisses on her throat. She moaned.

"I want you as much as you want me, Edouard, but I want to wait until after the wedding."

He straightened and stared blankly at her. "What wedding?"

Renée saw the confused look in his eyes. "Yours and mine!"

At first she thought he was going to hit her, his eyes blazed so with anger. Then he burst into laughter. "You'll have to find a new strategy, my pet, that one doesn't work anymore."

"I don't understand . . ."

"Of course you do."

"I'm afraid I don't!"

"Then let me explain it to you. Not once to my recollection have I ever mentioned the word 'marriage' or 'wedding' to you. Don't look so stunned, Renée, you knew very well what you were getting into when I moved you here. You've held out on me longer than any woman before. I indulged your little game because it was a lark for me—and it kept your meddling aunt out of my hair."

"I don't understand this at all!"

"I seriously doubt that," he said, stepping over to the

cherrywood bombé bureau where he withdrew a flat velvet box. He handed it to her. "Perhaps this will alter your attitude."

She opened it. "Diamonds?" She picked up the wide bracelet containing at least a hundred diamonds. "Why are you giving me this?"

"Come now, chérie. You're no different than Fifi or the others like her. You know the rules. Why don't you wear the diamonds while we make love?" he asked blithely, not seeing her mounting fury.

"You thought you could buy me with jewels?" she said angrily and dropped the diamonds into the case and snapped it shut. She jammed the box into his hand. "I don't want diamonds!"

He howled with laughter. "All women want diamonds!" He paused. "Sapphires! You want sapphires!"

"Edouard!" she exploded. Tears of anger and pain stung her eyes. "I thought I was going to be your wife! You told me I was special . . . and I am! I'm not like the other women. I could make you happy. Why are you treating me like this? Why did you lie to me? I thought we were all going to live together as a real family."

Edouard was aghast. "That's impossible! Surely you know that you would never be accepted by my family."

"Why not? What have I done?"

He stared at her. "Are you really so naïve that you don't know who the Ruilles are?"

"I know your family is wealthy and I'm poor . . . but . . ."

"Renée! You really don't understand, do you?" he asked suddenly, very shaken at her total innocence and his blindness. He'd thought her to be worldly and he'd assumed she knew how exclusive and elite was the sphere he and his family inhabited. But as he looked into her eyes, he suddenly realized that her artlessness was not a ruse. She was unsuspecting of his intentions and helplessly innocent.

Renée was a provincial girl, untouched by corruption. She was pure in mind and spirit. He realized that to her, virginity was more than an old-fashioned notion. To Renée her body and soul were one.

Normally, Edouard would have considered himself lucky to have stumbled into such a situation. She was totally within his power and he could easily take advantage of her.

But suddenly he found he wanted to protect her—both from himself and his mother. No one had ever loved him before. Renée truly did not want jewels or the things he could buy. She had wanted *him*. Not his body or his mother's bank, but *him*. Instantly, he became the defenseless party, for he realized what he had in Renée. He realized he loved her in return.

"I didn't lie to you—exactly. But I did let you think I was going to marry you. I wanted you, Renée. But more than that I know now that I love you."

He put his arms around her, but she shunned him angrily. "What kind of love is this that you must lie and deceive me?"

"I lied to you before because I didn't know myself what I was feeling. Now I do. I suppose I sensed all along what you wanted. I was desperate to have you. I felt I had no choice."

She turned and faced him again, her eyes formidable and resolute. "Everyone has choices, Edouard. I was fool enough to let my heart make my choice. Céleste was right about you. She told me that the people I met when we were together were not part of your real life. But I didn't believe her, because I'd never heard of such a thing. I'm beginning to understand many things now. Your family thinks I am your whore, don't they, Edouard?"

"Renée . . . I . . ."

"That's what I thought. At least we can enter this bargain as equals. I deserve that much, don't you think?"

"Yes, but you *must* believe that I *do* love you. I don't care about your lack of background, but my family does."

"And I care what my family thinks too. I can't tell my aunt that she was right about you. You're forcing me to lie to her about my situation. I've never lied to anyone until I met you. I'm sure in time she will discover the truth, but for now I don't want to cause her any worry."

Renée sipped the brandy then settled steely eyes on him. "There's one more thing. Tomorrow morning I want you to enroll Pierre in a private school just as you said you would."

"Of course," he answered quickly, still not trusting her altered behavior.

"And Edouard, when you pay the headmaster, tell him that Pierre will remain there until his matriculation. In other words, pay the school for seven years' tuition."

"I'll do anything you ask." For the first time in his life, Edouard felt ashamed and guilty.

The following night, Renée held a written receipt from the Ecole St.-Denis for Pierre's tuition. She would do whatever it took to provide the best for both her brothers.

Renée despised Edouard not for robbing her of her virginity but for taking the innocence of her spirit. Because of him, she had learned how to survive in his world—a place where prejudice and selfishness reigned. She doubted she would ever trust in the way she had only yesterday. He had robbed her of the qualities that had made him love her. She had learned to be cunning and demanding. She was now just like the polished cosmopolitan women he'd always known.

Chapter Five

Renée wore a pearl gray silk dress with decorated collar, cuffs, and hem she'd beaded herself the night Edouard booked reservations at La Tour d'Argent. But even her skillfully applied makeup did not hide the dark circles under her eyes. For days she and Edouard had done nothing but argue.

He told her he loved her and that he would marry her, but when she inquired about a meeting between them and his parents, he informed Renée that his mother had turned him down.

"This is the twentieth century!" he said more to himself than to Renée. "She has always given me more and indulged me more than Lucienne or Emile. I'm her favorite. She's often told me that if I needed anything to call on her. I cannot think of a single instance when she's denied me. When she sees how beautiful, mannered, and capable you are, she'll accept you in an instant. She'll relent. She always has before."

But the days passed and still he skirted the issue whenever Renée brought it up. Renée could not tolerate the idea that she was a man's mistress. Nothing in her upbringing condoned any facet of this life she led. Her mother would have been horrified; her father would have disowned her. She felt a keen pressure to be married as soon as possible. To right the wrong, somehow. She worried that Céleste would somehow discover the truth. She wondered how she would ever face her aunt bearing this shame. Worst of all, she began to doubt Edouard's love for her, something that had justified her lies and actions in months previous.

"If you love me, you'll make your mother see us," she screamed at him.

"I do love you. Don't worry. I can handle my mother."

Finally, he'd done the only thing he could to stop Renée's badgering—he lied.

"You told me you had arranged for your parents to meet me," she said as they drove through the city streets. "You deliberately lied to me."

He pulled the Isotta to a stop. "Not exactly."

Renée stared straight ahead, nerves tensed. "Either you did or you didn't."

Edouard got out of the car and opened the door for her. "Renée," he pleaded. "I've gone to special pains to make this evening pleasant for you. Couldn't we talk about this later?"

Before Renée could let loose with her objections, she found herself being ushered to their table. The waiter held her chair while she seated herself. Edouard sat across from her and had just signaled the wine steward when he froze in midmotion.

"Edouard? What is it?" she asked, following his gaze to the exquisitely dressed woman seated two tables over. The woman's back was ramrod straight. Her eyes were cold and penetrating as she glared at Edouard. "Who is that?"

"My mother," he answered, a deadly chill in his voice.

Often when he spoke of her, Renée sensed that mother and son were not bonded by love but by fear. Always when he spoke of his mother, even while praising her, Renée noted that Edouard's jaw would tighten just enough to make a slight twitch at his temple.

As he looked at the formidable and undeniably magnetic woman across from them, she saw that his twitch was there again.

"Excuse me," he said and rose and went to Virginie's table.

He said something to her. Virginie whispered to Claude who nodded and remained seated while Virginie stood and reluctantly followed her son back to his table.

"Mother, this is Renée." His smile was strained.

Virginie's emerald eyes bored straight through Renée as if she were nonexistent.

"How do you do?" Renée said politely.

Virginie did not answer and immediately picked up her conversation with Edouard without missing a beat. "We could go to the balcony."

He nodded.

Renée was dumbfounded! She had expected hostility or coolness, but her utter lack of acknowledgment of her presence at all was far more unsettling. It took only seconds to realize that Virginie was not threatened by her in the least.

To Virginie, Renée was just another in Edouard's long line of mistresses, a temporary situation. She had no intention of accepting her as a future daughter-in-law, because she wasn't going to be one.

Renée watched as they walked outside the restaurant to the terrace that overlooked the Seine. Boldly, Renée rose and followed them. She found a small alcove where she could watch and listen without being seen.

Edouard sat on the balustrade listening to his mother. At one point he stood as if to protest, but Virginie simply laid a delicate hand on his sleeve, stated a few words, and he was under her control again.

". . . you're twenty-six years old, for another thing. I think an eighteen-year-old girl is a bit young for you, both in maturity and experience."

"Why don't you quit beating around the bush and get to the point, Mother."

"You must understand there is more at stake than your flirtations with a shop girl. There's the family name and business to consider. One day your heirs will be required to handle millions of francs the world over. You must look to the future and see what I see. The St. John family and ours have been close for over fifty years. Your grandfather Louis and Sir Jason went to school together. Since my father died, Sir Jason has been a comfort to me and this family for many years. I received a letter from him just this week intimating that he wanted to begin plans for an engagement party. How could I possibly inform him that he must delay everything because of your untimely dalliances?"

"I've never proposed to Lady Jane. In fact, she's the last person I'd choose."

"It's my place to do the choosing, not yours. What I don't understand is your current disregard for your duties."

"Well, I don't understand why you're being so harsh. You've never been like this with me."

Virginie's exasperation almost exploded. "I've allowed you to do as you please when it came to inconsequential matters. You aren't stupid—you know very well what's going on. I get the impression you're testing me—stalling for more time to play with your whore."

"She's not a whore. I've tried to tell you that I love Renée and I'm going to marry her."

"Love is for fools, Edouard, and no son of mine is a fool. Get rid of your encumbrances or face the consequences." Virginie did not wait for an answer and walked away.

Renée was stung when she heard Virginie call her a whore. She wasn't like that. She wasn't evil nor was her love for Edouard wrong. At least, it hadn't been in the beginning. She admitted her love had changed. Perhaps she was a whore now. Whether it was Virginie, Edouard, or herself who was to blame, she didn't know. The truth was ugly, but she could not turn away from it.

Renée had followed her heart, a perilous move on her part. She'd always believed love should be a simple matter. Two people met, fell in love, and were married. But her love affair was complicated and twisted because of Virginie's interference. She realized now that Edouard was not strong enough to stand up to his mother. Virginie was not only telling him that he could not marry Renée, but that he could not live with her either.

More than Edouard's weakness or Virginie's coldness, Renée despised the circumstances that made her and her brothers vulnerable to them. If she were more powerful and rich, she could vanquish this woman who wanted to eliminate her. She had to beat Virginie. She must make Edouard see that together they could fight her.

Renée's legs were shaking as she turned around and went back to their table.

Edouard returned shortly, spoke not a word, and quickly escorted her out of the restaurant. Just as they got to the door, Renée looked back at Virginie. She thought that for the rest of her life, she would never despise anything as much as the victorious grin on his mother's face.

"What did she say when you told her we were going to be married? Is she going to stand in our way? Will she give us her blessing? And what about your father? Why didn't you talk to him?"

"He doesn't get involved in family matters. Or business ones either."

"I don't understand that. Why not? And why won't your mother speak to me like a person?"

"Goddamn it, Renée! I can't answer a hundred questions at once! That's the trouble with you. You know that? You're constantly badgering me about everything. Especially these asinine minor details about our wedding!"

"I do not consider your family's blessing 'a minor detail'!" she screamed over the roar of the car's engine. "Just who is Lady Jane St. John anyway?"

"Jesus! You were eavesdropping! And you know, you're beginning to sound like a shrew and I won't have it! Do you understand me?"

Renée would not give up. "Of course I was listening. I'd do it again too. What 'consequences' was your mother talking about?"

"That's it!" he yelled as he pressed the accelerator flat to the floor and sped down the street.

Renée tried to get him to talk to her, but he ignored her and drove more furiously every time she opened her mouth. Afraid she was placing herself in greater jeopardy, she finally did as he asked and remained silent.

When they arrived at the apartment, Edouard stormed about for the rest of the night and then went out at three in the morning. He did not return for three days. When he did, he was unshaven and drunk. It was the beginning of a nightmare.

Two raging sleetstorms racked Paris that December, but inside the St.-Honoré apartment, Renée wrote a letter filled with lies to Céleste, then read stories to Michel in front of a warm fire and sipped hot chocolate.

"I want peppermint in mine," Michel said as he watched Renée top her cocoa with whipped cream.

"All right. And what else?"

"Two hugs and a kiss!"

"Easiest thing I've had to do all day." She complied and handed him his stuffed bear.

Michel was a happy baby with an even temper and curious mind. He was quick and bright and she knew one day he would be very successful—if he were given the chance. Every time she looked into his clear lavender eyes she reaffirmed her vow to secure proper educations for her brothers.

Pierre was stimulated by his courses at school and was respected by his teachers because of his efforts to catch up with the rest of his class. But even more importantly, he had met several boys with whom he'd formed friendships.

Since their encounter with Virginie, Renée saw little of Edouard for he stayed away for days on end and when he came home he was always drunk. They would fight for hours, Edouard smashing crystal vases into mirrors and then storming out of the house.

Most of Paris was buzzing with the story of Edouard's falling out with his mother over his newest mistress and the majority of the Ruille family friends had ostracized Edouard and Renée. This along with Edouard's new restrictions on their spending, Renée surmised, was what Virginie had meant by "consequences."

One night, Edouard came in, drunk and smelling of cheap perfume. The next morning, Edouard was oddly remorseful. "I don't understand what is happening except that I can't go on like this."

"It's no good . . . you and I," Renée said, lowering her eyes.

"You're wrong. It's not you at all. My mother has been pressing me to marry Lady Jane St. John and I've flatly refused. Somehow I must make her understand that in order to keep me, she must accept you."

"It will never happen and neither will you be able to live without her money. That's why you drink so much, isn't it?"

He shook his head. "That's all going to change. I am my mother's Achilles' heel. She needs me, she always has. I'm the only one she can depend on at the bank. In fact, I have a keener sense for international banking than she does. But she needs me for other reasons too. She has no one besides me. My father cares nothing for her and she only tolerates him. She has never been close to Lucienne . . . and Emile, now there's a waste of one's emotions! No, Mother will come around."

"You're so sure . . ."

"Very sure."

"Then it's a matter of who can wait it out the longest," Renée said, knowing Virginie was stronger.

"Exactly. In the meantime I must settle this matter of Lady Jane. If I go to London and tell her face-to-face there will be no engagement, I know we will be rid of her."

"That's wise," Renée said, thinking that with Lady Jane out of the way, perhaps Edouard would quit drinking and be able to face his mother. Her hopes were feeble these days—needing signs and reassurances from Edouard that theirs would be a happy ending. Unfortunately, Edouard failed her—again.

Chapter Six

Renée picked up the *Paris Herald* and read about Edouard's marriage to Lady Jane St. John on December 21, just two days after her sixteenth birthday and approximately thirty minutes before Virginie's servants arrived with orders to close the apartment and dismiss the servants. Virginie's stone-faced butler was surprised to find a two-year-old baby living in Edouard's house, not to mention Pierre, who came bursting in the front door momentarily interrupting the verbal eviction.

"We have no place to go!" she protested.

"That is not my concern," the butler replied icily.

"Make him go away!" Michel cried.

"Shhh. Everything will be all right. I'll take care of us." She carried him to the bedroom.

Trembling and in shock, Renée quickly stuffed their belongings into an old suitcase and two cardboard cartons. Under the butler's scowling gaze she dressed Michel and instructed Pierre to gather his things.

As she packed the clothes she had made to please Edouard, tears stung her eyes. She had loved him, believed in him. This couldn't be real, she thought as her throat constricted with unshed sobs.

She looked at the damask-draped bedroom one last time, remembering that it hadn't all been bad. There had been nights when, lying in Edouard's arms, she had wanted nothing else from life. She remembered his smile when they'd gone horseback riding in the Bois, and how in those first weeks, he'd followed her around like a puppy.

Never, she vowed, would she love a man again. Never would she trust anyone but her family. And never would she let Virginie beat her down again.

Surely nothing could be worse than this feeling of being used, invaded. She could remember days at Worth when she would have given her life for only a few moments with Edouard. As she looked back on it, she was amazed that she was once that naïve.

In less than two hours the three Dubois children found themselves without a home. Walking aimlessly toward the Seine, Renée was beside herself with anger, disillusionment, and fear.

"Where are we going?" Pierre asked.

"I don't know. We don't have any money for a hotel," she said despondently, looking up at the darkening skies.

"I have money," Pierre said, pulling a small wad of francs from his pocket.

"Where did you get that?"

"I stole it from Edouard. Just a little bit every night so he wouldn't know it was missing. I was going to use it for Christmas presents for everyone. I know it was wrong—"

Renée grabbed the money. "Not all that wrong!" she said and quickly counted it.

There was almost a hundred francs.

"It isn't much but it's enough to rent an apartment until I can find a job again. We'll go to the Left Bank where we can find something cheap. We'll need some of this for food. That means no bus."

Pierre looked at her and then at the three boxes and two suitcases.

"All right," she relented, "but just this once."

By the time they found an empty apartment they could afford, it was sleeting and all three of them were soaking wet. Pierre immediately stripped Michel of his wet clothes, bathed him, and dressed him in warm flannel pajamas. Renée went out to buy food and coal for the fire since there was no central heat.

After they finished their sparse meal of cheese and bread,

Renée counted the money and found she had only fifteen francs left. She would have to write to Aunt Céleste for a loan, and she would try to get her job back at Worth. That night they slept on the floor in their one-room apartment huddled together beneath the blanket.

Renée was awakened the following morning by a knock on the door. A sleepy man in his midtwenties with tousled brown hair and hands on narrow hips stood in the doorway.

"Would it be too much to ask to keep the noise down? I couldn't sleep because of you," he sputtered angrily, and then stopped abruptly and smiled as he eyed Renée appreciatively from head to toe. His temper quickly faded even though Renée continued to glare at him.

"I don't know what you're talking about," she said as Michel began crying.

"*That* is what I'm talking about," he said, pointing to Michel and pushing his way into the room.

"I heard nothing last night. There must be another baby in this building."

"No there isn't. Yours is the only one."

Pierre held Michel and nodded. "It's true, Renée. I was up with Michel all night. I thought I was keeping him quiet since he didn't wake you. I know you have been very tired. I think he caught a chill on the way here."

The stranger's expression changed to one of concern.

Renée went to Michel and laid her hand on his cheek. "He has a slight fever."

"I have some aspirin and fruit. That should help," the man said.

"Oh, yes." Renée smiled for the first time.

He left and returned moments later. While Renée rocked Michel in her arms, the man said: "It's Larousse."

"What is?"

"My name. Jean Larousse."

"I'm Renée and this is Michel and Pierre."

"I'm an artist. I said that first because that was going to be your next question."

She looked at his patched jacket and threadbare slacks.

"I'm not successful yet, but I will be." He smiled charmingly.

His brown eyes were intense and honest. "I believe you will. Could I see your work sometime?"

"How about now?"

Before she could answer he had dashed out of the apartment and was back with a painting of a beautiful woman clad in pastel blue lingerie. Renée could see he was talented.

"The woman is very sensual. I like it."

"You're of an extremely small minority, I'm afraid. There isn't much call for work like this."

"Ahead of the times?" she asked.

"Something like that."

"Are you from Paris?"

"North of the city." He nodded. "My father was a horse breeder. My mother was a socialite. I was seven when my father died. He left my mother enough money to live on for the rest of both our lives *if* she'd have invested wisely. She didn't."

"What happened?"

"She spent it all on maintaining ties with her wealthy friends. Couture clothes, lavish parties, expensive jewels. She even sold the house to keep up appearances."

"Then where did you live? Here?"

"No. With friends. I've been inside nearly every château, town house, and mansion in or near this city." He sighed sadly. "It was too much for her in the end. She accidentally died one night from too many sleeping pills and champagne."

"I'm sorry. My parents are dead too."

Renée felt so comfortable with her new friend that she soon found herself telling him all about Edouard and her current situation.

Later that afternoon, Jean took Pierre to the park where they shot pigeons with a slingshot and brought them home to eat. With half a bottle of cheap wine and the apples Jean had stolen the day before, their stomachs did not growl quite so much when they went to sleep.

The next day, Renée knew she must find work, but Michel's fever had not lessened. She took some of the money and bought more aspirin and cough medicine. Jean promised to keep an eye on Pierre and Michel, which gave her a measure of peace of mind as she set out for Worth.

The familiar gold "W" looked like Mecca, until Rénee was

informed by the directrice that her position had been filled and there were no openings available.

Renée had no choice but to keep searching.

When she walked in the worker's entrance at Paquin she found she was in luck. A nearly completed beaded cape designed by Jean Cocteau was due to be finished the day before Christmas and two of the seamstresses had taken ill. The position was temporary but she had to start immediately.

Renée took up her needle and tried to join in the seamstresses' happy chatter about their holiday plans, but as her fingers stitched the golden bugle beads onto the pale pink nubby silk crepe, she worried constantly about Michel.

She should be with him to hold and rock him. She wondered if Pierre was giving him the proper dosage of medicine. If the fever rose, Michel would need cold compresses. She forgot to tell Pierre to make certain Michel drank enough liquids. With fever came dehydration. She wondered if Jean would know about such things. How she wanted to go home, but still, the money she earned would pay for food and medicine.

As the hours passed and the design took shape, she thought about where she would go to find another job when this was over. Renée's anguish over her situation grew and a clear vision of Virginie loomed over her. She could see Virginie laughing at her, pleased with the havoc she had wrought.

It was nearly ten when she returned home, exhausted and worried. Jean and Pierre were waiting impatiently for her.

"Where have you been?" Jean demanded.

"I found a job, but it's only temporary. How is Michel?"

"The same. No better, no worse." Jean held out an apple. "Do you want something to eat?"

"Stolen?" She tried to smile, but failed.

Jean shrugged his shoulders as she took the apple.

"I want to see Michel," she said.

Renée went across the hall to Jean's apartment where Michel was asleep in Jean's bed. She touched his cheek. His fever was lower, but his breath rattled like a worn-out machine. Just like Papa, she thought.

Renée knelt beside the bed. "Please, God. Don't take him away. Let him stay with me. I know you aren't pleased with me right now. But don't make Michel pay for what I've done."

Tears streamed down her cheeks as she covered him with the blanket. With her hope buffered by prayer, surely Michel would be safe.

The following morning when Renée left for work Jean assured her that Michel was in good hands.

"He'll be all right. This time, if you're going to be late, telephone the concierge and leave a message for me. Then I'll come for you and walk you home."

"That's not necessary. I don't want you to be our nursemaid."

"I don't much care for your choice of words. Guardian angel sounds better. And while we're at it, no one asked for your opinion in the first place." He put his arm around her, but she was unable to draw comfort from the gesture.

Renée felt the world was against her. She kept searching for the way, the means to fight back, but she failed. She felt she couldn't do anything right. She kept praying and still Michel was no better. She had always believed in herself, but her confidence had fled along with her ability to trust.

By Christmas Eve Michel's breathing was extremely labored. Renée was frantic. Her meager earnings were gone, all spent on food and medicine. She could not afford a doctor. She didn't know what to do or where to turn.

Jean remembered a doctor he'd met years ago, but after walking across the Seine in the sleet and snow, he found the man had gone to the provinces for the holidays.

When he returned, Michel's fever was raging. Renée applied cold compresses to Michel's forehead. "This is just like it was with Papa. He'll die if we don't do something!"

"But what?" Jean asked.

Suddenly, Renée's whole face lit with hope. "Aunt Céleste told me once that the American Hospital had treated her and didn't ask for money."

"We'll try it!"

Quickly, they bundled Michel in blankets, borrowed an umbrella from the concierge, and set out.

As soon as they reached the hospital, the nurses rushed the flush-faced baby to emergency. Within seconds, a doctor arrived. While the doctor examined Michel, Renée could only think of

Virginie sitting in her warm house. She thought of Edouard and how secure he must be now with his new wife.

Suddenly, Michel's breathing became terribly constricted.

"You'll have to leave," the doctor said to her.

She looked down at Michel. His eyes were filled with terror.

"Renée," he rasped and reached out his tiny hand, but the nurse was pulling at her arm.

"You'll just be in the way," the nurse was saying.

Once she was in the hallway, Michel's cries increased. She slammed her hands over her ears so she couldn't hear them. He was calling for her. Renée was ravaged with panic and guilt. Had loving Edouard been such an awful deed that Michel must suffer like this? She knew the unfamiliar faces of the doctors and nurses must be frightening him. She had to be with him, to calm him.

His screams kept slicing through her heart. She thought she was being ripped in half. She wished she could trade places with him. She was stronger, healthier. She could withstand the fever—Michel couldn't. His breathing sounded like a freight train.

She paced. She bit her nails. Long moments of silence terrorized her, but then his frightened screams echoed through the hall again, making her glad for the deadly silence.

The doctors were taking so long—too long. They should have worked a miracle by now. Michel had always looked to her for miracles. Almost since the day he was born, she had taken care of him. She had fed him, changed him, rocked him, and sung to him. She wanted to sing to him now. Maybe then he wouldn't be so frightened. Maybe then he would get better. Maybe then she would work *the* miracle.

Renée was strung like piano wire. Never had she known hours to lag this slowly. She watched Jean pace up and down, lighting one cigarette after another. Pierre slumped in a chair opposite her, fighting to stay awake. Evening became night. She still was not allowed to see Michel. Mercifully, his cries had abated. She was unsure if that was a good sign or not. She fought tears but every time she saw the faces of the nurses who rushed in and out, she lost the battle.

Pierre watched her crying but his face was granite. He was an emotional volcano ready to erupt. He clutched the chair's arms and stared at the wall.

It was almost dawn when the doctor emerged.

Renée took one look at his face and screamed hysterically. "No! He can't be!"

Jean held her back but she broke free and raced into the room and clutched Michel's body to her breast. "He's so tiny and limp," she whispered through her tears. "Why aren't you flushed anymore?"

Then she remembered that the fever was gone. "Thank God you are better now, Michel. Pierre and I will take you home with us."

She smoothed his hair away from his forehead and kissed his cheek. It was velvety smooth—baby's skin always was. He was so young, with his whole life ahead of him, she thought. She would make certain he'd have all the advantages. Michel would have the education Papa had wanted for him. Maybe he would decide to be a doctor. Doctors were such a noble breed, saving lives. Michel would save lives one day just as these doctors had saved his life. Hadn't they?

Renée's thoughts sped through her head, jumbling her dreams with reality.

"Someday we'll have a nice house like we had on St.-Honoré and I'll buy you all the toys and chocolate you want. Won't you like that, Michel?"

She stroked Michel's arm, wondering why tears filled her eyes and blurred her vision. Everything was fine now. Wasn't it?

Pierre stood by the door watching his sister. "He's dead, Renée. He's . . . dead!" Finally, tears streamed down his cheeks.

Pierre was telling the truth, but her mind couldn't accept it. Her heart would never let Michel go. She would always keep him close. Renée focused horror-stricken eyes on Michel. It wasn't Michel's crying and whimpering she was hearing, but Pierre's. She looked over as Jean picked Pierre up and hugged him tightly.

"Why do we have to lose everyone we love?" Pierre cried. "I want Maman and my papa. I want Michel back. It isn't fair! It isn't fair! Maybe they hated me. Maybe I did something wrong."

"No, Pierre. NO! Nothing you have ever done or been has caused this."

"Oh, Jean. I'm so alone."

"No you aren't. You have Renée. You have me."

Pierre clung so fiercely to Jean's neck that he left red imprints.

Jean thought Pierre's unleashing could have lasted days, but Jean's soothing words and strong arms finally calmed the boy.

Jean pried Reñee away from Michel's body and pulled her into his arms. She had never felt so desolate in all her life. Her guilt beat at her insides, pounding her, making her wish *she* were dead, not Michel. Not innocent Michel. She thought of all the things she should have done for him. She should never have loved Edouard so much. Pierre had seen the truth. He had known Edouard was stealing too much of her time. Too much of her. She should have been clever like Pierre and stolen more money from Edouard. She should have gone to London with Aunt Céleste. She should have made God hear her.

Jean tried to comfort her and say the words that would reach inside and calm her. "It's not your fault, Renée. It was meant to be like this. There was nothing you could have done to stop it. Don't blame yourself."

She looked at him incredulously as images of Edouard's drunken fights and Virginie's cold eyes flashed before her. Suddenly she realized Jean was right. She *had* done all she could. She was only a young girl at war with probably the most powerful family in Paris. She had never stood a chance against them. Virginie had always known that. Now Renée knew it too. But it wouldn't always be so.

Jean felt Renée's back tense, and when she looked up at him, her eyes were filled with a ferocity that sent chills down his spine.

"I swear to you this day, on my brother's dead body, I will never let this happen to me or any of my family again. I'm going to be rich and powerful so that no one, not even Virginie Ruille, can ever hurt us again."

Chapter Seven

When the particularly discriminating Baroness de Beauchamps commented to the vendeuse at Paquin that the beading on her evening cape was superior to anything she'd ever seen, the vendeuse told the fitter who related the compliment to the directrice, who in passing mentioned it to the first assistant who told Madame Paquin herself.

Renée Dubois was hired as a permanent employee and promoted immediately to first hand seamstress.

In the weeks that followed Michel's death, Renée struggled with her grief and anger. She found that as long as she submerged herself in work, she did not have to deal with her emotions. Slowly her plans for the future took shape and she put the past behind her.

Every week she budgeted her household money and always put a portion aside for savings. She never bought sugar or coffee; she walked everywhere. She volunteered for extra hours at work and did handwork at home.

Pierre continued at the private school Edouard had paid for, and with Jean's gentle encouragement, he bore his grief more openly and his wounds began to heal.

These days, Renée did not trust the people she met. When men approached her at a café, she declined their invitations, emphati-

SINS OF OMISSION

cally making certain they would not bother her again. After Edouard, she vowed never again to be so foolish.

She made certain she did not reveal her vulnerabilities to anyone. She buried her fears deep inside. She found it was easy to keep a rein on her emotions, if she had any left. Edouard had murdered the Renée she had once been. In her place emerged a woman of purpose whose goals were clearly defined within the context of the business world. She became a woman with a façade. Coworkers liked her efficiency, knowledge, and style. Though she was pleasantly warm, she retreated when anyone tried to know her better.

Her grieving over the death of her innocence was second only to her mourning for Michel.

Only Jean and Pierre knew the truth. Only they were allowed to love her and she to love them.

With so many voids in Renée's life, Jean's friendship was vital. He was father, brother, and friend rolled into one. He joked one time that even he could not understand their relationship, since he'd always made lovers of the women he met. His paintings were still not selling and if it weren't for Renée he would not have been able to eat.

One night in January after Pierre was asleep, Renée went to Jean's apartment and found him immersed in his work. He hadn't heard her knock nor the door open as she entered.

He worked by candlelight since that was the effect he was hoping to convey on canvas. The woman in the painting had huge childlike eyes that seemed to smolder at Renée. Jean had once again successfully breathed life into his unnervingly sensual subjects. She watched as he used short feathering strokes to give the illusion of candleglow around the woman's breast. She wore a lavender teddy, dropped to her waist, as she sat on the edge of the bed, which Jean had darkened as much as the surrounding room so that upon first glance the woman looked like an angel suspended in darkness. Peering closer, Renée realized the light in the room was from a match, not a candle; lying next to her was a wad of francs, and the woman was not an angel but a whore.

"It's magnificent," Renée whispered in awe.

Jean spun around, his mouth agape. "Oh, Renée! I didn't hear you." He turned back to his painting. "You really like it?"

"Very much."

"I call it 'Smoldering Innocence.'"

"I think you succeeded. Would you like a break? I've got some wine and a very warm fire I'll share."

Jean quickly put his brushes away. "How could I refuse?"

Renée poured the wine while they talked about the future.

"I can't imagine ever not painting. And yet, I think I'm going to have to find something else since the public does not appreciate my talent," he said, mocking himself.

"And I refuse to spend the rest of my life being a seamstress for someone else."

Jean glanced at her and once again saw that look of cold determination he'd seen so often since Michel's death. "What do you want to do?"

"I want my own boutique with the finest clothes in France. I'll be as famous as Chanel or Vionnet. It will be elegant, chic, and very expensive."

"Your ambitions are very lofty for such a little girl."

"You find it hard to take me seriously," she said angrily. "Let me assure you, this is not idealism or naïveté. I *will* have my shop and no one, not even you, can stand in my way!"

She spoke with such resolve he believed her. "What kind of clothes will you have in your shop?"

Renée thought for a moment, then spying the painting he'd given her for Christmas, her eyes lit up. "Lingerie!" she said, scrambling toward the painting. She held it up to the firelight. "Negligees that you will design for me, Jean!"

"You're crazy! I'm not a fashion designer!"

"Of course you are! Every time you paint one of your pictures you put different lingerie on the women. Where did you get the ideas for them? Do the models wear these things when they pose for you?"

"Well, no . . ."

"I thought not. They pose nude and you put the clothes on the subject later. Don't you see, Jean? This is our ticket out of here!"

Her enthusiasm was catching and what she said was true. He did design the clothes, using bits and pieces of peignoirs and negligees he'd seen all his life on his mother, his lovers. The idea was a good one, but implementing it was another matter.

"Even if I could come up with designs for you every day, where are you going to get the capital to buy the material, rent the shop, and hire people to do the work?"

"One thing at a time," she said and went off to a corner where she opened a box and brought forth yards of beautiful and expensive chiffon and silk.

"Where did you get this?" he asked.

"This is the last of Edouard's gifts to me. While he was in London I went on a shopping spree at Bon Marché and charged him for it. I should have bought more. But I have two boxes filled with materials, all of which were intended for lingerie."

"That hardly stocks a store, chérie."

She smiled coyly at him. "I know that. A store is out of the question right now, but we could make this apartment into a workroom and fitting room, while the three of us lived in your apartment."

"I don't know . . ."

"Listen to me. When I was with Edouard I met a lot of wealthy people, and I know that if I approached them in the right manner, there would be enough who would buy my clothes."

"My clothes, you mean."

"No. Your designs. *My* clothes," she said sternly.

"This is the craziest thing I've ever heard, but just to make you happy, I'll draw you one gown and if you can make it up and sell it at a good price, then you have yourself a designer. But you have to prove to me you can get couture prices."

"It's a bargain!" she said, but when she bent over to hug Jean, her knees buckled and she sank to the floor next to him.

Not realizing what was wrong, Jean joked, "You'd better save some of that energy for all the work you're going to have."

Renée suddenly felt nauseous and clutched her stomach. "Help me to the bathroom. I'm going to be sick."

Jean scrambled to his feet and lifted her off the floor, but before they could make it down the hall to the bath they all shared, she vomited.

Jean took her back to his room where she lay down next to Pierre. He surmised it was the cheap wine, and by the time he cleaned up the mess and returned, she was fast asleep.

"Some entrepreneur you are, Renée Dubois," he mumbled as he made up his pallet and wondered why he allowed this young girl to dominate his life.

The next evening when Renée returned from work, Jean presented her with a sketch of a negligee cut straight across the breasts, with beaded straps and a beaded detachable waistband that ended in a V at the navel. Renée searched through the fabrics and found a celadon silk satin and began work.

Between the lack of a sewing machine and bouts of nausea, it took over two weeks for Renée to finish the gown. When she produced the finished garment for Jean's inspection, they both agreed it was magnificent and equal to anything found in the best shops of Paris.

When Jean surprised Renée with four additional sketches, he was so immersed in an excited explanation of his ideas that he was slow to notice Renée's preoccupation.

"Are they really that bad?" he asked, looking first at her then at the drawings.

"Jean, I'm pregnant."

The sketches fell out of his hand and scattered at his feet as he stood there dumbstruck. She looked so young and innocent standing before him; a child herself. She was the little sister he'd never had; he'd pretended all these weeks that Edouard was just a story she'd made up like children often do. His part in Renée's life had been easy to forget. Now Edouard was making his presence known and Jean didn't like it one bit. He wanted to protect Renée from Edouard, from pain, but he didn't know how. He gathered her in his arms and said nothing.

Renée had thought about nothing else for days and in her mind she dismissed the fact that Edouard was the father. This was her child and in her heart she believed that God had sent this baby to her to take Michel's place. She knew it was a blessing, but she doubted God's wisdom in His timing. They were doing well as long as she had work and a paycheck coming in. She wouldn't be able to hide the pregnancy for long before the directrice discovered her secret. She could not afford to lose her job nor could she give up the work she was doing at night. She told herself the nausea couldn't last forever and that somehow she would find the energy to make up Jean's new designs. He was solidly behind her now, and if it took every ounce of her will, she would not disappoint him.

As she stood in the circle of his arms, it was she who strengthened her hold and said: "We'll make do the best we can."

In the weeks that followed, their luck began to turn. For the first time in months, when Jean actively sought buyers for his paintings, he was successful. He purchased expensive cream-colored stationery and hand-painted unusual announcements that Renée sent to prospective clients. When the box of fabric was emptied, Renée had produced four nightgowns, two peignoirs, and two pairs of silk pajamas. All were exquisitely made. Jean hung the collection on the eight nails he'd hammered into the wall of Renée's apartment. He purchased a used table and chair for twenty francs, placed an order pad and pencil on it, and declared themselves in business.

The following Saturday afternoon Carrie Baldwin and Ursula Ames arrived with announcements in hand and purchased one gown apiece. Two nights later, Carrie returned with three friends who purchased the remainder of the collection. One week later, Renée and Jean found themselves with customers, orders, and operating capital.

Renée quit her job at Paquin, bought a sewing machine, and placed her first order with M. Vernet, the owner of a Lyon silk plant.

To her delight, M. Vernet gave her a discounted price as a favor and sent her a sample of a watered silk whose dye had "run," creating an unusual print in mauves, blues, and lavenders. He informed her the silk was a "mistake," but should she be able to use it, he could offer an excellent price.

Jean and Renée spent three nights struggling with a design that would display the silk to its best advantage. Their collaboration resulted in a severely tailored nightgown and masculine-cut robe to match. Renée quickly ordered M. Vernet's "mistake."

Renée read Céleste's month-old letter which had been sent to the St.-Honoré address and then forwarded to her new general delivery address. Lies were boomerangs, Renée thought. Céleste had read of Edouard's marriage to Lady Jane. She demanded an explanation. Renée felt guilty and sad for she not only had to admit to her lies, but the time had finally come for Céleste to learn of Michel's death.

Taking up pen and paper was an arduous task. Renée spent all of Sunday afternoon explaining and pleading for Céleste's understanding. She told Céleste about Jean, their fledgling business, and her hopes for the future—her shop. Renée told her of the pregnancy and, as she wrote, tears filled her eyes. Just as regret filled her heart, the baby moved. Renée placed her hand on her stomach. This baby was hers and hers alone. She would protect it from all harm. If Céleste could not understand, then Renée would protect her baby from her aunt too.

In less than a week, Céleste's reply arrived. She did not condemn her. There was only sadness over losing Michel. Céleste did not send for Renée and Pierre, wisely sensing that Renée would not come. Her life was in Paris now, as she struggled to make her shop a reality. Céleste stated adamantly that she would come to Paris to help out when the baby arrived.

Every month Renée went to Dr. White at the American Hospital who told her that both she and the baby were healthy. By her seventh month Jean had cleverly designed clothes with low hip sashes and pleated bodices that almost completely hid Renée's protruding abdomen. Under no circumstances did Renée want any gossip about the baby. She could not afford Virginie's wrath either psychologically or financially.

Dr. White was sworn to secrecy in exchange for a design especially for his wife. In her eighth month, Renée brought him a cream silk negligee trimmed in peach piquot ribbons and a cream satin robe to match. To her surprise, Mrs. White called on Renée personally to thank her and ordered two more gowns. The following month, Mrs. White sent a dozen of her friends to Renée and they all placed orders too.

As Renée neared the end of her pregnancy, she and Jean had become known for their avant-garde lingerie. The Americans especially responded to their designs with enthusiasm and a seemingly endless supply of money.

Renée was placing weekly orders with M. Vernet, and in his last letter he teased her that soon he would have to "run" silks on purpose for he had shipped her the last of his "mistakes." Renée wrote him back, including silk samples from the previous two shipments, and told him to do exactly that. She would pay full price.

As their fame grew so did their overhead. Renée found it necessary to hire two seamstresses and a fitter. They needed larger quarters.

Jean wondered if he would ever have any privacy again, but he was accomplishing something tangible for the first time in his life and it *almost* made up for the lack of women in his bed.

When school began in September, Pierre was forced to study in the library near the school to avoid the noisy apartment. He slept on a cot since Renée's pregnancy was so advanced she needed the bed. Using Renée's ideas and suggestions of color and fabric for each client, Jean usually sketched until late into the night. More often than not, he fell asleep at the table. What money they had went back into the business to purchase fabric, trims, beads, lace, and pay salaries. Renée was caught with no cash in hand and saw no answer to their predicament.

Céleste arrived in Paris a week later than planned and found Renée two days overdue.

"I can't believe that the three of you are living in such cramped quarters! And where did you expect to put the baby—in the hallway?" she exclaimed. "I can see I arrived none too soon. It's time I took matters into my own hands!"

Céleste rented a large apartment just off the boulevard du Montparnasse on the rue de Vaugirard. There was an excellent view of the Jardin du Luxembourg, ample room for the seamstresses, a kitchen, bath, and two bedrooms; one for Jean and one for Renée and the baby. She found two used white iron beds with mattresses, a battered chest of drawers which she repainted herself, and a wicker basinette for the baby. She purchased two screens to mark off a private area for Pierre and one for Jean's new drafting table, stool, and lamp. She found a storage trunk for Pierre and together they pasted old theater posters on it, and she then filled it with three new pairs of trousers, a tweed jacket, two shawl-collared sweaters, and four cotton shirts.

Pierre did not ask her where the clothes came from and she did not volunteer the fact that "an old friend" of hers had a son two years older than Pierre who seldom wore his clothes longer than a season before his father replenished his son's wardrobe. Céleste did not believe in blackmail, but she was not above exacting a little "pressure" for a favor that she felt due her—especially when it benefited her family.

In all, Céleste spent slightly over eight hundred francs, the last of her household spending money, and considered it a wise investment.

* * *

On September 20, 1926, Edouard Ruille splashed his seventh brandy into a Lalique glass and continued his pacing. It was medieval for a woman to give birth at home, he thought, as he listened to Jane's screams tearing through the house.

Virginie tapped her red-lacquered fingernails on the overstuffed black moiré upholstered sofa, causing Edouard to glare at her.

"I swear to God, Jane can be so pigheaded about the most asinine things," he said.

"Agreed. But there isn't much we can do about it now. When I last went up the doctor said it would be any minute now."

Edouard finished off the brandy, poured himself another, and lit a cigarette. "That was over two hours ago."

"Must you drink so much, Edouard? After all, women give birth every day. What I can't understand is this production Jane has to make of it all. With you three children I was never in labor over four hours and I certainly never carried on the way she is."

"You're a paragon, Mother," he said sarcastically.

Virginie let the remark pass. "You will be glad to know I have made all the arrangements for the christening and I thought a luncheon at the château afterward would be nice. That way we could invite more guests."

"I thought Jane was planning a small reception here?"

"Your town house may be big enough for you and Jane, but it's hardly suitable for entertaining a large number of people. I suppose that if it's a girl it wouldn't matter much, but if it's a boy, and I think it will be, certain matters of protocol must be maintained."

"Mother, this is not a dauphin we are talking about, but my son."

"Precisely! *Your* son, Edouard. Heir regent to the Ruille fortunes. He will be our future, yours and mine."

Edouard eyed her gravely. "Sometimes you really frighten me, Mother. You act as if none of us really matters. Not me, or Jane or the baby—only the business. Is that all there is to you, Mother, a ledger of credits and debits?"

"Don't be absurd, Edouard. I love you and I'm thrilled about my first grandchild. Can't you see I just want him to have the best advantages?" She rose gracefully and put her hand on his rough cheek. "You are my firstborn, Edouard, and I'm sure you have always known that you are my favorite. Everything I've done has been for you."

He looked into the dark depths of her eyes and shuddered. "For me, or for yourself, Mother?"

Just then the doctor burst into the room, flinging the doors aside. "Monsieur Ruille! You have a son!"

Edouard shoved the brandy glass into Virginie's hand and raced up the stairs. Virginie sighed with relief at the news. A son. How right she had been to insist on this marriage!

"Thank you, Doctor!" she said exuberantly. "Remind me to call especially for you when Jane has her next son!"

The doctor's face fell, causing Virginie to ask: "What is it? Is there something wrong with the baby?"

"No, not the baby. But I'm afraid Lady Jane won't be having any more children."

"What?"

"She had a very difficult time. She is a small-boned woman to begin with. There has been damage. I strongly suggest we transfer Lady Jane to the hospital, where I can watch her more closely. Let me assure you, I do not expect any complications. But I do believe she should be allowed to recuperate without intrusions from visitors."

"Yes, yes, of course."

Virginie heard nothing of what he said about Jane's condition other than the fact that Edouard was to have only one child. There must have been some mistake! This was all too incredible, she thought, as Edouard walked into the room with his son.

Virginie looked down at the fair-haired, blue-eyed baby. Virginie's disappointment was written all over her face. He had Jane's bland features and possessed none of his father's dark good looks. There was not a single characteristic that stamped him as her grandson. She could only hope he would inherit her brains along with the Ruille name. When she looked up, Edouard was watching her intently. She forced a smile.

"What's the matter, Mother? Doesn't he meet your standards? You wanted Jane to be the mother of your heirs. I should think he was made to order."

He placed the squalling child in her arms and took the brandy glass from her. "Here's to you, Mother. You got what you wanted." He sneered and stormed out of the house.

* * *

On the other side of Paris in the American Hospital, Renée Dubois gave birth the same day after three and a half hours of labor to an eight-pound three-ounce baby boy whom she named Gaston. Had Edouard Ruille known about Gaston he would have been pleased. Gaston had a full head of dark hair, thickly lashed dark brown eyes, and looked exactly like his father. The nurses commented at every feeding that Gaston was the handsomest baby they had ever seen—not to mention the healthiest.

Renée had to agree with them, but then, she had expected nothing less.

The announcement of Gaston's birth did not make the society columns of the newspapers, but Virginie heard about it three months later through the gossips. Virginie immediately ended speculation about the paternity of the child by calling attention to the fact that Renée had reportedly been living with a man, now her "business partner," since the day Edouard left her.

Edouard paid no attention to the rumors for he had remained perpetually drunk since the day Henri was born. When Edouard brazenly appeared at a dinner party with his new dark-skinned African mistress, all gossip about Edouard's former mistress died instantly.

Chapter Eight

Since its origin under Louis XIV, the Bois de Boulogne has been the setting against which rational men and women have succumbed to the madness of romance. Thus it was in 1927 on one of the last fine days of autumn when the sun still warms the face and the air is so crisp it stings the eyes, that Edouard Ruille fell in love for the second time in his life.

His horse came galloping out of the Bois forest, its hooves crushing fallen leaves into golden dust, when he saw her. She was dressed in khaki jodhpurs and a heavily cabled wheat-colored pullover. Her lavender-blue eyes would put any sunset to shame, he thought, when she turned and saw him. Not until he reined in his horse and jumped to the ground did he notice that she was not alone.

The dark-haired little boy toddled toward his mother with outstretched arms and wide, terrified eyes. She protectively scooped him up in her arms, quieting him with soothing words.

"Your horse frightened him," she said coolly and stooped to gather her blanket and the baby's toys.

"Don't leave. Please, Renée, I must speak with you."

"I have nothing to say to you, Edouard."

He looked at the boy and instantly knew the child was not the son of her new lover as he'd heard when the child was born; the boy was *his*.

"I think you do," he said.

"Gaston is *my* son!" she said vehemently and moved to walk away.

"Why didn't you tell me?"

"It was none of your business. And in case you've forgotten, you have a son. Henri, isn't that his name? I think I read that in the newspaper along with the extensive list of noted guests at his christening."

Renée's voice was filled with so much venom, Edouard recoiled from the onslaught.

"You hate me and I don't blame you after what I did."

"Well, at least we agree on something. Let's just leave it at that, shall we?"

"I must make you understand."

Renée laughed sarcastically. "I understand a lot more than you give me credit for, Edouard. I didn't have enough money or the proper background for you. I was and still am a nobody, so why'd don't you leave us alone?"

This time when she turned away from him, he grabbed her arms and held her steady.

"I love you, Renée. I didn't know how much until after I married Jane. It was a horrid, stupid mistake. My life has been miserable since the day I left for London. I know I should have stood up to my family, and if I had it to do all over again, I would!"

"Ah! But you don't have that luxury anymore. How convenient! I'm sorry you aren't happy, Edouard, but that's your problem, not mine."

He could say nothing to refute the truth she spoke. He released her. "I don't want to hurt you anymore, Renée. I know this is a lot to ask, but could I visit you and my son sometime? I beg you, please don't refuse, just think about it."

He was truly despondent, and for the first time in his life, Renée thought he was telling the truth. He was not a happy man. She had heard rumors about him from her friends and clients. His drinking had become worse, which seemed impossible. Then there was the story about his arriving at a party with a cold-cream jar of cocaine.

The unprinted stories about Edouard's supposed love affair with a well-known homosexual artist had been more than Renée could stomach. She was not convinced it was true, since Edouard had as many enemies these days as he used to have friends. Still, she was wary of him and the trouble both he and his family could cause. Most of all, she didn't want anyone taking Gaston from her. She wanted to get away from Edouard. She wished she could find someplace where she and Gaston would never see him. But Paris was a small city.

"I'll think about it," she said, hoping to put him off.

"Fair enough. Let me get you a cab."

Renée gathered her things and walked alongside Edouard as he continued with small talk. Though her demeanor was cool, she was seething inside. Once she was seated in the cab and they drove away, she finally relaxed. She held Gaston close to her. It was pointless to hope they could rid themselves of Edouard. For almost two years they had enjoyed peaceful anonymity. But now, Edouard wanted them. There was no escape.

In the days and weeks that followed, Renée found herself living the life of the hunted, for Edouard followed her every move. She avoided his phone calls and never returned them. She altered her normal routines and sent her seamstresses or Jean on errands rather than risk being seen leaving the apartment. She noted Edouard's car parked outside their building three times in one week. She discontinued her evening stroll through the park and sent Pierre to school in a cab rather than the bus where Edouard could easily approach him.

Edouard's obsession with her finally came to a head when he pushed his way into the studio, sending gasps of outrage from two Italian women who were being fitted in yards of fuchsia silk.

He boldly walked up to Renée, who was inspecting alternative silk prints for the Italians, and said: "You can't avoid me any longer! I have a right to see my son!"

"You relinquished all rights when you abandoned me! And I forbid you to come into my place of business and upset my customers like this." She stalked into the hallway outside the apartment.

Edouard apologized to the startled Italian women, whom he

knew would feed the gossips an earful by evening. He shut the door and stood next to an enraged Renée.

"Can't you take the hint or are you just that dumb, Edouard? I don't want to see you, talk to you, or even hear your name."

"Please hear me out. I was wrong and I apologize for my behavior. It won't happen again. But you can't stop me from loving you. That's all I wanted to say. I don't want you to feel threatened by me and it's the last thing on this earth I intended. Ever since that day in the Bois, I haven't been able to think about anything but you or my son."

"Stop calling him your son! He's *my* son!"

"All right. Gaston, then. I want to do what's right by you both. I know I'm to blame for all that's happened to you and I want to make it up to you. Do you think you could see your way to just being friends?"

"I don't think so, Edouard." If anything, she wished she had a knife so she could rip his heart out, the way he had hers. It took every ounce of self-control to rein in her anger. She had to remain calm and keep him out of her life.

"I won't bother you here anymore, if you'll promise to meet me for dinner so we could talk."

"I don't see any point in it."

"Then I'll show up here anytime I damn well please!" he growled.

"All right," she said, relenting. She could not afford the emotional or financial repercussions of his unannounced "visits." "Next Wednesday I'm free. Where should I meet you?"

"I'll send a cab for you at eight and we'll have dinner at Maxim's."

"Until then, Edouard," she said, then opened the door and rushed to her apartment. She had bought a week of peace but that was all. Her stomach churned with the thought that she had been forced to bargain with that devil again.

The night at Maxim's turned out not to be quite the nightmare that Renée had feared. Edouard was on his best behavior; he made no further threats about visiting the workrooms, not did he push to see his son. When the evening was over Renée was certain he would soon press for another rendezvous.

* * *

Lord Arthur Wellesley and Lady Wellesley arrived at Claude and Virginie Ruille's home for a quiet after-dinner game of cards.

"Claire, how lovely you look," Virginie greeted her longtime friend from London.

"So do you, dear," Lady Claire replied.

"How was Maxim's?" Claude asked.

Claire's bland lashless eyes rolled in her heavily jowled face. "As usual, the exquisite food was not the topic of conversation."

"And who was?" Virginie asked purposefully.

"Your son."

"Edouard? He didn't tell me that he and Jane were going out this evening."

"He wasn't with Jane."

"Then who . . . ?" Suddenly, Virginie noted the glint in Claire's eyes and felt her own nerves tingle. As always, she kept her composure.

"It was that young tart he was seeing before he married Jane. You remember, what was her name—" Claire tapped a blunt finger to her cheek as she watched Virginie struggle with herself. Claire had heard others speak of Virginie's vendetta against Renée Dubois, but this was the first she'd seen of it. Claire was delighted.

"Dubois," Virginie whispered.

"Ah, yes, Renée Dubois." Claire knew Virginie would not ask for the details, but Claire wanted to be the one to tell her. "They sat in a corner, which is unusual since Edouard normally gets a better table. He seemed very attentive to her, though she was quite restrained. I've heard a lot of talk about her, but this was the first time I'd actually seen her. I was surprised."

"Surprised?"

"She's more beautiful than I'd been told. Lovely clothes, well mannered, graceful." Claire seated herself at the card table. "I think it's appalling how the lower classes believe they can bluff their way into our world."

Virginie was seething, but she managed to concentrate on her cards and pretend that nothing was wrong. When Lord and Lady Wellesley left two hours later, her head was splitting. She was determined to put an end to Edouard's affair.

She inundated Edouard with work during the day, scheduled

two evening meetings with board members, and made certain his social calendar was filled with dinners and parties where Jane's presence was also expected.

For fourteen days her plan succeeded.

Renée answered the phone on the second ring. It was Edouard. He suggested they attend the theater.

"I'm told it's a marvelous comedy," he said.

"Yes, I'd love to go," she said instantly, thinking that her reentrance into Edouard's life must have angered Virginie. The thought was a sweet one. Renée was certain his mother was the reason she hadn't heard from him for two weeks.

As Edouard rambled on about his busy schedule, Renée became acutely aware of the tug-of-war Virginie was waging. This time Renée would not be the loser.

"Edouard, after the play could we have late supper at Le Grand Véfour?"

"Of course, darling."

"You should make reservations then."

"Yes! And we'll have champagne!"

"Of course," she replied and hung up. A hard smile parted her lips as she thought of the havoc she would create at the Ruille household.

The night at the theater was enjoyable because Renée was successful in blocking Edouard's presence out of her mind. The dinner was romantic and festive. Renée noted that half the patrons at Le Grand Véfour were Virginie's intimates. When she and Edouard left, she could hear the buzz of their gossip.

When he returned her home, his eyes were filled with love. She thought about what she was doing—using him to exact her revenge. She pitied him for being the pawn, but even more she hated his weakness that allowed her to use him.

Edouard was enough of a romantic to believe that a life with Renée was possible. She could see he had convinced himself that his dreams would come true.

In that instant when he held her, kissed her, and told her that he loved her, tears filled her eyes for she remembered a naïve Renée who had once loved him back. It was too late now. That had been a lifetime ago—before he and his mother had taught her to hate.

* * *

When Edouard approached his mother and told her he wanted to divorce Jane and marry Renée, he felt it unimportant that he had not discussed his plans with Renée at all. Handling his mother would be far more difficult than convincing Renée.

Virginie's glacial eyes stared incredulously at him as he stood before her, watching cold fury ignite. With her lips curved upward she hissed through clenched teeth: "Impossible!" And she returned to her papers.

"I don't think you heard me correctly, Mother."

"Yes I did," she replied without looking up.

He lunged across the desk and grabbed her chin in his hand, jerking her face close to his. "I mean to do what I say. You can't stop me this time. I don't give a damn about the family or the money. She's the only shot at happiness I've got. You nearly destroyed it once. I won't let it happen again."

"Don't do something you'll regret."

"I have many regrets, Mother. This is *not* one of them!"

For the first time in her life Virginie felt powerless, but she cleverly hid the fact from her son. She should have paid off the Dubois girl long ago. She blamed herself for not taking stricter measures with Edouard when the problem first arose. She had always been too lenient with him. Now he thought he could take advantage of her preference for him. Edouard had to learn that he was powerless. He must know that only through her was he anything at all.

In his irascible state she would not be able to deal with him rationally, a tack that had always served her well. She freed herself from his grasp, and stood up.

"You seem quite firm on this matter, Edouard, but I advise you to weigh all the consequences before you take any action."

"That ploy won't work again, Mother. You have manipulated me for the last time. I only came here today to tell you goodbye. I felt I owed you that."

"You came here hoping I would tell you that your ideas were just dandy and that I would allow you to keep your money, your son, and your slut. The answer is no, Edouard, nobody gets it all, least of all you. You haven't earned it."

"Then I guess the war is over, Mother. And we both lost."

That was the last time Virginie was ever to see her favorite son, for that night Edouard got roaringly drunk in the Ritz bar, complaining to the bartender about his agonies with his family. He left the Ritz and raced his blue Bugatti down the Champs-Elysée, crashed into one of the historic chestnut trees, and died instantly.

Four days after Edouard's fashionable and well-reported funeral, the immediate members of the Ruille family sat shocked and aghast in the attorney's office as he read Edouard's last will and testament bequeathing the title to his personal villa at Saint-Jean-Cap-Ferrat to Renée Dubois and a lump sum of twenty-five thousand francs to Gaston Dubois. To his wife, Lady Jane St. John Ruille, he left the bulk of his estate, including the house on rue St. Anne, and to his rightful son, Henri Ruille, he left a trust of thirty thousand francs, only slightly more than the bequest to his bastard son.

The scandal over the public disclosure that Gaston Dubois was a Ruille was more than Virginie could stand. She swore to her closest friends that Edouard had been duped by the "Dubois whore." Few believed her this time.

Virginie quickly initiated proceedings to contest the will, but was informed by a bevy of attorneys and judges that the will was legal and her efforts would only prove futile and costly. Virginie refused their advice, and when her efficient attorney returned from court four months later with the distressful news that she had lost her case, Virginie showed no emotion, thanked him, and handed him a check for two thousand francs. She turned to the mullioned window that overlooked the city and yanked the brocade drapery shut.

"You'll pay for murdering my son, Renée Dubois, and the price will not be cheap. Crushing you will be the sweetest pleasure I'll ever know."

Book Two

The Thirties

Chapter Nine

1931–1938

The thirties blew into Paris on the dreamy South American strains of the samba and rumba. Cole Porter penned one Broadway musical smash after another, hemlines fell to below the calf, and Paris designers stripped their dresses of trimmings. The great adventure of the twenties ended when the American stock market crashed two days after Countess Cécile d'Itagnio married Alvin Thorpe, who wisely had never participated in the speculative hypertension of Wall Street.

Renée Dubois was not able to expand beyond lingerie and accessories due to the worldwide depression. However, she had been successful in keeping her doors open at a time when many businesses and older, more established firms were filing bankruptcy. Renée carefully clocked the trends producing bias-cut lingerie that fit the body like a second skin, so that the mere act of breathing invoked sensuality. Necklines plunged, waists were defined, and backs were nonexistent. In the few short years it had been in business, Maison Dubois was noted for the most daring and original lingerie in Paris.

The American artists, journalists, poets, and novelists fled the city with memories of a Paris that would never come again. In their wake came Hollywood movie stars and the capricious sons and daughters of the "New York Four Hundred" who dubbed themselves "café society."

Since the inception of the business partnership between Renée Dubois and Jean Larousse, Maison Dubois primarily owed its financial stability and its impeccable reputation to the American trade. Though the faces of the customers were new and the names of this select group had changed, their desires and needs had not. Nor had their spending power.

Renée often wondered if the "Depression" wasn't just a state of mind to the Americans. From what she saw, the lifestyles of her wealthy American clients had not altered in the least. The recklessness of the twenties was replaced by an ennui that was relieved by luxurious ocean voyages to Paris that ended in spending sprees in the couture houses.

For the past three years Renée had made her business her life. She handled every aspect of management: bookkeeping, ordering, hiring, payroll, and supervision of the workrooms. Whether it was pride or fear that made her unwilling to relinquish any authority to an assistant, even she did not know. Her determination to someday see Maison Dubois accepted as one among the select group of the haute couture drove her. Her impeccable eye found the most minute flaws, causing seamstresses to burst into tears and fitters to mumble curses. But as time passed she gained their respect, for when she discovered mistakes she proved to everyone that she could and would rectify them herself with her nimble fingers. More than once a midinette had arrived in the morning to find Renée still in the workroom, hand beading a particularly delicate chiffon, or embroidering rhinestones to the back of a coup de velours gown. When orders were backed up and an important client, like the wife of M. Rodier, the textile magnate, could not be put off, Renée would sit at the tables with her seamstresses, sharing their work and proving to everyone that Renée Dubois was no ordinary employer.

Slowly Renée was being accepted by the Paris elite but strictly on a commercial basis. Every month Maison Dubois would have an order from another of Virginie's friends. It was a slow climb, but Renée was determined to make it.

Renée knew that she and Jean were only a step away from branching into evening gowns, which would place them in competition with Vionnet and the rest. Jean's designs were in fact party gowns adapted for the boudoir, which was the reason for their popularity. However, she correctly surmised that she was still too inexperienced and their finances were not stable enough to risk all she had built thus far. When the timing was right, she would know it and nothing would hold her back.

For a long time Renée had successfully swept men out of her life by simply immersing herself in work. As time passed she became increasingly beautiful. Many men fancied themselves her suitor but none succeeded. Wealthy husbands and lovers of her clients proposed everything from jewels to villas, but she politely refused them without giving it a thought, until one unsuspecting day at the shop.

An aristocratically boned auburn-haired young woman was in the shop, clearly undecided about the shade of green she should use for the peignoir she had ordered. As Renée walked forward she noted the woman's alabaster-smooth skin, the ripe peach tint to her cheeks, and her flawless figure.

Rightly, she guessed the woman was American and spoke in English. "Perhaps I could be of some assistance," she said, noting the blue flecks in her emerald eyes. She was an unusually beautiful woman and Renée could understand her desire to purchase exactly the color that would benefit her most. Renée selected a dark teal silk satin and held it to the woman's eyes. "This is the only color for you. It not only enhances your eyes but makes them appear innocent. In the design and cut, I will display your body to its best advantage. It will smolder."

The woman's eyes grew wide with excitement. "This I have to see to believe!"

"Certainly," Renée said and signaled the vendeuse to usher the woman to the fitting rooms where her measurements would be taken.

From the moment he walked through the door, he commanded the attention of every woman in the showroom. He was tall, with well-proportioned wide shoulders, slender torso, and long muscular legs that advanced across the floor to Renée's counter in only three steps. Despite his Savile Row suit, the Italian shoes and French silk tie which he wore with casual ease and aplomb, he was indisputably American.

As Renée looked up into his eyes she was reminded of the blue one finds in the center of a fringed gentian that opens its petals only on a sunny day. He wore his thick honey-colored hair parted to the side. An errant lock continually fell across his forehead, causing him to push it back into place, and when he did, she noticed he wore no wedding band.

It was an unusual observation for her to make, she thought, noting how the sunlight played against the rugged planes of his face. His smile was wide, displaying straight white teeth as he stumbled over French phrases in conveying his needs.

Finally Renée put him at ease by speaking in Herbert Simcox's Queen's English.

"Is there something I may show you?" she asked.

"You speak English! Wonderful. I'm afraid my high school French leaves a lot to be desired."

"I think you're doing fine."

"Thank you," he said, taking a long moment to assess her face.

She could tell he was pleased with what he saw. Her smile grew.

"I was wondering if my companion was still here," he said, glancing quickly about the showroom.

"I don't know," Renée replied. "What's her name?"

"Amanda Sommers."

"Ah! The beautiful red-haired woman." Renée hoped her disappointment didn't show in her voice. She should have guessed his taste in women would be exquisite. "She's being fitted at the moment."

"Will it take much longer?"

"An hour I'd guess. She's very particular."

"I know," he said. "I have some errands. I'll come back for her then."

Renée went about her duties, and found that never had an hour passed so slowly. She couldn't take her mind off the handsome American. It was silly, she thought. Why, she didn't even know his name.

Renée made special pains to be at the same counter when he returned. She felt like a schoolgirl as her breath caught every time the door opened. And then he walked in.

"Hello," he said in that husky voice. "I'm back."

Renée thought she would tumble into his deep blue eyes.

"Miss Sommers is almost finished. I'll tell her you're here, Mr. . . ."

"Morgan. Grant Morgan." He smiled.

Renée liked the sound of his name as she repeated it in her mind while going back to the fitting room. She returned with Amanda.

Amanda was beaming as she possessively slid her arm through Grant's. It was a gesture Renée did not miss.

"Grant, if I'd known you had so much clout with Mademoiselle Dubois, I would have brought you earlier."

"What are you talking about?"

It was Amanda's turn to be confused.

"Don't you realize you've been talking to the famous Renée Dubois? Owner of Maison Dubois."

"You're not . . . a sales clerk?"

Renée chuckled. "I'm afraid not."

"I feel foolish."

"You had no way of knowing. Perhaps I should have said something."

Keen-eyed Amanda didn't miss the smoldering look in Grant's eyes. Nor did she miss Renée's reluctance to leave. Amanda moved closer to Grant, making certain her ample breast rubbed against his arm.

"Grant, wait till you see the negligee I'm having made," she purred.

Her words hit their mark and jostled Renée out of her dreamy state.

"The gown will be finished on Monday, Miss Sommers. Thank you so much for coming to see us. Mr. Morgan . . ." Renée nodded and walked away. Grant Morgan was another woman's man, she thought, and did not look back.

On Monday, Grant Morgan arrived at Maison Dubois just as the doors opened.

"I'd like to see Mademoiselle Dubois, please," he told the vendeuse.

Renée came into the showroom carrying the box with Amanda's gown.

"Here you are, Mr. Morgan. On time, as promised."

"Miss Dubois, I didn't come here for that."

"You didn't?"

"No. I mean, well, I think there's some confusion here. A misunderstanding about Amanda and me . . ."

"I don't think so," Renée said politely.

"Oh, yes there is. Amanda is not my . . . uh . . . Amanda is my employee. You see, I'm a movie producer and Amanda is the lead in a film I'm making here in Paris."

"Oh? I thought movies came from Hollywood."

"They do. I do. I mean, I'm from California, but I have this idea—a better way to make film. I want to capture more realism for the audience. It's a new concept . . ."

"I don't know much about making movies," Renée said. There was something endearing about his inability to explain himself. It meant she was important to him. She liked that.

He fumbled in his pocket. "Here's my card. Ever hear of Monument Studios?"

"No. Should I have?"

"Not really. It's pretty new. But someday I'll be famous. Like you."

"I'm not famous, my clothes are."

"I don't know much about making dresses, but I'd like to. Would you have dinner with me tonight?"

"I don't think so, I have piles of paperwork I've neglected and I'd like to spend the evening with my son." Renée felt herself being drawn to him. But as always, she'd found it safer to withdraw from men. Grant Morgan was especially dangerous. She couldn't take the chance.

"I didn't know you were married," he said with deflated spirits.

"I'm not."

"Good!" he exclaimed. "What about tomorrow night then?"

"I already have plans," she lied.

"I see."

Just then Jean walked up. "Renée! I've spent two weeks with Mademoiselle Gentilly and now, suddenly, she can't make a single decision without you." He took Renée's arm to stress the urgency.

Grant didn't miss the gesture. It was clear to him who Renée's "plans" were.

"I trust Mademoiselle Sommers will be happy with her purchase. Do let me know if I can be of any further assistance," she said.

Grant smiled. "I will," he said. "I most definitely will."

The following day Renée sat at her desk making out an order to M. Ducharne, whose looms in Lyon were creating the most sought-after silks in the world. Every designer in Paris used his silks and Renée was grateful that he felt her designs worthy of his fabrics. M. Vernet still worked his people overtime keeping Renée supplied with unusual prints but his was a small factory and could not supply her with enough fabric. With his blessing she had turned to M. Ducharne to fill the surplus.

Renée had made a small coup that morning when the Marquis de Cholmondeley had placed an order for two dozen beaded handbags to be given as party favors. At a thousand francs apiece, it was an expensive endeavor. She instructed the seamstresses to give their all to the project and asked Jean to design each one individually with her sleek logo woven into a graphic design.

Gaston sat in a chair opposite her, drawing pictures in one of Jean's sketchbooks, when a florist delivered an enormous bouquet of tulips, daffodils, and narcissus. Before she read the card she knew they were from Grant Morgan.

"What happened, Maman? Why did they bring these flowers to you?"

"Just a happy customer, Gaston, showing his appreciation."

Her answer seemed to satisfy him, and he went back to his sketch. Fifteen minutes later a second florist appeared at her door. This time it was pink and yellow roses. Renée read the card from Grant requesting her presence at a cast party that night.

She had no more than turned around when a third delivery boy handed her a wildflower bouquet.

"We must be rich! So many happy customers!" Gaston said gleefully, taking the wildflowers and sniffing them.

When the telephone rang, Renée was not surprised to find Grant on the other end. "The flowers are beautiful, but if you keep this up, you won't have enough money to complete your film."

"If you'll come to the party, then it was well worth the investment."

"I'm afraid I'll have to decline. I have too many things pressing me here at work. It's going to be a long night as it is."

His voice was cool with disappointment. "Perhaps another time, then."

"Yes. Perhaps," she said and hung up.

"Why do you look so sad?" Gaston asked.

"I didn't know that I did," she said, trying to dismiss Grant from her mind. "Why don't you show me what you've drawn?"

He held up his drawing for her approval. Renée gasped with stunned delight when she saw a pair of knickers and a blouse whose detail was quite intricate.

"Gaston, did you do this all by yourself?"

"Yes." He smiled.

"Jean didn't help you at all?"

"No."

"This is fantastic!" She hugged him. "I'm so proud of you. I think you are a better designer than me already."

"Do you really think so?" he asked excitedly, looking at his sketch again.

"Yes. And I think the time has come for you to learn more about the different fabrics and which ones you should use to bring out the best in your design."

Renée selected several swatches of wools in a variety of colors. "Any of these would be good for the knickers."

Gaston flipped through the wools, noting aloud the qualities of the various weights.

"Because of the pleats you've drawn at the waist, you'll want to use a lightweight wool so that the gathers are not bulky and make the woman look fat. The nubby cream sample you seem to favor won't do."

Gaston's excitement grew along with his comprehension of what his mother was telling him.

"Now, let's see about that blouse . . ." she said as she picked up a stack of silk pieces.

Just then the phone rang. It was Jean calling from the button makers.

"What do you mean they lost the order? Now what are we to do? Stall the customers or tell them the truth? Either way won't be easy, Jean."

"Maman," Gaston interrupted. "I think the blue silk."

Renée nodded. There was a knock on the door.

"Come," Renée said, holding her hand over the receiver.

"Maman . . ." Gaston said impatiently.

"In a minute, Gaston. I'm busy. Yes, Jean."

Two vendeuses, who were arguing loudly, burst into the office. Jean was shouting on the phone and the vendeuses would not stop long enough for Renée to get a word in. The tension in Renée's face increased.

"Maman . . . the silk . . ."

"In a minute, Gaston! Jean, place the order and get back here. From what I can tell, the Vicomtesse de Milay is *not* happy. I need you . . ." Renée stood and tried to quiet the vendeuses. "Everything will be fine. Just let me handle the vicomtesse," she said, as she ushered them out the door. As she turned to close the door she noticed Gaston staring disbelievingly at her.

Once again she felt that knife of guilt run through her. "I won't be long, Gaston. Then we'll see about that silk."

"Sure," he said and looked away.

"I'll make it up to you," she said, but as she walked into the showroom she wondered when the day would come when she wouldn't have to make promises to Gaston that they both knew she could not keep.

It was well after eleven when Renée finished her paperwork and turned off the lamp. Her muscles ached from the long day. Jean had left early, the invitation for dinner with his new lover, Mariane Gentilly, and friends too good to refuse. Pierre had come in after school, chatted briefly about his weekend plans to attend a party at the home of his classmate André Mallot's parents, and she had given her approval.

By now, both Gaston and Pierre were sound asleep upstairs. The lights were still burning in the showroom. As she walked to the front to switch them off, she noticed a man standing outside the door. It was Grant.

She unlocked the door. "How long have you been there?"

"I just walked up," he said, pointing to a waiting cab. "I was driving by on my way back to my hotel when I saw your lights. You weren't kidding about a long night. Have you eaten?"

"No."

"Neither have I. The party was a bore. Is there someplace you know where we could get something this late?"

"It's been ages since I've had onion soup. I know a café near Les Halles that serves the best."

"Sounds great!" he said, noting that she didn't go back for a jacket or purse, which was unusual for it seemed every woman in Paris feared crucifixion if she weren't perfectly dressed no matter the hour. As they rode in the cab, he thought that never in his life had he met anyone as beautiful as Renée.

If any of Grant Morgan's California friends had been asked to describe him, they would have used words like "realistic," "modern," "conscientious," and phrases like "a self-made man." Though he was only tweny-six, he had been to Paris over half a dozen times in the last four years. It was a city he liked, and he often spoke about its peculiar lighting and the mist that added both clarity and softness to the city. None of them thought it necessary to warn him that people, especially young people, fall in love in Paris. "Romantic" was not an adjective used to describe Grant Morgan, and so they failed to mention that one goes to Paris to have one's heart broken.

They ordered a red bordeaux at À la Grenouille and looked at the silver moon.

"They don't have moons this romantic in California."

"They don't? I thought it was the same moon."

"Nope. Everything is different here. Even me." He leaned back in his chair thinking her violet eyes fascinating. They were sensitive and wary of him, as they should be, and he sensed a kind of pain he knew she thought was hidden.

"How is work progressing on the movie?"

"Slow, but we're getting excellent work out of everyone." He took her hand. "You don't really want to talk about my work."

"I don't?"

"No. You want to talk about us."

"I didn't know we were an 'us.' "

He grinned. "You will in time. And I'll wait."

"You're pretty confident about all this."

"I can see things more clearly than you. And I'm not afraid."

Four years of eliminating all but the least threatening of men from her life had left Renée unsure of how to deal with her emotions. In fact, it had been so long since she'd reacted at all to a man that now she was confused as much as anything. She didn't want to feel anything. But she was succumbing to him, had been since the moment they met.

It was odd, she thought, how certain people, strangers, could walk blithely into one's life and turn everything upside down. It wasn't logical.

She knew she couldn't trust herself. She had made such a horrid mistake with Edouard. She could never let that happen again.

Perhaps, though, she and Grant could have a physical affair. He was certainly handsome. Then, when it was over, they would go back to their former lives and nothing would have changed.

She could handle an affair, she told herself, as long as she kept her emotions in their proper place.

Renée drifted through her days in a dreamy netherworld, battling with her heart, hoping to focus on work and not Grant. It was a ploy she'd used successfully for four years. It had to work again.

She spent her evenings with Gaston and Pierre while Grant continued with his night shoots. Therefore their suppers were unusually late and at posh places like La Tour d'Argent. Because of the hour, the last person Renée expected to see was Virginie Ruille.

The Ruilles had been to an overlong Ballet Russe production and were enthusiastically discussing the ballet with their dinner companions while the maître d' seated them. It wasn't until after their wine had been poured that Virginie glanced around the room and realized that one of the remaining couples was Renée and Grant.

Renée had seen them the moment they walked in. Grant had been ordering dinner and didn't notice Renée's eyes widen or her back stiffen.

"Do you want the sole?" He nudged her when she did not respond.

"I'm sorry," she said, but could not tear her eyes from Virginie who had now noticed her.

Conversation at the Ruille table ceased as all eyes locked on Renée.

Grant followed Renée's gaze and saw a sophisticated raven-haired woman staring back at them with the coldest eyes he'd ever seen. Her ruby lips parted in a malicious smile that made his skin crawl.

"Who the hell is that?"

"Someone I don't care to see." She glanced at the menu. "I'll have the sole and . . . the escargots for appetizer. No salad . . ." Her voice was strained.

Grant eyed her suspiciously, noting the sudden flush to her face. He placed his order.

Renée could not see Virginie's imperious glares but Grant did. Though Renée presented a cool façade to the other diners, she didn't fool him.

"Here. Drink this." He poured more wine.

Renée's stomach churned as she sipped her wine. "How did the shooting go today? You said you were having trouble with Amanda. That she didn't take direction well. Is that going any better now? Did the rain this evening slow anything down?"

"Do you always ask this many questions?" He chuckled.

"Sometimes."

He glanced over at Virginie. "When you're nervous?"

"I never thought about it."

"Oh."

She knew he was curious about Virginie, but he didn't ask any more questions, only spoke of his movie. Renée picked at the sole, listened to Grant, and doubled up on the wine. Her head pounded as the minutes dragged on.

Finally, Grant reached over and took her hand. "We don't have to stay any longer. I'd much rather have coffee and dessert some place else. What do you say?"

Flooded with relief, she answered: "That sounds wonderful!"

He signaled the waiter and paid the bill.

Once they were in the car, Grant asked again: "Who was that woman?"

"Her name is Virginie Ruille. She's the high priestess of Paris, you might say."

"Really? What's she to you?"

"She's my son's grandmother."

"Brother!" He sank back into the seat as the information hit him.

"She despises me because her son loved me once."

"Do . . . you . . . still love him?"

"He's dead," she answered flatly.

"You didn't answer my question."

"No . . . I don't love him."

"Why does she still have a hold on you?"

"She doesn't," Renée lied. She wondered if she or Virginie would ever rid themselves of each other. They were like panthers squaring off for the fight. She feared that, at times, she needed the tension, the suspense of their feud. Her rage gave her purpose, impetus to achieve more; to win. It frightened her when she delved into herself like this. Revenge was not good motivation for one's work or life.

For the first time in years, she realized she had allowed herself to cross dangerous boundaries. She was just as guilty as Virginie. Renée had to reset her priorities. She had lost sight of the fact that her friends were far more precious to her than her revenge. She knew that friends like Cécile and Carrie Baldwin had helped her when she'd thought everything was lost. If she didn't act now, she would lose them.

She looked at Grant with clear and resolute eyes.

"Tonight has shown me that this game Virginie plays was most embarrassing for the Ouidinots, the people with her. They're also my friends. It's unfair of both Virginie and me to put them through this. They couldn't possibly have enjoyed their dinner."

"I'll agree with that. I think everyone in the restaurant was tense."

"That's what I mean. Virginie may not care about anyone but herself, but I do. Until tonight, I'd never thought about the fact that many of my friends are caught in the crossfire between Virginie and myself. It's time I put a stop to it."

"Couldn't you and Virginie bury the hatchet, try to be friends and all that?"

"Never! I'd rather be dead! As far as she's concerned there isn't enough room on this planet for the two of us."

"Is that Virginie's feeling—or yours?"

"Both."

He was shocked at the intensity of her anger, but once again he saw that sadness and pain. It made him want to protect her. Renée was very much an independent woman, the only kind he liked. He admired women with whom he could interact, share experiences, thoughts, and desires. He wanted a woman who could think for herself, make her own way, and dream her own dreams. He despised those cloying women who lived only for and through a man. And so, it confused and fascinated him that he should feel protective toward Renée. When she looked at him with those sad eyes, she only had to ask and he would do anything for her.

He wanted all of her. He didn't want to share her with another man's ghost or his mother. He wanted to fill her heart, mind, and body with himself.

"Perhaps it's time you thought about something besides Virginie Ruille." He pulled her hand to his lips and kissed her fingertips. "I know you don't trust me yet, but if you ever want to talk to me about this or anything that bothers you—I'm here."

He leaned over and kissed her. Slowly, she sank into him. It seemed he was everywhere around her and inside her head. She heard his breathing, felt his heartbeat against her chest. She closed her eyes, but his face was imprinted on her mind.

Gaston watched as his mother prepared breakfast.

"Why are you always singing in the morning, Maman?"

"Don't I usually?"

"No," he said when she suddenly turned around and gave him a crushing hug.

"I love you, Gaston. And I love the sketches you left on my night table."

"You must have worked very late. I waited until ten, but then I guess I must have gone to sleep."

"Don't do that anymore. You need your rest," she said and went back to humming a song.

"You really liked my drawings?"

"Of course! I could tell you've practiced a lot."

"Three hours yesterday! Jean said he would give me a book on anatomy so that they will be even more real."

"That's wonderful. You make me very proud and happy when you work hard."

Gaston smiled back at her when she kissed his cheek. He knew his drawings must have been very good, indeed, for what else could explain his mother's high spirits?

* * *

It was while Grant was bargaining with the fat, loud-voiced vendor over the price of leeks that Renée realized that she was in love with him.

"Fourteen francs is too much! Look at these ends! They're wilted and the whites have been crushed!"

Caught off guard by the slow swelling of her emotions, she pretended to examine a polished stack of apples and mangoes. It was an odd place to fall in love, she thought, surrounded by stalls filled with neatly stacked radishes, artichokes, and lettuce. The woman standing next to her was still dressed in her housecoat and her hair was in curlers as she cheerfully settled on a price with the vendor then opened her small change purse and counted out her coins.

"Come on," he said, taking her arm.

"What about the leeks?"

"Oh, I didn't want them. I just wanted to dicker with him. Nasty negotiator that bugger. Wouldn't drop a centime!"

They stopped at Sylvia Beach's bookstore, where he borrowed a copy of Browning's love sonnets.

"The only decent love lines I've ever read. All the rest I've forgotten."

When they reached Le Sélect they stopped and ordered rum cocktails.

"Right over there"—Renée pointed to the corner near where they were sitting—"I saw Hart Crane, the American writer . . ."

"Yes, I know." He smiled.

"Anyway, he picked a fight with a man and they nearly tore the place apart. Aunt Céleste said that Crane spent the whole weekend in jail. . . ."

Grant placed his fingers over her lips. "I'm in love with you."

She was stunned, but happily. He kissed her hand and she traced the outline of his lips with her fingers. The look in his eyes went beyond desire and need. Their intense sincerity pulled at emotions she'd thought were long since dead. She should have been afraid, but she wasn't.

She *wanted* it to happen—and with him. Especially with Grant. The dangers of such thinking seemed less perilous with every moment they shared. This love was different than the love she'd felt for Edouard. She was breathless, but curiously calm all at once. She felt as if she'd always known him; always been a part of him and always would be. She didn't feel as if she had to become someone she wasn't as she had for Edouard. He accepted her as she was—faults and all. When she looked at him she was thunderstruck at the emotional upheaval within her. Everything was intensified. And yet, everything seemed gloriously *right*.

"I love you," she said and smiled.

It was crazy, she thought. They had known each other less than two weeks and already she could envision herself growing old with him. He was like no other man she'd ever met. She was twenty-two, and other than Edouard, there had been no lovers. She hadn't wanted a man and she had thought there would never be anyone again. But Grant had a magnetism about him that broke down her defenses. She found it incredible, insane, and wonderful.

He leaned closer and caressed her arm. "Your mind is running a mile a minute. Don't be afraid of me."

"I'm not," she said, knowing her tentative smile gave her away.

"I don't blame you if you were. I was until last night. And then I realized how stupid I would be to throw all this away."

"I've never told anyone I loved them before."

"Neither have I. And I can't explain how or why it happened but it did. I do know that love is rare. I've seen people in lust, in greed, and in need, but not in love."

"There really is a difference, isn't there?"

"It's a gift and we can accept it if we're strong enough."

"What happens now?"

"Everything, my love, everything."

The next afternoon Grant and Renée drove in his gray and black Delage to the rue de l'Université on the Left Bank.

"I rented this really great place. Sorta small, though. It was just painted. I hope you like pink."

The walls were pink, and the trim and ceilings were white. There were two green and pink flowered chintz sofas facing each other with a low mahogany table between. The kitchen was only large enough for the sink and a two-burner stove and oven. The apartment had been remodeled and contained a shower, toilet, and bidet. The bedroom was outfitted with a pickled-oak armoire and brass bed. A vase of violets sat on the stand next to the bed. There was a skylight in the center of the room.

"If you put your head at the foot of the bed, you can see the sky and clouds," he said, demonstrating.

"I hope you like it," he said, taking her in his arms. "We can't go to your apartment, and my hotel is always filled with directors, scriptwriters, and a legion of errand boys. It seemed the only solution. This is where we'll live whenever I'm in Paris. It's yours just as much as mine. No one will ever come here but you and me."

He kissed her eagerly, his tongue probing and tasting the interior of her mouth. Her body could not resist him and, as he pulled her closer, her doubts and reservations melted. She felt secure and safe, as if she'd found the harbor she'd always sought. She loved him and nothing else mattered.

Just as the moon's shadow passes over the sun and consumes its light, so Renée felt as Grant eclipsed her heart. They were irrevocably joined and she knew nothing would ever alter her love for him.

He unbuttoned her blouse and let it fall to the floor. He pushed the narrow straps of her slip off her shoulders and massaged her breast through the thin silk.

She removed his jacket and unbuttoned his shirt and let them fall atop her blouse. In a moment her skirt and his trousers joined the pile of clothing.

He sat her on the edge of the bed and removed her stockings. He pushed up her slip and kissed the inside of her thighs. She fell back on the bed, her head sinking into the pillow. She spread her legs farther apart as his lips and tongue continued to tease her. He brought her to a frenzied pitch.

She clutched his head and pulled his face up to her breasts. Her nipples grew hard and taut as he sucked and licked them.

Effortlessly, he slid inside her and for a moment he stopped.

"What's wrong?"

"Nothing. I wish we could stay like this forever," he said.

She felt him growing stronger inside her. He stroked her slowly at first, then his rhythm increased. He kissed her ears, cheeks, and throat. She raised her hips to meet him. Never had she believed that lovemaking could involve such tenderness and beauty. She felt a prick of tears as their love burst in a shuddering fusion.

Afterward, with the sun streaming through the skylight, lacing intermittent locks of her hair with red-gold, he reached over and withdrew the violets from the vase.

"When I saw these they reminded me of you," he said and placed a violet in her hair. Then he took another and another until he'd wreathed her face in the delicate blooms. He wove a violet chain and laid it between her breasts and down over the creamy white roundness of her stomach.

"I'll always love you, Renée. Never forget that."

"And I'll love you for eternity."

He moved over her, placing his weight on his elbows and knees. He made love to her through the violets, and that evening when she returned home Renée placed the flattened violets in the book of love sonnets.

Renée tried not to count the minutes every day until Grant arrived. She tried not to pick up the phone and call him when she knew he had a break from shooting. She tried not to hold him just a bit tighter when he greeted her and she tried not to love him so much. And she failed.

She believed she was unique in the world. Surely no woman had ever loved a man this much and no man had ever loved her the way Grant did. In the month's time they had known each other, she thought love had been reinvented by them and them alone.

She reclined on the brass bed, satiated from their lovemaking, while he opened the champagne to celebrate the end of the shooting.

He wore a navy silk robe piped in black. He sat on the edge of the bed, leaned over and kissed her hungrily. "I love you."

Before she could answer, his smooth hands caressed her thighs and breasts while his tongue parted her lips, sending shock waves through her body once again. Suddenly, he stopped and pulled her to his chest.

"I don't want us ever to be farther apart than this. Tell me again that you love me."

She nuzzled her face into the crook of his neck. "I'll always love you."

"Then say you'll marry me."

She pulled away and looked into his eyes. Her own were filled with tears. "Yes, I'll be your wife."

Grant was so excited he let out a whoop. He jumped up from the bed, grabbed the champagne and glasses, and in his exuberance spilled wine on himself, Renée, and the bed.

"Everywhere but in the glasses!" he joked and licked champagne off her nipples and belly. "I do love you, Renée. You are wonderful . . . Paris is wonderful! Love is wonderful!" He kissed her over and over, thinking he was about to take on the very adult responsibilities of a family and he felt and acted like a kid. But he didn't care. Renée had made all the jumbled pieces of his life fall into place. She made him feel invincible. For the first time he had buried that scared kid from Nebraska who set out for Hollywood with the fool notion that he could run a movie studio—one that was bigger and better than Metro or Paramount put together. He no longer felt as if he were flying by the seat of his pants, but that he finally had solid ground beneath him. He wanted to do everything for her, give her everything, and be everything *she* wanted. She made him believe.

"We'll have the biggest wedding you ever saw," he said.

"I want a simple ceremony . . ."

"Right! Like I said—a simple ceremony. Just the family and friends."

She chuckled at him as they clinked their glasses, sipped the wine, and kissed again.

"You're going to love California. The palm trees, the sunny weather, the people . . ."

"California?" she asked as she sat up straighter, her smile replaced by a sense of dread.

"Of course. That's where my work is—my studio. I just assumed that we would live in California."

"But my work—my shop and my family are in Paris . . ."

"You could open a shop in California."

Renée shook her head adamantly. "American seamstresses don't know the first thing about couture. It's a little more than slapping two pieces of cloth together." She was growing tense as her mind raced ahead of her. She knew there was no answer to their dilemma and neither of them wanted to face it.

"I didn't mean to belittle your work. You know that. I was just hoping—" His words caught in his throat. They looked at each other.

"I know. So was I . . ."

For Renée the bittersweet edge of reality was like a razor slicing through her heart. The qualities that had drawn them together, their ambitions and convictions about their careers, were now about to tear them apart.

Grant read her thoughts as he watched her eyes fill with tears. The answers eluded him. He could no more give up his fledgling studio, that part of himself he'd dreamed and worked for all his life, than she could give up her shop. It was her ambition that fired her enthusiasm which excited him. He'd never met anyone like her and now he was losing her and he didn't truly understand why.

He had assumed too much; assumed she would give up everything for a life with him. And yet, he wasn't willing to do the same for her. Only a week remained before he was to sail for America. He gathered her in his arms and they clung to each other.

"I'll think of something. There must be a way."

She nodded and tried to speak but the sob in her throat strangled her words. She knew there was nothing he could do, but for a week she chose to believe otherwise.

Grant had been gone for only six days and never, Renée thought, had she been so miserable. Though she still had her work and her family, she'd never felt this alone. Her most vivid memories were of their last week together when she would meet Grant at their apartment and they would make love and talk until dawn.

She tried not to taste desperation in his kisses or complain that time passed too quickly. Grant would hold her for hours not speaking, but his thoughts were so loud they seemed to fill the room with commotion. He refused to allow her to wear the pretty gowns and peignoirs she had brought, wanting nothing to separate them. With skin next to skin, they would lie together and stare out the skylight.

"If we set our sights on the stars—keep our goals high—then maybe . . ." His voice trailed off as she pulled him to the safety of her arms.

Renée often thought during those last days that their separation was going to be more difficult for Grant than it would be for her, because she had Gaston and Pierre.

"I'd like Gaston to meet you."

"I can't, Renée. From the way you talk about him, I know I would love him. And if I got close to him even for an afternoon . . ."

"When will I see you again?"

"I'll come back to Paris as soon as the movie is finished in late August. And we should be together for Christmas. New York, maybe. Promise me you'll meet me there."

"I will."

"You know, California doesn't seem nearly as far away as Christmas."

"Time and distance. They both sound awful to me," she said.

Amanda Sommers was what was known in Hollywood as "a smart cookie." She was beautiful, young, and as an actress, she was quite talented. Until the part in *Paris Moon*, all she had lacked was a break. The big studios were inundated with enough would-be actresses to fill the Hollywood Bowl, and after three years of knocking on doors she had almost given up when she met Darma Logan.

Darma was the daughter of the wealthy California investor James Logan, who was reportedly worth over eleven million dollars. Literally owning half the real estate upon which Hollywood was built, James Logan could and did buy anything his daughter wanted.

In a quirk of fate under the guise of an arranged date by Metro-Goldwyn-Mayer studios, Amanda Sommers was escorted to a party at the Logan mansion by a lowly contract player, Clark Gable. Over two hundred guests meandered through the sprawling Spanish-style house with its open interior balconies and lofty ceilings. Around the fifty-foot swimming pool lounged every notable movie star, agent, and studio executive in Hollywood. Amanda saw Edward G. Robinson giving poker tips to Lionel Barrymore; Norma Shearer, Leslie Howard, and Spencer Tracy conversed amicably while standing next to an eight-foot ice sculpture.

Talent agents Ruth Collier and Minna Wallis were combing the crowd for new faces, but since Amanda had already struck out with them she turned away and headed for the bathroom. It was too early in the evening to be depressed and she needed a "lift."

The only unoccupied bathroom was one upstairs which connected to a lush salmon and beige sitting room. Amanda had never seen anything like it in her life. The walls and doors were upholstered in tufted beige satin and a thick white wool rug with at least two inches of pad covered the floor. A glass and chrome dressing table easily held over two hundred bottles of French perfume. And resting in an armchair was Darma Logan.

"I'm sorry. I was looking for a free bathroom. I didn't know anyone was up here," Amanda said.

The fabulously beautiful platinum blonde raised a slender arm, pointed a well-manicured finger, and said: "Go ahead. It's in there."

Amanda said nothing, went to the bathroom, withdrew a vial of her "vitamins" from her black beaded handbag and swallowed two yellow oval pills. When she emerged she noticed that her hostess was still staring out the window.

"It's your party, why aren't you out there having fun?"

A pair of dark brown oval-shaped eyes stared at Amanda. "You don't look as if you're having too much fun yourself."

Amanda laughed. "I'll be all right in a few minutes. I have my friends with me," she said and showed Darma her pills.

"What are they?"

"Just some vitamins my doctor gave me for when I get a little low. He said it was something about not enough sugar and too much protein in my bloodstream, or maybe it's the other way around."

"You think they would help me?"

"They couldn't hurt," Amanda said and went to get a glass of water.

And so it was that Amanda and Darma became friends.

For months James Logan speculated with the idea of investing in a business venture with Grant Morgan. He brought the young man to dinner at his estate on several occasions and introduced him to his daughter.

When Darma realized that she was falling in love with Grant Morgan, she pressed her father to bankroll Grant's studio. Ordinarily, James would not have thought twice about spending the money, but going up against well-established studios like M-G-M, Warner Brothers, and RKO was another matter. James thought it best for Grant to make one movie first; if it did well then he would back the young man.

When Grant needed a leading lady for *Paris Moon*, Darma suggested Amanda to both men. After a screen test which Grant insisted upon, Amanda signed a one-year contract renewable for two years should the movie succeed.

When Amanda and Grant sailed for Paris for the location shots, Amanda promised Darma she would keep her hands off Grant and plead her cause whenever the opportunity arose.

During the crossing Amanda figured that what Darma didn't know wouldn't hurt her and made a play for Grant herself. In one quick rebuff she found that Grant Morgan already had a mistress—his movie. Amanda decided that if Darma wanted this one-track-mind bozo, she was more than welcome. When Grant began seeing the French designer Renée Dubois, Amanda was only too pleased to inform Darma about it. She also told her that Grant had been letting everyone in Paris think that he already owned his own studio when in reality he was as much on trial as was Amanda.

Darma had always gotten whatever she wanted and she'd never wanted anything as much as Grant. His Achilles' heel was his studio and his ambition. If she was subtle and very careful, she had a good chance to win him.

In her favor was the fact that he was coming back. She had taken it upon herself to rent office space suitable for a movie mogul and have it completely decorated upon Grant's return. He may have fallen for a Frenchwoman, she thought the day he viewed the offices for the first time, but he was *here* now and she was going to do everything in her power to keep him here.

She smiled broadly as he surveyed his dark-paneled office.

"I like it, Darma," he said, checking the view of the studio grounds outside his window. He sat in a leather swivel chair. He folded his arms behind his head and grinned. "Hell, I love it!"

"I'm glad. I pictured you in that chair a hundred times while you were gone. The real thing looks even better."

"Thanks for everything. It saves me a lot of time. Now, how can I pay you back?"

"Lunch?"

"That's all? Of course. Anywhere you want." He checked his

watch. "I need to make some calls, check the mail, and talk to Bob Zimmermann."

Darma pouted. "Bob again? He's the most temperamental director in Hollywood. That'll take hours."

"No it won't. Meet me back here at one."

"It's a date," she said as she blew him a kiss on her way out.

Grant shook his head. Darma made no effort to hide her desire for him even though he'd never encouraged her. But she'd never pressured him or asked for more than she knew she would receive. He hoped they would still be friends after he and Renée were married . . . whenever that would be.

Thinking of Renée he snatched up the stack of mail and quickly flipped through it. There were three letters from her!

He read through them quickly and then, figuring the ten-hour difference, which meant it was eleven P.M. in Paris, decided to call her.

"Renée? Did I wake you?"

"No, and even if you did I wouldn't care. How are you? How was the trip? Do you miss me? I love you, Grant!"

"Fine, fine, yes, and I love you too." He paused. "Renée, I've thought about nothing else but us on the voyage back. Really, it wouldn't be so difficult for you to move to California."

"We've been all through this, darling. It's impossible."

"No it isn't! There are such things as telephones and two or three times a year we could make the trip back for you to check on everything."

"Grant, you don't know what you're talking about. It's more complicated than that."

"I don't think so, Renée," he said impatiently. "Christ! We're talking about *us*, Renée. Our future is at stake here. I want us to be together. You act as if your damn nightgowns are more important than I am!"

"Grant, you know that's not true!"

"Prove it. Think about this for a couple days. Think about how we could work this out."

"All right."

"I'll call you on Thursday."

"Goodbye, chéri."

"Good night."

On Thursday their telephone conversation was much the same,

and Grant's frustration increased. "What's the matter with you, Renée? Why can't you come to America? You keep giving me excuses but no reasons."

"You won't give up your studio. It's the same thing."

"There's a big difference in our situations." He paused, trying to control his mounting anger. "Do you know what I really think? I think it has nothing to do with me or your being needed at work every day. I think your reluctance is all tied up somehow with your hatred for Virginie Ruille."

"That's preposterous!"

"Is it? I've analyzed everything I could about our problem and this is the only thing that makes sense to me. That night at La Tour d'Argent I didn't understand exactly what was happening, but I think I do now. I don't have all the details, but common sense tells me there is more to this than what the gossips told me in Paris."

"You're getting into something that doesn't concern you, Grant."

"Are you saying it's none of my business?"

"Exactly."

"I guess that tells me all I need to know right there."

"What do you mean?"

"Obviously I don't fit in to your life as much as I thought. I'm not as sophisticated as you Europeans. Call it naïveté, but I really believed there was a chance for us."

"Grant, there's so much you don't understand."

"No, Renée." He cut her off. "I understand more than you do. You're the one who's not facing the truth. And it's painful too."

Renée's voice quivered with the shock of realizing that she was losing him. "Please, listen to me. I would change everything if I could, but it's not in my hands."

"I think it is. And I think it's pointless for us to go on with this. . . . Goodbye, Renée."

"Grant! Don't hang up—" But the line was dead.

Chapter Ten

Renée called Grant back twice, but he never took the message or returned her call. She sent cable after cable, but his message became clear as the weeks passed without an answer. Now, a year later, she felt nothing but grief, the same kind of mourning she'd experienced when her parents died.

She admitted to herself, by now, that she had been unable to commit to Grant because of the scars left by Edouard. She was a driven woman; her shop was not simply a career but her purpose for living. It kept her safe from heartache and it sheltered her family from ever being vulnerable to people like Virginie. She could never give up her shop, or her dream. The risk a commitment to Grant demanded of her and her family was too great. She also easily remembered that once she had loved a man and, when *he* decided to end the affair, she had been turned out onto the street with nothing.

The picture of herself, Pierre, and Michel walking through the icy sleet was as fresh in her mind as if it had happened this morning. She could never allow herself to be that vulnerable again.

As determined as she was to protect herself and her family, that did not lessen the pain she felt every time a vision of Grant spiraled unwanted into her brain. He was all around her, taunting her, forcing her to remember his voice, the touch of his lips, his love. She thought she would go insane from the torture. For weeks she cried until she thought her eyes would never unswell. She couldn't eat, sleep, or think. She thought she might as well be dead.

But then, as always, she slowly realized that her salvation could be found in her work.

After the first two months, she scheduled herself into a strict regimen which allowed her no time to think about Grant. She worked late into the night doing backlogged hand beading, which eliminated dreams about him. When she slept, it was only for a few hours and then she would return to her office.

It took over six months before she felt she could ease the reins on herself. In that time, she had neglected not only herself but Pierre and Gaston. She felt as if she'd been in a closed tunnel with no way out and no one to help her. Then suddenly, one day, she decided it was time to make changes.

She and Gaston went on picnics, went to the movies, and watched Pierre play Hamlet in a school play. They went to the zoo, went bike riding, and talked of everything and nothing during long walks through the Bois. But as they became a family again, Renée noticed that Gaston was never satisfied with what she gave him. He demanded more and more of her time.

"I want to see the puppet show."

"I have three consultations tonight, Gaston. I told you that yesterday. I can't possibly get out of them. Don't you remember I had canceled them all earlier in the week because you had wanted to go to lunch on Monday and Wednesday?"

"But tonight is the last night!"

"We went to the ballet on Saturday night. And in two weeks we'll be going to the country so you can ride horses. I can't do everything."

"I want to go to that show."

"Jean could take you."

"I don't want Jean to take me. Or Pierre either."

"I'm doing the best I can, Gaston."

"It's not good enough!" He stormed out of her office.

She watched him go. Somehow, she had to make him realize there must be give-and-take on his side too. Right now, however, Gaston was in the right. For weeks, she had not been there for him. His retaliation was understandable. She wished she'd been a woman of simple dreams and needs. Then she wouldn't feel this stinging guilt every time she placed the customers' needs and her ambitions over her son.

The months passed, and eventually Renée was able to see her friends again without fear of boring them to death with her depressed spirits. In time, she almost believed she had rid herself of Grant's memory. Then, one summer afternoon, one of her seamstresses, who had taken a maternity leave, telephoned to inform her that the handwork she'd been doing at home for the Vicomtesse de Paulo was finished. Since the vicomtesse was due at Maison Dubois at four o'clock, Renée herself drove to the seamstress's apartment.

It wasn't until she was outside the woman's house, work in hand, that she realized that she was just two blocks from the apartment Grant had rented for them.

In a daze, Renée walked toward the antique shop on rue de l'Université. She mounted the narrow stairs to the second floor, remembering the sound of Grant's laughter and the way he would grab her from behind and steal a kiss on the steps. She pulled the key from a concealed inner pocket in her purse and opened the door.

The impact upon seeing the pink and green room, the particular way the sun glinted through the windows, and the wilted and dried flowers in the vase on the coffee table overpowered her.

"It even smells like Grant." She moaned and sank down on one of the sofas.

As she sat there barraged by a thousand memories, she realized how wrong she had been to try to push him out of her heart. Grant was a part of her life, an important part. She looked at the key in her hand and promised herself to come back on the sixteenth of every month, the day on which he'd left Paris, to clean and air the rooms. She would keep the key, and if he ever came back . . .

Virginie's Hydra head rose again that summer of 1931 and this time her victim was Pierre.

Through André Mallot, Pierre met Suzanne Chemaine, a beautiful and aristocratic girl whose only fault was she'd fallen in love with Pierre Dubois.

It had been one of those gloomy days just after the Christmas holidays when boxes of decorations were still stacked in the vestibule of the Mallot mansion awaiting the attention of the servants. It had been sleeting and Pierre was warming his hands over the fire in the salon. André came bursting into the room tugging on the arm of the most delicate female creature Pierre thought he'd ever seen.

Her hair was the color of moonbeams and when juxtaposed to her intense onyx eyes the effect was dramatic. The moment she saw Pierre, she stopped dead still and stared at him.

Then she smiled and never, Pierre thought, had he seen anything so beautiful.

"I'm very pleased to meet you," she said.

Pierre was dumbstruck and he found that her riveting eyes somehow affected his speech. "Me—me too," he replied.

"I'm Suzanne. André never told me about you."

"I'm Pierre."

"Pierre what?"

"Huh? Oh! Dubois . . . Pierre Dubois. Would you have coffee with me tomorrow after my classes? About three?" he said, stuttering.

"I'd love to, Pierre, but what are you doing this afternoon?"

"Today?"

"Yes." She giggled. "I'd like to spend the afternoon with you."

"You would?"

"Yes. I've never met anyone quite as nervous as you seem, Pierre. It's the most sincere compliment I've ever received. You won't mind if we leave you alone, André?"

"Not at all. Something tells me no one would pay much attention to me anyway," he said, glancing at Pierre who hadn't taken his eyes off Suzanne.

Suzanne took Pierre's hand. "Shall we?"

"Yes . . . yes," he answered sheepishly, thinking it unbelievable this angel could be interested in him.

Pierre and Suzanne met the next day at Deux Magots after his classes. The following day he took her to lunch. On the third day he asked her to dinner, but she declined. On the fourth day

Suzanne looked into Pierre's handsome face and said, "I love you, Pierre—more than anyone in the world."

Tears filled her eyes and he took her hands, trying to comfort her. Both of them were keenly aware of the social barriers between them.

Pierre had been seeing Suzanne for two weeks before Renée realized what was happening. At first he told her he was staying late at the library to study for exams, but that didn't explain the rapturous look on his face.

"What's her name?"

Pierre glanced at his sister quizzically. "I don't know what you're talking about."

"Whom, not what." She grinned.

He didn't flinch. "I was studying."

"With . . ."

"Aren't you going to give up?"

"No."

"Suzanne."

"Is she nice?"

Pierre sighed and fell back on his bed. A smile lit his face. "She's an angel. She's absolutely perfect. Beautiful, intelligent, fun, and in love with me." Suddenly he looked down at his hands, which were clenched.

Perceptive to his swing in mood, Renée asked, "So what's the problem?"

"Her family . . ." Pierre gulped. "She's Suzanne Chemaine."

Renée's eyes widened. "Not Guillaume Chemaine's daughter?"

"You know them?"

Suddenly the impact of Pierre's predicament hit her. "Pierre, he practically owns half the commerce in France! Their family can be traced back to Charlemagne. Of all the loves you could have had, why did you pick one so hopeless?"

"It's not hopeless! She loves me and I love her."

"Oh, Pierre, you know as well as I the futility of all this. Her parents will never allow it. It wasn't that long ago that Edouard and I—"

"Just because it didn't work out for you doesn't mean it won't work for me," Pierre broke in.

He sank onto the edge of the bed knowing everything Renée

said was true. He knew he would never be accepted by Suzanne's parents, but he nevertheless clung to his illusions.

Renée put her arms around him. "All I ever wanted was for you to be happy."

They were both crying now; she because she knew the reality of her past, and he because he feared a future without Suzanne.

Had Pierre not graduated with such high marks he would not have been invited to the great number of parties, teas, and dances given by the parents of his classmates. Thus, at the impressionable age of seventeen, he discovered that sphere of social elite governed by Virginie Ruille.

One of the purposes of the numerous and lavish parties was parental perusal of marriage candidates for their respective sons and daughters.

Emile Ruille was now twenty-one years old, a graduate of Oxford University, a miracle in itself in Virginie's eyes, and soon to become an executive at the bank. The correct wife was essential for his acceptance among his peers both at work and in society. Virginie narrowed the field to three choices: Danielle Vollet, Amie Beauchamps, and Suzanne Chemaine.

Of the three, Suzanne's parents were not the wealthiest, but her father's lucrative raw-mineral importing and exporting business would be an asset to Crédit de Paris.

As Virginie watched Suzanne, dressed in a cerise silk gown, glide across the ballroom floor at the home of Denis and Marguerite Corbeil, she decided that capturing Suzanne for Emile would not be half as delightful as eliminating the young girl from Pierre Dubois's life.

In Virginie's favor was the fact that Guillaume Chemaine was a ruthless businessman who believed he would benefit greatly from an alliance with the Ruilles. Moreover, he was vehemently opposed to his daughter's infatuation with Pierre. Virginie took advantage of her "edge."

She arranged dinners and parties at which Emile and Suzanne would be thrown together. As the weeks passed, she was delighted at the course her plan was taking.

When Pierre told Renée about Suzanne being "forced" to see Emile Ruille, she tried to prepare him for the inevitable.

"It's more than just class barriers this time, Pierre. Once Virginie starts, she won't stop, no matter who she destroys in the process."

"I won't listen to this!"

"Please, I'm trying to keep you from being hurt."

"No!" he screamed at her. "You're just trying to keep me from Suzanne. You couldn't marry your way into that world and so now jealousy is eating you up."

Renée grabbed his shoulders and shook him. "Stop it and listen to yourself! I'm not your enemy, Pierre—Virginie is!" Crying, Renée raced from the room, slamming the door behind her.

Pierre felt as if everything in his life had gone haywire. He fought with Renée and said horrible things he didn't mean. He didn't want to hurt her, but she kept telling him not to hope when he knew he must. He was not afraid to battle Virginie. He only feared losing.

Emile became genuinely entranced with Suzanne and embarked on a program of dieting and exercise which resulted in eliminating over fifty pounds in a few months. He hired a private dancing instructor, spent endless hours perfecting his dressage on horseback, and took a crash course on the ballet, which Suzanne frequented every chance she could get. Emile went to London and had his new body fitted with an entire wardrobe by master tailors. He sent Suzanne enough flowers to sink the *Mauretania*, escorted her to the most expensive restaurants and lavished her with gifts of perfume and exquisite, but not costly, jewels.

Suzanne refused to succumb to Emile's barrage of a courtship; she loved only Pierre.

By the end of July, Virginie realized that more drastic measures were necessary. When Guillaume Chemaine mentioned that he was taking the family to Cap d'Antibes for the summer holidays, Virginie suggested he use their yacht, which was harbored at nearby Cannes. Guillaume accepted.

Yachting was Emile's forte and Virginie arranged for Emile to pilot the boat around the Mediterranean and give the Chemaine family "an unforgettable vacation."

After two weeks of slicing through the blue-green waters, docking at one resort after another, and watching Emile's bronzed arms hoist sails, Suzanne's overt aversion to him began to fade. She thought of him as a friend and believed he could be quite pleasant when he wanted to be. The fact that only four days of their vacation remained before she could return to Paris and Pierre had a definite impact on her attitude toward both Emile and her family.

Suzanne and Emile remained on board one night while the elder Chemaines went ashore to travel up to Aix-en-Provence to the Vendôme restaurant.

Emile had the cook prepare a delicate sole Véronique, which was accompanied by a bottle of Perrier-Jouët. With the chocolate mousse, which Emile declined, they drank a second bottle of champagne. With coffee he poured her Napoleon brandy. By nine o'clock, Suzanne was stinkingly drunk and Emile gladly carried her to her stateroom.

When Guillaume and his wife returned, they discovered their daughter in a very compromising situation. They demanded she and Emile announce their engagement immediately and set the wedding date for September first, two weeks hence. Should a pregnancy result from Suzanne's indiscretion, it would be explained easily.

Suzanne's tears and tantrums aside, Emile thought he had never been happier in his life, and to celebrate, he stole into the galley and devoured the two remaining chocolate mousses and half a dozen petit fours.

On a sunny September afternoon at Deux Magots, Pierre sat across the table staring disbelievingly into Suzanne's tear-filled dark eyes while Renée's words rang in his ears. "It's all right to believe in love, Pierre, but love can't conquer all things . . . especially family ties."

"You told me you loved me, Suzanne!" he hissed, allowing only his anger to escape. His pain he harbored inside.

Her voice was filled with despair. "I've never lied to you."

"Then how can you sit here and tell me you're going to marry Emile in two weeks if you love me?"

"I think you know the answer better than I." She looked away, at the shoppers passing by. Her eyes were dry when she spoke again. "What fools we were, Pierre, to allow ourselves to become this involved. We should have known . . ."

Pierre was about to explode. "Love is never wrong! God help us all if it ever comes to that. You can't tell me we wouldn't be good together. We could fight your family—"

"You know as well as I that we could never do that," Suzanne interrupted. "How many times did you tell me your sister tried to do just that and look where she ended up!"

Pierre didn't miss the sarcasm in her voice. "Renée did all right for herself."

"She's alone, isn't she?"

"That's spiteful and you know it!"

Suzanne nodded and fought to suppress her tears. "I'm sorry."

Pierre was beside himself. He would have done anything for Suzanne and yet she didn't seem at all inclined the same way. He wondered if perhaps there wasn't some feeling for Emile after all. She was evasive about too many things. Pierre knew she was hiding something from him. She seemed ashamed more than hurt, as if she had done something wrong. She was dumping him for a future with a man who would provide her with everything she could ever want or need. She would have furs and jewels, beautiful houses and cars, months on end of travel, and through his family she would meet the most exciting and influential people in the world. He had been a fool to ever think he could be more than just her lover.

Suddenly, all the social restrictions he'd fought against for months engulfed him, making him feel unworthy. He felt as if he were being smothered—by Suzanne, her parents, and his anger.

As he looked at her now he wondered how many of her tears were for show and if any were from the heart.

He stood and gripped the back of his chair. "I have to go, Suzanne. I think if I had to listen to you any longer, I'm afraid of what I might do. But I want you to know I'm going to do us both a favor. I'm leaving Paris. When you get bored with your rich husband, I don't want to be there the day you decide to go slumming again."

Pierre spun away from her, stormed out of the café, and jumped onto a bus.

Suzanne couldn't tell him the truth. She knew Pierre's fury was nothing compared to the rage he would feel if he knew Emile had raped her. Her parents called it something more polite, but she knew he'd used her. She believed she was protecting Pierre.

If Pierre discovered the truth, he would kill Emile. Of that she was certain.

She raced out of the café. "Pierre, I do love you!" she yelled as she ran after him. But he never heard her and he never looked back.

"Insulation!" Renée flung the word at Jean like a hand grenade. "I've got to find a way to protect my family from Virginie! I swear, I have never seen Pierre so devastated. He won't sleep or eat or talk to me."

"Do you want me to talk to him?"

Renée looked into Jean's concerned and sympathetic eyes and sank back onto the sofa. "It seems the Duboises are always coming to you with their broken hearts."

Jean pulled her to him and she rested her head on his shoulder. "I know I wasn't much help when Grant . . ."

"I wouldn't let you—or anyone. You tried. You always do."

He kissed the top of her head. "Pierre just needs some time and this idea about going to Munich to study is a good one."

"But I'll miss him . . ."

"Let him go. You know as well as I do that he can't stay here. Suzanne and her life would confront him at every corner. Virginie will see to it that her new daughter-in-law is the princess of society. Pierre is right. He's got to leave—for everyone's sake."

"You're thinking the same thing I am. Suzanne does love Pierre."

"No question in my mind. I've seen them together twice, though they don't know that. If ever there were two people in love, it's them."

"Then you agree with me that we need to protect ourselves. This meddling into Pierre's life only proves to me that Virginie has no intention of leaving us alone. She's just been biding her time, toying with me. I wondered why she didn't try to overtly shut me down. There were times when our position was so rocky, two bad months would have sunk us. Virginie could have put out the word and, with no business, we would have folded."

"I'm beginning to think the one thing we have underestimated is the extent of her desire for revenge."

Renée stood and walked to the window and lifted the drape. "Virginie wouldn't gain much satisfaction from vanquishing a small businesswoman from Lyon—a shopkeeper. She is waiting for me to grow and expand. She knows what I have not known all this time. I will be rich and powerful someday! At that time the game will take on new meaning. There is no question that she intends to destroy everyone dear to me—but not me, not my business."

"If that's true, Renée, you're dealing with a very twisted mind," he said, alarmed by her observations.

"I made my first mistake by underestimating her. She made hers by allowing me to establish my business. I'm going to beat her at her own game." Renée's eyes were glassy with determination.

"I want you to look into those shipments to America you talked about a few months ago. Perhaps we could take Saks Fifth Avenue up on their offer. I'll write to Aunt Céleste. She mentioned in her last letter that there were two businesses she wanted to invest in and wondered if I would be interested. One was a bed-linen company that has gone bankrupt. I could buy it under Céleste's name, which would give us anonymity until we are firmly established."

"What in the hell are you going to do with sheets?"

"Sell them! I'm going to do what I do best and that's sell. I don't care if it's ponchos to South American gauchos, I'm going to make money! Virginie has made it clear she isn't done with me yet. But I will tell you this: my family is more important than the business and I'll do anything to protect them."

"You're talking about a lot of work and some long hours."

"That's never stopped me before."

"Maybe you should be spending some of that time with your family, Gaston in particular, rather than spending it to build your empire."

"What good would that do if Virginie can ruin his life as she did Pierre's?"

"Ever heard of inner strength?"

"Gaston has plenty of that. The point is that he won't need it if I can stop Virginie."

"I'm not sure about that."

Chapter Eleven

Pierre enrolled in the university in Munich where André Mallot was already a member of the freshman class. In 1931, Schwabing, the university center, was a virtual regulator of the rising political power of the Nazi party. Often when Pierre walked to class he would see Josef Paul Goebbels, the Nazi party spokesman, accompanied by Adolf Hitler, the party leader. Many of the SA rallies were held in the Schwabing area, sometimes drowning out the sound of music and laughter from the many beer halls and taverns nearby.

From his dormitory window Pierre could look down over the Osteria Italiana, the oldest Italian restaurant in the city at Number 62 Schillingstrasse and farther to Number 54, to his favorite coffeehouse where he, André, and Pierre's new roommate, Randolf Heilmann, would play chess and skittles.

Pierre had studied the German language along with English in high school, and other than learning a few new slang phrases in German, none of his studies proved difficult.

In his free time, Pierre roamed the city, reveling in its history and grace. On his way to the university, Pierre often passed through the Englischer Garten, which was more beautiful and larger than anything in Paris. Somewhere between the Marienplatz and its soapbox orators, and numerous mugs of Löwenbrau beer he consumed in the Alter Simple, Pierre's memory of Suzanne began to blur.

On the first Sunday in October the streets of Munich exploded with the *oom-pah, oom-pah* of dozens of brass bands. It was the last day of Oktoberfest, and the beer halls and fair grounds at Theresienwiese were crowded with boisterous folk singing and dancing.

Pierre came away from the window, peered at his roommate, who was reading *Mein Kampf* for the fifth time, and said: "Randolf! Surely you have that thing memorized by now! Look outside! This is our last chance to wallow in gluttony and revelry!"

Randolf's ice blue eyes looked up from the book. "You foreigners are all alike. We are here to study and learn about what is happening in the world. All you ever want to do is play. I have more important things on my mind."

"Spare me!" Pierre said. "If you had better study habits, one reading would be enough," he taunted.

Randolf flung his pillow at Pierre, who ducked and burst into laughter. "You need target practice too!"

"I give up! I'll go with you and drink to the fact that I have a full year's reprieve until Oktoberfest comes again."

"Don't be so dour," Pierre said as they walked out of the room. "André is going to meet us at the Burgerbraukeller."

As soon as Pierre mentioned the name of the beer hall that lately was most noted as a Nazi meeting place, Randolf's eyes brightened.

"He's meeting two girls there, Randolf. There's no political gathering on the last day of Oktoberfest. Honestly, there is more to life than being a Nazi!"

Randolf's expression turned determinedly serious and he stared malevolently at Pierre. "Not to me there isn't." He spun on his heel, went back to the room, and slammed the door.

In the months that followed, Pierre was to discover how all-encompassing Nazism was to Randolf and his fellow party members. Randolf rattled off the names of the leaders and meeting places. He extolled their convictions of anti-Marxism and their dream of a unified German rule throughout the world.

At Randolf's urging Pierre attended a meeting of the Hitler Youth, of which Randolf was a member. As Hitler spoke, Pierre realized that not a single original idea passed Hitler's lips, though Pierre did think the man was a genius at feeling the pulse of the German people. He struck the hardest in bad economic times and blamed all personal and national ills on the Marxists and Jews.

Now that a year had passed since the elections, it seemed that most of Munich's young men marched with impassionate, nondescript faces in brown-shirted uniforms. After living so many years in the Parisian couture world of originality and individuality, Pierre was frightened by the Nazi rallies with thousands of identically dressed Germans. Centuries of German traditions and culture were being erased, and replaced with a people who had subordinated their individualistic will to the will of the party.

When Randolf first approached Pierre with the idea of coming home with him for the holidays, Pierre refused. Pierre was wary of Randolf and his political views, but more than that, for him, Paris was always connected with Suzanne.

Too many nights he'd awakened suddenly and found himself drenched in sweat, his hands clenched in tight fists, and his penis hard and erect. He kept pushing her and the memory of her soft body against his into the back of his mind. Suzanne kept breaking out of that prison and haunting him. It was too soon to return to Paris. He had to bury Suzanne first and only when he was strong, would he go home.

When Randolf offered a skiing trip to the Alps as an enticement, Pierre jumped at the bait.

Renée was glad Pierre was not coming home for Christmas. Not that she didn't miss him tremendously, for life had not been the same since he left. But there were rumors about Emile's cruel treatment of his wife, and she feared Pierre's reaction to them.

Earlier that autumn Renée was frequently escorted around Paris by Lord Richard Ellingham, a dashing young Londoner who had found a wonderful companion in Renée. "I find that I'm less apt to be badgered by overly eager mothers who want both a title and a husband for their daughters," he once confided. Richard respected Renée's need for privacy and both were grateful for a nonpossessive relationship like theirs.

One evening in October, before Suzanne announced her pregnancy, Renée and Richard spied her at the Comédie Française wearing, in Renée's opinion, much too much green eyeshadow.

Later that night, Jean had the opportunity to observe Suzanne more closely as he was the guest of the Marquesse de Rouchfauld, who arranged the party with, among others, the newly married Ruilles. Jean told Renée there was no mistaking the cut and bruises on Suzanne's eye. Emile was the perfect adoring husband afterward when they ate at Le Grand Véfour, but Suzanne had demurely caught Jean's eye with such an imploring look that Jean wanted to tear into the bastard himself.

Weeks later, Coco Chanel's fitter told Renée's fitter about the bruises on Suzanne's arms when she came for a final fitting. Twice Suzanne was "too ill" to attend charity functions of which she had been the chairwoman. Virginie explained that Suzanne was having a difficult pregnancy, which was accepted by almost everyone. Others knew of a darker, more terrifying explanation.

The once powerful electors of Trier who first built Schloss Zell, a castle on the Moselle River, also built a "guest house" south of Munich near Fussen on the Austrian border. Situated in the shadow of the Zugspitze Mountain, it was in a breathtakingly beautiful spot, but access was nearly impossible. It sat unused for two hundred years, its turrets and fortifications on the verge of crumbling, when the Heilmann family, industrialists from Frankfurt, bought the small castle in 1880.

Friedrich Heilmann installed a road which was later paved for motorcars, shored up the foundation, and tore down the imposing collar wall and ramparts. He installed Gothic bedsteads, Renaissance wardrobes, new leaded-glass windows, and had the ceilings rebeamed. For three generations, the Heilmanns lived and loved amid the splendor of the Alps.

The interior was nothing like Pierre had imagined. Almost the entire first floor was open, with no walls dividing library, dining, and living rooms. Overstuffed chintz sofas surrounded an enormous stone fireplace that soared to the second story. Aubusson rugs defined conversation areas. Fires burned in every bedroom, and on particularly cold days, central heat kept owners and guests warm.

When Pierre sank into the featherbed and snuggled beneath a down-filled comforter, he felt as if he were floating on a cloud.

The Heilmanns employed two housemaids, a cook, and a handyman. Linens and fresh flowers were replenished every morning and the meals were more Continental than German and exquisitely prepared.

In the evening they all gathered around the fireplace on the first floor for cocktails and admired the twenty-foot Christmas tree adorned with electric lights in the shape of animals and houses, and generations-old glass ornaments.

Pierre believed that no two finer people existed on the face of the earth than Friedrich Heilmann III and his wife, Lisle. Well-traveled and educated, they delighted him with their sense of humor and their obvious caring for each other and the welfare of their guest. Friedrich was an enormously successful man whose concern over the rising Nazi party was, if anything, understated during Pierre's visit. Pierre sensed alarm in Lisle's face whenever Randolf discussed politics. Pierre admired them for the manner in which they approached Randolf, always assuring him he was to follow his own beliefs and reiterating their love for him.

Randolf, on the other hand, scoffed at his parents' lack of foresight and aversion to change. When he referred to them as conservative, capitalistic, and traditional, he nearly spat the words out. Pierre wondered what had happened that two such wonderful people could have raised, in Pierre's eyes, a fanatic. He was soon to discover the reason.

Karl Heilmann was Randolf's thirty-year-old brother. When he arrived two days before Christmas, bearing a carload of presents, Pierre thought him a Nordic god. Karl stood six foot three, with blond hair and blue eyes.

As Karl embraced his mother and father, Pierre noted the chilling look of hatred in Randolf's eyes. Pierre was soon to learn that Karl was everything Randolf wanted to be and couldn't.

Karl possessed a brilliant business mind and, in five years of managing and running the family steel business, he had trebled their profits. Two years ago he sold the business for a sizable fortune against Friedrich's wishes and deposited the money in a Swiss bank. Karl started his own investment house with branches in Berlin and Munich and was currently seeking other cities in which to locate. Friedrich and Lisle no longer objected to Karl's business decisions. Karl had also been a champion skier. Following in his footsteps would be difficult for anyone. Randolf had decided long ago he was not equal to the challenge.

That night, when Pierre and Randolf were alone, Randolf

drank too much Moselle wine. "They love Karl more than they do me."

"I think you're wrong."

"Karl has always been their favorite!"

"I think your parents love you more, but you won't accept their love. It's much easier for you to hate your brother than to admit you were wrong."

"I can't be like him," Randolf said ruefully.

"Who asked you to?"

"It's what they expect! I see it in Mother's eyes all the time. 'If only Randolf were more like Karl—how proud we would be.'"

"I think they just want you to be happy and they know you aren't."

"I am happy! How could I not be? I'm becoming an important person in the party. You mark my words! Someday people will look up to me with fear and respect!"

Randolf's eyes held that glassy frenzy they often did when he spoke about the party. It seemed that lately his zeal was overpowering him.

Christmas Eve dispelled all of Randolf's sour mood. He was like a child, ripping through green and red wrapping paper, finding a new pair of skis, poles, and boots; a down-filled parka; a sheared beaver hat; three sweaters; and cologne.

"Pierre! Tomorrow you and I will go to Innsbruck and test my skis!" Randolf said.

"It's a date." Pierre smiled as Randolf hugged his mother, overjoyed at this material show of love which strangely meant so much to him.

After dinner, Karl and Pierre found themselves alone in the library.

"I must tell you I'm relieved to find you aren't another of Randolf's Nazi party friends."

"Far from it."

"I worry a lot about him. Randolf has always been impressionable. He likes to think he's a leader, but he isn't. He lets other people do his real thinking for him. He's overly involved with the Nazis and I'm sure it's apparent none of his family is pleased."

"I can understand your concern."

"What about his classes? Does he attend them?"

"Yes. Faithfully. But he never has any fun."

"No girlfriends?"

"None that I know of. He's become a loner. He's abandoned our weekend chess games and he never goes to the taverns with our friends."

"This isn't good at all, Pierre. I'm hoping you won't give up on him. Keep inviting him to go with you."

"I'll do my best. It won't be easy."

Karl lit a cigar and stared at the fire. Pierre liked this soft-spoken man. As the evening progressed, he found they had many things in common.

"If you plan to manage your sister's business affairs, you should request Professor Holbein for your corporate management course. He's an unbearable taskmaster, and you'll plan his execution at least twice during the course, but it's worth every painful moment."

"Thanks for the advice."

"Not at all. Listen, I get to Munich on business a couple times a month. Randolf is always too busy to see me, but perhaps we could have lunch. I could show you all my old haunts when I attended classes there."

"I'd like that." Pierre smiled.

"I'm glad we had this talk, Pierre. And I'm glad Randolf has you for a friend." Karl rose. "I'll see you in the morning."

Pierre sat in the lift looking back at the glorious sight of the Austrian Alps around him. Randolf was in his element, relating which slopes were the best, the fastest, the most treacherous. He had been raised in this area, and Innsbruck offered the finest slopes and most convivial chalets for their overnight stay.

Since Pierre had only a rudimentary understanding of skiing, the first afternoon he spent most of his time skidding down the slopes on his backside. Finally, he mastered a short slope. The next morning Randolf wanted him to venture onto a more challenging mountainside.

"This will not be a difficult run for you, Pierre. I picked the east side of this mountain, because there aren't too many trees for you to break your neck on and there are two jumps I particularly like."

Pierre adjusted his goggles and checked his boot lacing. "If you say so."

"Remember everything I told you and just follow me. When I get to the jumps, I'll signal to you and you veer to the left. There are no obstacles on the left side, except for some scrub pines."

"I think I can manage."

The slope was not smooth, with intermittent patches of ice and barren grassy areas where the snow had drifted away. It was far more difficult than Randolf had made it sound. Pierre had a hard time keeping his balance. Then he saw Randolf give him the signal. Pierre angled off to the left, darted through the "scrub pines" that were actually tall skinny trees, and wondered if Randolf's memory was that poor or if he just hadn't been here for a long time.

Pierre looked back over his shoulder in time to see Randolf take the jump. It was magnificent watching him soar in the air, propelled by the force of his downhill run. Randolf leaned far over his skis, pushing for extra distance. It was a perfect landing and Randolf took it with ease.

Together they began their descent, Randolf always taking the lead. Pierre now knew why both Heilmanns loved the sport. The air was clean and crisp and the view was magnificent. He felt a sense of power and pride surge through his veins as his body learned the terrain and mastered the mountain. Rabbits and squirrels darted out of his way into the surrounding trees. The lake below was like a mirror reflecting the blue sky above. More than ever, Pierre's affinity for Bavaria swelled.

The second signal came and once again Pierre veered off to the left. Randolf looked like an eagle soaring into the skies. Suddenly, something happened. Randolf tried to break his speed in midair and turn toward Pierre. His arms flailed, and he screamed.

Pierre braked, jerking his knees so quickly he nearly turned his ankle. Clumsily, he skied over to where Randolf had disappeared, thinking he would find him lying in the snow.

He found nothing. Where there should have been the side of a mountain, there was nothing but a sharp, ragged abyss.

Pierre unbuckled his boots and removed his skis. He crawled to the edge of the cliff, afraid to look. He called Randolf's name but there was no answer. He screamed and crawled on his belly until he was nearly half over the cliff himself. There, on a three-foot-wide ledge, several feet below him, lay Randolf.

His face was bloody and Pierre could not tell if he was dead or alive. He called Randolf's name again. This time, his roommate stirred. Frantically Pierre yelled for help, but it was futile since Randolf had already told him few people skied here. Pierre now understood why.

Then Pierre saw Randolf ease himself onto his elbows, shaking his head to clear his brain.

"Randolf! Is anything broken? Can you stand?"

"I think my leg is broken!"

Pierre grabbed his ski pole and lowered it over the side. "See if you can reach this."

Randolf stood up, but the pain was too much, and he almost slipped on a patch of ice.

"Take it slow, Randolf. Try to stand on the good leg."

Randolf maneuvered his body close up against the mountain, clutched at the icy rock, and stood on the ball of his foot. He reached for the pole and missed it by three inches.

"It's no good! I can't reach it. Go for help, Pierre!"

"You'd freeze to death before I got back and you know it!"

Pierre backed away from the edge and took off the small backpack that held the lunch the cook from the chalet had prepared. Pierre knew he was grasping at straws, but it was his only chance. "Hold on, Randolf! I'll get you out of there!"

With a knife that was packed with the lunch, Pierre began chopping into the ice and snow. He made two holes and then planted his skis upright into the sturdy earth beneath the snow. As best he could he packed the dirt around the base of the skis and fortified it with large hunks of ice. He took off his boots, cut off the straps to the backpack, and then tied them around his stockinged feet. He then buckled the straps to the skis. He grabbed the ski pole and on his belly lowered himself once more over the edge of the cliff.

"You've got one shot at this, Randolf, and that's all. Grab the pole and I'll pull you up. Take off your gloves!"

Randolf looked at him, blood oozing from a deep gash on his cheek, yanked off the gloves with his teeth and stuffed them in his pockets. This time the pole reached. Randolf firmly grabbed the leather hand grip on the pole.

"Pull! Now!" he yelled.

Pierre used his stomach rather than his arms to raise Randolf up the cliff. Inch by inch, Pierre moved backward and arched his back like a cat, sitting more erect with every move. He pulled again. The muscles in his arms burned as if they were on fire, and perspiration soaked his woolen knit cap. The tension in his back and neck muscles threatened to betray him. He pulled. He clenched his jaws so tightly he felt part of a tooth chip off.

He kept his eyes shut, straining with the effort. Randolf was a good twenty pounds heavier than he, and his clothing and boots could account for another ten. He pulled. His arms and thighs quivered as he took another deep breath and pulled again.

Suddenly, his body jerked up and the pole flew out of his hands and over his head. *He'd lost him!*

But when he opened his eyes, there was Randolf lying belly down on the snow, his legs still dangling over the cliff. Pierre grabbed his hands and pulled him to safety.

"I owe you my life, Pierre."

"Don't be silly."

"I'll never forget it. I promise."

"We've got a long way to go, my friend. That gash needs looking after, not to mention your leg."

Randolf stood up and put his arm around Pierre's neck as they stumbled their way back to the lodge. Not once did Randolf look back for his new skis and poles.

Chapter Twelve

Lamb's blood might have kept death at bay, Pierre thought, if he had still believed in the Bible, but he didn't.

He had bribed the groundskeeper with fifty francs to allow him into the private cemetery where Suzanne rested. He laid a bouquet of pink roses on her tombstone and ached to shed the tears that would not come.

For months he'd tried to forget Suzanne, but his mind was no match for his heart. If she'd lived, he would have done anything to see her, be with her, make love to her. Where Suzanne was concerned, he had no pride. He was certain now that eventually he could have convinced her to leave Emile. Even if it took a decade, they would have been together, he knew. But Emile had robbed him of that chance.

Pierre had always believed himself to be a gentle, loving man. But now he understood the rage that drove humans to commit murder—without regret.

He balled his trembling hands into fists as he remembered Renée relating Suzanne's story.

Emile had beaten Suzanne because she refused to tell him that she loved him. Virginie had kept the stories out of the newspapers and away from the public in general. Only a few close to Virginie knew the truth.

Renée had seen Suzanne's bruises with her own eyes when Suzanne had boldly defied Emile and Virginie and come to Maison Dubois for maternity clothes. Suzanne had been discreet about her visit and had told Renée nothing, but Renée's curiosity was piqued when Suzanne asked question after question about Pierre. It didn't take a genius to see that the girl was still in love with him, Renée had said.

When Cécile Thorpe visited Paris with her husband, Alvin, one of her first stops was Maison Dubois.

"I would have come sooner," said Cécile as she peeled off a pair of fuchsia kid gloves, "but getting away from the château isn't easy."

"And how is Virginie?" Renée asked as she poured tea.

"She's got her hands full with Emile."

Renée paused midmotion, already sensing the direction of Cécile's thoughts.

"Have you seen Suzanne?" Renée asked.

Cécile placed her cup on the table. Her eyes were troubled. "Last night, as a matter of fact. I couldn't sleep, and while on my way to the kitchen, I found her crying in the solarium. Once she knew she had my sympathy, she told me everything, Renée. And it's incredible!"

Cécile told Renée that Suzanne had *not* become pregnant that night on the yacht when Emile tricked her, but later, after they were married.

One day Emile had a terrible argument with his mother about his being passed over for a promotion he believed he deserved and one which his mother had been long promising him. Virginie had chosen that day to inform Emile of his "ineptitude," "lack of talent," and his "dismal chance for advancement" while she was alive. As she often did, Virginie lamented aloud that Edouard was dead.

"Emile came home drunk and not only raped Suzanne but sodomized her as well. Suzanne spent three weeks in a private sanatorium arranged for by Virginie. If she hadn't hemorrhaged, she wouldn't have been there as long. She told me it was the most peaceful time in her life since she'd married Emile. When she returned to the château, she was pregnant. Virginie was overjoyed. Emile was not."

"I knew it was bad for her, but this is like a horror story! What do her parents have to say about this?"

"They don't know! Suzanne is afraid to tell them since they think Emile is the perfect son-in-law. And then, they've been on their trip around half the world. They've been gone for seven months."

"So Suzanne hasn't been in communication with them."

Cécile shook her head. "No."

Cécile promised Renée she would keep her informed of news of Suzanne.

Then in June, just a week before Pierre was due home for summer, Emile had a second angry encounter with his mother. This time, Suzanne did not escape her husband so easily. Three weeks before her delivery date, Suzanne was rushed to the hospital, where the baby was delivered prematurely. The unnamed baby girl preceded her mother in death by three days.

From Jean, Pierre learned that Angélique de Lemare, the wife of a highly successful psychiatrist, had requested Jean to design her a gown for the Ambassador's Ball. It was an unusual request for Maison Dubois since they did not specialize in evening gowns, but the fee was handsome and Jean couldn't pass up the opportunity to display his creative abilities.

During her sessions with Jean, Angélique made several overt advances toward Jean which he shunned until one afternoon she mentioned a tea she'd attended at the home of Virginie Ruille. Further investigation disclosed that the woman's husband was a close friend of Virginie's. Jean discovered that Virginie had paid the doctors and police to keep Emile's assault of Suzanne out of the papers and police records.

Virginie sent Emile to Dr. de Lemare, who saw Emile for a total of five visits and then never returned. Dr. de Lemare diagnosed him as a homicidal schizophrenic, which Virginie dismissed as quackery, and she paid the doctor handsomely to burn his files. He accepted the check with gratitude and locked a copy of the files in his wall safe at home.

Jean thought he'd seen enough of life not to be shocked any longer. What he learned from Angélique repulsed him. He intended, however, to keep Angélique as a client and a lover until he could get what he wanted from her wall safe.

* * *

Pierre left the graveyard and walked the street for hours. He passed the café where he'd last seen Suzanne, the day she told him she was going to marry Emile. He remembered her eyes, her smile. He remembered the acid taste in his mouth when he envisioned her in Emile's arms. Jesus! Would he ever be able to forget?

The next morning, the milk in Pierre's cold coffee curdled as he stared at Emile's slovenly face grinning out at him from the society page.

Renée slowly filled her cup all the while keeping an eye on his trembling hands. "Pierre . . . what is it?"

Pierre slammed the paper on the table. He jabbed his finger at Emile's picture.

"He doesn't deserve to live! If I had a gun—"

Renée went to him and put her arms around him. "You can't do this to yourself! I know this has been a shock. I wish now I hadn't told you."

"I should have done something."

"Pierre, she was another man's wife. She had her family. It wasn't your place."

"Not my place? What is my place?" he yelled, his rage searing the air. "Suzanne loved me, but her family wanted me to 'know my place.' Look what happened."

"Oh, Pierre, there's nothing I can say . . ."

"No, there isn't."

She rubbed his neck. She felt helpless. Only time would help. What a platitude that was, but so painfully true.

Pierre's eyes riveted on her and conviction resonated in his voice. "My brooding here in Paris won't do either of us any good. Suzanne is gone. I have to think about the future, not the past."

"What are you going to do?"

"I'm going to double up on my courses and graduate early. The sooner I put college behind me, the sooner I can join you at Maison Dubois. Together, we'll find a way to stop Virginie. We have to."

"Yes," she said. "And we will."

That autumn Renée successfully filled the orders placed by Lord and Taylor and Saks Fifth Avenue in New York. Despite the Depression in the United States, it appeared that women would never outgrow their need for luxurious nightwear. Renée hired six new seamstresses and expanded her workrooms. The investment was a wise one, for their profits from the New York sales were nearly double that of goods sold in Paris.

Eighteen months earlier, the perfumery next door to her shop had been forced to close due to the poor economy. Renée made the owner a ridiculously low offer to purchase his stock and facilities. The short, pudgy M. Dumain surprised her by accepting her first offer. She kept his name on the door, paid him a salary, and asked him to develop a new fragrance solely for her. It was called "Noir"; Renée shipped the first samples to the United States, and the response was overwhelming; the perfumery was back in business. She decided to send samples to Harrods in London, the gift shop at the Gritti Palace Hotel in Venice, the Palace Hotel in Milan, and two boutiques located on the Via Veneto in Rome. The response was just as brisk. She incorporated Dumain's shop into Maison Dubois by tearing down the wall between the two shops. Now when patrons entered her salon, they were engulfed by clouds of "Noir." Perfume sales soared. M. Dumain developed scented body lotions and creams and was currently at work on a scented shampoo.

Renée was overworked and exhausted. In his last letter, Pierre had asked her to consider a holiday in Munich. She wrote to him at the end of October stating she barely had the stamina to get through the Christmas orders and would love to visit Munich. She would take Gaston out of school for one week, no more.

Pierre and Karl were having lunch together when Pierre read Renée's cable stating she and Gaston would be on the two o'clock Friday train and to make hotel reservations for her.

"I can't believe you finally talked your sister into coming to Munich!" Karl said.

"Neither can I. The rest will be good for her. She's sounded terribly overworked in her letters. That's why it's important for me to choose the right hotel. Got any suggestions?"

"No hotel. I insist you all stay at the 'guest house.' "

"Karl, that's very generous, but—"

"I'll hear no more about it." He laughed, knowing Pierre would not take much persuasion.

"I'd love a quiet weekend in the mountains away from my studies—and the goose-stepping Nazis!"

A worried frown crossed Karl's face, but he was quick to hide it. Pierre was as concerned about Randolf as Karl, but he took his cue from the German and kept the topic light. "You don't think Lisle will mind?"

Karl shook his head. "That's the last stupid remark you're allowed for the day. But just to be sure I'll telephone them now."

Before Pierre could stop him, Karl rose and went to the lobby. He returned a few minutes later.

"You see? I never lie. Everything is in readiness for your sister's visit!"

Karl knew now he *had* lied. *He* was not ready at all for the vision that alighted from the train that rainy day in Munich.

"Pierre!" Renée hugged him. "You look wonderful—and rested. Are you sure you've been studying enough? I thought college students were supposed to have perpetual bags under their eyes."

"Those are from hangovers, not studying." He laughed as he hugged Gaston. "How've you been, fella?"

"Fine," Gaston replied lamely as he glanced again at the stranger who was staring at his mother. "Who's he?"

"Oh! I almost forgot. Renée," he said, taking her hand and leading her toward Karl. "This is Karl Heilmann. Remember, I told you about him?"

"Yes." She shook Karl's hand. "So pleased to meet you. And this is Gaston, my son."

"I've heard a lot about you both." Karl reached for Gaston's hand. Though the boy smiled at him, Karl was aware of the wariness in the boy's eyes. "How was your trip, Gaston?"

"Fine."

Pierre gathered the luggage. "Your first train trip and all you can say is 'fine'?" he teased.

Sensing something had altered her son's earlier excitement, Renée put her arm around him. "Sometimes he's a bit shy around strangers."

Karl strained to see the road through the worsening rainstorm, thinking his concentration would have been a lot better if Renée weren't sitting beside him. Was it possible for a human to have eyes *that* color of lavender? Pierre's were violet, and since they were brother and sister, he supposed it was the same color, but on Renée he could swear it was different.

Whenever Pierre had spoken about his sister, it was always within the context of her business. Karl had expected to meet a buttoned-up spinster whose lover was work. Not once had it occurred to him that she would be young, beautiful, and alarmingly sensual.

"Karl is in the middle of a business expansion himself, Renée," Pierre said.

"Oh?" She turned to Karl.

"Yes!" Pierre piped in before Karl could answer. "His investment house is such a success that he feels Germany is not big enough for all his ideas. Karl has contacts and clients all over Europe."

"That's very impressive. . . ."

"And you should see him ski! Say! There's an idea! Maybe Karl could teach you to ski, Renée."

"Pierre . . ." she began.

"I'd like to ski," Gaston interrupted.

"You're still too young." Pierre brushed him off.

"No I'm not. Am I, Maman?"

"I don't know anything about skiing, chérie. If Pierre says . . ."

"You can stay with me while your mother goes with Karl," Pierre replied.

Gaston's lip curled down in a pout. He didn't like being treated like a child. He could learn to ski—probably better than his mother. Pierre was acting strangely, Gaston thought. Very strangely.

Karl and Renée exchanged an amused smile at Pierre's obvious matchmaking.

"I'm not really the deity Pierre thinks I am," Karl said.

"In what way?"

"I eat peanuts in bed. The shells are very messy."

"Ugh! That's disgusting!"

"There's no one there to tell me not to."

"Oh," she said and then forced herself to look away.

She knew he'd purposely made the sexual reference to stir a

reaction. But rather than being put off by it, which was her usual response, surprisingly, she found she was flattered—and intrigued.

Why had she never bothered to ask Pierre more about Karl? She was responding to more than just his looks. It was something in his voice. It was soothing and, stealthily, it surrounded her like a cocoon. Absentmindedly, she wondered what it would be like to be held in his arms. They looked very strong—very muscular.

What was she thinking? She didn't need to be held. She didn't need a man and certainly not this man. She had plenty of male companions, and they were all so . . . safe. Was that what intrigued her? That Karl was not safe?

The rain had stopped by the time they arrived at the "guest house." Renée remembered most of what Pierre had told her about the ancient castle, but still she gaped at its beauty and the surrounding mountains.

"Pierre was right. It's like a fairy-tale kingdom," she said to Karl.

"I'm glad I was able to impress you," he said, taking her arm and leading her inside.

Renée and Gaston met Friedrich and Lisle, who showed them to their rooms. By the time Renée finished unpacking, it was time for dinner, during which Pierre continued a ceaseless heralding of Karl's accomplishments. Gaston was unusually quiet during the meal, answering in monosyllables. She knew this time his despondency was not due to his characteristic "moodiness."

After dessert when everyone adjourned to the living room, Renée walked Gaston upstairs to bed.

"Is there anything wrong?" she asked him as she tucked him into bed.

"No."

"Certain?" She bent down and kissed his cheek.

"Yes," he replied, but when she started to go, he grabbed her hand. "He looks at you funny."

"Who?"

"Karl. I never saw anyone look at you like that."

"Really?" She smiled to herself, thinking his attraction to her was not just her imagination.

"Jean never did and not Pierre or me. He thinks he is special and he's even fooled Pierre. You should warn Pierre to be careful."

"That's silly. Pierre and Karl are friends."

Gaston folded his arms across his chest. "I don't like him."

"I don't think he's so bad. And if you'll be honest, it isn't Karl you don't like, but Pierre's friendship with him. Hmm?"

"Well . . . Pierre didn't ask me about school or the shop at all! And he always does whenever we see each other. It was 'Karl this and Karl that.' "

"Chéri," she said, "Pierre is just excited to have us here. He wants us to like his friends as much as he does. That's all. But I'll talk to him for you. Okay?"

Gaston nodded sullenly as she kissed him and turned off the light.

"All the same," he said as she opened the door and the hall light illuminated his concerned face. "Karl looked at you funny."

"Is Gaston all right? I noticed he didn't say much at dinner," Karl asked when he and Renée stood on the terrace drinking brandy.

"I think he's experiencing jealousy for the first time." She chuckled.

"Oh?"

"Gaston couldn't understand Pierre's effusiveness about you. Pierre normally spends his praise on Gaston. Gaston felt a little left out. I also feel I must apologize for my brother's behavior. I know he embarrassed your parents. He means well. I'll speak to him tomorrow and explain the situation."

Karl crushed out his cigarette with his heel. "What situation is that?" he asked, easing closer to her.

"You know very well."

"Do I?"

He was even closer now. "Yes, well, I mean thrusting us upon one another the way he has . . ."

Karl placed his hand over hers. She jumped.

"Am I frightening you?"

"No, not at all," she said and snatched her hand back. "I'm rather tired—the trip and all."

She backed away but he kept closing the distance between them. She could almost feel his body heat, he was so close. His eyes were maddeningly blue. Renée fought the impulse to fling her arms around his neck. She wondered what his lips tasted like and unconsciously she licked her own. She didn't realize how seductive she appeared to him at that moment.

"Ah, yes. The trip." He nodded, relishing her discomfort.

Panicked by the enormous attraction she was feeling, she wanted to flee. She handed him the brandy glass. "If you'll excuse me . . ."

"Of course."

She turned back just for an instant to see his eyes again. "I'm looking forward to the drive through the mountains tomorrow."

"Good night, Renée," he said earnestly, dropping his bantering inflection. "Sleep well."

It had been a long time since Renée had felt these sexual impulses. She had to be careful. Stay on guard. When would she *ever* learn to restrain herself? Every time she'd reacted like this—Edouard and then Grant—it had always spelled disaster. She had to learn to take sex for what it was, a release of tension. Or better still, she should ignore it—and him.

Renée liked the touch of Karl's hand on her shoulder as he pointed out different mountain peaks, explained their history, and showed her where he skied every year.

"Come with me, Gaston," he said, offering his hand.

Gaston stood rigid.

"I want to show you a special cave."

"What's so special about it?"

Karl leaned forward conspiratorially. "Legend says a dragon still lives there."

"I don't believe it."

"I do. I've seen it."

"You have?"

"Yes. Are you sure you don't want to come with me?"

"Well . . ." Gaston hesitated only momentarily. He grasped Karl's hand firmly. "If you think it's safe."

"You'll be with me. I'll keep you safe."

Gaston felt frightened going into the dark cave, but Karl held his hand and talked to him constantly, using his voice to calm him. Karl asked him questions about school, his friends, his chores at Maison Dubois. Karl did not ask a single question about his mother. Gaston liked that. He didn't like men who were only nice to him so they could find out stuff about his mother. He never answered their questions, though. He had to protect her. Pierre had told him to.

Gaston listened as Karl told him about the time he'd come here to see the dragon when he was six years old.

"I was scared, too, because I was alone. This is much better, don't you think?" Karl asked.

"Oh, yes," Gaston answered and gripped Karl's hand even tighter as they stepped gingerly over loose stones.

Twice Gaston lost his footing, but Karl was there to help him and all the while Karl never stopped talking.

Gaston's trust grew slowly. Gaston pondered the decision to be friends with Karl during the entire trip through the cave. Once they saw "the dragon"—actually a stone formation—Gaston decided Karl was just as special as Pierre had said.

Karl had warm hands and they never got clammy. Karl never talked down to him and Gaston liked that too. He was sincere like Jean and he was interested in what Gaston had to say as if he, Gaston, were important. Gaston decided it would be all right to like Karl.

Emerging from the cave, Gaston and Karl made their way up to the ridge where Renée waited for them with a picnic lunch. On the way, Karl picked up squirrel-eaten walnuts, pine cones, and acorn pods.

"Why do you want all this stuff?" Gaston asked, stuffing another cone into his pocket.

"Not me, my mother. It's a tradition with us. She makes Christmas ornaments and decorations from them and puts them on the tree or gives them to special friends. It wouldn't seem like the holidays without Mother making ornaments, baking cookies, and decorating the tree. You know, all those things that mothers do during the holidays."

"No, I don't know."

Gaston had responded with such a puzzled look on his face that Karl pressed the boy further.

"What are some of the things your mother does at Christmas?"

"Mostly she works late."

"On Christmas?"

Gaston nodded. "We have a big dinner and there's presents in our shoes in the morning, but usually she and Jean talk about work while we eat and then they go down to the workrooms after I go to bed. It's no different than any other day."

Karl stopped and sat on a sun-warmed rock while Gaston stood next to him. "Who decorates your house?"

"We live over the workrooms."

"Your apartment, then."

"No one. Well, that's not true, really."

"I thought not."

"I made some stars with glitter at school and hung them from the light in the dining room. And we have chrysanthemums on the tables. But then, Mother always has fresh flowers in the dining room."

"I get the impression that you don't talk to your mother very much."

"We talk all the time," he said defensively.

"About things that trouble you?"

"Sometimes . . . but it's hard for her because she has to work. And . . ." Gaston paused. Karl could tell he was fighting tears and he realized the boy desperately wanted to talk to him.

"And what, Gaston?"

"I used to think she avoided me because I was a bastard. But," he added quickly, "I don't think that now, because I know she really loves me."

"Of course she does! Anyone can see that. Who told you that you were a bastard?"

"The boys at school. They call me that a lot because my mother wasn't married to my father."

"What does your mother say about your father?"

"Only that he died. She doesn't like to talk about him at all. I think she hates him."

"Did you tell your mother about your problems at school?"

"No. It would only hurt her. She gets very upset when anyone mentions my father or my grandmother. I hear her and Jean talking at night sometimes and my mother cries about it. She hates my grandmother." Gaston stopped and looked into Karl's eyes. Suddenly he was frightened as he realized how much he'd told a stranger. "Please promise you won't tell my mother. She doesn't know I know about my father and grandmother. My father was an evil man and my grandmother hates my mother too. But I don't know why."

"Gaston, I doubt seriously your father was an evil man." Karl took Gaston's hands and pulled him a bit closer and, with his fingertips, tilted the boy's chin up so that he could look into his eyes. "You are the finest young man I've ever had the pleasure of meeting and if your father were all that terrible, he couldn't have been your father, now could he?"

A tear slid out of Gaston's eye. He liked the way he felt protected around Karl. Gaston had never thought about what a father should be like. He'd never had one, so he felt no loss. At school functions, soccer games, and picnics, he'd always had Jean or Pierre or both to stand in as "father." Gaston wasn't sure about what he'd do with a father if he'd had one. He did know he liked Karl, and since he was unable to find a niche for the big German man, Gaston raised his head and said in a low voice: "I wish you were my father."

Karl hugged him fiercely, needing the contact perhaps as much as Gaston. "If I had a son, Gaston, believe me, I would want him to be just like you."

Karl pulled away. "You should remember that sometimes people say things about other people when they've been hurt, but it doesn't mean they're true. I'll bet that when your mother says things about your father, it's because he hurt her, not because he was evil. I don't believe there are any evil people in this world. There are some pretty crazy ones and sick ones, but sheer out and out evil is rare. I hope never to see it in my lifetime."

Karl stood on the balcony, smoking one of his father's imported cigars, and looked up at the clear October sky. This was his favorite time of year, when the days were still warm and the nights crisp and clear. He couldn't help thinking what it would be like to lie next to Renée and have her body keep him warm through the chilly night. He blew the smoke out and leaned over further, watching the moonlight play among the pines below. A greensilver light decorated the tips of the trees, making them appear much closer.

"You weren't at all what I expected," Renée said.

Momentarily startled, Karl turned to see her standing by the leaded-glass door. Even in the shadows, her lavender eyes gleamed at him as if lit from an inner flame. He had a feeling if he never saw her again they would haunt him for the rest of his life.

"Disappointed?"

"Not in the least. I suppose I had confused you with your brother, Randolf. I anticipated a sparse lifestyle, even austere—with an uninteresting German family." She laughed lightly. "I suppose I've read too much about the Nazis and failed to realize that Germany was here long before this new political party. It truly is a beautiful country. I understand now why Pierre is so enamored of it. And your home, your parents—just wonderful."

He nodded. "If I lived two lifetimes, I doubt I could live as happily as they do. They seem to have found the right balance between work and family. I've never felt neglected or unduly pressured by them. I always knew they loved me just for myself. I think that's a hard thing to do for a child."

"It is, believe me," Renée said, looking off into the distance and thinking of Gaston.

"I understand from Gaston that you work some very long hours. Isn't there some way you can spend more time with him?"

Renée's shoulders tensed and Karl didn't miss the defensive turn in her voice.

"What I do with my time and family should not concern you."

"I apologize. That's one of my faults—I'm forever sticking my nose where it isn't wanted."

"I'm sorry too. I'm overly protective of my family."

"You should be. I know if I had a family I'd do the same."

"Trying to give my son everything he needs plus run the business and handle the expansion seems an impossible task to me most days. I can only take things day by day, crisis by crisis. Somehow, we're surviving."

He peered at her. "Doesn't sound like you have much fun."

She laughed. "I wish my schedule would allow for some!"

"Fear not. That's an area that's been severely lacking in my own life. I was wondering if you would care to join me in an alteration of lifestyles?"

"What *are* you talking about?"

"No questions please. A simple 'yes' or 'no.' You'll have to take this one on good faith."

"That's not fair! How can I answer without knowing all the details and repercussions? I'll have to say 'no.' "

"I'm crushed!" He laid his hand over his heart and rolled his eyes upward. "But not discouraged!"

"Perhaps next time you'll allow me a few questions!"

"Perhaps . . ." he said seriously. "Next time." He bowed and walked away.

Renée felt an excited chill run down her spine as she watched him disappear inside. Karl was intriguing, but more than that, she sensed that once she left Germany she would not easily forget him.

Chapter Thirteen

Karl Heilmann owned the patent on persistence, Renée decided as she slid his last letter into the top drawer of her desk. Through the remainder of October, all of November, and most of December he had unabashedly showered her with telephone calls, notes, and letters. True, none of them were overly committal, most dealing with trivialities or news of Pierre as he crammed for his final exams. However, he strategically timed all his missives, making certain Renée never forgot him or her visit to Munich.

Pierre had finally graduated, and Renée was beside herself with relief for she had enough year-end paperwork to keep them both busy for months.

Pierre shot the first arrow through her balloon when he said: "I'm not working through the holidays and neither are you."

"Don't be ridiculous, Pierre. There's too much to be done."

"After the New Year," he retorted.

For hours they argued until finally she did the only thing she could—she gave in.

When Pierre began to unpack, he made an exaggerated display of the many gifts the Heilmann family sent to Gaston and Renée. From Lisle there were dozens of homemade ornaments for Gaston, and two hand-blown glass angels for Renée. Lastly, he handed Renée three beautifully wrapped boxes from Karl.

"I think it only proper we have a Christmas tree this year. Lisle would be heartsick if she knew we didn't put her gifts to good use." Pierre winked at Gaston who whooped his approval.

Pierre and Gaston went straight to work creating whimsical decorations for the tree they'd placed in the living room next to the fireplace. Pierre wired fruits and nuts to long ropes of greens and festooned nearly every doorway and window.

On the twenty-third of December, an enormous poinsettia was delivered to Maison Dubois for Renée from Karl. Later that evening, a messenger delivered a fruitcake and a two-pound box of chocolates. Both were from Karl.

Each time the bell rang, Renée did not miss the eager look on Pierre's face. She had the feeling he knew more than he was letting on. Frequently that day, she'd caught him whispering to Gaston in the kitchen while they iced cookies. Later, Renée distinctly heard Pierre mention her name while he and Gaston wrapped presents in the bedroom.

Gaston seemed unduly excited about something, but she attributed it to the "fuss" Pierre was making over the decorations.

Jean stopped in at the end of his day to share a glass of champagne and placed his gifts for Renée, Gaston, and Pierre under the tree. When Renée returned from the kitchen, she heard Jean say: "I won't let on. You can count on me."

"Count on you for what?"

"I've been sworn to secrecy. Besides, that's what Christmas is all about—mysteries and secrets." He put his arm around her. "I'll be back Christmas for dinner," he said. "Right now I have a lovely lady waiting."

"You'd better be here. It wouldn't be Christmas without you." Renée kissed him and walked him to the door.

Later that night after Gaston was asleep, Renée sat on the sofa in front of the fire and hugged Pierre especially close.

Pierre sensed a veil of melancholy descend over his sister. "What is it, chérie?" he asked, stroking her hair.

"I've always hated Christmas ever since Michel died. It's a perpetual reminder and I keep thinking if I rush through it, it won't hurt as much. But I miss him just as much now as I did the day he died. Logically, I know there was nothing I could have done, but my mind keeps going over it and over it. If I hadn't had to work, if I'd been there with him . . ."

Tears sprang into her eyes. "I'm always afraid something dreadful will happen to you or Gaston or Jean on Christmas. I'm so tense for weeks ahead of time that I can't possibly enjoy it the way other people do."

Pierre held her closer. "I know."

"I don't want Gaston to think that I deliberately try to cheat him out of anything."

"He doesn't think that."

"But I feel that way! He's a good boy and he deserves more from me—more of my time. But it seems there are never enough hours in the day. Sometimes, I feel like I'm being crushed under all the responsibility. So many people need me, depend on me. Sometimes, Pierre, I don't see how I'll make it through the next hour, much less the next day."

"I'm here now. I hope I can take some of those pressures away. Together we can build Maison Dubois even bigger and without so much stress on you."

She looked over at the lighted tree. "It really is beautiful, isn't it? From now on, we'll have to make our times together more special."

Christmas morning Gaston awakened his mother and uncle, then raced into the living room and began ripping through packages before Renée was in her robe.

"Maman! Karl sent me an electric train with boxcars, an engine . . . and here's the caboose!"

Renée rummaged through the box. "Look at all these pieces, Gaston! Here's a tiny kiosk, a train station, trees, even telephone poles. This is a wonderful gift!"

They opened the remaining gifts and then Renée went to the kitchen to prepare a fruit plate and make coffee. Pierre helped Gaston set up the train track.

At the knock on the door Renée asked, "Who can that be?"

"I'll get it." Pierre smiled a bit too broadly as he bounded toward the apartment door. "Karl! Glad to see you made it!" Pierre said, taking Karl's coat and turning to catch Renée's reaction.

She instantly felt dowdy standing in the doorway to the kitchen with no makeup, her wavy hair still tangled from sleep, and dressed in an apricot robe. Somehow she had known for a long time that he would be here on Christmas. Perhaps it had been a slip in one of his letters or calls that tipped her off. Or perhaps she had wanted him with her. She wished desperately she had paid attention to her intuition.

"Merry Christmas, Karl," she said, running a hand through her hair. He was more handsome than she remembered. She couldn't think of anything to say.

"Merry Christmas, Renée."

"I'm happy to see you," she said, still not moving from the spot. His blue eyes seemed to penetrate her.

He could only nod, his tongue caught by the same cat.

Gaston pulled on Karl's arm. "Thank you for the train! I've never seen one so grand!"

Not once did Karl take his eyes off Renée, and not until he sat on the floor with Gaston did Renée feel her heart beat again.

They sat at the best table at Les Princes at the George V Hotel surrounded by ultrarich Americans, scandalous Parisian lovers, the Turkish ambassador and his mistress, and an avant-garde Russian novelist.

Karl had arrived in Paris virtually unannounced, spent Christmas day with Renée, and then all but disappeared for over two weeks.

He had telephoned twice at her office and left messages since she was out. Three weeks ago he suddenly appeared again, stating that business had kept him occupied, but he very much wanted to see her. That was the beginning of what he referred to as his "gastronomic tour of Paris," but Renée thought she knew courtship when she saw it.

"Actually, I'd planned to come to Paris for over two years," he said, sampling a particularly delicate wine, "so it wasn't a sudden decision at all."

"Is that so?" She knew he was lying.

"In another two months all the papers will be finalized and my new branch will be open for business."

"I'm intrigued," she said, noting that his eyes were anything but businesslike. "The prawns are especially creamy," he said.

She had noticed all evening that his mind seemed to flit from one topic to another. "Karl, what's bothering you?"

"Why, nothing," he said, his smile withering. "That's not

true, either. I spoke with my father today and he's quite concerned about Randolf."

"What about your brother?"

Karl lowered his voice. "Over the holidays he and Father had a terrific argument. Randolf stormed out of the house accusing Father of being anti-German, when exactly the opposite is true. Father is anti-Nazi, which he'd never say to Randolf. My brother is very volatile and we're afraid he will say something about our family differences at the wrong place and to the wrong people. It could be dangerous for my parents. I hope it doesn't go that far, but Randolf has become quite militant in his thinking."

"Pierre has often said the same thing. From what little I know, I doubt your father can stop him."

"Family opposition only seems to egg him on."

"Is there anything I can do?"

It was the first time that evening that a genuine smile lit Karl's face. "You can be there when I need to talk to you."

"That doesn't sound too difficult."

When he held her hand, a now-familiar feeling of protected warmth engulfed Renée. Karl brought a sense of stability to her life she'd never known. What surprised her most was her willingness to accept it.

It had taken Renée and Céleste four years to find the kind of linen company they wanted to purchase. Finally, their search had come to an end.

Renée sat at her desk and tore open Céleste's letter.

> Dear Renée,
> I've done as you asked and have the pertinent information on my desk waiting for you. I can't tell you how anxious I am to purchase this company.
> Hammerly Linens is over two hundred years old and has always produced the finest in English bedding. Their handwork is beyond compare and I can guarantee that we can rehire all the old employees. I have also found a warehouse in Chelsea that bears looking into. I can honestly say that Hammerly Linens would be the only company on or off the Continent that could compete with Porthault. It will take us a while to get reestablished and there is much that needs overhauling,

though not in the manufacturing end. Most of the problems were in management, which I doubt we will have any difficulty in reorganizing.

I'm looking forward to your visit on the first. Hug Gaston for me and tell Pierre I expect to see him soon when he comes to look over the facilities.

Love to you all.
Aunt Céleste

Renée had just put the letter away when Karl walked in. Though only eight months had passed since his arrival in Paris, Renée couldn't remember what it was like without him. He was smiling as he leaned down and placed a kiss on her cheek.

"Are you free for lunch? I know I should have telephoned . . ."

"As a matter of fact, I am. I have something I want to discuss with you anyway."

He hailed a cab, instructed the driver, then leaned back and hugged Renée to him. "Mmm. You smell good." He tilted her chin up to his face and kissed her deeply.

Renée held him close, savoring the feel of his body next to hers. Karl's kisses were like a tranquilizer. No matter how rushed she had been all day, he had a calming effect on her, as if he were asking her to stop and enjoy this one moment of life that could never come again. Karl was good for her and she sensed he knew he had nearly beaten down all her defenses.

When they were escorted to their table at Café de la Paix, every male eye was riveted on Renée and she did not miss the covert female glances Karl received. After Karl placed their order he smiled at her.

"Mademoiselle Dubois, have you ever noticed what a striking couple we make?"

"Humble, aren't you?"

"Observant."

"What else have you observed?"

He scrutinized her face and said, "Something is bothering you."

She nodded. "Karl, I have to go to England on business."

His jocular mood vanished. "How long will you be gone?"

"Only a week. Do you remember I told you about a linen company I was looking to purchase?"

"Yes."

"Céleste, Pierre, and I have agreed that the timing is right for it now."

"Why do you need more businesses to run? It seems to me that you have more than you can handle as it is. Perfumes, lingerie—now bed linens. Where are you going with it all?"

"Let's say I have an innate fear of poverty."

"More like an insatiable desire for revenge, if you ask me."

Renée was stunned and knew it showed in her face. "I don't know what you're talking about."

Karl's voice was thoughtful and precise. "I told you once before I know a lot more about you than you think. I know Virginie Ruille is more than just another society matron to you and Pierre. I don't know all the details but I know enough about what drives you. What do you think I've spent the last eight months trying to show you? There is a great deal more to life than getting even, Renée."

Renée's eyes were shadowed and she closed her mind to what he was saying. Karl grabbed her arm.

"Goddamn it! I'm talking to you! For once in your life listen with more than your ears!"

"Don't manhandle me, Karl!"

"I love you, you idiot! Or can't you see that either? I want you to marry me!"

Renée continued to stare at him as his words sank in.

"I wanted to propose to you in a romantic setting, not in the middle of an argument."

Renée laughed. "Do you suppose that's an omen?"

"Don't even think such a thing!" His eyes were pleading as he looked at her.

Renée wanted so desperately to jump into his arms, smother his face with kisses, and shout "Yes" so that all of Paris could hear her. Instead, she looked deeply into his eyes and said, "Could I think about it this next week while I'm in England? I promise I'll give you my answer when I return."

Karl was disappointed, but he brightened. "I can't believe I'm going to say this, but I *do* want you to think about it. Look at your factory, think about me and what a life together would be."

* * *

After Renée gave her approval on the factory, Céleste bombarded her with questions about Pierre and Gaston. Then she asked: "And how is Karl? Your last two letters didn't mention him at all . . . your brain is too much on business, as you said. I didn't want to bring him up in case he had gone back to Germany."

"Quite the contrary. He's asked me to marry him."

Céleste's smile was immediate, but it dimmed when she saw the concern in Renée's eyes. "You don't love him?"

"I'm not sure. I'm so cautious about everything these days. Pierre complains that I dawdle over which marmalade to have in the morning and Jean is constantly threatening never to involve me in the designs again because I'll spend hours choosing colors. I'm at a standstill. I'm terrified of risking my feelings again. Twice I believed in a man and twice I was hurt."

"I don't know what advice I can give you."

"Perhaps there just isn't any for my situation. I care very much for Karl. We enjoy each other's company, and yet . . . I don't feel that same kind of magic I had with Grant."

Céleste scowled and folded her arms.

"You don't like Grant," Renée said.

"How can I say? I never met the man. But I will say I never was partial to fools, no. Edouard was a bastard and got what he deserved. This Grant . . . I only know from your letters. I know you loved him, but he still sounds like the greatest fool on the earth to let you go."

"You're just prejudiced because you love me," Renée said.

"Not only that, but I'm old and can say and do just about anything I please. There are compensations for being over fifty."

"Well, Karl asked me to think about his proposal while I'm in London and I promised I would do just that."

"Perhaps London will show you the way," Céleste said.

"I hope so," Renée said. "I really hope so."

Chapter Fourteen

Years of scientific research had produced enough data to substantiate the belief that just before one dies, one's life passes before one's eyes.

That was how Grant Morgan knew he *must* be dying as he watched her cross Brompton Road and dash into Harrods. She was dressed in a white linen suit with a white silk blouse that tied in a soft bow at the neck. Her hair was longer now, falling in shimmering waves over her shoulders. He held his breath, thinking it impossible she could become more beautiful, but she had.

He walked into Harrods and peered round one counter after another. He searched aisle after aisle, but couldn't find her. He knew he must look strange, running through the departments, ignoring the scowls from the salespeople and twice mistaking a customer for Renée. He wandered through the store wondering what he would have said to her if he *had* found her. He couldn't decide which he would rather do: grab her by the shoulders and shake her until her teeth rattled, or take her in his arms and kiss her as he'd dreamed of doing every day for the past four years.

Two years, three months, and one week ago he'd come to the conclusion that she was superstar material. He'd dealt with actresses nearly all his adult life and prided himself on knowing when they were "on" and when they were "off." Renée Dubois was an actress's actress for she had fooled even him. *He had believed her when she told him she loved him.* But she had lied. All she really wanted was her business, which he was convinced was an excuse to continue that feud of hers with Virginie.

Many times he thought he should come back to Paris and flaunt his affair with Darma so that Renée would know she hadn't won the prize. But that plan would have backfired on him too. Even if Renée saw him at this moment, she would know the instant their eyes met that she still held his heart.

He walked out the front door and almost fell over a woman who was crouched down picking up the contents of her purse that were scattered on the sidewalk.

Reflexively, he excused himself and offered to help. He'd just picked up a gold tube of lipstick and turned around when he heard her sharp intake of breath.

"Grant?" She uttered his name in that way that made his nerve endings explode.

She looked like a goddess, her eyes wet with joyful tears and a smile on her lips that made him ache to touch her. Words were leapfrogging over the lump in his throat, but only faint mumblings exited.

"I . . . I can't believe it's you!" she said, reaching to touch his hand.

When her skin met his, he felt as if they were fused together by that same electricity he'd tried for years to forget.

"What are you doing in London?" she asked.

"We're shooting a new movie. It looks promising."

She smiled. "Oscar material?"

"I'm always hoping," he said. She seemed so at ease and in control while his stomach was churning. "Are you here for long?"

"A week—just while I attend to some business matters." She felt marvelously calm and seemed to know all the right things to say. She had been right not to deny herself memories of him. And she knew he'd never really left her. It had been the specter of Grant that had loomed over her relationshp with Karl. She smiled again. "Can I tell you something?"

"Of course."

"You know the apartment where we used to go?"

"Yes—how could I forget?"

"I go there once a month to clean it—and when I do, well, I think about you and what it was like. I guess the landlord doesn't mind because no one has ever stopped me."

His smile was tremulous. "I shouldn't guess anyone would. You see, I bought it outright. You can go there whenever you want."

Renée was astounded. From Cécile she'd heard bits of information about Grant, but never much more than the projects he was working on since Alvin invested in films from time to time. Grant apparently led a low-key personal life and his name was seldom mentioned in the newspapers. In fact, it wasn't until he announced his engagement to Darma Logan just two weeks ago that Renée had read anything about him. The papers had stated Grant was a "young man with a dream. This union with James Logan's fortune would make him the movie mogul Morgan was destined to become."

At that moment, Renée couldn't think about Darma or Karl. She couldn't remember why they had remained apart for over four years. Suddenly, it was 1931 again and Grant was holding her in his arms, kissing her passionately.

Renée laughed. "Don't you think we've drawn a large enough crowd?"

He grabbed her hand and together they raced to the Basil Street Hotel.

At midafternoon, only the desk clerk was present in the antique-filled lobby. He nodded as he watched Grant and Renée mount the Georgian mahogany staircase that led to Grant's second-floor room.

For more than a thousand days and nights, Renée had expertly expelled desire and passion from her life, so that now their unleashing could be nothing less than explosive. She clung to him, telling him with her mouth and tongue and body how much she wanted him. When they finally stood naked, she thought she had never felt this complete.

"God! How I've needed you!" he said and scooped her up into his arms and carried her to the bed, and at that exact moment, Renée knew it would not be possible to live another day without him.

* * *

"Grant has finished *Murder in the Streets* and he wants to celebrate."

"Celebrate what?" Céleste asked stiffly. "For two days you've been walking around with your head in the clouds. You've missed appointments, you were in a daze at the attorney's office, and you haven't thought once about your family—or Karl—since you met Grant."

"I'm in love, Aunt Céleste."

Céleste's eyes were glacial. "And is he in love with you or with his fiancée?"

"I know he loves me," Renée declared.

"And Darma?"

Renée quickly turned away and gathered her cloak and gloves. "Grant is taking us to Boulestin's," she said, referring to the restaurant on Southampton Street, on the border of Covent Garden Market, founded by Xavier Marcel Boulestin who was, in 1934, at the apex of his culinary career. For those who wanted to be "seen" and for those who wanted to impress, Boulestin's was *de rigueur*.

"Lovely," Céleste grumbled and joined Herbert who was waiting for them in the vestibule.

They sat at a corner table in the luxurious restaurant, attended by a very polished staff, and no one said a word. Twice Renée tried to start a conversation, and though Herbert tried to keep it going, it was clear Céleste was not pleased.

"I'm pleased you could come along tonight," Grant said to Céleste and Herbert. "I'm told the food is excellent. Have you been here before?"

"Yes," Céleste replied coldly.

"Dealing with your caliber of clientele, I suppose you've been just about everywhere in London."

Céleste remained silent.

He glanced at Renée, who was feeling every bit of his tension, and then spoke to Céleste again. "That's a lovely dress you're wearing."

"Thank you. Renée made it for me."

"I could tell. The color enhances your eyes."

Céleste did not reply as her jade green eyes continued to examine him.

Just then the wine steward appeared.

"Would you care for wine, Céleste? Herbert?"

"Yes," Céleste replied crisply as she placed her napkin on her lap.

"Champagne. Your best," Grant ordered.

"Aunt Céleste, Grant has been working on a new movie here in London."

"Oh? Probably has a bland plot and trite dialogue."

"Aunt Céleste! What's gotten into you?"

Grant peered at Céleste for a long moment. "Why don't you like me, Céleste?" he asked.

"I don't know you, Mr. Morgan. I only know what I see and hear from Renée. She's in love with you. I saw her like this once before and she was left with a broken heart. You, in fact, left her before. I have always been protective of her and I guess I'm too old to change."

"But I don't want to hurt Renée. I love her. Maybe once you get to know me, you'll be able to see that. What happened before . . . well . . . that was then. And now—"

"Now is what I'm talking about," Céleste interjected. "How can you change who you are so easily?"

"I can't and I don't want to. But I can move to Paris."

"What?" Céleste's eyes flew open.

"You can?" Renée exclaimed as she held her breath.

"Why not? I think I can arrange my business from Paris at least for a portion of the year. Perhaps you could rearrange your schedule and live in California for a few months out of the year."

"Grant, I . . ."

"Say yes," he said, taking her hand.

Renée's smile filled her face. "Yes," she whispered as he kissed her.

He turned to Céleste. "I'd like to have you on my . . . our side, Céleste. Something tells me you'd be a good ally. Lord knows, I've seen all the combat with you I'd *ever* care to have." He chuckled.

Céleste gasped. "I'm not *that* formidable!"

Everyone at the table laughed.

"When it comes to your family, you are." Herbert patted her arm and smiled. Then he picked up his champagne glass. "A toast to us all."

* * *

On Tuesday nights in London everyone who was anyone would not think of dining anywhere but Boulestin's. It was not by accident but by custom that Lady Sara, aunt of Lady Jane St. John, was seated at her usual table with Lord and Lady Wellesley and the Earl of Ducingham.

Lady Claire leaned over to Lady Sara and said, "Isn't that Renée Dubois?"

Lady Sara prided herself on knowing faces, connecting them with their proper names, and remembering backgrounds. "Why, yes. And the Simcoxes of course. Renée is Mrs. Simcox's niece. I don't know who the man—" She peered more closely. "If I'm not mistaken that's Grant Morgan, the American film producer. There was an article in the *Times* about his work here."

"Ah! I remember reading about that." Lady Claire glanced again at the American just as he held Renée's hand. "Seems odd that the Dubois woman would be interested—him being engaged and all."

"Yes, it does," Lady Sara replied but she had known of the Morgan-Dubois affair of years ago when Virginie first told her about it. Like Lady Claire she was surprised to see them together, but she was pleased.

Over the years, Lady Sara had learned more than she cared to know about Virginie and her obsession with Renée from her godchild, Lady Jane. Lady Sara now employed caution whenever she dealt with Virginie.

Six months after Edouard's death, Sir Jason had implored his daughter to return to England with her son, Henri. Jane declined, stating she feared retribution from Virginie. At the time, Lady Sara thought Jane was being melodramatic. When Henri was six years old, Sir Jason died in his sleep from a heart attack. This time, Jane was more than ready to leave France. But it was too late, for Henri was Virginie's protégé first and Jane's son second.

For a long time, Jane wrote to Lady Sara about the strange affinity between Virginie and her exceptionally intelligent grandson. And on her last trip to Paris, she understood exactly what Jane had meant. . . .

They were ten for dinner, seated on the massive terrace of Virginie's château that overlooked the royal forests.

"Henri should be getting his grade card soon," Lady Jane said. "I'm very proud of his work."

"What is your favorite subject, Henri?" Lady Sara inquired.

Virginie spoke first. "Mathematics seems to provide him the most stimulation. In fact, he has advanced to algebra."

"Is that right?" Lady Sara asked the pale-faced boy.

Henri turned to Virginie. "You were right to ask my tutor to introduce me to algebra. I like it so much more than geometry."

"Do you like any other subjects, Henri?" Lady Sara asked.

"Grandmother, I'd like to know if that abacus has arrived yet?"

"No. It hasn't."

Lady Sara thought the child was being rude. "Henri, I asked if there were any other subjects that interested you."

Henri was still turned toward Virginie, his eyes intent upon her questions and responses. They spoke to each other not only in words but in slight gestures and mannerisms. They had formed a language all their own.

"Grandmother, I found a theory about percentages that we might possibly use at the bank."

Lady Jane's tension was visible. Sheepishly, she said, "Henri, don't be impolite to our guest."

He glanced sideways at his mother. "Please do not interrupt me when I'm speaking with Grandmother." He spoke as if he were addressing the servants.

In the five days Lady Sara stayed at the château, at no time did she see Henri play with other children, nor did she ever him see treated as a child by Virginie. Eerily, Virginie looked upon Henri as her equal.

Halfway through dinner another evening Virginie said, "Henri has been a tremendous help to me in fighting our enemies."

"Enemies?" Lady Sara asked.

"Surely you don't think that someone as powerful as I am can exist without enemies! I'm constantly on my guard against people . . . like Renée Dubois. People who have nothing try to create havoc for those who have acquired wealth, property, and power. It's always been that way."

Henri turned to Virginie. "Renée Dubois killed my father."

Lady Sara gasped.

"That's right, Henri," Virginie replied, pleased with his mimicry of her views.

"Edouard's death was an accident!" Lady Sara protested and looked around the table for support. Jane hung her head and said nothing.

Emile poured himself his fourth glass of wine. His smile was twisted, as if it had been scribbled on his face. "That's not a popular view in this house, Lady Sara."

Virginie's voice was even when she spoke. "I won't go into it at length here, Sara, but I'll excuse your remark simply because it's impossible for you to know all the facts. The Duboises are responsible for a great deal of heartache in this family. I'm sure Emile could enlighten you about Pierre Dubois and how he tried to steal his wife from him. Suzanne was forever throwing him in Emile's face. I don't believe in scapegoats, Sara, only in revenge."

Wisely, Lady Sara said nothing. The malicious glint in Virginie's eyes made her glad she was going back to London the next day. . . .

Lady Sara glanced once again at Renée and noted the particular smile she gave Grant Morgan. Lady Sara would have liked to see Renée Dubois remain happy . . . and strong. Lady Sara wanted the best for Virginie's adversary.

Renée couldn't sleep that night. She tossed and turned, hearing voices—first Darma's, then Karl's. She dreamed that Darma tried to kill her and that Karl kidnapped Gaston. Renée bolted awake. She was panting and out of breath.

"How absurd! Karl would never . . . it meant nothing. Dreams aren't real!" she mumbled to herself as she pulled up the covers and eased her head onto the pillow. "Dreams are *not* real," she repeated over and over, hoping she would sleep again. She did not. "He loves me. I know he does. He has too. . . ."

Renée met Grant for lunch the next day knowing it was time they dealt with reality. He sipped his wine and looked at a very pensive Renée. "You've been rather quiet today. What's on your mind?"

"You can't guess?"

"No. I should think you'd be all smiles."

"Well, I'm not. You and I have avoided mention of Darma for

three days. I've pretended she doesn't exist—but she does.'' Renée dropped her eyes to the table and stared at the flowers. A sob caught in her throat but she choked it down. The idyll was over. This special world of timelessness—of no past, no future— she'd lived in for three days was gone. She was confused. Now, as once before, she wanted Grant to splice it together and make the fantasy last.

"I'm not sure what to think. I don't think you could make love to me the way you do if you loved her."

"I don't love her. I never did. I've never loved anyone but you. You have to believe that."

His eyes were pleading. She did believe. God help her, she did.

He sighed regretfully. "Now that I've seen you again, the whole thing seems crazy. I'd lost all hope for us. I couldn't see any way to rectify our problems. But I never stopped loving you. Never." He laughed one of those cynical, self-deprecating laughs. "Funny, none of my reasons make *any* sense now."

"Why did you ask Darma to marry you?"

"I didn't. She asked me."

"All right. Then why did you accept?"

"I'm not proud of it, but my motives were mercenary."

Renée was incredulous. "For money? You would marry a woman to benefit your studio?"

"Don't look at me like that! People marry for hundreds of reasons—the least of which is love."

"But not you."

His eyes were hard. "Why not me? I'm not perfect, like some hero in a book. I can be as much of a bastard as the next guy. Besides, I learned the hard way that nice guys finish last. If I couldn't have you, I'd have my studio. It's not as if I don't like Darma. We have a lot in common. She was brought up in California, she knows movie people better than I do. She's a nice woman, intelligent and fun. Any man would be proud to have her for a wife."

"But you don't love her. . . ."

"I care about her. She's become important to me. I don't want to hurt her, either. Can you understand that?" He grasped her hand. "I do love you, but when you weren't there . . ."

"You learned to care for someone else instead . . . ," she said, thinking of Karl.

"It was better than nothing," he said bitterly.

"You *have* changed, Grant."

"I had a good teacher."

"What's that supposed to mean?"

"I don't like being the heavy in all this. You ditched me once because your business was more important than I was."

"That's not true!"

"You know I'm right. At first I thought you couldn't wait to get rid of me. I thought if I had stayed in Paris, I would have taken up too much of your time. I thought that was the problem. It took me years to figure out that it wasn't the business at all—it was your little feud. You could never give up your hatred. Not for me, anyway. By the way, I forgot to ask, did you finally get even with Virginie? Is that why you suddenly agreed to marry me?"

"Grant! Why are you saying these things? Why are you being so cruel? None of this is true!"

"When are you going to understand yourself enough to realize that there's nothing noble in your crusade? You're after revenge, Renée. It's what drives you and makes you successful."

"You're no better! Your ambition makes you do things that are far from honorable!" She wanted to hurt him for the things he'd said, for having a fiancée, a movie studio—a life without her.

They glared at each other, their angry words crackling around them. Suddenly, with tears streaming down her cheeks, Renée jumped up and raced away.

Grant was frozen to his seat, trying to understand his own anger. He did not run after her. It puzzled him, this lack of action. At that moment he felt all the fury of their earlier breakup plus his own guilt over his decision to marry Darma. How could he stop her when he wanted her to hurt; to feel the pain he'd felt for so long.

Before this London trip, he'd had everything neatly tied up. He and Darma would marry, Monument Studios would treble in size, and he would be racing with the big boys. He would have made his own dreams come true. Now he thought of Renée and what it would be like to share a life with her—in a world where he could not be king.

He wanted Renée desperately, but with the same ferocity, he wanted his studio.

Renée rushed into Antiques World. Céleste took one look at her niece's stricken face and quickly ushered her into the office.

"Tell me everything, chérie."

"I don't know what happened except that Grant and I had a horrid argument. I think the damage is irreparable."

"An argument about what?"

"Darma, the past, Virginie. Everything. He said some terrible things and what makes them so awful is that they're true. I can't give up my business—I can't."

"He asked you to do that? I thought he wanted to move to Paris."

"I think that was a grand gesture for your benefit. He says the only reason I want the business is to exact revenge on Virginie. But that's not true! I've dreamed of that shop all my life!"

"I know, chérie. I must admit I was impressed with Grant last night, but then I have always been fooled by handsome, charming, and persuasive men. As much as I want to like him, I have to tell you that I don't think he is good for you."

"You don't?"

"Karl is the man you need. He hasn't asked you to give up anything for him. In fact, he has already moved from his own country to Paris just to be near you. He is only asking to be a part of your life. He's a mature man, with successes of his own. You need someone like Karl—not this volatile movie tycoon who appears in your life every few years."

"I just don't know. My head is pounding with all this."

"Don't think about anything now. Your work is finished here. You need to be alone for a while."

Renée nodded. "I need to go home. I need to see Gaston and Pierre—talk to Jean."

Céleste patted her hand. "I agree. Even though I'd like to have you stay longer, London is not the place for you now."

Renée hugged Céleste. "I don't know what I would do without you, Aunt Céleste. I love you."

She kissed Renée's cheek. "Find your answers, chérie, and be happy. That's all I want."

"I will."

Herbert drove Renée to the Simcoxes' town house, where she packed, and then they headed for the train station where she would catch the train that would take her to the channel boat. She cabled Karl to meet her. Luckily, she was in time to catch the three o'clock train.

"Thank you, Herbert. You and Céleste have both been wonderful to me."

"We're family, Renée. We'll always be here for you."

She hugged him one last time and jumped onto the train as it pulled out of the station. She waved and then settled back in the seat. This felt right, she thought. She was going home.

At the moment Renée waved goodbye to Herbert, Grant walked into Antiques World.

"Is Renée here?" Grant asked of Céleste.

"No, she isn't."

"Where is she?"

"She went home to Paris."

Grant's face paled. "Is there some way I can contact her?"

"I don't think so."

"You mean you won't give her a message from me?"

"I didn't say that."

Grant's shoulders slumped. "She told you then?"

"Yes. Everything."

"I need to see her. Apologize to her. She was so upset . . . I said . . ."

"Perhaps it's best she not see you for a while. I'm not saying this just for Renée, but for you too." She paused, noting his dubious look. "Grant, I get the impression that you're in competition with Renée." She held up her hand. "Hear me out. I want what's best for my niece. Lately, she's been seeing a man whom she cares for."

"I don't believe you."

"It's true. I have no reason to lie to you."

"Well, he can't be very important—she never mentioned him to me."

"Grant, for the past few days, she hasn't even remembered

she had a child! She's not rational. That's what I'm talking about. She needs some stability in her life. Karl can give her that constancy she desperately needs. You can't do that for her or yourself. You are a very ambitious man and you want to reach all those horizons you see before you. And that's a good thing. But when you reach your goal—and you will—you'll find another goal and another. It will never end for you. Think about that.''

Grant shook his head. "You don't understand. I love her! Surely there must be something we can work out."

"I think you both need time to think. Renée is much too vulnerable now. She needs to sort out her emotions. And so do you. You owe that to yourself and to her."

"Perhaps you're right."

"I want what's best for my niece. You have accused her of choosing her career over you. Don't cast stones, Grant."

For a long moment he stared at her, marveling at her insight. She knew him better than he knew himself. "I have to leave for the States the day after tomorrow. I don't have much time. Tell her I want to see her—now."

"Leave her alone, Grant. If she wants you, she'll find you."

"And in the meantime?"

"Keep hoping."

"I know I should believe, but something tells me I've already lost."

The train was early and Karl was late. He rushed to the station and pushed his way through the waves of passengers who had just disembarked the train.

Renée looked like a lost kitten to him as she lugged her suitcase. She hadn't seen him yet and it gave him a minute to observe her. He hoped she had missed him even a fraction of how much he missed her. He'd made a point of seeing Gaston and Pierre every day, but whenever he walked into her apartment, the knowledge that she wasn't there only made it worse for him.

He decided on the third day she was gone that he wouldn't take no for an answer to his proposal. He loved her and she would have to see that being his wife could be wonderful.

Just then she looked up and saw him racing toward her. She dropped her suitcase on the ground and, slump-shouldered, stood there, tears in her eyes, until he came to her and lifted her off the ground.

"Karl . . ." She buried her head in his shoulder. "Oh, Karl."

"I missed you, Renée. I'm so glad you're back."

Renée felt weightless when he lifted her—as if she were a little girl. She needed his strength now more than ever. She needed a foundation, not passionate dreams. Grant could never understand her the way Karl did; his studio would always stand between them. Karl was her rock. This was the right thing and he was the right man.

"Karl, say you still want me."

"I've never wanted you as much as I do right now." Gently he placed her on the ground. "I take it this means you'll marry me?"

"Yes, Karl. Yes. The sooner the better."

Renée squinted at the flashing cameras thinking she would never get used to photographers. She wondered why she was suddenly the target of reporters and what was so important about her marriage to Karl that anyone would be interested in printing it.

If Renée had not been so interested in dashing for the waiting taxi, and had bothered to ask one of the reporters, she would have found the answer to her questions.

Most of the group that stood outside the public registry were representatives from British *Vogue*, French *Vogue*, *Harper's Bazaar*, and *Vanity Fair*. Renée Dubois was gaining considerable recognition on the Continent for her lingerie and perfume. She was also one of the few young and unmarried couturiers. Her wedding day was news.

It was the beginning of a love-hate relationship Renée was to have with the press and they with her and which would span the next forty years.

Renée cabled Céleste to inform her of the wedding on the morning of the ceremony. Knowing Grant was due to leave that night, Céleste rang the Basil Street Hotel and asked him to meet her immediately at the shop.

In less than twenty minutes he arrived.

One look at Céleste's face told him more than he wanted to know.

"You've heard from her."

"Yes. A cable arrived this morning. I wanted you to hear this from me and not read it in the papers."

"I don't like the sound of this."

"Renée is married," she stated bluntly.

He was incredulous. "This is a joke . . . or a lie!" He ran a trembling hand through his hair. "This can't be happening!"

"I only received a brief cable myself. I, too, am stunned."

He looked at her and decided she was telling the truth. "I thought maybe in a month she would see I was right. . . ."

"Grant, did you honestly think there was a way?"

"Yes! Yes . . . I don't know." His eyes were wild as his emotions ate at his insides. "I just don't know." He sank into the chair. "Jesus! She didn't waste any time!"

"Grant . . . I . . . maybe I was wrong to advise her . . ."

Anger jolted him to his feet. "Maybe you were. But you and I no longer have anything to say to each other. The less I see of a Dubois, the better off I'll be!"

"Don't blame her . . . or yourself." She ran after him. "Please, Grant . . ." But he was out the door before she could stop him.

Grant leaned over the rail watching the play of the sun on the ship's wake as he sailed away from England. His eyes were a steely blue and there was an unfamiliar hardness to his features. It was the third day of his crossing and he still had not spoken to any of the passengers nor shown any desire to do much other than remain in his cabin. When someone did approach him, they were put off by the tense set to his mouth and the angry gleam in his eyes.

Grant wondered if he would be able to make pictures without leaving California. If he had an assistant . . . one he could trust to oversee location filming. He never wanted to see London or Paris again.

As he glared at the ridiculously blue sky and voluminous clouds, he thought that for the first time he would be genuinely happy to see Darma. She *loved* him. So she pressed him a little to get married. What woman didn't these days?

He'd been a fool long enough. When he got back to Los Angeles he and Darma would have the biggest, splashiest wedding Hollywood had ever seen.

Chapter Fifteen

The explosions were deafening. Gaston threw his hands over his ears. Three loud simultaneous blasts caused Renée to jump, as she, Jean, Karl, Pierre, and Gaston watched the awesome Bastille Day fireworks.

"This is the largest display they've ever had!" Jean said.

"No it isn't. When I was eleven, *that* was the best. Wasn't it, Renée?"

"I'm not getting in the middle of this," she said, laughing.

Gaston clung to Karl's thigh, shut his eyes, and tried not to tremble when over two thousand firecrackers were set off at the grand finale. "It's too loud! I only like Roman candles!" he yelled over the noise.

"You aren't afraid of a little firecracker, are you, Gaston?" Jean teased.

Pierre leaned down and grabbed Gaston under the ribs. "You're almost seven years old—" he began but Gaston jerked away and kicked Pierre in the shins.

"And I'm faster than you—old man!" Gaston raced away with Pierre in fast pursuit.

Karl and Renée laughed as they made their way through the crowd. In a little over a month, Gaston had grown close to Karl in a way Renée had never thought possible. Always a quiet child, he had come out of himself and spoke his mind more openly. He and Karl raced bicycles on Saturday afternoons, went horseback riding in the Bois, and every chance they got, they talked. And in the afternoons, he took the bus to Karl's office. The world of investments fascinated him, though he found it difficult to understand. Karl understood and was patient with his eager student.

"I got you this notebook to put your information in. Some things you can memorize, but the more complicated points we'll write down."

"This is great! Then I can look it up any time I want."

"Precisely." Karl would then explain about corporate profits, formulas, and percentages one should invest. Gaston filled twenty pages in his notebook the first month. What had begun as a game, became a quest for Gaston.

Soon he began asking Pierre questions about business and he wrote that information in his notebook. He asked Jean specifics about designing and how he could improve his sketches. More than ever Gaston was fascinated with the entire fashion business, from the clothes themselves to management of the offices and workers to investing the profits. The only thing that bothered him was that he was only seven years old.

Renée smiled to herself as she went back to the kitchen for the chocolate cake. She placed neat, thick slices on cut crystal plates while she listened to the sound of male voices in the living room.

At no other time in her life had she felt so protected and loved. And never had she felt so unworthy. Every night she went to bed with Karl's arms wrapped around her, and thought of Grant. It was Grant's voice she heard when he told her he loved her, it was Grant's lips that kissed her and it was Grant she made love to.

After Karl was asleep she would fall victim to hours of torment and tears. *She wanted to forget*. It was a simple request to make of oneself. Oblivion. She wanted to push Grant into oblivion, but he wouldn't go away. He haunted her days at the office and her nights in bed with the man she *should* love.

Her head was swimming with guilt as she placed the cake plates on the table centered . . . with sweet-smelling . . . roses. . . .

The sickeningly sweet smell filled her nostrils and suddenly the room was spinning and everything seemed the color of the red roses.

She didn't feel any pain when her head hit the floor with a thud.

"Renée!" Karl yelled. In one swift movement he lifted her and carried her to the bedroom.

Pierre raced to the kitchen for a cold cloth and Jean telephoned the doctor. Gaston stood staring at the lifeless form of his mother, tears streaming down his shocked face.

"Is she dead?" Gaston cried.

Karl placed a reassuring hand on his shoulder. "No. She just fainted."

"Why would she faint?"

"I don't know," Karl answered tersely.

Gaston didn't miss the panic in Karl's eyes though he tried to remain calm. Something terrible had happened to his mother and no one was going to tell him.

The doctor arrived forty-five minutes after Renée regained consciousness and scolded everyone for making a fuss.

"I've been a bit tired lately, that's all," she explained as she held Gaston.

"I think she should have some tests run. Perhaps there isn't enough iron in her blood," Pierre said to Karl, who was silent.

Jean only smiled to himself.

Dr. Bressard put his stethoscope away and sat on the edge of the bed. "You seem in good health to me."

"There's nothing wrong?"

"Not unless you call being pregnant 'wrong.' "

"Pregnant?"

"You do know what that means?"

"A baby? Karl and I are going to have a baby?" She couldn't believe it. It was the answer to all her prayers. A baby would make it up to Karl. She knew she didn't deserve this blessing but she was thankful . . . very thankful.

Renée sat in her office battling waves of remorse and confusion. There was a real possibility that this child could be Grant's. She couldn't be sure, not yet. She tried not to think about it. For over three months she had successfully kept the idea buried. But it was always there, gnawing away at her.

She told herself that it had to be Karl's child simply because God rewarded good people. Karl was innocent of any kind of deception and she knew it would be his goodness that would outweigh her duplicity.

Karl lavished her with attention. When he had the chance, he waited on her constantly. He cherished her and loved her even more now that she was having his baby. He asked Jean to design a maternity wardrobe especially for Renée, which he did. Every week Karl came home with something new for the nursery.

In the middle of her fifth month, Karl decided that once the baby arrived there would not be enough room for them all in the cramped apartment above the workrooms. He began searching for the "proper house" for his family.

Renée did not try to dampen his enthusiasm. Instead she let him go about his plans as he wanted. She was afraid if she didn't that he might suspect something. She vowed she would do anything and everything to protect Karl . . . even from herself.

To escape her personal hells, Renée, as usual, threw herself into her work. Jean took his maternity line a step further and convinced Renée to offer ready-to-wear maternity clothes. She agreed with little persuasion. Jean was delighted and instantly hired on the four extra seamstresses they would need.

Pierre suggested they turn the storage rooms between their shop and the perfumery next door into a maternity boutique. Jean leapt at the idea. Renée agreed just to keep them off her back. She had enough to do with the linen company.

Céleste shipped her samples of the new textiles from America. There was also a new range of colors available to them and Renée experimented with patterns for the first time. The D & S Linen Company became known for its printed borders and exquisite handwork. Each month brought innovation to her London-based company and she was more thrilled than ever over the quick upturn she'd made. In January of 1935 Pierre announced they were purchasing another facility in London and buying more equipment.

It had taken her a decade, but Renée believed she was poised on the edge of her dream.

"To hell with the business!" Karl stormed at her and then continued his pacing.

"You needn't yell at me, Karl. Honestly, I don't know what has gotten into you lately. It's not like you to lose your temper."

"Perhaps is should be more like me than I let it. I'm not going to stand around while my pregnant wife works herself into a miscarriage."

"Thanks a lot!" She was getting tired of his daily recriminations about her long hours. She was healthy and the baby was fine. "You care more about the baby than you do me!" She *was* exhausted and she should go home and rest but she was damned if she was going to let Karl know it.

"That's not true and you know it!"

"All right. I'm closing my files. See?" she said as she shoved them into her desk.

His voice mellowed and his eyes softened. "I don't want to argue with you like this," he said and came around to hold her close. "I don't know why you can't be satisfied like other women," he said and then wished he'd kept his mouth shut.

She turned on him with eyes full of venom. "I'm not like other women. If I were, you wouldn't want me. Why must you always demean my business?"

"I wasn't doing that," he said in defense. "But you are pregnant now. Surely that—"

"I want to go home," she said and stalked out the door, refusing to discuss what they rehashed every night.

Sometimes she wondered if Karl would ever understand. He had been born into money and making more of it was a pastime for him. Renée was driven by passion. Passion to be the best at whatever she did; passion to build a world where her family would be safe from harm; passion for revenge that was born a decade ago. Renée would never relent and the sooner Karl understood that about her the better off they would be.

Time seemed to bear down on her as never before. Perhaps it was the baby coming, perhaps it was the fact that everyone in her life wanted such large slices of her time . . . Karl, Gaston, Pierre, Jean . . . even Grant.

It was amazing how he managed to invade her life. He came to her in the early morning to remind her that she wouldn't see him that day and then again in the early afternoon when she and Karl ate lunch at a café and watched lovers walk past with their arms around each other. Always he loomed over her happiness with

Karl, preventing her from loving him the way she should. As the months passed and she saw Karl give more of himself to her, she feared that God would exact a price from her. She prayed endlessly that the punishment would not be spent on her children.

Her screams flayed the night like a cat-o'-nine-tails.

Karl grabbed the nurse's arm. "What's happening to my wife?"

Exasperated with the expectant father's constant questions, she said: "Monsieur Heilmann, your wife is fine. All women in labor sound like that."

"Why can't I see her?"

"Because it just isn't done!" she replied righteously and stalked away.

He paced, then sat on the edge of the worn leather chair and ran his hands through his hair. Renée was at the other end of the corridor in the delivery room. Sometimes her cries sounded so pathetic and weak, then only instants later, she would scream at the top of her lungs. He thought surely she would die.

At four o'clock in the morning the doctor came into the waiting room. "There have been complications. It was a frontal presentation."

"What does that mean?" Karl asked.

"The forehead is coming first and the baby is lodged in the birth canal. I think we can save the baby, but Madame Heilmann is weak."

"Are you telling me that my wife is going to die?"

"We are doing everything to save her."

"No you aren't!" Karl boomed. "You're standing here talking to me!"

When the doctor saw tears well in Karl's eyes, he turned away and rushed back to his patient.

At four-thirty Karl asked the nurse again for news of his wife.

"I'm sorry," she said as she shook her head.

Fifteen minutes later Karl saw an orderly. "Stop! Young man! Have you been to the delivery room? Do you know anything about the woman in there?"

"No, sir. I don't."

Just then Karl realized that the screaming had stopped. He released the boy. Four nurses came running up the stairs and disappeared into the delivery room. Another orderly appeared pushing a gurney.

Karl was panic-stricken. "Damn the hospital rules!" He ran down the hall.

Before he reached the door, the doctor emerged with a smile on his face.

"I was coming to get you. You are the father of a nine-and-half-pound baby girl," he said and then noticed that Karl's frightened expression had not altered.

"My wife?"

"Will be fine after some much-needed rest. It was a difficult delivery."

"Thank God!"

"You can go in."

Karl walked into the room and found a very weak Renée staring at her daughter. Karl took one look at the blond, blue-eyed baby and beamed.

"She's beautiful! My hair . . . my eyes. Shows what good genes I have," he said, leaning over to kiss Renée.

Renée smiled wanly. "She's quiet now. She was crying before . . ." Renée turned away so that Karl could not see her tears. *He must never know,* she told herself. She loved Karl and she loved her new baby daughter with the golden hair and dark blue eyes . . . eyes so blue . . . like the inside of a fringed gentian that only opens its petals on a bright summer day.

Chapter Sixteen

"All newborns are ugly, chérie," Céleste said, trying to reassure her niece.

"No they aren't. Gaston was breathtaking. All the nurses said so. Don't you remember?" Renée pulled herself into a sitting position for the fifteenth time and then lowered herself back to the floor. She had locked her feet beneath an overstuffed chair, but it didn't help much. She continued on with her sit-ups while Céleste bathed the baby. "Besides, Juliette is almost seven months old—hardly a newborn."

Céleste carefully rolled the cooing baby over and rinsed her back. Renée was right. Juliette was the ugliest baby she'd ever seen. Her pudgy cheeks overwhelmed her almond-shaped eyes and her mouth was a long slash that almost looked painted on. Her nose was thin and nearly nonexistent. Her head dangled at the end of a long neck that was disproportionately lean and attached to an overly large body. For a female she had huge hands and feet. Renée thought she looked like a turtle. Karl thought Juliette the most beautiful baby in the world.

By the twenty-fifth sit-up Renée was huffing. "I'll never be the same," she said with a groan. Renée had always taken her slender body for granted, but years behind a desk and two pregnancies had taken their toll. Her muscles refused to respond to discipline, much like a mischievous child. She pushed herself twice as hard and added another set of ten. Then she stood up and began a series of waist twists. She still had twelve pounds to lose. She looked down at her milk-filled breasts and wondered if there really was any benefit to exercise. So far, all she had noticed was an increase in her appetite. Karl didn't seem to mind, though. He was happy about everything these days.

"There you are, Mademoiselle Juliette," Céleste said as she dried the giggling baby with a soft terry towel. "I have to admit she is the happiest baby I've ever seen." Céleste chucked Juliette under the chin. "Just like your papa!"

Renée froze in midtwist just as Céleste spun around and looked at her. "I'm sorry, chérie. I didn't think . . ."

"It's all right. Karl *is* Juliette's father," Renée said determinedly. "The only father she will ever know."

"It must be so difficult for you . . ." Céleste began but Renée cut her off.

"Only if I make it so. No one knows the truth except you and me. Not even Pierre suspects. He remarked on her unusual eye color and I told him it was a blend of my violet and Karl's ice blue. He accepted that. Frankly, she doesn't look like anyone—me, Karl, or Grant. I promised myself that I would do everything in my power to keep her from the hell Gaston has known over his bastardy. Karl has been so good for Gaston."

"Karl has been good for you too," Céleste said, wrapping the baby in a blanket and placing her in the crib. "But don't sell yourself short. You are what he needs. I've had a chance to get to know him these past weeks. He's an extraordinary man. I think if he knew the truth about Juliette, it wouldn't devastate him as much as you seem to think it would."

Renée looked shocked. "I'll never do that to him. Karl is the best thing that ever happened to this family. I'll never hurt him. Promise me you'll never say the slightest thing that could jeopardize his happiness."

"Of course I won't!"

Karl Heilmann's crusade for the perfect structure in which to house his growing family had consumed his free time for the better part of a year. He had crawled through tiny rooms, looked at peeling paint and enough mansard roofs in need of repair to last a lifetime. He had very specific needs and he was extremely particular. Having grown up in a castle, he wanted open rooms and high ceilings, hand-carved woodwork, solid doors, central heat and plumbing par excellence, and he wanted history. Above all, he wanted a bargain. Karl did not believe in buying real estate unless it was a good investment.

Renée went with him the first two weeks of his investigations. Once she discovered that Karl was looking for the impossible, she left him to his pursuit and she went back to running Maison Dubois.

When Karl told her he'd found what he'd had in mind, though it would need more renovation than he'd planned and a good deal of interior decoration, Renée breathed a sigh of relief. As finicky as he was, there was probably a door that was slightly askew or a rug that needed replacing.

Juliette was three weeks old when he showed her the house, located in a splendid row of seventeenth-century speculator-built houses on the Ile Saint-Louis. It was six stories high and every one of its many windows offered a thrilling view of the Seine and the city. The ceilings were high, the woodwork and painted frescos magnificent. Karl had spoken with an architect and had already contracted to have the kitchen enlarged, the salon, library, and study combined and new ones incorporated on the upper floors. The master bedroom was to encompass almost the entire third floor, with an adjoining nursery until Juliette was old enough to move to her own room on the fourth floor with Gaston. Pierre was to have the fifth floor to himself and the sixth was to be used for storage for the time being.

Renée sat down on one of the wide curving stairs and looked around her. This wasn't a house, but a life's project!

"Karl! This is much too large! We'll never need all this room. Who is going to take care of it?"

"Trust me. I practically stole the property. Can't you see the potential here? If anything should ever happen, financially, I mean, we can rent out enough rooms to sustain us. I'm thinking of the future. If we should have more children, I won't have to be so damn cramped!"

He was so happy with the house, Renée was not about to dampen his enthusiasm. They would have to employ at least two maids just to dust! She wasn't used to this kind of life, but Karl was. For the first time she realized how much it must mean to him to finally be able to duplicate the kind of lifestyle he'd always known. Wisely, she kept her misgivings to herself and agreed to help with the decorating. It might even be fun.

Now, six months later, the decorating was finished, the new furniture had arrived, and they were in the process of moving the last of their clothing. Jean had persuaded her to let him move into the apartment they were vacating so he could be closer to work. It would be perfect for him, and already he'd bought a new drafting table and planned to turn Pierre and Gaston's room into a study.

Renée had used a palette of pastels throughout the house, with an abundance of white to keep the rooms airy and springlike. Voluminous balloon shades in pale rose hung over the many windows and French doors. She wanted to be able to look out and see the sparkling Seine winding below her. The pickled oak floors had been refinished and polished to a gleam. In the family areas she used powder blue and cream patterned rugs and a solid blue carpet up the stairs. The upholstered pieces were modern, huge, and overstuffed with thick down cushions.

Each bedroom was outfitted with an armoire, bed, and nightstand. Renée used mountains of matching fabric for dust ruffles, canopies, draperies, throw pillows, comforters, and sheets. The master suite was executed in white satin and black watered moiré, giving the room an opulent, sophisticated look. Gaston chose beige and chocolate brown, Pierre picked a deep hunter green and camel, and for Juliette, Karl chose three colors of pink. Renée assigned two seamstresses to the special duty of sewing for her new house. It took four months, two hundred and sixteen yards of fabric, one and a half cases of thread, one hundred and thirty-three and a third yards of fringes, bindings, and tape to accomplish the job.

As Renée looked around her she wondered what kind of profit could be made in the home-decorating market. It was something to consider. She would speak to Pierre.

They were playing in the garden when it happened. Juliette had been taking steps for the past two months and was nearly able to maneuver across any given area on her own. She was an awkward baby, her head bobbing from one side to the other as if her puppet strings had not been adjusted. She was clumsy, overweight, and extremely tall for her age. The walled-in garden was centered with a huge flowing fountain which was ringed with a cement seat.

It was unusually warm for early March, some of the trees were budding and the purple tulips threatened to blossom any day. The breeze carried the beginnings of sweet lilac perfume. The sun was warm on Gaston's face as he took another bite of his cookie, laid it on the plate, and went back to his sketch. Juliette went darting past him, chasing a blue jay which flew up into the bare tree branches and then stared down at her.

"Birrrda!" she said, pointing upward and then looking over at Gaston. He did not look up and so she toddled over, grabbed his knee, and shouted at him. "Gastie! A birrrda!"

She was teething and spittle rained across his charcoal drawing, ruining his work. Gaston's anger exploded. The nursemaid had the afternoon off, and he had to sit and watch after Juliette instead of going to the shop with his mother. He grabbed his sister's wrist and squeezed it—hard. She squealed in pain.

"Shut up, you ugly pest!" He jerked on her arm again and then shoved her away.

Juliette planted her heavy bottom on the ground and wailed. Gaston ignored her. She rubbed the tears in her eyes and looked at him. Still crying, she placed her hands on the ground and pushed herself up. She sat on the fountain's edge on the opposite side of Gaston so that he could not see her, and continued to cry. Her frustration mounted and she kicked her heels against the fountain wall. She turned around and looked at him. He ignored her. She glanced down into the clear water and, for the first time, saw her own reflection. Instantly, she stopped crying. She stared for a long time, leaning over farther and farther, inspecting the vision she saw.

Gaston heard the splash and then Juliette's cries. The water was over three feet deep and Juliette could not swim. She was a defenseless baby. And he hated her. Karl gave Juliette all his love, until Gaston felt there was none left over for him. Ever since Juliette arrived his mother had had less and less time for him. She had immersed herself in work again. Gaston did get the impression that his mother didn't like Juliette all that well, probably because she was so ugly. Gaston thought his mother stayed away from home because Juliette was there.

Juliette splashed and gulped water. He could hear her choking. He didn't move from the spot, but watched, mesmerized, while his sister drowned in the fountain.

Karl had finished his meetings early and decided to have a late lunch at home. When he arrived at home, he saw that the maid was not doing her chores or watching the children, but reading a mystery novel. She didn't hear Karl come in.

"Mademoiselle Souveau! I do not pay you to read! Perhaps you would rather work someplace else!"

When angry, Karl's mellow voice could boom from the rafters. The irresponsible young woman was instantly on her feet. "I'm sorry, sir. It won't happen again."

Karl went to the kitchen and had just taken a plate of cold chicken from the refrigerator when he heard Juliette's cries coming from outside. He quickly glanced out the window.

"What the hell . . ." In stunned terror Karl realized that Gaston was allowing Juliette to drown.

Karl broke for the door and leapt over the three steps to the garden. He covered the area in four giant strides, shoved his arms into the frigid water, and retrieved his daughter. He placed her face down on the ground and pushed on her back.

"Juliette . . . please God!" He pushed again, but she was deathly still.

Suddenly, she gasped and choked. Water spurted out of her mouth.

"Thank God!" Karl cried and hugged her close to his chest. Karl glared at Gaston, whose eyes were glassy and mechanical-looking.

"What are you doing?" Gaston asked in a stupefied tone.

"Saving your sister from death!" Karl boomed at the boy. "What in the hell were you thinking? Weren't you going to help her?"

"She wasn't going to die. I was just teaching her a lesson."

"What kind of lesson?"

"She has been too greedy. She's taken everyone's love and she must know she can't do that."

Karl gaped at Gaston and realized the enormity of the problem he had. There was more here than sibling rivalry and yet he didn't think Gaston was demented or twisted. But if he didn't handle him correctly, he could be faced with just that. Karl realized that he *had* been giving Juliette all his attention. With the new house, the opening of his new branch in Zurich, and Juliette's arrival, he had neglected his stepson. Gaston was not to blame here—he was. And so was Renée.

She had thrown herself into the business again, burying herself under stacks of work. She spent no time with Juliette, gave nothing to Karl, and if anyone did receive attention it was Gaston and that was only because Gaston went to Maison Dubois and demanded it. A great deal had to change.

"Gaston, come with me while we both change Juliette into some dry clothes."

Gaston nodded, his head now bowed in shame, guilty tears in his eyes and hands trembling.

In the nursery, Gaston sat in the rocker staring at the floor. By the time Karl had dried Juliette and dressed her in warm clothes, she was so exhausted she fell asleep. He placed her in the crib, kissed her cheek, and walked over to Gaston.

"It was a horrible thing I did today."

"It was a sin of omission," Karl said.

"A what?"

"A sin of omission is when you don't do something that causes someone harm. Like you not trying to save Juliette. But I'm guilty, too, Gaston."

Gaston looked at him quizzically.

"I should have let you know how you are loved. I've been negligent with you and I'm sorry. You were right. Juliette *has* taken most of my time, because I think she needs it, but you need it, too, and I didn't see that. It was my sin of omission. All that is going to change."

Gaston's tears were silent rivers on his face. "You're the only father I ever had, and it seemed that just when I'd found you, Juliette came along and stole you away from me. Maman doesn't have time for me, she hardly ever does." He paused. "I don't want to hate Juliette."

"I don't want you to, either. In fact, I want you to join with me and protect Juliette."

"I don't understand."

"Juliette is not a pretty girl, Gaston. I never want her to hear me say that. For a woman beauty is an important thing. I keep thinking that if she knows all the while she is growing up that she is loved, truly loved, her ugliness won't hold her back. I don't want her to be afraid of life or loving. She is looking for affection from you, it could mean a great deal to her."

"I called her an ugly pest today. Now I feel terrible for doing that."

"I also think that if you and I combine forces we can get your mother to spend more time with us. Next weekend the Lipizzaner horse show is coming to Paris. I could get tickets. . . . Do you think she'd like that?"

"Of course! Who wouldn't!" Gaston threw his arms around Karl. "I guess there is room for us all in this family, isn't there?"

"Always, Gaston. Always."

Chapter Seventeen

On October 15, 1937, Claude Ruille finished his third Napolean brandy, kissed his nineteen-year-old mistress on her naked buttocks, and suffered a massive coronary. In less than ten minutes he was dead and Virginie faced not only the worst scandal since Suzanne's death, but the Crédit de Paris presidency was left vacant and she had no one to fill the position.

Two weeks after Claude's burial and the reading of his will—leaving everything to Virginie as per their bargain made during the first year of their marriage—Emile stormed into his mother's office.

Virginie, now forty-eight years old, confident with her power and vastly increased personal reservoir of money, glared at her obese, weak-willed son. She found it incredible that she had mothered the monstrosity. At times she actually believed the nurses had switched babies on her. It was the only explanation that made sense. She looked down at the papers on her desk. Just the sight of him made her sick.

Emile was twenty-five and looked forty. Already he was balding, due in part she was sure to his unhealthy diet and massive drinking. Though he had tried to hide it, she knew about his gambling, and the debts he owed. That was the reason he wanted his father's position so desperately. He needed the increase in salary to divest himself of his "obligations." Had he been a stronger man, he would have realized his limitations and tried to remarry someone of wealth. The family name alone could have brought prospective women flocking to his door. However, his reputation and the unfortunate circumstances surrounding Suzanne's death rendered him undesirable and unmarriageable. Not a decent woman on the Continent would have anything to do with him. As for sex, she knew he had resorted to purchasing it, just as he had to buy his friends. Emile lived an expensive lifestyle.

"What is it this time, Emile?" she asked without looking at him.

He hated being treated like a piece of furniture. He hated his mother even more. It took all his stamina to be civil to her. Trying to wrest this presidency out of her was becoming an impossible goal. He hated that too. It should have been his by birthright, but somehow the old crow had gotten his father to sign all the control at the bank over to her upon his death. It gave Emile the chills. It was almost as if his mother had known Claude would die before she did. She certainly had been prepared for it.

"I was wondering if you'd come to any decisions yet."

"Not yet. I'll let you know," she said coldly, as if speaking to the mail boy.

Emile wanted to strangle her. How he wanted to feel the crush of her bones beneath his hands.

Then she looked up and glared at him as if she'd read his thoughts. Her smile was perfunctory. She knew she would always win. "If you don't mind . . . I'm very busy."

Emile hated himself for backing down like this. He felt helpless and very, very angry. He slammed the door to his mother's office.

"I'm late for a meeting," he told his secretary as he headed out of the bank. He wondered if the red-haired prostitute would be at her regular café. She liked him, he could tell. And he could tell she liked the things he did to her.

Virginie had not been idle in the past five years since Emile's deterioration had begun. She knew she would need an energetic younger man with foresight and guts to help her run the bank. It was time she began paving the roads for the international empire she desired.

Lucienne was twenty-eight and Virginie thought it time she accepted her responsibility as a Ruille. Virginie had pampered Lucienne for too long.

Antoine Junot was thirty-three years old, handsome, educated, and in love with Lucienne. He was very distantly related to the banking Rothschild family. He was talented and extremely well educated. He was golden. Virginie knew for a fact that when Lucienne dashed off to St. Moritz to ski or Capri to sun, Antoine waited faithfully for her return. He was beguiled by her beauty and charm, which had grown over the years, and counted himself fortunate to be considered by the press as the number one suitor to "the most beautiful woman in Europe."

Lucienne made certain her life was well covered by photographers and reporters, especially when she was with Antoine. Virginie was aware of the ploy her daughter used. Virginie also knew that Lucienne seemed to delight in Antoine's misery every time she was asked when they were to set a wedding date and she replied with her usual evasions.

Antoine was not a weak man. His only misfortune, as far as Virginie saw it, was that he'd succumbed to emotion. Virginie liked Antoine and wanted him as a member of the family. Lucienne, however, would not commit to anything or anyone.

The day of reckoning had finally come for Lucienne, and Virginie had appropriately chosen the dining room at Le Grand Véfour in which to pass sentence.

"You can't do this to me!"

"I can do anything I please," Virginie replied.

"I don't want to get married! I can't think of anything more hideous to happen to a woman." Lucienne grasped the table edge to keep her from throttling her mother.

"You have done as you pleased all these years. The bank needs new blood and Antoine is very willing to help. He would be an asset to the family and the business."

"I won't do it, I tell you. I'll move out immediately. You can't run my life for me."

"And what will you live on?" Virginie's dark eyes looked like pieces of hard coal.

"My allowance," she said, and hesitated.

"Which I disperse as I choose."

"You wouldn't do that."

"Count on it." Virginie watched her power slowly graze its way into Lucienne's awareness.

Lucienne could feel the walls moving in on her. The palms of her hands became clammy and it was only her hatred of her mother that kept her from fainting.

She looked Virginie straight in the eye. "What did Edouard say when you gave him the same alternative?"

"He got rid of his mistress."

Lucienne raised a finely plucked eyebrow. "I mean the second time. The time that really mattered."

For the first time, Lucienne saw her mother falter. It was a nervous, imperceptible flick of the wrist, a tick in her eyelid that gave her away. But Lucienne knew she had her. Lucienne found she liked power too. She knew she must find a way to have more of it.

"Did you hear me, Mother?"

"Edouard had his foolish moments. That was one of them. Be careful you do not make the same mistake."

Virginie's gaze was deadly and Lucienne backed down beneath it. She vowed that day at Le Grand Véfour that it would not always be so. She would find a way to beat her mother at her own game. At the moment she wasn't so sure that marrying Antoine was such a bad thing, either.

"I'm having dinner with Antoine day after tomorrow. We'll set a wedding day immediately. I expect the most lavish wedding of the year. Of course, with Father's death, we will observe the proper period of mourning. That should be ample time to make the arrangements and select a new house."

Virginie was surprised. "A new house?"

"Yes. Something expensive, and large, I should think. Antoine and I have standards we must uphold. Don't worry, I won't let you down, Mother."

Karl carefully placed three white shirts atop his beige cashmere sweater and closed the suitcase.

"I don't like this at all. I feel very uneasy about this trip you're making," Renée said and impulsively threw her arms around him, feeling a need to protect him, rather than be protected.

"I don't like it either, darling, but I have no choice. I must go back to Germany."

By the fall of 1938 the political situation in Europe had grown extremely tense, and Karl's father sent him an urgent cable to return to Munich. Friedrich would meet him at a friend's house on Theatinerstrasse at eight in the morning on October ninth. It was a strange and ominous message from his father and Karl lost no time in making plans.

Renée worried about Karl, for in recent months he'd shed his usual optimistic air. He worked long hours locked away in his study next to their room and rarely spoke of his business. Late at night he talked of ridiculous things . . . a family trip to America, sending Gaston to school in England, and closing down his business.

"You shouldn't be making this trip," she said as he packed his razor and shaving mug. "You're overworked and exhausted. Please, don't go, Karl."

"I have to. You don't understand the situation like I do. You're like all the rest of the French."

"I don't believe in borrowing trouble."

Angrily he jammed the suitcase lid down. "Quit acting like the ostrich you've become lately! War is inevitable!"

"And France will win!" she broke in. "The newspapers stated just yesterday that our armies are greater than anything Germany has!"

"Propaganda! And you believe it!"

She spun away from him but he grabbed her arm. "I'm sorry for snapping at you. I don't take these things lightly. I speak with important men all over Europe every day. If you were interested in anything besides Maison Dubois, you'd see what's happening."

"You've become obsessed with politics and the result is that all we do is argue!"

He sighed. "I know."

"Perhaps it's best you make this trip. You need to know that your parents are safe. Then you'll see how needlessly you've worried."

Had it really been three years since he'd been back to Munich? Karl wondered as he rode the taxi to his hotel. So much had changed. Gone were the troubadours in the Marienplatz and the smiling children who used to scamper from one café to another. Gone were the pretty girls who winked at eager young men as they strolled down the narrow streets. Grave-faced soldiers covered the city like black spiders, their eyes darting from corner to corner, always suspicious.

Instead of pots of bright geraniums to decorate balconies of apartments, there were red, black, and white Nazi swastikas everywhere. Posters with pictures of Hitler, blond youths reaching for glorification through Nazism, and announcements of yet another party rally plastered the kiosks and brick walls of abandoned buildings.

The taxi pulled to a stop in front of the Bayerischer Hof. Karl paid the driver and walked into the century-old hotel.

He wasted no time in contacting his father at the telephone number he'd sent. The man on the other end gave Karl convoluted directions to the address at Theatinerstrasse. Karl was to ride in a cab to the north side of the city where a car would be waiting for him. The keys were hidden beneath the right front wheel. He would then drive to four blocks from the appointed house and walk the rest of the way. Karl was even more anxious about his parents' well-being after the phone call.

Karl followed the instructions, making certain he was not followed. He knocked twice on the red-painted door. The door opened and he slipped inside unnoticed.

Friedrich Heilmann embraced his son for an inordinately long time.

"Karl, I'm so glad you've come."

"So am I, Father," Karl said, trying to hide his shock at Friedrich's physical appearance. His hair had gone completely gray and deep lines creased his face. He looked thinner and was stoop-shouldered. But it was the anxiety and fear in his eyes and voice that unnerved Karl the most.

"Father, what's happened?"

Friedrich sat in a worn upholstered chair and turned to the old man standing near the door. "Oskar is a friend of mine. You've never met him but we fought together in the last war."

Karl shook the man's hand and suddenly realized that Oskar was a Jew—a German Jew. Karl was beginning to understand a lot of things.

"You've always been a clever man, Karl. I needn't tell you how opposed I am to the Nazis. I'm afraid that my views have placed me in a precarious situation. I have many loyal friends like Oskar. For the past three years I have purposely not allowed you to come for a visit, because I have lived with the fear of discovery. Oskar has been secreting Jews out of Germany and I have been bankrolling his efforts. It's as simple as that."

"And now—"

"Your brother has reason to suspect my involvement."

"Come now, Father. Surely you can't mean that Randolf would arrest his own flesh and blood!"

"Randolf is as power-mad as the Führer. He has risen in the party, and I have no doubt he will be one of Hitler's favorites one day. He willingly trusts anyone connected with the party and does not believe his family wants what is best for him."

"Randolf *must* know that his family is more trustworthy and loyal to him than the Nazis!"

"How naïve you are, Karl. This isn't Germany any longer! Look around you. No one thinks the same anymore. There is no love of life, of country; there is only the party and its goals. I'm glad you went to Paris when you did, but you must realize that France offers no safety. I saw that a few days ago when the Munich Pact was signed. It was the end of Europe—and the Heilmanns."

"What does that mean?"

"Lisle and I are going to America. Oskar has arranged our trip to Switzerland. Then we will make our way to Marseilles and sail from there. I have signed a power of attorney to you. I have sold the 'guest house' . . . don't look at me like that, it was difficult enough for me to do. I thought I had broken your mother's heart. The Heilmanns will never come back here after the war, which you must know to be imminent."

Friedrich reached in his coat pocket and pulled out a long envelope. "Here is the number to my account in Zurich. Should anything happen to us, you are to have the money. I want none of the family money to go to Randolf, who would turn it over to the Nazis anyway. Give some to my granddaughter. Tell her I especially enjoyed seeing her last Christmas. I'm afraid this Christmas will be a bleak one for all of us."

"Is there anything else you need me for?"

"Yes, Karl, and it involves some risk."

"It doesn't matter. I just want you and Mother to be safe."

"I want you to see Randolf . . . tonight. That's when I plan to leave. Your mother will follow me in the morning. I thought it unwise to be seen together for fear the Nazis would know we are planning an escape. She is out now shopping for a new dress, as if nothing were wrong. We have taken a small apartment in town and she will be there tonight. Near dawn she will leave with one of Oskar's men." Friedrich handed Karl a small slip of paper with an address scribbled on it. "She would like to see you before she has to leave, but she also knows the danger. Only go if you think it's safe."

"I'll be careful," Karl said as his father rose.

"When you see Randolf, suggest a family dinner for the following night at a very public restaurant. He won't suspect your motives and that will buy us time to escape."

Karl hugged his father again, and before he could say anything more, Friedrich signaled to Oskar who pulled back a tapestry and revealed a back door.

"Godspeed, Father," Karl said, and with a nod, Friedrich vanished behind the tapestry.

Facing his brother over a tall mug of beer, Karl couldn't help but notice the differences between himself and Randolf.

Randolf never eased the restrictions he held on himself, not even in front of Karl. He was as unemotional as stone. Stiff-backed, jaw tensed, and mouth set in a sterile smile, Randolf probed his brother with one question after another.

"Why would you pick this particular week to come to Munich when you have nearly abandoned us for three years?"

"This was the first chance I've had to get away. I do have a family now, you know." Karl tried to hide his sweaty palms and act nonchalant. "What is so significant about this week?"

For the first time Randolf appeared flustered. "Then you haven't spoken with Father?"

"No, why? Should I have?"

"I was just wondering."

Karl drained his beer and ordered another round. "I told you, I didn't know until this morning I was coming. The branch here had problems they could not handle alone. I didn't have time to wire Father. I knew your office was here in town and I thought you would want to see me." Karl smiled, trying to keep matters light.

"I just think it's a bit odd. . . ."

"I think *you* are a bit odd, Randolf. Do you always question everyone as if they are being interrogated?"

Randolf's eyes were like glaciers. "I'm very good at my job."

"I'm sure you are the pride of the SS."

Randolf's chest puffed out. "I'm told I could be colonel in less than six months."

The chills Karl had been experiencing increased as Randolf detailed his climb through the ranks over the past three years. It was true what his father had said about Randolf, nothing mattered to the man except his career in the party. He nearly stated point-blank that not even his family would stop him from accomplishing what he wanted. Twice Karl brought up the subject of their parents and each time Randolf quickly changed the subject. Karl was convinced Randolf was hiding something. It took considerable effort to persuade Randolf to join in the family dinner Karl had planned. When the two brothers finally parted late that night, Karl fully understood his father's fear.

Karl had Randolf's driver deposit him at the hotel and once the man left he started out on foot for his mother's apartment. It was not a long walk, less than nine blocks from his hotel, but it was a cold night and a dense fog covered the streets like cotton candy. Karl pulled his collar up and shoved his hands into his pockets. Had Karl's eyes not been so keen he might not have noticed the man sitting in the car parked across the street. He was watching the third-floor far right window: Lisle's window.

Karl was wondering how he would slip into the building when suddenly, at the street corner, a pair of drunken soldiers approached the car. The drunks were singing as they staggered down the sidewalk. While the man in the car watched the drunks, Karl darted into the building.

Lisle was overjoyed to see her son. She held his hands constantly while they talked and Karl assured her that Friedrich was safe.

"I was afraid I wouldn't see you, Karl. They are having me watched." She nodded toward the window. "But I have fooled them." She motioned for him to follow her to the bedroom. She pointed to a woman's dress form which she'd rigged into a dummy, perched in a chair, and then pulled the window shade so that the burning lamp would create a silhouette. "The man downstairs thinks I read a lot." She giggled.

"That was very clever of you, Mother," Karl said as he glanced down at the man in the car. "In fact, I think it will help us to get you out of here on time."

Before Lisle could question him, Karl was crawling across the floor to unplug the lamp. "Toward dawn we will turn the light on again so that he will think you couldn't sleep. Then we will slip out the back."

"Somehow, I'm not as frightened as I was before."

"I wish I could go with you to Marseilles."

"Oh, no! It's too dangerous. Your father has made very specific plans. I will be all right if you can keep Randolf occupied tomorrow. Make him think we have spent the morning together."

"Mother, are you certain it was Randolf who turned you in?"

"Randolf did not intentionally try to harm us, but we know for a fact that after one of his rows with your father, he said far too much to some of his fellow officers. I think they have pressed him to gather information on our comings and goings. Your father has learned that we are to be arrested tomorrow night. Randolf knows this. After an hour a call will come in for you at the restaurant that I have taken ill. If Randolf insists upon accompanying you here, I will have had a fourteen-hour start."

"I'll be glad when it's over," Karl said, holding his mother again.

In the morning luck was with Lisle and Karl for the fog was thicker than before and the Nazi in the car had fallen asleep. Karl was able to take his mother to the appointed rendezvous and then return to his hotel before Randolf called him at eight in the morning. They made plans for lunch.

Karl went out, making certain the desk clerk was aware of his plans to spend the day with his parents. It was not difficult for Karl to lose himself in the Schwabing. Karl telephoned Randolf and canceled lunch, keeping his brother at odds all day. At dinner, Karl thought he was engaging in mental warfare with every statement. Randolf hedged answers to Karl's questions about everyday things like hobbies, friends, and women. Randolf wanted only to talk about politics. Karl was an expert at circumventing undesirable topics and Randolf was a supreme interrogator. It was a stalemate.

After about an hour, Karl checked his watch. "This isn't like Father to be late," he said, noting his brother's accelerated nervousness. "I've always liked the food here at Cafe Luitpold, haven't you, Randolf?"

Randolf tore his eyes away from the doorway and glared at his brother. "You should. Father brought you here more often than he did me."

"Are you never going to realize you were loved even more than I?"

"Don't delude yourself, I never have."

"Randolf, you can't go through life being so bitter . . . or distorting the truth like you do."

Karl watched as Randolf's hands shook while he lit his cigarette. Randolf's control was being strained to the limit for he could not handle criticism—especially from Karl.

"I don't need you to tell me what I should and should not do!" he hissed. "You'll never know what a thrill it was for me when you announced you had gotten married and were staying in Paris. I no longer had to feel that you were watching over my shoulder, counting my every failure."

"Randolf, you've always imagined a rivalry between us that has never existed. At least not to me."

"But it did exist and your ignorance—your inability to hear the tone in Father's voice when he spoke of you and his disdain when he referred to me. Mother adores you and tolerates me."

"If that's so, it's only because you make it so damn hard to love you!"

Randolf's eyes were filled with anger and pain. "It was a mistake my coming here tonight. You tell Father I will see him some other time, when you aren't around!" Randolf tossed his napkin on the table, glared at Karl, and stalked out of the restaurant.

At twelve-thirty Karl arrived at the train station just as the train was pulling out. The Nazi guard checked his passport and let him through. It was not until he crossed the border into France that Karl consciously remembered breathing again.

They were all safe now: his parents and himself. He wondered if Randolf would be demoted when it was discovered that Lisle and Friedrich had escaped. Karl thought of the courageous, quiet Oskar and if he had been detected. He prayed for them all, for he sensed that this was not the end of his fears but only the beginning.

Chapter Eighteen

André Mallot, Etienne Landreaux, and Pierre Dubois, inseparable since high school, had continued their friendship after graduation from college, André's marriage to Amie Beauchamps, and Etienne's engagement to Mary Anderson, an American girl whose father was a reporter for CBS. As the Christmas holidays approached, and the invitations to parties rolled in, Amie and Mary took it upon themselves "to find someone for Pierre."

The girl they found to be stylish, intelligent, and witty, Pierre found to be a self-centered pseudointellectual whose taste in clothes was abhorrent and who wore too much makeup. There was nothing real about the woman at all, except for her vanity.

Disliking the feeling of being a social pariah because he was unattached, Pierre left André and Amie's party at eleven o'clock, walked along the snow-covered streets until he found himself, cold and frustrated, in front of Philippe's. The place was almost empty save for a pair of lovers at a far table and a lone woman at a booth. It was warm inside and he ordered café crème and a brioche.

He warmed his hands on the hot cup and looked over at the girl in the booth. He was unaware that he was staring at her, until she looked him squarely in the eye and stuck out her tongue at him. Pierre had never been so shocked! Upon closer inspection he noticed that her dark hair was shot with coppery highlights and her skin seemed to glow in the lamplight. She was quite petite, with delicately formed hands that she used gracefully. Though she was not strikingly beautiful like his sister, she was pretty, with huge dark eyes that seemed to fill her face. This time when she looked up at him, she smiled, giggled to herself, and then lowered her head as if embarrassed by her earlier outlandish behavior.

Pierre rose and went to her table. "I always make it a practice to ask for the name and address of pretty girls who stick out their tongues at me."

She was blushing when she glanced up at him. "It was all your fault for staring at me! I really hate that!"

He sat down opposite her. "I'm sorry . . . I didn't realize I was . . . my head in the clouds as they say."

"I can't believe I did that. Truthfully, I've never done such a thing."

He placed his elbows on the table and watched as she finished her sandwich. He noticed the faint beginnings of lines at the edges of her eyes and realized she was no girl. She could possibly be even older than he. He was intrigued. She had long eyelashes that fluttered up and down like bees' wings, and when she smiled at him, he thought he'd never seen a smile so genuine.

"Are you going to sit there all night and stare at me?"

"No." He stood, went to his table, retrieved his coffee, and went back to join her. "I'm Pierre Dubois."

"Annette Fouquet." She offered her hand.

Her skin was smooth, moist, and white, like none other he'd felt. He was reluctant to let go. Quickly, she pulled out of his grasp and looked down again as if she were afraid of him.

"Do you come here often?"

"No."

"Do you live around here?"

"No."

"Do you work around here?"

"No."

"Chock-full of information, aren't you?" he quipped.

"Not especially."

"Is Annette Fouquet your real name or are you incognito?" he teased.

"It's real," she said and gulped the last of her coffee. "I have to go."

Pierre stood immediately. "Let me walk you home."

"No, thank you."

"You certainly can't go about the streets alone. What if some stranger accosts you?"

"You're a stranger," she said, with a finely arched eyebrow raised in accusation.

"So I am. But I'm trustworthy! All my friends will attest to that."

"Too bad they aren't here to plead your cause," she said and glided out the door.

Pierre dashed after her, and when he stood next to her on the sidewalk as she hailed a taxi, he was stunned at just how tiny she was. She couldn't have been five feet tall, he thought, and surreptitiously glanced at the high heels on her fur-lined ankle-high boots. He was certain he could pick her up with one arm, for he guessed her to weigh less than a hundred pounds. Pierre was utterly fascinated.

When the taxi pulled up, Annette stood back to avoid being splashed with slushy snow. Pierre was so busy watching Annette that he wound up with wet dress pants and snow in his boots. He held the door for her.

"I'd like to see you again," he said. She smiled, grabbed the door by the handle, slammed it shut, and, before Pierre realized it, she was gone.

A few questions put to the owner of Philippe's informed him that Annette was a regular who worked a few blocks away. Pierre stood outside the café the next morning, determined to wait all day if necessary to see her, but he didn't have to wait that long. Early in the morning, he saw her go into a red brick building. After following her inside, he found out she was the assistant librarian. He waited until she was reshelving a stack of poetry before walking up behind her.

Before he said a word, she looked over her shoulder and didn't seem at all surprised to see him. Her expression did not alter and she returned to her task.

"I told you I wanted to see you again."

"I thought you would find me here."

"You seem very sure of your feminine wiles, Mademoiselle Fouquet," he said stiffly, not liking the fact he was so readable.

"I was most certain of the look in your eyes—you wanted me." She turned and looked up at him, a tiny bird of a woman, but so strong, so unafraid.

Pierre's defenses rose into place. "Overconfidence has lost many battles."

"I wasn't aware this was war," she teased and placed the last book on the shelf.

Pierre liked her, probably a bit too much, and he was wary of the fact that she was winning him so easily. He didn't want her to think he was too pliable.

"Monsieur Dubois, I have a lot of work to do this morning, so if there was some point to your visit . . ." She waited for him to finish.

"Point? No, there is no point."

"Thank you for coming by," she said casually, but as Pierre turned to leave he was positive he'd seen a flicker of disappointment in her eyes.

"Forty-eight hours is *only* two days!" Pierre said to himself as he paced up and down in his office. When he'd first restricted himself from seeing Annette for two days, it had seemed a simple enough task. Out of the accumulated days of one's entire life, two days was but a speck of time. How, then, was it possible for the time to be this unbearable for him?

He went to lunch yesterday with André to discuss Renée's wills and endowment funds for her children and new incorporation papers for another offshoot of Maison Dubois—a cosmetics firm. Pierre was glad he'd taken notes, for he couldn't remember anything other than André asking him four times why he wasn't hungry. He had finished a stack of paperwork and didn't remember doing it. Breakfast this morning with Karl and the children was a blur as was lunch in Renée's office. She'd asked him if he was bringing a guest to the Christmas Eve party they were giving. Like a fool he'd told her yes. Her name? Annette Fouquet. No, no relation to the assistant ambassador to Spain.

There was no getting around it. He wanted to see Annette, and if she was too overconfident about him, then he would worry about that later. He grabbed his tweed overcoat and dashed out the door. His self-imposed sentence was over.

He reached the library just as she was coming down the steps with . . . a man. They were laughing, but she saw Pierre, waved, and walked over to him.

"Pierre! How nice to see you. I'd like to introduce Guillaume Breton, my supervisor."

The men shook hands. Guillaume said to Annette, "If you don't mind, I have some errands. Perhaps Pierre will see you home."

"Do you mind, Pierre?" she asked.

"Not at all."

They strolled for several blocks before either said a word. "I am very glad to see you. I want to apologize for my behavior."

"I'm the one that should apologize, Annette. You were right. You did see something in my eyes . . . I . . . I want you to . . . to want me back."

She dropped her shoulder bag on the street, jumped onto the first step, threw her arms around his neck, and leaned into him. "These last two days have been the longest in my life! I do want you, Pierre!"

She kissed him then and he was startled at the force of her passion. For a woman so small, she packed every inch with an intensity the next fifty women could only wish for. *She* outlined his lips with her tongue and probed the recesses of his mouth. *She* pulled him to her. *She* smothered his face in kisses and *she* suggested they go up to her rooms.

Renée clipped a pair of Cartier amethyst and diamond earrings to her lobes as she finished dressing for her Christmas Eve party. They were a gift from Karl and her first "substantial jewels," he called them. Next year he promised her a square-cut amethyst necklace to match and told her he wanted her to have the kind of jewels his mother had owned. Karl often spoke of Lisle since his return from Munich. As the days passed and still there was no word from America, Renée promised God every day she would give up all the jewels she would ever own if only Karl's parents were safe.

Just then Karl came into the room cursing in German about the ineptitude of the caterer, but when he looked at his wife he fell silent. She was beautiful with her dark hair piled in a modified Gibson atop her head and dressed in a black crepe skirt and silver beaded draped-neck blouse. Light refracted off the bugle beads and seemed to dance in her violet eyes. He was glad she had kept some of the weight she'd gained with Juliette, for he liked the soft inviting curves of her fuller breasts and hips. She was intoxicating, he thought as he put his arms around her.

"It was worth the three hours it took to get ready just to see that look in your eyes," she said, kissing him.

"I always look at you like that."

"Oh, no you don't. If you did, there would be half a dozen Juliettes running around here."

He smiled. "Nice idea."

At that moment the bedroom door was flung open and three-year-old Juliette came tumbling in. She landed flat on her face and instantly began howling.

"Juliette, how many times must you trip on that rug before you realize it is there?" her father said, helping her up.

Juliette, dressed in red velvet and white lace, was still plump and ungainly. Her hair was a shoulder-length mass of corkscrew golden curls with individual pursuits. Renée could not decide how one would describe her daughter. She was not plain or ordinary looking by any means, nor was she deformed or horribly ugly. Juliette was *different*. She had beautiful skin that seemed to glow as if lit from within, but her facial features still resembled a lump of clay waiting for the sculptor to work his craft on her.

Renée didn't care. Juliette was her little girl and she loved her with all her heart. She was a happy child, not given to brooding spells as Gaston was, and she was smart. Juliette adored the attention given her, especially by the men in the family. At times, Renée thought Juliette was jealous of the time she and Karl spent alone, for Juliette had recently developed the habit of coming into their bedroom late at night. The excuses were many, the results the same. Karl would always get up and take her back to bed and read or sing to her. Juliette was very smart.

"Come give me a kiss, chérie," Renée said as Juliette waddled to her and smacked her cheek with her lips. "You look so pretty tonight."

"Not as pretty as you, Maman."

"To me you are." Renée smiled and kissed Juliette again.

"Juliette and I will go downstairs and supervise the caterer."

"And light the tree!" Juliette squealed.

"Only if Gaston is there."

Juliette frowned but immediately scampered off. "Gaston! Hurry! We're going to light the tree!"

Karl reached for Renée's hand and they descended the curving staircase to the main floor.

When Pierre and Annette arrived at the Ile Saint-Louis, she clung possessively to his arm as he introduced her to the many guests. He pointed out his favorite ornaments on the twelve-foot lighted Christmas tree and offered her a silver mug of brandy.

Jean Larousse was playing carols on the white baby grand piano.

"Does he always sing off-key?"

Pierre nodded. "Part of our Christmas tradition."

She laughed. "And who is the woman with him?" she asked of the dark-haired, middle-aged woman.

"Vicomtesse de Marin. Jean is her designer. She wears nothing unless he designs it for her. They are very good friends."

Annette saw the seductive gleam in the woman's eyes as she rubbed Jean's thigh. "I can tell."

"Renée, I'd like you to meet Annette Fouquet. Annette, this is my sister, Renée."

"I'm delighted to meet you," Renée said.

"Thank you for inviting me. I've never seen such beautiful decorations and everyone has been so nice to me."

Renée noticed how Pierre beamed and stole his arm around Annette's waist. She also noted how the slightest word from her sent Pierre scurrying for another eggnog, a light for her cigarette, an ashtray. Renée chuckled to herself. Her brother was in love.

"Next time, I would like for your parents to come. Do they live here in Paris?"

"My mother died when I was young and my father died three years ago after we moved from Bordeaux."

"I'm sorry. I know what it's like to lose someone. I didn't mean to upset you."

"It's all right," she said and brightened when Pierre pulled her a bit closer. His eyes were filled with sympathy and love.

When the party was over, it was Annette who remained behind

to lend a hand, for she was quick to notice that everyone in the family was expected to aid in the cleanup. It was after midnight when Pierre and Annette finished washing the last of the crystal.

"This must be serious, Pierre."

"What are you talking about?"

"I hate doing the dishes. I must want to impress you more than I thought."

"Come here," he said, taking her in his arms.

"Excuse me," Karl said, peeking his head in the door, "but you're wanted in the salon."

Annette started to follow Karl when Pierre grabbed her arm and pulled her back. "Before we go in . . . there's something I've been wanting to ask you."

She placed her fingers on his lips. "Of course you can spend the night with me."

"No, it isn't that. Annette, would you marry me?"

She stood there dazed as if she hadn't heard him clearly. For a moment he thought she was going to refuse him. Perhaps she never wanted to be married. He didn't really know that much about her—they had only met each other three weeks ago. All he knew was that he loved her.

She continued to look at him, debating her options, he supposed. Suddenly he was afraid she'd only wanted his body. He had to admit they made very passionate love, despite her size. Every time he thought about her, he wanted her. He had never had this now-or-never feeling about anyone, not even Suzanne.

Her eyes were growing huge. She looked like a zombie. He wanted to shake her and make her give him the answer he wanted.

"What's the matter?" he finally asked.

"Is it the eggnog? The season of the year perhaps?" Her voice was raspy.

"What are you talking about?" He noticed the tears in her eyes.

"I don't make it a practice to marry men whom I've known for less than a month. Especially those who don't love me!"

"But I do love you!" he shouted.

"Really? Funny, I've never heard you say anything to that effect."

"So that's it." He sighed, relieved.

"What does that mean?" she said agitatedly.

"I love you, Annette. And just to keep the tally straight, you never told me that you loved me."

"Men are supposed to say it first."

He kissed her and felt a now-familiar fire leap through his body and burn in his heart. "If you only knew what you did to me."

She pressed her hips into his. "I've got a good idea."

"Shall we go into the salon and tell the family?"

She nodded and took his arm as they walked to the hall. Then she stopped. "Pierre, promise me all our Christmases will be this happy."

He kissed her. "I promise. How could they not?"

Book Three

The Forties

Chapter Nineteen

June 1940

In the first months of the Occupation, many shops and couture houses in Paris closed. Renée refused to be intimidated by the Nazis. Her doors remained open but her clientele was composed now of the wives and mistresses of Nazi officers.

One of these was in the shop now. A thick red-gold curtain of curls fell nearly to her waist. She could not have been more than seventeen, Renée thought as she watched her being ushered from counter to counter by a handsome young Nazi lieutenant.

She had huge doelike eyes that she kept lowered, but as the girl glanced around, Renée detected a purposely concealed ferocity that intrigued her. She approached the couple.

"May I help you?" she asked in her best German.

"I am Lieutenant Hemmel. This is Yvette and it is her birthday. I promised her a gift. She wants a negligee to please me."

Renée was quick to note the soft lights in the Nazi's eyes as he looked down at the girl. He wasn't as formidable as he'd like her to think. The girl never took her eyes off the peach silk print she was inspecting.

"If we use this fabric, which would be beautiful with Mademoiselle's coloring and hair, it could be quite expensive."

"I can pay," the Nazi said defensively.

"Of course, you will want my designer to fashion something special."

"I want the best, pretty, like Yvette."

"We'll need her measurements and a consultation. It could take a while."

"I have a meeting. I will be back at four. Will that be enough time?"

"Yes. That will be sufficient."

The Nazi kissed the girl on the apple of her cheek. She did not flinch nor did she speak. Curiously, just as he started to walk away, her arm shot out and without turning she grasped his hand and squeezed it. He nodded solemnly and left.

While Yvette went to the dressing room, Renée called for Jean.

Ordinarily, Renée did not sit in on consultations, but something about the girl compelled her to want to know her.

"You're the most beautiful girl I've seen in years," Jean exclaimed when he walked in.

Yvette's smile was radiant. "You needn't flatter me."

"I don't believe in flattery, only the truth," he said as he coldly assessed her features and coloring. "Good bones, even skin tones. Slender torso, we'll need to enhance the small waist. I should think something very romantic—lots of lace, in a deep cream shade. Something with a turn-of-the-century sepia quality, like a Victorian bride. . . ." His voice trailed off as he peered into her eyes.

Yvette made no move to extricate herself from his gaze.

"The peignoir should be buttoned high around the throat to emphasize your long neck."

Yvette's eyes followed his every move.

"The sleeves should have lace cuffs banded with ribbon at the wrist."

"I'll be covered from head to toe. Lieutenant Hemmel had something else in mind."

"I'm sure he did. But you should be wearing something . . . virginal."

"I don't think so."

"I do. And I'm the designer."

Renée never did know at what point during the next hours it happened, only that it did. Her forty-three-year-old best friend was falling in love with a girl, barely seventeen. A beautiful girl and a dangerous one, for Yvette was Nazi property.

"Why are you crying, Papa?"
"Because I'm sad."
"Why?"
"I've heard some very bad news. Your grandmother Lisle and grandfather Friedrich are dead."

Juliette flung herself into Karl's arms as she burst into tears. She looked up at her mother, who was standing behind Karl. Renée's eyes were red and swollen.

"It's not true!" Juliette cried, looking from face to face. Gaston sat on the edge of the chair staring silently out the window. He was trying to be brave, but Juliette saw the sun glint off his face and betray his tears. "Was it an accident?"

Gaston spun around and faced Juliette. His voice was angry. "No. The Nazis killed them over a year ago. Randolf has been keeping the truth from us."

"Juliette doesn't need to hear all this," Karl said, putting her on his knee.

Gaston bit his lip and turned back to the window. Juliette noticed his clenched fists. She'd overheard him talking to their mother about going off to join the Resistance. Juliette didn't know what the Resistance was, but she was glad her mother refused to listen to him. She didn't want him to go away.

"Come, Juliette," Renée said. "Let's go downstairs and make some strudel for Papa."

Juliette looked at her father. He nodded his head. Juliette reluctantly scrambled down off his knee. Juliette knew that death was a terrible thing, but she still believed that if she shut her eyes very tight, she would see her grandparents. Perhaps later, she would go to her father and tell him that. Then Papa won't be so sad, she thought.

September 1941

It was raining when Renée opened the shop for the day. She flipped on the chandeliers, noting that somehow they didn't seem to burn as brightly as they did before the war. She remembered when they could dispel the bleakest day. She passed the glass cases filled with pink and mauve silks, satins, chiffons, and crepe de chines. The demand for frivolous fabrics had decreased while they could barely make enough warm flannel gowns and robes. There were still fabulously hand-beaded evening bags so incongruent with wartime and yet there were no stockings, only a silver tray filled with bottles of leg makeup.

She walked into her office, where Jean was waiting for her.

"Where's Pierre? He left the house before I did."

"He had an errand. He should be back soon."

"What errand?"

"I don't remember," Jean said, taking out his sketches. "Could you look these over?"

She took the first sketch.

"This is the peignoir for Fräulein Schmidt."

"You don't think these lines are too narrow for her? She gets heavier every time she walks in the door."

"I thought we'd keep her coming back if she outgrew her nightgowns every few months or so."

Renée smiled. "I like the dark eggplant color. It will complement her silver hair."

"I made these up for the sweater line you suggested. What do you think?"

"I don't care for the narrow lapels on the cardigans. Let's go with wide shawl collars—ones big enough to wrap across the chest when it gets really cold. I think we'll sell more that way."

"Good point."

Just then Pierre walked in.

"Where have you been?" Renée demanded.

"An errand. I'm here now."

Renée saw the quickly exchanged look between Jean and Pierre. "What's going on with you, Pierre? I swear, you're away more than you're here."

"I thought you were the one who wanted me to get more woolens."

"I do."

"In case you haven't heard, there's a war on, which means I have to use more than an order form to get these fabrics."

"I'm sorry." She paused. "Well? Did you?"

He laughed. "Yes, so you can relax."

"Pierre, you never cease to amaze me. Where are they coming from?"

"Lyon. We're using the black market there. I've hired Etienne Landreaux to be our driver. He says he could use the money. They're expecting another baby."

"Etienne is a good man. I'm surprised he's not too proud to accept such menial work. I know his law practice has come to a halt with the Occupation."

"I told him this job would require a lot of courage."

Renée nodded. Lyon was in unoccupied France and the woolens were stolen off Nazi ships and trucks. She felt a tingle of power when she thought of how she would fashion the woolens into designer clothes and then stick a fat price on them. The profits they made off the Nazis would keep their doors open, support their workers and other Frenchmen like Etienne and his wife, Mary. There was some justification in price gouging, she thought.

"If you don't need me, I've got to run," Pierre said, moving to the door.

"Where are you going now?"

"Business, dear sister. Just business." He was gone.

She slammed her fist on the desk. "Why does he make such a mystery of everything?"

"I don't know," Jean replied, gathering his sketches.

"Where are you going?"

"Business."

At two o'clock Pierre still hadn't come back and Jean had left the store twice, but returned within half an hour each time.

Renée didn't know why but suddenly she felt as if Jean and Pierre were conspiring against her. As she went through the day, she realized that their actions were not new but had been going on for a long time. She had just been too busy to notice.

Pierre returned at three and worked in his office until six, when she closed the shop.

"Jean"—she stopped him on his way out—"could you look at these sketches I've done? It won't take long."

"I'd love to, but I'm late already. Yvette and I don't have much time as it is."

"I hope you know what you're doing."

"I'm a big boy now. I can take care of myself."

"I'll see you tomorrow." He walked away waving his arm over his head. "And be careful!" she called.

Renée stuck her head inside Pierre's office. "I'm going home. How long will you be?"

"I've got a lot of paperwork here. Probably an hour or more."

She started for the front door when she remembered she'd left some sketches of Gaston's she wanted to discuss with him. She went back to her office. Just as she was about to leave again, she heard Pierre mount the stairs to the apartment upstairs.

"That's odd," she mumbled to herself. She waited until he was all the way up the stairs before starting after him. She waited until he was inside the apartment before she crept any closer.

She could hear Jean's voice.

"She's getting wise to us. We can't hide from her much longer. I say we tell her."

"No. It's too dangerous. We've already taken too many risks. I'd never forgive myself if anything happened to her. We can't tell her."

Renée threw the door open. "Tell me what?"

Jean nearly jumped out of his skin. "I thought you'd gone home!"

"Well, I didn't. The time for your bluffs and games is over. Whatever this is all about, you have to tell me."

Jean shrugged his shoulders. "She's right."

Pierre sighed. "Sit down, Renée. I'll make this as simple as I can. Jean and I are members of the Free French. We take information as it comes out of Berlin and see that it gets to de Gaulle in England."

"How?"

"By the radio receiver and transmitter in this apartment."

Jean spoke. "We've been using Maison Dubois without your knowledge."

Renée listened while they told her of their work. She found there never had been any wool in Lyon, but that the strongest bands of the Resistance were located there. It was there the Maquis gathered information by torturing Nazis and Vichy government-backed French informants to the Germans.

Etienne Landreaux was not in need of a job. He was the man they were protecting; he and his father-in-law, Garrett Anderson, the American reporter for CBS.

Garrett had both press cards and "neutral" papers that allowed him to travel to Berlin and Switzerland. His work was vital in getting the truth to America so that the United States would back England with ships, guns, and munitions.

Jean and Pierre chose Maison Dubois as their headquarters simply because it was so visible to the Nazis. There were officers coming and going every day. Working directly under their noses offered the underground a good smokescreen.

She learned that Yvette was an informant to the underground. Her Nazi lover was the son of a high-ranking general stationed in Berlin. She had not come to Maison Dubois for lingerie but as part of her work. She led an even more dangerous life than Renée had realized. Yvette was an important girl to Jean in more ways than she'd imagined.

"What can I do to help?"

"It won't be easy because you can't act any differently than you did before. You can't say anything that will bring attention to our activities," Jean told her.

"Now that Karl's brother is here, you must be doubly careful," Pierre said. "One slip could be fatal."

"I understand."

"Above all, you can't tell Karl," Jean said.

"Karl is not a Nazi! There's a big difference."

"I know that. But the more people that know about us only increases our chances of discovery."

"I hope I can make you as proud of me as I am of you," she said. "But you won't mind if I add extra prayers every day until this is over."

Pierre took her hand. "Maybe that's the only thing that will matter . . . in the end."

Chapter Twenty

"Where are you going?"

"None of your business."

"Lucienne, I will not tolerate your attitude."

"Oh, really, Mother? I suppose you don't like the coffee, fresh cream, and new Italian leather shoes I brought home for you last week either," Lucienne hissed.

Virginie looked away momentarily. "This isn't fair to Antoine."

Lucienne angrily shoved her hands into a pair of white kid gloves. "Since when have you concerned yourself with what is 'fair'?" Lucienne headed for the door. She turned. "I told him I was working as a volunteer at the hospital. It was the part about the refugee children that got him."

"He's still suspicious."

"He's your problem, Mother, not mine," Lucienne said as she slammed the door behind her.

Virginie went into the salon and poured herself a sherry. Lucienne was getting out of hand. She must find a way to curb her daughter's newest bid for independence.

When the Nazis first took Paris, Virginie had struck a bargain with her friends in Berlin. She would allow them to use her house in town and the facilities at Crédit de Paris in exchange for the assured safety of her son-in-law, who did not register as was required of all other French Jews.

Every Friday, a small group of Nazi uniformed accountants opened Crédit de Paris, used the bank for eight hours to reconcile their books, and then closed the bank until the next Friday.

For eighteen months Antoine had been content to remain at the château. Not until Lucienne began work as a volunteer did he confess to Virginie he felt confined. Suddenly he wanted to go to Paris. He wanted to roam through Crédit de Paris where he'd worked for seven years, he told Virginie.

She knew he wanted only to confirm his suspicion that his wife was having an affair.

Randolf Heilmann leaned his head against the damask chair. He looked down at the thick file on his desk. Across the top was the name: COLONEL A. F. WEITZEL.

In less than a year he'd nearly accomplished his mission. He hadn't arrested all the Jews on the list Berlin had given him, but his main objective had been to find the head of the black market. By the end of this day he would have arrested them all.

Weitzel's network had been hard to crack, for Weitzel paid his "men" in product not promises. The idealist in Randolf liked to think that Nazi officers would rather be rewarded with promotions and glory, but the realist knew that alcohol, food, and cigarettes bought loyalty.

The war was not going well in 1942. The victory in the Balkans had cost the Reich dearly. Too much time, munitions, and men had been squandered. Nearly everyone agreed that efforts should have been focused on the Russian front. Only now with winter approaching did Hitler agree to march on Stalingrad. The major error of not invading Britain at Dunkirk had even caused Randolf to question Hitler's intelligence.

Because of the military situation, Weitzel had increased his network tremendously. Nazi soldiers were too easily bought, Randolf observed.

At this very moment, every one of Weitzel's men, except for Weitzel himself and his most valued man and accomplice, Lieutenant Gunther Milse, were being arrested.

Randolf wanted to personally see Milse's face when he told the traitor he would no longer be selling conscription goods on the black market. Then he would deal with Weitzel. It was a major triumph in his career, sure to win him a commendation from Berlin, perhaps from the Führer himself.

Luxuries, lust, and lovers were rare in wartime. The day Lucienne found all three, she thought her luck equal to the night she'd won half a million francs at the Casino in Monte Carlo.

His name was Gunther Milse. He was six years her junior, endowed with an incredible body, indefatigable sexual stamina, and he was in charge of all supplies for the German High Command. Gunther could and did provie Lucienne with everything from silk stockings to Swiss chocolates.

Twice a week, on Tuesday morning and Thursday afternoon, Lucienne unlocked the back door of Crédit de Paris, led Gunther to her mother's office, and there, on the beige watered moiré love seat, they would unleash their passions.

Lucienne began stripping off her clothes the moment Gunther walked into the room.

Half an hour later, he was still hard and demanding more. He kissed her rapaciously and teased her nipples with his tongue.

"I can't decide which is better," she said, stroking him, "the fact that we screw in Mother's office or your skill."

"I'll show you which is best," he said, picking her up and slamming her down hard on Virginie's desk. He rammed himself inside her. She only laughed at him.

"Show me!" she demanded.

He grabbed her legs and put them around his neck while he continued to pump her. She moaned and then screamed as she climaxed. "Which is best?" he asked gruffly.

"You are! God! You're the best!"

He pulled her up to face him and, still joined, he carried her to the love seat. She straddled him. "Now you show me how good you are."

Suddenly, the door flew open and Antoine burst into the room.

"What are you doing here?" Lucienne demanded righteously.

"Catching my adulterous wife with her Nazi lover!" he yelled.

Gunther shut his gaping mouth as he pushed Lucienne off his lap and scrambled for his pants. He was still hard.

"You fool! Don't you know how dangerous it is for you to be here? What if someone saw you?"

Incredulously, he stared at her. "Did you ever think what I would do to *you* if I caught *you?*"

Lucienne's bare breasts were lightly glowing from a thin layer of perspiration. Her color was heightened to a bright peach and her perfectly coiffed hair had come undone and hung in thick, wet curls down her neck. She was magnificently beautiful.

"No."

Antoine's dark good looks were shadowed with humiliation and frustration. "Are you totally incapable of feeling? Don't you care about anything, anyone but yourself?"

"I didn't ask you to love me, Antoine. That was your mistake."

At that moment, before Antoine could thrust his hands around her neck and squeeze the life out of her, and before Gunther could defend his position, the halls of Crédit de Paris thundered with stomping jackboots.

"Halt!" Randolf Heilmann boomed.

Lucienne looked up to see the doorway filled with high peaked caps with the death's-head insignia and soldiers dressed in preposterously cut charcoal breeches with shiny black leather belts angled across their chests. There was a machine gun leveled at her face.

She held a pale pink chiffon blouse over her naked breasts, screamed, and fainted.

"Arrest him!" Randolf ordered as his soldiers dragged the stunned Gunther Milse into the hall.

"Your name!" Randolf demanded.

"Junot. Antoine Junot. I run this bank for Virginie Ruille. This is my wife, Lucienne Junot."

"Seize them both and take them to headquarters. I will deal with them later."

Two hours later, Lucienne was released. Antoine was charged with being an unregistered Jew and imprisoned.

"You simpleminded slut!" Virginie screamed at her daughter when she heard the story. It was the first time in over eleven years she lost her temper. "Do you have any idea what you've done?"

Lucienne belted down a jigger of brandy and leaned back in the sofa. "I can guess."

"Can you? I doubt it." Virginie paced in front of the marble fireplace. "I should have stopped you long ago."

"Don't hand me that crap, Mother. You liked all the goodies I brought home. You wouldn't sell your body for food and clothes, but you were more than happy to let me do it for you. We understand one another."

"I don't think I'll ever understand you."

"It's not so tough, Mother. All you've ever wanted from me is a child. An heir for your precious dynasty. You pushed Antoine on me. I never had any say in the matter . . . not if I wanted to continue to live in the manner I'd been accustomed to." Lucienne lit a cigarette. "It didn't work out the way you'd planned, did it? When you choose my next husband, perhaps you should check to see if he's sterile."

"Lucienne!"

"Too graphic, Mother?" Lucienne taunted and smiled. There were very few times in her life when Lucienne held the upper hand with her mother. She wished she could take further advantage of her edge, but she felt too wretched.

She poured herself another brandy. It would take a lot of liquor to calm her nerves. She had never been this terrified in her life. She didn't love Antoine, but she wasn't quite the cold-hearted bitch she portrayed to her mother.

For the most part her life with Antoine had been surprisingly satisfying. Lucienne had wanted only to needle her mother by taking up with Gunther. She hated Virginie. She did everything she could to make her mother's life miserable. Lucienne wanted nothing more than to be free of her mother's power and manipulation. But Lucienne was too weak to break all her ties. Virginie had taught Lucienne to appreciate and need all the luxuries life as a wealthy woman could offer. Lucienne could not tolerate deprivation of any kind.

Lucienne watched her mother pacing. She wondered which one of them would win this game of impossible tasks—Virginie in wresting Antoine from the Gestapo or Lucienne at besting her mother.

"Perhaps all isn't lost. I have many friends in places that count. People who can free Antoine with a phone call." Virginie went to the phone and dialed.

It took over an hour and a half to reach her high-placed

contacts in Berlin, but all her pleadings did no good. Then she made another call.

"André? Could you drive out to the château this evening? I need to speak with you. Good. I'll see you then."

She went to her study and unlocked the desk drawer. She pulled out thirty thousand francs. "Perhaps I can buy Antoine's freedom," she said to herself.

André handed the packet of money to Pierre.

"How does Virginie know we're part of the Resistance? Or that we would help her?"

"I don't know that she does. She knows I have connections. Beyond that, your guess is as good as mine. I can't imagine Virginie Ruille not knowing every man we have."

"I haven't even told Renée you're involved."

Just then Renée came into the office and found André and Pierre. "I didn't know anyone was in here," she said, eyeing the half-concealed francs in Pierre's hand. "What's this?" she asked, knowing instinctively this money had nothing to do with Maison Dubois.

André turned away, leaving Pierre to make the explanations.

"This is our revenge against Virginie. This is our chance to strike back for what she has done to us."

"What are you talking about?"

"Antoine Junot has just been arrested. Virginie is willing to pay the underground thirty thousand francs to free him. No questions asked."

Renée looked at André. "She called you?"

"Yes."

"She knows you would come here?"

"I'm not sure."

Pierre's eyes were hard. "I'd like to refuse her and let her know it is the Duboises who have the power. But the fact is that there is nothing we can do for Antoine. Once the Gestapo makes their arrests, those people are shipped out of here within hours. There are no trials and no justice. And there is no confusion in the ranks as they are ushered onto the trains. *Every* name is read off by Nazi soldiers so that *every* person is accounted for. Antoine was arrested by Randolf himself. Antoine would not be just another face in the crowd. My men risk their lives every day for hundreds. But to try to engineer an escape for Antoine would surely result in the loss of many of my men. I'm plagued with too many informants and not enough guns and provisions as it is. We are not that well organized, or as powerful as you think. We're just a few untrained men doing the best we can with very little support."

Renée looked at the money and turned to André. "Take the money back to Virginie and tell her the truth—that the risk is too great for the underground. Perhaps if we'd known of him earlier we could have gotten him out of the country. It's too late for her son-in-law."

André took the money. "The underground could use this money just as Pierre said. We could keep it and tell her we tried, then later we could tell her we were unsuccessful."

"André! I can't do that! How could I ever live with myself again? I would be reducing myself to worse than her level. Whether I refuse her or accept her, the result is the same. The Gestapo has seen to it that Antoine is a dead man. I think Virginie already knows this—in her mind. Right now she's living on hope. For seventeen years I wanted revenge, but never like this! Not at the expense of a man's life. Tell her the underground sends it deepest regrets for Antoine. We will all pray for him."

"We'll be at home if you need us again tonight," Pierre said.

"Good luck, André," Renée said as he left.

Pierre put his arm around her.

"For the first time in my life, I feel sorry for Virginie." She shivered. "Take me home. I want to be with Karl and the children."

Virginie looked at the packet of money on her desk as if it were contaminated.

"Did you speak with those who have the influence—the kind of power we need in this situation?"

"I did everything I could. I was told that had you requested to send Antoine out of the country earlier, before he was arrested, that measures would have been taken to insure his safety."

"Exile? I couldn't have Antoine exiled when I needed him here!"

André was flustered. "I don't understand. Crédit de Paris was closed."

"Antoine was like a son to me!"

As he watched her struggle to control her anger, André realized that Virginie and her selfishness were to blame for Antoine's predicament. There had been no *real* reason for Antoine to remain at the château with Virginie, except to amuse her and satisfy *her* needs. It was a fact he knew she would never admit to herself.

Just then Lucienne knocked on the library door. "I saw your car outside, André."

Her eyes were puffy and he could tell she'd been crying. She had tried to mask them with eye makeup. Her smile was strained and she was drunk.

"Lucienne," Virginie said, "take André into the salon and fix him a drink. I'll be there presently."

"Wonderful idea, Mother," Lucienne said sarcastically, and then took André's arm. She leaned heavily into him, trying to maintain her balance.

Once in the salon, Lucienne sat on the sofa.

"Why are you here, André?"

"Amie and I were wondering if we couldn't get together for some cards this weekend."

She wasn't listening. "Antoine has been arrested by the Gestapo . . . or did Mother already tell you that?"

"She did. I'm sorry, Lucienne."

"Did she tell you it was my fault he was discovered?"

"No." He sat next to her and held her hand. He glanced into the hall. Virginie was still in the library. He sensed something was not right. Perhaps it was because he didn't trust Virginie. Perhaps it was his work in the underground that taught him to stay sharp.

"You and I go back a long way, don't we? Parties at your family's estate. I remember when you were five. And your father gave you that pony. I had always wanted a horse of my own, but Mother would never allow it, though Edouard had one. I hated you then. You were five years younger than I and already you'd accomplished the impossible . . . you had a pony."

Tears sprang to her eyes. "How did it all become so horrid? I never wanted to hurt Antoine. I keep thinking of all the rotten things I did to him . . . the lies . . . the cheating. He didn't deserve any of it."

"What makes you do such things, Lucienne?"

Suddenly, her lips curled into a snarl as her eyes traveled to the portrait of Virginie over the mantel. "You have no idea what it's like being her child. None of us, not even Edouard the favorite, are real people to her. We're just objects to be maneuvered and used in her schemes."

"I think I'm beginning to understand."

"Really? Sometimes I'm not sure I do." She sighed and wiped her eyes. "Antoine loved me. I see that now. No one has ever loved me, especially not anyone in this family. I think I was so frightened by his feelings that I did everything I could to turn him away. Mother told us that emotions would weaken our character, make us vulnerable. God, what a fool I was . . ."

André pitied her and everyone else who lived in this cold house. Lucienne had never had a chance to become anything but the spoiled, spiteful woman she was. He watched her as she glared at her mother's portrait. The hateful look in her eyes gave him chills.

"I think we could both use a drink."

He poured two drinks and stopped. Virginie had been in the library much too long. "Perhaps your mother would like a drink. I'll go ask her."

"Do that," Lucienne said, trancelike.

The library door was still ajar, just as he'd purposely left it. He listened. Virginie was on the telephone.

"Colonel Weitzel, you needn't know who I am. Call me a friend of the Reich. The dissidents you seek can be located on the rue du Faubourg-St.-Honoré—at Maison Dubois. I leave the rest of the investigation in your capable hands." She hung up. She was smiling.

André tapped on the door, then opened it farther. "I was pouring drinks. I thought perhaps you might want one—tonight especially."

She looked at him. "Yes, I would. Tonight especially."

Randolf Heilmann watched as his sergeant left the office. Milse had cracked during the first hour of interrogation. Now he had more than enough evidence to convict Weitzel. The Jew arrested with Milse had shed no light, though Randolf suspected the man was involved with the black market somehow. Perhaps he was involved in the underground. Three hours of questioning still had revealed nothing. Junot would not break.

When Randolf spoke with Berlin he was ordered to have both Milse and Junot sent to Berlin. Randolf's next task was to arrest Weitzel.

Randolf opened the venetian blinds in time to see Junot and Milse being ushered onto a military truck that would take them to Berlin. Randolf did not want anything to happen to these prisoners and therefore decided against sending them by train. Randolf believed in an ounce of prevention. . . .

He picked up the telephone and spoke to his secretary. "Order the men who accompanied me this afternoon to meet me in front of the building in thirty minutes. We have another assignment."

Jean stepped into the hot shower and lathered his hair. In an hour he would be meeting Yvette. The water pelted his skin as he washed the soap off. He wished she were here now. He'd like to wash her back, her breasts. She had the most wonderful creamy skin. If he lived to be a hundred he thought he would never see such skin again. He'd tried twice to paint her but failed to capture her particular essence. After the war was over, he would have the rest of his life to paint Yvette. He would keep a chronicle of her over the years, knowing that her beauty would not age—only mellow.

He found it incredible that they had fallen in love. If it were possible, he loved her more now, after a year, than he had when they first met. With every woman he'd ever known, the "romance" had worn thin after only a few weeks. Nothing was the same with Yvette and he was glad.

Tonight would be a special night for them—it would be their last for a long time to come.

Lieutenant Hemmel was being transferred back to Berlin, and Jean decided that it was time for Yvette to leave France. He had arranged for her to be hidden behind the backseat of an old Renault and driven to Toulouse on the Garonne River. From there she would cross the Pyrenees and make her way to Spain. She would be safe until the war was over. It didn't matter to him if she agreed or not. He wanted a future with her and this was his insurance it would happen.

He turned off the shower and then realized he'd forgotten a

towel. He went to the linen closet, and as he did, he happened to look out the window. Parked in front of Maison Dubois were two black Citroëns with yellow wheels. He knew immediately it was the Gestapo.

He wrapped the towel around his waist, got his loaded revolver, and listened for the sound of footsteps.

Like jackals storming the gates of hell, the Gestapo charged into Jean's apartment. Shiny black gun barrels stared at him and in their center was Lieutenant J. Hemmel.

"Search the premises!" he ordered.

Jean knew better than to protest. He glared at the young Nazi . . . Yvette's lover.

The soldiers ransacked drawers, closets, and slit furniture cushions with long silver knives. Draperies were ripped from the windows, his drawing table overturned, his oil paintings slashed. Jean did not flinch.

Hemmel turned just as one soldier picked up the painting of Yvette.

"Let me see that!"

The soldier handed him the canvas. "Yvette?" He looked closely at the painting and then at Jean.

The soldiers went into the bedroom where he kept the radio. Jean could hear them slitting the mattress.

"You . . . and my Yvette?" Hemmel's hand was shaking. Jean watched as Hemmel's finger tightened on the trigger of the gun he was aiming at Jean.

"Sir!" one of the soldiers shouted. "We've found the radio and the transmitter. It was hidden in a wall."

Jean's eyes were riveted on Hemmel.

"You are under arrest for being a member of the Resistance."

Hemmel tried to level his gun, but still his hand was shaking.

Jean started to raise his arms over his head, but went for his gun instead. He got off two shots before Hemmel fired his gun at Jean's heart, killing him instantly.

Hemmel clutched his arm where he'd been hit. "Take the radio and the body to Colonel Weitzel. Say nothing of the painting."

André made the fourteen-mile journey from Saint-Germain-en-Laye to the Ile Saint-Louis in record time.

"She turned you all in. I heard her talking to Weitzel!"

"My God! She has no heart at all!"

Pierre rushed back into the salon. "The line is dead at the apartment. I have a feeling we're too late. André, you have to get out of here. It's not safe for you, either."

"I've already thought of that. I'm taking Amie and we'll leave Paris tonight."

Renée hugged him closely. "God go with you."

"My good friend," Pierre said. "We—we'll be together after the war."

There were tears in André's eyes. "Yes."

"Hurry, André. You must leave now."

André dashed out the door to his car and sped off.

Just then Karl came into the salon. "Juliette wants to see you, Renée." He saw their anxious faces. "What is it?"

"We're in terrible danger, Karl," Renée said, but before she could continue with her explanations, the sound of screeching tires and slamming doors filled the still night.

The soldiers banged loudly on the door. "Open up in the name of the Führer!"

A very pregnant Annette waddled hurriedly into the hall, wiping her hands on a kitchen towel. She was enormous with child. "Pierre! What's happening?"

Karl opened the door, and Colonel Weitzel and his men filled the hallway. Their guns were leveled at Pierre and Renée.

Annette screamed, which brought Gaston and Juliette running to the top of the stairs.

"Stay where you are!" Karl ordered the children.

"Renée Dubois Heilmann, Pierre Dubois, and Karl Heilmann, you are under arrest."

"On what charge?" Karl demanded.

"Subversion and sabotage against the Reich."

Roughly, the soldiers grabbed Renée and Karl, and shoved them down the front steps. Annette tried to reach out to Pierre but a soldier grabbed her around the stomach and held her back.

"Take your hands off her!" Pierre started for the man, but another soldier shoved his rifle butt into Pierre's stomach. He doubled over in pain.

"Pierre! Pierre!" Annette screamed as they dragged him off.

They shoved Renée into the truck with Karl and Pierre. Two

soldiers followed them inside and then pulled the canvas flaps down over the back. In seconds, the trucks, the Citroëns, and the soldiers were gone.

Gaston raced down the stairs with Juliette clad in her nightshirt directly behind him. "Annette! Where are they taking them? What have they done?"

Annette stood in the doorway staring into the night. "I don't . . ." She clutched her abdomen and fainted into Gaston's arms.

Chapter Twenty-one

Pierre and Renée were ushered to a mildewed basement room which contained a bare overhead lightbulb and a battered desk in the center with two austere wooden chairs on either side. There were no papers on the desk, and Renée got the impression that no record of the business conducted here would ever exist.

"Sit down," Weitzel ordered them. He whispered something to the two guards and left.

Karl was taken to a plushly appointed office, given coffee with cream, and was asked to wait.

Suddenly Karl heard shouting in the hallway. It was not Weitzel who burst into the room, but Randolf.

"Karl! What in the hell is going on here?"

"I've been arrested."

"On what charge? And by whose order?"

"Conspiracy . . . I think. Colonel Weitzel was not all that clear about things when he came to the house tonight to arrest us."

" 'Us'?"

"Pierre and Renée were arrested along with me. I thought it was some trick. . . ."

Karl watched as Randolf slowly sank into his desk chair. "I'm afraid we have a real problem."

"Are you crazy? We haven't done anything!"

"I just came from Maison Dubois where an arrest was made. Jean Larousse was shot trying to escape. A radio transmitter was found concealed in a wall."

"Jean is dead?"

"Yes. Renée and Pierre are naturally suspected of being coconspirators."

"I . . . I can't believe . . ." But he could. He would have gambled his life that Renée would not have kept something this important from him. And yet, somehow he knew she had. She was French after all, and he was German.

"You must know, Karl, how much I want an end to this underground. It has caused a great deal of trouble for me. Pierre is guilty, I would stake my reputation on it. But the thing that angers me the most is Weitzel's interference in my affairs!"

Randolf pounded his fist on the desk. "Weitzel thinks he can outsmart me by rousting the underground. He knew I would arrest him tonight. He hopes to win support for himself by his courage. I'll teach him never to aspire to levels he is incapable of reaching."

"What are you going to do?"

Randolf leveled his gaze on his brother. "It is not I who must sacrifice, Karl, but you—if you want to save your wife."

"I'll do anything!"

"I have asked you several times over the past months to consider enlisting in the German army."

"Nazi army."

Randolf glared at Karl. "If you enlist, it will convince my superiors of your loyalty. Your actions will be a direct reflection on your wife. If evidence does prove she is involved in the underground, this will give me some leverage . . . not much, but some."

"What of Pierre?"

"I owe Pierre a debt from long ago. He saved my life once. After this, however, I owe him nothing. You will advise Pierre to leave Paris."

"Of course. Where do you think they have taken them?"

Flecks of conquest studded Randolf's eyes as he headed toward the door. "Remain here," was all he said and was gone.

* * *

They pelted Pierre's chest and ribs with hard jabs. Again and again the soldiers rammed their fists into him with sadistic smiles gnarling their faces.

Renée screamed when the larger of the two Nazis drew back to hit him again. Instead, he whirled around and struck her in the side of the face. She felt her eye swelling. With each painful throb, she thought of how much worse it must be for Pierre. She squirmed against the Nazi who held her. She wanted to kill them all. She looked at Pierre and wondered how much longer he could last.

Weitzel hovered over Pierre. "Tell us about the Resistance. Who are your contacts?"

Pierre was very weak. His face was mangled, he barely breathed. Blood poured out of a split lower lip and a deep gash over his eye.

"Nothing," he mumbled. "I know nothing."

Frustrated and angry at Pierre's resilience, Weitzel grabbed him under the chin and jerked his head up. Renée thought she heard his neck snap. "Watch while we cut off your sister's ears."

Weitzel nodded to the soldier who held her. She struggled to free herself, but the soldier was too strong. Out of the corner of her eye, she saw the blade fly up to her neck. The Nazi taunted her with the sharp blade, reveling in her terror. He jerked her to one side so that her head bobbed to the left.

She braced as the Nazi began to slice at her right ear. He had just pricked the skin when Weitzel yelled at him.

"Not that one," he said, watching a fine line of blood trickle down her neck. "The other ear."

The soldier jabbed his elbow into her spine while he switched the knife in his hands. Searing pains shot up her back and she felt her legs crumble. The Nazi was forced to hold her up.

She was weakening but she swore to herself she would never give Weitzel, or any of them, satisfaction. If Pierre could hold out, so could she. She tried not to think of the knife as it flashed in front of her. She told herself there was no pain as the sharp steel slit her skin.

She concentrated on Pierre. She wanted him to be strong and not give in for her sake. She saw tears slide out of his bruised eye. His mouth was trembling. He wanted to cry out. But she willed him to silence.

She thought about Lyon and the warm sunny days when they used to play in their mother's garden. She could smell hyacinth and lilac. She heard Michel's giggles and Pierre taunting her as they chased each other underneath the blossoming trees. Pierre pulled on her braids, causing her to let out a loud yelp.

She opened her eyes.

Suddenly, the door burst open.

"Colonel Weitzel!" Randolf stormed. His shoulders filled the doorway. With the hall light shining behind him the way it did, he looked like God. His eyes were filled with glacial rage. Renée cringed.

Randolf looked at Pierre. "He has confessed?"

Weitzel hesitated. "No, but he will."

Randolf snickered. "The man is half dead. If he's guilty, a competent man would have had his confession by now. But then as we all know, you are not a competent man."

"I can make him confess . . . when he hears his sister's screams. Pity she is your brother's wife."

Randolf's expression was oblique. "Pity Lieutenant Milse is such a weak man. He confessed without much persuasion at all."

Renée watched as Weitzel shrank away from Randolf. What were they talking about? Why had the soldier loosened his grip on her and lowered his knife?

"I prefer to conduct my own investigations. It was bad judgment on your part to interfere. You ordered Larousse's death."

Renée was in shock. Jean was dead? André had not made it in time. She trembled.

"Release them!" Randolf ordered. He did not look at her as he preceded Weitzel out of the room.

The soldiers exchanged a quizzical look and then untied Pierre. Renée raced to him and he slumped into her arms. His breathing was labored and she tried to help him stand, but she sank under his weight. One of the soldiers took Pierre's other arm and helped them up the stairs.

A Citroën pulled up in the alley behind the building. Discreetly, Renée and Pierre were put into the car and driven home.

*   *   *

Karl paced. How foolish Renée had been not to tell him. What could Jean and Pierre have been thinking—using Maison Dubois as their base? It was insanity; it was dangerous, and yet, it was perfect. For nearly three years they had gone undetected. A long time even for a professional espionage agent. Now Jean was dead and God only knew what would become of Pierre. Karl believed Randolf when he said he could get Renée out. He had to believe in something.

At that moment the door opened. Randolf was not smiling. "Your wife and brother-in-law have been sent home. You will be contacted within the week regarding our bargain."

Karl nodded.

"A car will drive you home." Randolf hesitated. "Karl, I—I hope I wasn't too late."

"She *is* all right, isn't she?"

Randolf's eyes revealed nothing.

Karl grabbed his brother by the collar. "Answer me, you son of a bitch!"

Randolf pried Karl's hands away from his neck. "Go home, Karl."

Karl turned and raced out of German headquarters and into the awaiting car.

Randolf Heilmann watched from the window as his brother rode away. It had been an excellent day for him and his career. He had discovered a key link in the Free French and eliminated it. As far as headquarters was concerned, the guilty party, Jean Larousse, had been apprehended and executed. Intensive interrogations of "other suspects" revealed nothing. He would have to shut down Maison Dubois, but he believed he could convince his superiors that Larousse was the only one involved.

Colonel Weitzel was taken into custody as a traitor to the Third Reich. On the basis of the confession from Gunther Milse, Weitzel would face execution within the month. Randolf had lied to Milse, telling the young officer he would only face a prison sentence for his part in the black-market ring. Randolf knew Milse would die before Weitzel.

Best of all, Randolf had forced Karl into compliance with a destiny Randolf had long believed Karl's only salvation. Since that day in the Alps, Randolf had "owed" Pierre. It was a debt he had been anxious to eliminate.

Randolf was certain that when his reports reached Berlin, he would be transferred back to the High Command. More than anything Randolf couldn't wait to get out of Paris.

Chapter Twenty-two

Pandemonium greeted Karl when he arrived home. Dr. Bressard and his nurse had been summoned by Gaston when Annette went into shock after the Nazis had come.

"She's been in labor for the past two hours, but has only dilated a centimeter. It's going to be a long labor," the doctor said.

It was Gaston who first saw Pierre and Renée drive up. He called the doctor as he bounded down the stairs, and they carried an unconscious Pierre into the house. Renée's calm was deceiving, and wisely Dr. Bressard recognized her traumatic state. He quickly administered a strong sedative.

Dr. Bressard spoke to Karl. "I've stitched the wounds behind her ears, and if there are any scars, they'll be hidden by her hair. The bruises on her face are not severe and I don't think there's any real damage."

"What about Pierre?" Karl asked as they walked down the hall to Pierre's room.

"His condition is much worse. He's got four broken ribs, a broken jaw, and severe bruises. I suspect a concussion. He needs X rays so I can determine internal damage. He's going to need a long time to recover."

"We don't have a long time."

"What are you talking about?"

"I have to move him. When can he travel?"

"Travel?" The doctor was astonished at the suggestion. "This man needs to be in the hospital! In fact, I insist on it! I must wrap his ribs and wire his jaw."

Karl went to see Renée, who was groggy from the injection but was still awake. He sat on the edge of the bed, and held her hand.

"Karl," she mumbled. "They didn't hurt you?"

"No," he said, the words catching in his throat.

"Pierre? Tell me about Pierre."

"Pierre is going to be fine. The doctor wants to transfer him to the hospital so he can be cared for properly, but he's very much alive."

"Then everything is all right now." Her eyelids were heavy. The sedative had begun its work.

"Yes, my darling. There's nothing to be afraid of anymore. It's all over."

Renée slept for over twenty-four hours and when she awoke she felt as if the world had changed.

Annette's labor had been long and difficult. At five in the morning a six-pound two-ounce baby girl announced her presence with a piercing wail. Dr. Bressard informed Karl, Renée, and a woozy but pleased Pierre that the baby was perfect and, though extremely tired, Annette was fine.

Karl helped Renée bathe that morning and pressed her to remain in bed, but she was adamant about seeing the new baby.

She poked her head into Annette's room and caught the nurse's eye.

"May I see my new niece?"

The nurse approached the door with soundless steps. "Of course."

Renée crossed to the eyelet-swathed wicker bassinette. The dark-haired baby turned her head toward Renée as if sensing her presence and opened huge violet eyes. She had smooth skin with only a hint of that reddish color of most newborns.

"She's beautiful!" she whispered to the nurse, who smiled and nodded in agreement.

Just then Annette awoke. "Renée . . ."

Renée went to the bed, leaned over, and embraced her. "I didn't want to disturb you."

Annette gasped when she saw Renée's bruised and swollen face. "What did they do to you?"

"It's nothing. I'm not hurt, really."

"Karl and Doctor Bressard won't let me see Pierre. I want my husband! He should be with me . . . and his new baby!"

Renée looked at the nurse, who gave her a warning shake of the head.

"Annette, you need your rest. You've had a very hard time with this baby." She smiled and changed the subject. "You didn't tell me her name."

"Didn't I? We thought 'Désirée' was pretty."

"It is a pretty name . . . for a pretty baby. You should be so proud, Annette. I know I am." Renée held her hand. She had liked Annette from the first time they'd met. Now that they were all living together in the same house, she'd grown to love her.

Pierre was lucky to have found someone who loved him so much. Renée knew that Annette was jealous of the time Pierre spent at work, and rightly so. It hadn't been easy on Annette or Karl, sharing themselves with Maison Dubois.

Annette's passion for Pierre superceded everything in her life. She demanded nothing from him but his time . . . something that wasn't his to give. Renée now had even more sympathy for Annette's plight. Since the war began, Annette had been battling not only Pierre's ambition but his patriotism as well.

"You need your rest, Annette. Pierre will come see you when you're stronger."

"You're right. I am tired . . ." Annette closed her eyes.

Renée smoothed a lock of hair from Annette's forehead. "We all love you dearly. Never forget that," she said, but Annette was already asleep.

Renée tiptoed out of the room. She met Karl as he was coming out of Pierre's room.

"Renée, darling, there's something I haven't told you." He paused and held her hands. "Pierre must leave France."

"What?"

"It's too dangerous for him here. Randolf could have him thrown into prison at any time. I wish he were able to make the trip tonight, but he's not well enough. There's a taxi waiting outside to take him where he can recuperate safely. Later, he'll be transported out of the country."

"My God! What's happening?" Her mind was screaming with pain. "Jean is dead, Pierre's been beaten half to death, and before he can even see his newborn child, you're taking him away?" Renée felt as if she were being sucked in by a vortex she couldn't stop. "My—my family is being split apart! Why is this happening?"

He pulled her to him. "There's something else—I'll be leaving too."

"No!" she cried, clutching his arms and looking into his eyes. "You can't . . . I won't let you. . . ." Suddenly her last illusions of security shattered.

In that fetid basement she'd known something had saved her and Pierre, but she'd been unwilling to face it. Karl had paid for her life with his own. He'd given in to Randolf's demand to join the Nazi army. Karl had found a way to protect her and his family. But at what cost? Pierre would be helping the Allies and Karl would be fighting with the Nazis. She felt incredibly helpless.

Karl held her bruised face in his hands, his clear blue eyes penetrating her. She felt tears roll down her cheeks and onto his hands.

"I love you, Karl."

It was a statement she'd made over a thousand times in her life. She told Gaston and Juliette every day that she loved them. She told Pierre and Annette she loved them and Jean too. She'd told Karl she loved him every night before they fell asleep. But at that moment, she meant it more than the sum total of all the times and all the people in her life.

She saw huge glistening tears in Karl's eyes, and though he didn't say anything, only pressed his trembling lips to hers, she *knew* he was aware of the importance of those words. For the rest of her life she would not forget that particular kiss. He held her tenderly, but the communion of emotion between them was overwhelming. Renée leaned her body into his, needing to feel the entire length of him. This time she did not want his security, she wanted *him*. As Karl held her in his arms, she thought of the time she'd wasted; the days she could never recall. She wanted only to show him how much she loved him and she prayed God would grant her the time to atone for her sins of omission.

SINS OF OMISSION

* * *

With his jaw wired shut, his ribs bandaged, and his face a mass of stitches, Pierre wondered how he could disguise himself and make it out of France. He agreed with Karl that Randolf could have a change of heart at any moment. Not only was his own life in danger, but the next time, the Nazis might decide to arrest Annette and his baby daughter. He and Karl began making plans for Pierre's escape.

In order to make the plans work, Karl enlisted Gaston's aid.

"Gaston, I just received a call from Randolf. I told him Pierre was not conscious yet. If he telephones again, I want you to say the same thing."

"I'll tell him Pierre can have no visitors."

"Yes, that's even better. We have to hold Randolf off for a few days until Pierre can make the trip."

"I haven't said anything to Annette or Juliette, as you told me."

"That's good. Annette's delivery was very hard on her. And I'm afraid Juliette might say the wrong thing at school. I don't want to put her in any more danger."

"Has Randolf told you when you have to leave?"

"At the end of the week, but only your mother knows that."

Gaston felt a huge lump in his throat. "I don't even want to think what it will be like without you."

Karl put his arm around his shoulder. "You're going to be fine and you're going to make certain your mother doesn't get too worried while I'm away."

Karl visited Pierre at the hospital. He was in a private room at the very end of the maternity ward. Only Dr. Bressard and his private nurse knew of his presence. They had gone to great lengths for Pierre's safety.

"His name is Malroix. I don't know who he is or anything about him, except that he can arrange for the Renault with the empty cavity behind the backseat," Pierre said.

"You're going by car to Toulouse?"

"The route I'm leaving to my driver."

"Who is?"

"I can't tell you that. But take this message and have the mail carrier deliver it to 385, rue Madeleine."

"And then what?"

"We wait."

Just six days after his arrest, Pierre Dubois walked unassisted out of his hospital room, down the corridor to the back stairs, and to a side exit.

He approached an older model dark blue Renault. The driver stepped out. It was Garrett Anderson, Etienne Landreaux's father-in-law. Pierre smiled.

There were many in Paris who owed Pierre favors, but none felt as indebted as Garrett Anderson. It was because of Pierre that his daughter, Mary, and Etienne were now safe in Madrid. When the order came to 385, rue Madeleine to transport Pierre out of France, Garrett insisted he be the driver. Not only did he possess two sets of false papers, but his press card wore ragged edges from usage in crossing into Vichy France. By the time the Nazis would be expecting Garrett to recross into the occupied zone from Vichy, he would be well on his way south to Bordeaux where he had arranged for himself and Pierre to be privately flown to Biarritz.

Pierre huddled into the tiny space as Garrett replaced the backseat. He hugged his arms around his broken ribs, trying to cushion himself against the car's jostling.

As they left Paris behind and headed south, Pierre thought of the baby daughter he'd seen briefly on the day of her birth while his wife slept. He closed his eyes and thought of Annette. He wanted to be with her, hold her. He wished he could have taken her with him. Annette didn't know she wouldn't see him . . . perhaps for years . . . not until the war was over. But *he* had known. He prayed she would understand one day.

By leaving his family and his country, Pierre hoped he would be better able to save them all. As he reached into his pocket for morphine, he wondered which hurt worse . . . his broken ribs, or his conscience.

Karl ignored the soldiers while he stood at the front door kissing his wife goodbye.

Juliette clung to his pant leg, staring saucer-eyed at the soldiers. "Papa, please, please don't go!"

He lifted her into his arms and kissed her. "It won't be long. I'm sure I'll have a leave very soon."

"I don't want you to go!" she wailed.

"I don't want to either."

"Karl." Renée choked back the mountainous sob in her throat.

Gaston embraced his stepfather in a vise of a hug. "I'll take care of them just as you asked."

Karl nodded. He hugged Annette. She was still in shock over Pierre's sudden departure. "He'll be back. We all will."

"It's time to go," one of the soldiers said.

Renée followed Karl down the steps. The soldiers walked in front of Renée so that she could not get close to Karl again. They hurriedly opened the car door and nudged him inside.

Suddenly, Renée panicked. She looked back at the children. Their faces were pale and they were crying. She swung around to see the soldiers getting into their jeep. Karl was watching her from the window.

"Karl!" she cried and walked alongside the car as it pulled away from the curb. "Karl! Don't leave me! Karl!"

He spun around in the seat to watch her from the rear window. He mouthed some words and even though she couldn't make them out, she felt them in her heart. She ran down the street to the corner, waving her arm over her head. She was trying to smile, but she kept hearing herself screaming his name. She waved frantically and ran another block but she couldn't keep up with the car.

"Karl, I love you!" She burst into tears as the car disappeared around the street corner. She thought she'd never been so alone in her life.

Chapter Twenty-three

"Papa! Papa!"

Silence filled the room as Juliette bolted awake from her nightmare. She was drenched with sweat and was shaking.

The door burst open, and the light went on.

"Juliette, are you all right?" Renée asked, rushing to her bed and holding her daughter in her arms.

"I had a bad dream."

"Tell me about it. Sometimes it doesn't seem so frightening when you explain it."

"It was those boys again. They called me 'pig face' and 'Medusa hair,' just like they did last week at school. Then they started throwing rocks at me. They said anybody as ugly as me should be killed!" Juliette sobbed and covered her face with her hands.

"Oh, Juliette! How awful!"

"It's true, Maman. I'll never be beautiful."

"*I* think you're beautiful. Even more importantly, you're beautiful on the inside, chérie. You're caring, thoughtful, generous. Those are the parts about you that are the most beautiful."

"I want to be really beautiful by the time Papa comes home."

"He already thinks you're a very pretty girl. And so do I.

Someday those boys will be asking you to parties. You'll see. I love you, Juliette."

"I love you too. I just wish Papa were home."

"Me too. But the war will be over very, very soon. Pierre is already home from London, Paris was liberated way back in August. Pierre says it could be as soon as a month until it's all over."

"Oh, Maman, I hope it's true. I want to see my papa."

Karl Heilmann dodged Allied bullets and sprinted for the foxhole. He dove for cover as a hand grenade exploded in the place where his feet had just been. His lips were caked with frozen dirt and tiny icicles hung from his blond beard. He rolled onto his stomach, hunched over, and covered his head with his arms as bullets from rifles and machine guns fell like rain. He shook more from the cold than he did from fear. Almost three years of battle had numbed his emotions. Slowly, he raised himself on elbows and peered around the foxhole. The inhabitants were dead. His blue eyes were war-weary, but they contained hope.

Karl had lived through the worst days in Stalingrad thinking that the war could not get any worse. Fortunately for him, he'd been transferred to Holland before being captured.

For the past six months, ever since the Allies had landed in Normandy, the Nazis had been on the run and he along with them. They were calling this battle in Belgium's Ardennes Forest Germany's last stand and Karl couldn't agree more, for this, like Hitler's fiasco at Stalingrad, was the biggest and most confused battle of the war.

Mortar shells pounded the earth around him and the air filled with bullets. Dirt, ice, and clumps of snow showered the foxhole. Karl reloaded his machine gun with stiff, frost-bitten fingers. He raised his head enough to see a wave of soldiers bearing down on him. He started firing and hit two men. He wondered why the men in his platoon were not returning fire. He couldn't see far enough to the next foxhole to discover that the German soldiers there were dead, just like his companions.

Karl kept firing, trying not to think about the men he'd killed in a war he didn't want, for a cause he despised. He couldn't feel his fingers any longer as he squeezed off another volley of shots.

The machine gun rammed itself against his bruised shoulder like an air hammer. He was certain his collarbone was permanently damaged.

The Americans were shouting their now-familiar war whoop as they dodged around trees and jumped over fallen logs. Their pace was steady and they gained a great deal of ground as they advanced toward him. Karl continued firing but his mind was not on killing or dying.

He thought about his house on the Ile St.-Louis and imagined his children's laughter as they shared dinner every night. He envisioned his wife's face. He remembered how she looked that Christmas Eve when he'd given her the amethyst earrings. He'd been right about her from the moment they met; she was the kind of woman that would haunt a man from beyond the grave. He fired his gun again and killed another American.

Karl knew Randolf was responsible for his lack of leaves over the past two years. Twice Karl had protested to his superiors, only to be reprimanded and then denied leave for another six months. Each time he thought a trip home was a real possibility, something always happened that prevented him from seeing his family. Through Randolf's directives from Berlin, Karl was made aware of his brother's clout with the Führer.

Karl's anger had grown over the months and years until he decided to risk the four-month prison stint and went AWOL. He'd gotten as far as Reims before they caught him. If only he hadn't been so tired and had not stopped at the hotel in town. If only he'd stayed to the outskirts, but French farmers were not sympathetic to Nazi enlisted men who needed a soft mound of hay to sleep on. It was a serious mistake, and to this day he couldn't believe he'd made it. He guessed he must have been crazy to do such a thing. The four months in jail had been reduced to two . . . he was needed at the front.

Karl thought of all the things he wanted to do. He'd promised Gaston he would teach him to drive, and there were those skiing trips they wanted to take to the Alps, just the two of them. And Juliette—he adored her and spoiled her too much, but that's what fathers were for. He hoped she would grow up to be like Renée.

He was glad he'd written to Renée last night telling her all these things that were on his mind. He wondered if she ever received his letters. Not many of hers had found their way to him, but when they had, he reread them until the pages were torn and the ink nearly rubbed off.

Karl peeked over the edge of the foxhole and leveled his gun. Suddenly, he felt a presence behind him, and just as he turned to investigate, a barrage of American bullets whizzed through the air. The first bullet hit Karl in the shoulder and he instantly dropped his gun. As his hand shot up to cover the wound another bullet entered the side of his neck, another sank into his chest and spun him around. Two more bullets hit him in the back. Stunned by the impact of the bullets, Karl's body was thrown against the other side of the foxhole.

Paralyzed, Karl could not feel the pain as he stared into the bullet-riddled air above him. He felt a rising hot bubble in his throat. He began choking and gasping for air. He felt the earth shake around him as hundreds of army boots thundered over the ground. The Americans were taking the hill, just as he had known they would. He continued staring above him, watching the Americans trample over him, leaving him for dead.

He didn't want it to end like this, but he could do nothing to save himself. Then an American soldier with a red cross on an armband jumped into his foxhole. He looked at Karl for only a second and withdrew a long sharp knife.

Karl saw the blade as it came toward him. He knew he was dying and he had no remorse over the fact that this man was going to make death come sooner for him.

Karl didn't close his eyes as the American slit his throat. He felt no pain at all. Karl stopped breathing and the light began to fade . . . slowly. The last thing he saw was the American smiling at him.

Chapter Twenty-four

Since the age of six, Henri Ruille had been touted by his teachers at L'Ecole St.-Martin as a genius in mathematics. He excelled in all his classes, and though he was better than passably capable in sports, he was not interested in playing games except to keep physically fit. To Henri, a healthy body was important, for he wanted to live a long and productive life. Henri socialized only to the point where it was necessary to enhance his standing in the business world. There were many Parisian hostesses that welcomed his presence at the small gatherings they had during the war, for Henri was a good conversationalist and he was charming when he wanted to be.

Throughout the war Henri spent long hours tracking every piece of military, political, and international news he could get his hands on. He did not tell his grandmother or his reclusive mother about the radio receiver he had stored above the carriage house. When asked to explain his many trips to the garage, he answered that he was teaching himself the mechanical workings of a piston engine.

Henri was watching his grandmother's investments. Already he was plotting locations for branches of the bank. His first target would be Egypt. His research proved that outside the United States, crude oil was most likely to be found in the Middle

Eastern countries. He was particularly interested in the enormous development in Saudi Arabia by an American company, California Arabian Standard Oil, which in 1933 had been given the concession by King Ibn Saud. That the king was an acquaintance of his grandmother was all the more reason for a branch at Riyadh, the capital.

On Henri's sixteenth birthday, his grandmother handed him a formal document stating that when the war was over he was to become vice-president of Crédit de Paris.

Henri was fully aware of his attributes and talents and of his limitations, which were few, and unlike other young men of his age, Henri knew exactly what he wanted out of life. He shared his grandmother's hope to one day expand Crédit de Paris to every continent on the globe.

Raindrops struck a tinny chorus as they pelted the leaded-glass windows of the château the night the Ruilles gathered to celebrate the Allied victory. Two baroque crystal chandeliers with a circumference of over six feet blazed brightly over the elaborately set dining table.

Virginie sat at the head with Emile at the opposite end. Everyone knew it was her only deference to his position in the family, for Emile had no power. To Virginie's left was Lucienne, and to her right was Henri and his mother, Lady Jane.

For Henri it was a special night, but the faces around him were hardly festive, save for the sparkle of pride in his grandmother's eyes. She, as always, believed in him.

Lucienne was desperately trying to conceal the fact that she was drunk. Since the day Antoine had been arrested over three years ago, this had been a perpetual condition for Lucienne. Henri wished there was something he could say or do to comfort her. She had grieved terribly over the loss of the man she loved. To him, Lucienne and Antoine had been the "perfect couple." Before the war, they had been the most carefree and happy people he'd known. Antoine was forever bringing Lucienne flowers or perfume. When they remained at the château over the weekends, they would disappear into the cabana by the pool or up to their rooms to make love.

Once, when Henri mentioned to Virginie that he would like to have a happy marriage like theirs, his grandmother had stunned him by saying: "Take my advice and never involve yourself with matters of the heart. Your surest way to financial ruin is through diversion. Love diverts the energy you need to build your future. Romance is not for you, Henri. You are far too intelligent to be caught in that trap. Besides, Lucienne's marriage is not all that it seems."

Henri never understood what Virginie had meant until the Nazis had come and then he knew of Lucienne's arguments with Antoine. The Occupation caused many relationships to be strained and so he saw nothing unusual in their behavior.

"I hope to God we can have some decent meals in this house again." Emile harumphed as he mounded sauce over everything on his plate.

Despite the hardships of the war, Emile's girth seemed to have doubled. Emile told everyone it was "middle age." Henri knew Emile had food hidden in his rooms that he never told anyone about.

"That's all you think about," Lucienne snarled at him.

"That's enough, Lucienne!" Virginie stopped her. "Emile is right, in a way. Things are changing . . . and rapidly now that the war is over."

"Rapidly?" Emile suddenly forgot about his meal. "What is that supposed to mean?"

"Next week I will be opening Crédit de Paris again. I told Henri that when the war is over, he would head the bank for me. I'm making good my promise."

Sputtering, Emile said, "You can't be serious! He's just a boy! Not even twenty yet! He can't handle responsibility like that!"

Lucienne was smug. "Forget it, Emile. You can't win and you know it. Let it go."

"Never!" He stood, pushing the chair far behind him to make room for his enormous belly.

For the first time, Lady Jane stopped picking at her food and uncharacteristically broke into the conversation. "Don't make a scene, Emile."

Henri cringed. He hated the sound of her voice. For years she'd never paid attention to him, to Virginie, or to anything other than the dime novels she read voraciously. He wondered why his father ever married her.

"Shut up, Jane. This is none of your concern."

Surprised at Jane's comment, Virginie said: "Jane's right. You're ruining my celebration. Sit down, Emile."

Angrily, he picked up his napkin from the chair and sat once again. Still staring at Virginie, he finally backed down completely and went back to his meal.

"There will be a great deal of rebuilding all over Europe and Crédit de Paris will finance much of it," Virginie went on. "Henri will be in charge of these loans and our expansion into new cities."

Emile's hatred smoldered. His hand was trembling as he laid his fork down. A malicious smile wavered on his lips as he spoke.

"Yesterday when I went into Paris, I noticed that Maison Dubois was being reopened. They were installing new windows. I know we financed Dior's opening. At what rate did we lend money to Renée Dubois?"

Henri braced himself and he flashed Emile a chilling look. Not since they'd received the call from Berlin that Antoine had been executed, had anyone mentioned Renée Dubois's name in the Ruille household. Virginie blamed Renée for Antoine's death. From his grandmother's explanation of the facts, Henri had no reason to doubt her.

Virginie had gone to the underground, which Renée and her brother, Pierre, were involved with, to plead for Antoine's freedom, and the Duboises had refused Virginie's messenger. Henri thought he'd never heard anything so cold-blooded in his life.

Once he'd gone to Lucienne to talk to her about it, saying he blamed the Duboises for Antoine's death.

"Don't believe everything you hear, Henri," she had told him. "Nothing in this house is as it seems. Not me, and especially not your grandmother. I don't want you to mention Antoine's name around me again. I hear it enough in my sleep." She poured a drink and downed it. She was still stone sober. "You've aligned yourself with Mother. You've got your angles all figured, haven't you?"

"Angles?"

"Everyone in this house needs one to survive. I haven't figured mine out yet, but I will."

Now, as Henri looked from Emile to Lucienne to his mother and back to Virginie, he was only beginning to comprehend Lucienne's statement of years past. He wondered if her "angle" was her drinking. She'd always impressed him as more wily than that. It was obvious he would have Emile to contend with in the upcoming months. He wondered what Emile's "angle" would be.

Virginie kept her composure, something that always fascinated Henri and infuriated Emile.

"No, Emile, I did not lend Maison Dubois money, though they have been everywhere seeking immediate funds. They must have acquired the loan elsewhere."

Not getting the response he wanted, Emile tired of his game. "Unless you have further announcements for us, I have an appointment this evening. It's obvious you don't need me—for anything."

"You're excused, Emile," Virginie said to her child.

Henri watched as he lumbered out of the room. Virginie was not frightened of Emile or Renée Dubois. She was a competent and intelligent woman and Henri admired her more every day. She could handle any situation and any person. She had placed tremendous faith in him with this new position. He hoped in the years to come, he could prove himself worthy.

Book Four

The Fifties

Chapter Twenty-five

1950–1954

Renée placed a cool cloth on her pounding forehead and eased herself onto the mountain of bed pillows. "Calm," she mumbled, hoping her tension would ease and the headache would vanish. She reached over to the nightstand and adjusted the oscillating fan. The breeze felt heavenly. Slowly, she opened her eyes and looked out the skylight above. Fat, billowy clouds raced across the sky. A storm was brewing, she thought as she noticed a gray tinge to the edges of the clouds. Paris could use the rain. For thirty-three days there had been no respite from the heat and drought. She hoped it poured for days, then she could stay right here in this apartment. She wouldn't have to go back to Maison Dubois. She would be where she wanted to be—alone with her thoughts.

She felt weary and old these days. It was a new decade. The postwar period was over, but somehow she felt as if she'd merely passed through those days in a trance.

She remembered how Karl's death had plunged her into deep depression. For two months after the funeral, she felt as if she were sinking in a quagmire. Renée cried silent tears for days as her guilt over Juliette's birth whipped at her heart. She should have had another baby—Karl's baby. But she'd been too busy, too selfish. She spent too many hours at Maison Dubois and too little time with Karl and the children. She should have done a thousand things more for him. Most of all, she should have loved him more.

The days passed as Dr. Bressard gave her pills for her depression, pills for headache, and chalky liquids for stomach pains. But she knew it was only grief and guilt. She refused to see friends who came to call. She shut herself in her room and thought of the terrible wife she'd been. Eventually, she shut out Gaston and Juliette. She was unaware of what she was doing, only that she was in pain.

One day Juliette found her sitting in the chaise in her room, staring at the wall, idly twisting her wedding band on her finger.

"Maman, won't you come to dinner?"

"I'm not hungry."

"But I made it myself." Juliette knelt by her mother's side. Her deep blue eyes were filled with fear and loneliness. What she saw in her mother's eyes—the lack of hope, the loss of will, frightened Juliette more than anything in her young life.

"I can't eat."

"I made apple fritters." She forced a smile, but Renée continued to stare at her ring. Suddenly, Juliette's fear turned to anger. How dare her mother suffer more than she? Her father was gone and she needed her mother now more than ever. What made her mother so privileged that she was allowed to give up when Juliette would have to go on—perhaps without her. Juliette's eyes burned. She clutched the side of the chaise with an angry grip. Juliette wasn't going to pamper her mother anymore. She was sick of everyone tiptoeing past Renée's door. She hated giving excuses to friends and coworkers who called. It was wrong and what her mother was doing to herself was wrong.

"When, Maman? When will you try the fritters?"

"I don't know."

"Well, I do!" Juliette bolted from the room. In seconds she returned with the apple fritters. She tore off a piece and shoved it up to Renée's face.

"Smell it, Maman! Taste it! I made it for you!" Juliette forced the crumbling fritter into Renée's mouth.

"Stop it! Juliette, stop, go away! Leave me alone!" Renée pushed at her, but Juliette kept shoving the food into her face till it smeared on her lips.

"No! You want to die like Papa and I won't let you. I need you." Juliette sobbed and put her hands over her face.

Renée looked at her daughter. The veil that had covered her eyes for weeks lifted. Renée put her hand on Juliette's head, feeling the unruly curls. "Juliette, don't cry, my baby. Come here, let me hold you. Shhhh. . . ."

Juliette crawled into Renée's arms. They were both crying now.

"I get so lonely without Papa. But it's even worse when you won't talk to me. *You* always know what to do. I don't."

"I'm sorry, my baby. So, so sorry. I didn't know. I'd forgotten all the things I should be thankful for. Especially you, God, especially you."

A slow rumble of thunder filled the room. Renée could see flashes of lightning in the distance. The temperature in the room was dropping. She switched off the fan.

Renée was immersed in the past. She hoped she could find the answer to why she felt so weary these days. Nothing was fun anymore, not even the business. She remembered, after the armistice, how she and Pierre recovered Jean's paintings, now worth in excess of three-quarters of a million dollars. She recalled, too, the secret they had discovered in Jean's metal box, hidden in his apartment. Within it had been a letter from Dr. de Lemare, Emile Ruille's psychiatrist, and it had been Jean's legacy to the Duboises. To this day, Renée had the letter hidden away, ammunition she might someday need to use against her lifelong adversary.

Renée had never used the floor safe Karl had installed in their home, but she stored the psychiatrist's report in it. She remembered how it had taken over an hour of routing around in Karl's desk drawer to find the leather notebook where he'd written the combination. He'd told her once that if she ever needed the safe, he'd listed the combination as the international telephone number of his good friend Harold Stearns, who had been "Peter Pickum" for the Paris edition of *The Chicago Tribune*.

When Renée unlocked the safe, she had found a few notes she'd written to Karl in the early years of their marriage, a newspaper clipping about their wedding, an announcement of Juliette's birth, and an odd key with a tag attached. She placed the psychiatrist's report in the safe but she kept the key.

For two days she pondered the origin of the key, musing over the numbers on the tag—CZ 78654. Finally, she had mentioned it to Pierre.

"Let me see it," he had said. "This looks exactly like the key to my safe-deposit box. The CZ stands for Crédit Zurich."

Renée made the proper inquiries, and two weeks later, she booked passage for herself and Pierre on a train bound for Zurich.

With the necessary identification papers she had no trouble in gaining access to the box. Renée thought she would never forget the moment when she counted cash, securities, bank accounts, and gold coins amounting to over two million francs.

The money had been a miracle. Virginie's influence had been used to stop all banks but hers from giving Renée the credit she needed to reopen Maison Dubois after the war, and Renée had, above all, not wanted to go to her enemy. With Karl's windfall, she did not have to.

Renée found one crisis after another those first months at Maison Dubois. They were terribly understaffed and qualified people were hard to find. Renée had wanted Gaston to go on to college, but once he'd graduated from high school, she needed him at Maison Dubois.

He spent his days coordinating lines, selecting fabrics, and managing the growing design staff. His energy was limitless and he reminded her of Jean.

It was Gaston's idea, coupled with Pierre's persuasion, that convinced her to branch out to Milan, Rome, and of course, London. She had made several trips to London once the war ended. Seeing Céleste and Herbert still alive and well was worth her first frantic trip in 1945. The linen-company facilities had been damaged somewhat, but with Herbert's connections they were able to make speedy repairs. Just as easily as they had converted to wartime production, they slipped back to peacetime linens.

Thinking of Gaston as a grown man was difficult for Renée, if not impossible. And yet, she relied on his fashion intuition as much as her own. Renée recalled the day he burst into her office, his eyes crackling with excitement.

"I think I've finally got the ad campaign for the linen company right. You want to hear my idea?"

Renée smiled, dropped her pen, and leaned back. "Of course!"

Eagerly, he pulled out a mock poster ad he'd drawn showing a military uniform slung hastily over a chair and their signature linens on a turned-down bed.

Renée peered over it for long moments as Gaston waited. It was quietly seductive while making the clear statement that the war was over and D & S linens was back in business.

"I love it! Send it to Céleste and run it."

Gaston wanted to jump he was so excited, but he only beamed appreciatively at his mother—his critic—and then rushed out of the office to launch his idea.

In the first six months of the advertising campaign, the linen orders jumped seventy percent. Another coup for Gaston was his insistence on a line of low-cost linens. Since the postwar world seemed to have abandoned luxury in favor of practicality, few people were willing to pay fifty pounds and over for a set of sheets. Again, his idea resulted in profits.

By 1950, he inserted scented cards in magazine ads that made the entire magazine smell like "Noir." He mailed samples to every customer Maison Dubois had ever serviced. In early 1951, Gaston urged Renée to expand to a cosmetics line. The front counters in Maison Dubois now offered makeup, cleansing programs, and a licensed cosmetician to demonstrate how no one could live another day without Dubois Cosmetics.

The profits were quickly plowed into another shop located in Monte Carlo. Gaston had pressed for New York, but Renée refused. Since the eligible Prince Rainier was attracting wealthy, beautiful women from all over the globe, Renée wanted to utilize the prince's wife hunt as an impetus to sell clothes.

Once the shop opened, Renée was a guest of the prince. Prince Rainier was only one of the many famous men to become her escort during those postwar years when she tried to fill the void Karl's death had made in her life. Europe was overrun with exciting men. Cary Grant, Laurence Olivier, and the Russian nobleman turned designer, Oleg Cassini, were at one time or another linked romantically with Renée by the press. But Renée's heart belonged to the past.

Once she and the Aly Khan were in Cartier's, looking for an appropriate gift for one of his lady friends, when Virginie Ruille entered. It had been the first time Renée had seen her in many years. . . .

Dressed in a Dior cashmere suit with alligator shoes and bags, Virginie Ruille looked to be in her forties rather than the sixty-two she was. Gossip stated she'd recently been to Zurich for cosmetic surgery, but Renée doubted it. Virginie had always taken supreme care of herself, and during the war she had not deprived herself of any luxuries as the rest of Paris had.

Renée had heard that European political leaders consulted Virginie first when they began formulating postwar economic programs. Virginie's advice had been sound and solid. She had received honorary awards and commendations from the most influential minds in Europe and America. Politicians, Renée discovered, blithely overlooked Virginie's collaborative acts with the Germans.

Virginie stood in the doorway, her eyes riveted on Renée. It took every ounce of control to keep her venom choked down as she stared at the whore who had murdered her son and killed Antoine. She placed a placid smile on her lips so as not to draw Renée's suspicion. Virginie thought if her jaw tensed any more, her teeth would crack.

She hated Renée and lived for the day of her downfall. And it would come too. All in good time.

The smile on Virginie's lips grew and there was a flash in her eyes.

The manager saw it as he looked from one woman to the other.

Renée felt as if time had stood still. Suddenly she was not the powerful woman she had become. She was once again the girl from Lyon facing Edouard's mother. It was 1925 and she could hear Virginie calling her a "slut" and Gaston a "bastard." They were words she hadn't thought of for over a decade. Renée realized that nothing had changed between them. If anything, the tension was more strained. Suddenly, she felt fearful and immensely protective of her children. She wanted to run home and see that Juliette and Gaston were safe. Then she chided herself. Virginie didn't have supernatural powers. She was only a woman—despite her vast power.

The manager rushed up to Virginie. She was, after all, an older customer. "Madame Ruille, how lovely you look today! Come with me, I'm anxious to show you the necklace we discussed. . . ."

Renée watched as Virginie followed the manager to a private room. Just as Virginie entered the office, she turned again and shot Renée a deadly look.

Renée realized with a pang that the war between her and Virginie would never end. . . .

Renée looked out at the raging storm. She remembered being terrified of the thunder when she was a child. Thinking of Virginie, she remembered a time when she was afraid of her too. These days she was afraid of feeling too little. It was difficult to remember the passions she had known when she first came to Paris. That ambition, the energy for the business, the revenge she'd wanted against Virginie. Most of all, as she peered about the bedroom, she could barely remember the excitement she'd known in Grant's arms.

In the past eighteen months, she'd found herself thinking more about him than ever. She'd caught herself speaking his name aloud in the middle of a conversation. She daydreamed about him when her mind should be on business. She purposely asked friends for news of him and she clipped stories about him out of the newspapers.

In the past three years, Grant's fame had grown like an atomic cloud and with nearly as big an explosion.

For years, he'd been well respected in the United States, but unless someone was actively interested in the motion-picture industry, Grant Morgan was only a name on a list of credits at the end of a film.

Now half the magazines and newspapers ran stories on him. *Time* had run his picture on the cover in 1950, *Paris Match* did an exclusive in 1949, the London *Times*, the *Berlin News* and the *Madrid Express* had recently run interviews that included pictorials.

For twenty years, Grant Morgan's method of producing a movie had gone unrecognized by the big studios. Now that the "star system" was dying and actors were going free-lance and top money-making movies were being filmed more on location than on a studio sound stage, Grant Morgan was being touted as the "Movie Mogul with Magic."

Cécile, as expected of her dearest friend, had always kept Renée well informed about Grant. Last year on Cécile's buying trip to Maison Dubois, they had lunch at Maxim's, and Cécile told her that Grant's marriage was on the rocks.

"Cécile, I didn't ask."

"I saved you the trouble," she said. "Darma spent the majority of the war going from one sanatorium to another. Grant's public relations staff has successfully killed most of their public arguments and her outrageous antics."

"Ah! So that's why I never read about them."

"I never believe half the gossip I hear, but once I saw it for myself."

Cécile told Renée how she and Alvin had been guests of Carole and Tom Baker at the St. Regis to celebrate Tom's birthday. Among the twelve other couples were Darma and Grant Morgan, who were in town at Darma's request. She'd demanded a new fall wardrobe—though she had already purchased one the month before—and she insisted Grant fly her to New York that week.

Tom Baker, a wealthy entrepreneur, had instructed the maître d' to "keep the Dom flowing."

Darma, seated at the opposite end of the table from her husband, put an end to her eight-month-long dry spell and imbibed all too willingly of the expensive champagne. Before the entrée was served, she was making a spectacle of herself on the dance floor.

She began pulling on the swathe of gold silk that encircled her breasts, ran over her shoulder and cascaded in a shimmering river down her back. In minutes she was standing bare-breasted in the middle of the dance floor, and then started ripping away at the gold scalloped hem.

Renée couldn't help but pity Darma; she was a sick woman. It was even harder for her to imagine Grant, dynamic, vibrant Grant, caring for his disturbed wife.

How fate had contorted their lives, she thought.

Perhaps it was this lack of control that bothered her the most. Just when she believed things would go the way *she* wanted, fate always entered and twisted her future. She seemed forever at a crossroads.

For months Renée had sensed herself at another of those "crisis" turns. Perhaps that was why she appeared apathetic about everything. Her sixth sense was warning her that something was about to happen. But what?

She knew the answer to her question but refused to face it. It was easier to live in the past and deny the present. Both her children were grown. It was easier to think of them as children, needing her. But the truth was they were both anxious to make their own way. Gaston pressured her for the New York branch, hoping he would go to America and run it. He was exerting his personality and talents, and he believed Renée was holding him back.

She believed in him, maybe even more than he did himself, but she couldn't bear to let him go. Life would be too empty without him.

Juliette was only seventeen, but she, too, wanted more in her life besides school. Neither of her children were satisfied with what Renée wanted for them: an easier life than she'd had.

Renée rolled over on the pillow. She realized she'd been fooling herself. She was just as afraid now as she'd ever been of thunderstorms or Virginie. This time, she feared the future—the thief that would steal her children.

Chapter Twenty-six

Christian Dior slapped the postwar couture world awake when he dropped hemlines from above the knee to midcalf in one season. The "New Look" with its long, pencil-slim skirts, nipped-in waists, and stiffly interfaced jackets did more to set back the liberation of the female body than Worth's triple-hooped skirts of the 1840's.

At Maison Dubois the orders for waist cinchers, girdles, padded brassieres, and detachable shoulder pads quadrupled in the first month of Dior's showing. Four years later, Dior was still the leading fashion dictator.

Renée sat in her office with Pierre going over the accounting figures.

"It's a good thing our undergarments are doing so well," he said facetiously. "Our spring showing was a disaster. I told you it was too big a risk to allow Gaston to design the whole line."

Renée exasperatedly tossed her pen on the desk. "And you've certainly made your views clear to me every chance you could!"

"It was a bad move."

"I still think Gaston's designs are the coming trend. They're more casual, body skimming—not body remolding—and they're more comfortable. You're forgetting what made Chanel famous. Gaston's just ahead of his time."

"Maybe your crystal ball has slipped this time. After all, you aren't exactly dispassionate on the subject of your son's skills. I want him replaced."

"You're being too harsh," Renée said.

"Look at the figures, Renée," Pierre bellowed. "Our payroll alone must include half of Paris! It's my job to keep this enterprise afloat. If our sales don't pick up, we'll have to shut down. We can't sell what the public doesn't want."

"You're exaggerating again." She sighed, but she knew he was right. Their showrooms had been empty for months.

Pierre pressed the intercom button. "Marie, have Gaston come to Renée's office."

Renée looked at him. Again, her decisions were being made for her. She didn't want to replace Gaston, but the business demanded it. Had the designer been anyone but Gaston, she would have done this weeks ago. She felt a rumble in her stomach as she looked through the glass partition in the door and saw Gaston come in.

God! She would never get used to seeing him so grown. At nearly twenty-five he was excruciatingly handsome. She knew he had all the models in a dither whenever he walked into the room, but he kept his affairs discreet. He never dated any one girl for more than a month. In that respect he was much like her. His passion for success was greater than his sexual desires. Or perhaps, she hoped, he just hadn't met the right girl yet.

Pierre's face was stern. "Sit down, Gaston."

Immediately, Gaston's relaxed demeanor became defensive as he looked at the strained expression on his mother's face.

"Why do I get the impression I'm facing a firing squad?"

Pierre forced a chuckle. "It's not all that bad. However, your mother and I have been going over the books. . . ."

"Are we going to have this discussion again?" Gaston jumped to his feet.

"Gaston, please . . ." Renée pleaded. She hated acting as the intermediary between Pierre and Gaston.

"So, we didn't get the orders we had thought. So we got a couple of bad reviews."

"You call every major magazine from *Women's Wear Daily* to British *Vogue* to *Bazaar* to *Elle*, 'a couple of bad reviews'? We're the laughingstock of Europe!" Pierre shouted.

"I still believe women are ready for a change," Gaston retorted.

"You can't tell from our showrooms!"

Renée wanted to help defend Gaston but couldn't. Everything Pierre said was the truth. Pierre turned to her, and when he did, Gaston's eyes followed.

Renée gulped as she began to speak. She was about to ring the death knell for her son's designing talent. Ironically, it was the single most important thing in his life she had always encouraged.

"I have to replace you, Gaston."

"What?"

"I've hired Geneviève as head designer. I stole her from Dior with the explicit idea of utilizing his training against him. While Dior is calling the shots, I feel we have no other choice."

"I can't believe you're doing this, Mother."

"It's just for a while, Gaston," she pleaded.

Gaston was in shock. The word "replace" boomed through his brain. How could she do this to him? He'd always believed her when she'd told him his designs were good. She'd been there all through the designing and production. He couldn't have been wrong. His mother *believed* in his clothing, in him.

He'd read the reviews and he also knew his uncle was right. They didn't have the sales. His mother had to fight for Maison Dubois and he had to fight for himself.

"Okay. The sales are down. Let's bring them up," Gaston said. "I know we've had this discussion before, but can't you see the time has come for ready-to-wear?"

"Here we go again on this mass-market crap," Pierre said.

"Gaston, you know how Pierre and I feel about this," Renée said.

"Mother, times have changed. This isn't 1925 anymore. We have to move into the future. The newest movement is into ready-to-wear. Haute couture is archaic."

Renée was instantly on her feet. "Damn it, Gaston. I will not argue this anymore. If we moved into ready-to-wear, I would be denying everything I've spent my entire life to build. Do you have any idea what it was like to battle the great houses of Paris all those years? To take their ridicule? I know you've been upset by the reviews you got this fall, but they are nothing to what I was up against. Your ideologies and mine seem to move further away from each other every day."

"Yes, they do." Gaston sighed.

"Why is it so tough for you to understand my position?"

"Why can't you understand mine?" he countered.

Gaston looked at his mother. He loved her—but she had become the foe.

"I guess that's it then. I certainly don't see any alternative."

"What do you mean?" Renée asked, sensing something ominous in his tone.

"You want a new designer. I want to open a shop in New York . . . so I'll go there and do it myself. I'll make and sell my own clothes."

Renée was speechless. This was what she had feared all along. She had felt it coming for months. Suddenly she felt abandoned and terrified.

"You're leaving me?"

"Mother, don't say it like that."

"That's what you're doing!" she shouted. She had to stop him. She had to keep him in Paris. "This is foolish talk, Gaston. How do you propose to pay for all this? A shop takes money."

"You did it."

"That was a long time ago. Times have changed."

"I know."

"Gaston, think how ridiculous this sounds! You're just letting your emotions run away with you. I know you're upset about being replaced, but don't be so hasty."

"Hasty? Mother, I can't stay here anymore. I'm not needed here."

"But, Gaston, this is insane!"

"I have to go."

"What about me? *I* need you!"

"Only to be your little boy, Mother. I can't do that anymore, either," he said sadly.

Quickly, before he let his mother see the mist in his eyes, he turned away from her. He didn't want to hurt her. He'd never wanted that. He just wanted to leave.

Chapter Twenty-seven

"Your mother is going to kill you, Juliette Heilmann!" Annette was wild-eyed as she stared at the Helena Rubenstein ad featuring her niece as the model. "You might have gotten away with it if it had only been this one magazine, but they ran this ad in *Elle*, French *Vogue*, and *Feminina!*"

Juliette was all smiles and showed not the first sign of regret.

"Renée thinks you're much too young for this and you know it. She wants you to be going to parties and having fun. Not working like she did."

"I want to work. I love modeling more than anything I've done." Juliette looked at the photograph. "I hope Maman doesn't get too upset."

"Well, I would if I were her. You went behind her back—I'm mad at you myself."

"You used to side with me."

"You used to be two years old."

"You sound like Maman when you say that."

"I should. I am a mother, you know."

While Annette and Juliette continued their conversation, eight-year-old Désirée stealthily latched onto the copy of French *Vogue* and inspected every inch of the photograph. She was fascinated with anything and everything concerning her aunt Renée and cousin Juliette. She looked up at Juliette, dressed in a pair of toreador pants and a dolman-sleeved cyclamen sweater, her glorious golden hair framing a subtly made-up face in delicate peach tones and wondered what it was like to be so beautiful.

Désirée took the magazine and slipped away to the hall mirror.

Désirée's hair was dark chestnut like her aunt Renée and her thickly lashed violet eyes shone in the electric light. Often when she went to Maison Dubois with her mother, beautifully dressed women would place their expensively ringed hands on her head and comment that she was a carbon copy of her aunt Renée. Désirée would smile widely, knowing that her aunt had often been called the most beautiful woman in Paris.

But as Désirée looked at the photograph of Juliette, there was something else here, some elusive quality she could not name that existed only within the confines of the photograph.

Juliette was beautiful, but in the magazine, she was more—she was ethereal . . . like the fairy princesses in her storybooks.

Désirée scampered back to the kitchen and sheepishly handed the magazine back to Juliette.

"I guess I'd better be going," Juliette said.

"We'll see you Saturday at the de Vilandry ball." Annette kissed Juliette as she closed the front door behind her.

"Désirée, where are you?"

"In the dining room, Maman."

Annette walked in to see the table already set. There were paper hats and tiny place cards that Désirée had made herself. The flowers had arrived earlier from the florist and Désirée had placed them in the center of the table.

"Are we using the Haviland or the Sèvres tonight?" Désirée asked, eyes dancing.

"The Sèvres is prettier, don't you think?"

"And Papa likes it the best." Désirée quickly went to the glassed-in china cabinet and took out the plates. "Do you think we'll surprise him this year?"

"I think this time we will. Pierre has been so engrossed in the acquisition of the boutiques in Spain that the last thing he's thought about is his birthday."

"How could he forget his birthday?"

Annette turned away so that Désirée could not see the pain in her eyes. How many times had Pierre put business before her?

Before Désirée? How many parties had she attended by herself, or gone to only to have him arrive hours late. When they'd first married they lived an idyll for six months, but then Maison Dubois demanded more and more of Pierre. During the war, many wives had found an abundance of time with their husbands as industry shut down. But Annette was forced to share Pierre with an entire country. For over three years she hadn't seen him at all. When he'd returned home, Maison Dubois stole him again. Annette felt there were only crumbs left for her now.

So many times she thought of giving up, of leaving him. But her passion for him was overwhelming. If she were smart, she would learn to prepare herself for disappointments. But she would always be the fool for Pierre. She would always hope for a time when she came first with him.

Annette and Désirée spent the afternoon baking a chocolate cake for Pierre. Désirée hung streamers and colored a birthday sign to hang in the foyer. They both donned their prettiest dresses.

To be safe, Annette telephoned Pierre's office.

"And you'll be home at six?"

"That's what I said," he replied, but she could tell his mind was elsewhere.

"Promise you won't be late?"

"Yes."

"I love you, Pierre."

"I love you too."

Désirée's eyes were filled with anticipation as she watched out the front window. She checked the clock. It was quarter past six. "Maman, do you think he'll like the cologne I bought?"

"Of course he will, chérie. It's from you, isn't it?"

Désirée smiled. "I want this to be his best birthday ever!"

"It will," Annette said, glancing at the empty street. There was no sign of Pierre's Fiat.

Annette went back to the kitchen to check the roast the cook had left in the oven. Annette wondered if she'd ever get the hang of cooking. After all, how difficult could it be? You read a recipe and do it. But time after time, she burned the chicken, her gelatin salads melted before they hit the table, and her roux was always lumpy. When it came to domestics, Annette was out of her league.

She remembered when they first moved into this house. She had wanted Pierre to be proud of her and had insisted she do the decorating herself. Pierre and Renée both suggested a professional designer. Annette had refused.

For months she combed the furniture stores. She had wanted everything modern. Hardoy chairs, kidney-shaped glass coffee tables, S-shaped lounges. She'd chosen rust and olive green, the favorite combination of all the decorators. For the baths and kitchen she'd chosen turquoise and pink. It should have been fabulous. Instead, it was a disaster.

Annette thought she'd never forget the look on Pierre's face when he'd seen the finished product the day before they moved in.

"It's not what I expected," he said, his face growing paler from room to room.

As Annette looked at the house from his eyes, she had to admit the green was bilious and the pink looked dirty. None of it blended.

"Oh, Pierre! It's just awful, isn't it?" She sobbed.

He took her in his arms. "I know how hard you worked and I appreciate what you did . . ."

"You were right. I can't do anything right!"

"I never said that! I just wanted you to get some help. I can think of a lot of things you do right."

"Name one," she said, her eyes bursting with tears.

He kissed her deeply. Slowly, they sank to the thick wool carpeting. As always, her need for him overpowered her. In minutes she had stripped him of his suit and he'd tossed her silk dress over the turquoise "womb chair." They made love for the rest of the afternoon. Annette's decorating blunder had unwittingly kept Pierre from Maison Dubois for over six hours.

The very next day, Annette hired an interior decorator who turned her home into the spacious, elegant retreat she'd wanted for herself and Pierre. Annette vowed then and there to do as her husband instructed.

Since she knew little about entertaining, cooking, and decorating, Annette learned to consult those who did. She found the very best florists and caterers. When she needed clothes she relied on the fitters at Maison Dubois. Annette learned to leave nothing to chance. Within five years, she'd constructed a network of professional drones who catapulted her into notoriety as one of Paris's most accomplished hostesses. When she gave a party everyone in Paris hoped to wangle an invitation. It was the one time when Pierre showed up on time.

Annette turned the oven down on the roast and checked the clock. It was past seven and Pierre still wasn't home. She telephoned the shop, but there was no answer.

Seven became eight, then nine. Désirée fell asleep on the sofa in the living room, still waiting for her father to come home.

At nine o'clock the door opened. Looking haggard and exhausted, Pierre walked into the living room. Annette's fury had abated. Now there was that pained, hurt look that made him feel wretched.

"We waited . . ." Annette glanced to the dining room where Désirée's sign was hung.

"My God, I forgot."

"I know. You always do."

"It was a rough day."

"They all are, Pierre. When's it going to stop? When Désirée is too old to care anymore?"

"At the last minute the buyer from New York showed up. He was a day early. I had to meet him."

"I know . . ." Annette replied wearily.

He walked toward her, his arms outstretched, but she avoided him. "Take Désirée to her room."

Pierre watched as his wife left the room. He couldn't make it up to her . . . or to Désirée. He wished he wasn't so busy. But the expansion to seventeen international boutiques was a vast undertaking. He felt it necessary to travel abroad, but he didn't. Annette would never go for it. At least this way, he was home every night. Couldn't she see that? He felt he was making many sacrifices for his family.

He looked down at his slumbering daughter. She was a duplicate of Renée as a girl. Désirée was already showing the promise of great beauty. God! How he wished there was more of himself to go around.

Renée found no one home as she locked the front door after her. Ever since the Nazis, it was habit to live with locks.

She picked up the mail, and absentmindedly took the new issue of French *Vogue* with her to the salon. Wearily, she sat down in an overstuffed chair.

She flipped through the pages, but she couldn't take her mind off Gaston.

She knew he was earnest in his plan to go to New York, but she hoped once he realized the impossibility of the venture, he would come to his senses. Sometimes it was difficult to stand her ground, but Renée was convinced, as long as she gave him no money, he would be forced to stay in Paris. He would chafe under the restraints of being told what to create by another designer for a year, maybe two, but she honestly believed Gaston's designs would win out. If only she could convince him of that. His timing was off, that was all. She also believed that as he matured, he would come around to her way of thinking and realize that haute couture and mass marketing could never coexist.

Yes, she thought as she turned the page, Gaston would see it her way—eventually.

Suddenly Renée's mouth fell open as she stared at the full-page color photograph of her daughter.

She marveled that she had once thought her daughter ugly. Here was one of the most physically perfect faces she'd ever seen.

She remembered when at the age of twelve, Juliette's riotous curls relaxed, creating a thick head of hair that ranged in color from tawny beige and gold to the silvery shades of cornsilk. It was hair that demanded attention, elicited comments, and was envied by women. When the fashionable world was crimping their hair to fit under tiny hats with veiling spun like cotton candy, Juliette wore her hair as if it were a couture gown. With torrents of golden curls falling down her back and dressed in her brother's loose-fitting casual clothes, Juliette was criticized by the more staid fashion critics and outwardly attacked by Renée's detractors.

But Juliette listened to no one, for she was as rebellious and avant-garde in her own way as Gaston was in his.

Juliette worked hard on her looks. On Monday, Wednesday, and Friday afternoons, she took classical ballet and jazz classes. On Tuesdays and Thursdays she had one and a half hours of calisthenics and weight training. In the past year she had grown another two inches, making her five feet ten inches tall with legs as long as Gaston's.

Renée often wondered where her willpower came from. Juliette positively never went near a dessert or piece of chocolate—a feat Renée could never hope to accomplish.

Since she first explored Renée's pots of rouge and lipsticks as a child, Juliette was at home amid lighted makeup mirrors, pancake, and mascara. Juliette experimented with exotic eyeshadows, glittery rouges, and face bronzers. She owned a collection of over two hundred cosmetic brushes, most of them expensive sable. She adored mixing her own colors of nail lacquers. Just last year Juliette had come to Renée with her suggestions for a color palette for Dubois Cosmetics. Renée believed in Juliette's instincts and had everything ordered to Juliette's specifications.

In less than six weeks the line was completely sold out and the manufacturing plant doubled the order.

As Juliette had done in the past, she continued to absorb and dissect every ounce of information the models could give her. She read books on human anatomy, picked Gaston's brain, and queried him on his designs. She knew not only how to mold cheekbones into a face that was devoid of them but also how to use makeup on the body to create shade, shadow, and light. She studied poses; those that were flattering to the thighs, back, waist, and breasts. She could, with the proper use of lighting and position, increase the size of her normal-sized breasts, alter the form of her long shapely legs into thin pencils, and create the most prefectly rounded derrière in photography.

Renée had always encouraged Juliette to work with the mannequins.

Just last spring, she announced to the thirteen mannequins working for her that she was making Juliette assistant coordinator. It wasn't until many weeks later that she heard how much the mannequins resented Juliette.

Renée kept waiting for Juliette to come to her about the problems she was having with the models. Juliette never complained. Two months after Juliette began, Renée noticed that the friction among the models had lessened.

"Juliette," Renée said, "I've heard wonderful compliments from our customers about the new models and the way you organized their work. I knew you wouldn't disappoint me."

"But you're surprised."

"Yes, I am. What did you do differently?"

"I studied each girl's personality and then tried to fit their character to the clothes they wore. Rather than matching only skin tones and hair color to fabrics, I wanted something more dynamic. I wanted the girls to know the clothes they wore, even if it was only for a few moments. I think we sold more that way."

Renée was amazed. She leaned back with a smile. Juliette was a natural for this business, an idea she'd never dwelt long on as she had Gaston. But obviously Juliette had only been marking time at Maison Dubois.

Renée looked down at the copy of *Vogue*. Both her children held secrets and problems within themselves that they refused to face. Karl's death had greatly affected Juliette; since then, she had elevated Karl until now she likened him to a god. Renée feared she would never find a man to live up to her expectations, and she believed her ambition stemmed from an inner need to be loved. The choice of modeling told Renée that much.

"What do you think of the ad?"

Renée looked up to see Juliette's nervous smile. "It's marvelous!"

"You're not mad?"

"No. Disappointed."

"Why?"

"I wish you trusted me enough to come to me first."

Juliette sat next to her and put her arm around her mother's shoulder. "It's not that. It's more trusting myself, not you."

"Hmm." Renée nodded.

"Aunt Annette said she'd brain me if I were her daughter."

"Good thing for you you're not!"

"Désirée is going to have a tough life, the way Annette holds her reins."

"It isn't easy for any mother watching her children grow up . . . and away from her."

"I'm not going anywhere, Maman."

"Not this minute. But you will. You want to model and it will take you many places. You'll meet many exciting people. There will be room for many others besides me . . . and the family."

"Never. My family is very important to me."

"But someday you'll meet a man and have children of your own. Then that family will be the most important to you. And it should be that way."

Juliette considered this for a moment. "I don't know who he'd be."

Renée smiled. "When it's right, you'll know. I did."

"Did you, Maman? Did you love Papa from the first moment?"

Renée looked at her. Though she saw Grant's eyes in Juliette's face, she spoke of Karl. "I knew he was a most special man, Juliette. It was very right."

"Annette said it was like that for her with Uncle Pierre. He is everything to her, isn't he?"

"Yes. And I agree with her that he doesn't spend enough time with her. I think that's the reason she holds Désirée back so much. She's afraid of losing her too."

"So, Maman"—Juliette motioned to her photograph—"is that what you're doing with me? Letting up on my reins?"

Renée looked at Juliette but all she could think of was Gaston. "I've done enough of that for one day."

It was at that moment Renée accepted that she'd lost her son.

Chapter Twenty-eight

Gaston walked down the metal rolling steps of the Pan American airplane, thinking instantly that America even *felt* different. There was an electricity here that seemed to charge through him. He smiled as he bustled into Idlewild terminal with the other passengers. Gone were the self-recriminations over leaving his mother. He was beginning a new adventure; the kind he'd prepared for all his life.

It was too bad he hadn't prepared himself financially for this undertaking. It was while he packed his steamer trunks with his expensive tailor-made clothes that he realized where all his money had gone over the past few years. Their acquisition had been important when one was wooing models, debutantes, and daughters of staunch Maison Dubois customers.

Gaston was aware of his good looks and the power he exuded over women. He knew that most of the girls he dated were impressed with either his looks or his mother's legacy. He'd never been serious about anyone, so he never took the time to delve any deeper into his heart than the surface.

Loveplay was meant for the idle or the foolish—and he was neither. Gaston had no time or energy for courtship. He'd set his sights higher.

Gaston wanted to be a millionaire before he was thirty. He

wanted to own the equivalent of his mother's business, and as he saw it, he'd lost ten years already.

Involved with major life decisions, wrestling with guilt over leaving his family and bolstering his already flagging optimism, Gaston was now faced with finding a place to live.

He sat atop three suitcases poring over the "For Rent" section of *The New York Times*. Knowing little about New York, he used the most discerning of all criteria for choosing a residence—cost.

Gaston's search took him to Greenwich Village, where he rented the two upper floors of a four-story house built in 1840. Located on Charles Street, two blocks down from Seventh Avenue, the apartment was close to the subway to the Garment District.

"I've come about the apartment," he said in his heavily accented English to the elderly landlady.

She eyed him up and down, then smiled. "I'll let you see for yourself. My arthritis keeps me downstairs." She handed him the key.

Gaston bounded up the stairs and dropped his bags on the plank floor as he stared at the vast emptiness around him. There was a small apartment-sized refrigerator, a stove that surely was a relic from another century, a sofa with torn cushions, and a dried areca palm in the corner.

Gaston scratched his head. "Furnished" must mean something different in America than it did in France.

Quickly he dashed up to the top floor and stopped dead in his tracks. The roof had been raised and a wall of glass curved into the ceiling, allowing a tidal wave of sunshine to flood the room. The floors were newly sanded and waxed. A fireplace large enough to stand in and a small terrace accessible through French doors on the other side of the room were all it contained.

Gaston didn't care. The apartment was perfect.

"New York . . . I love you!" he yelled and raced down the stairs to give Mrs. Nelson his first month's rent.

A young man's enthusiasm coupled with an overabundance of nervous adrenaline can last only so long. Two months after his arrival in New York Gaston found the life of a struggling artist unpleasant, discouraging, unrewarding, and unprofitable.

His ten thousand francs converted into two thousand American dollars, and though he was not starving, his capital was dwindling, and he'd been unsuccessful in garnering the bank loan necessary for setting up his own shop. At First City Bank of New York he was told he needed citizenship papers. At New York Bank he was refused because he had no steady job and no income. The First National Bank and Trust Company refused all collateral except real estate, and the Federal Savings and Loan of New York told him they were "leery of the rag business."

Characteristically, Gaston found himself depressed and immersed in one of his "moods." He shut himself up in his new apartment, and other than trying to revive his dying areca palm, he was not interested in anything. It was the first time he'd ever been forced to bring himself out of depression. He did not have his mother looming over him with troubled eyes and solicitous demands that he eat and sleep correctly. Pierre was not breathing down his neck every hour pestering him back to life; Juliette was not banging on his bedroom door demanding his newest record albums as an excuse to come to him with her latest adolescent problems.

May slid into June and brought with it an early summer heat wave. Even with the windows open, there was no breeze. One such night Gaston sat on his terrace staring out at the city lights, wondering when the heat would subside.

One and a half floors below him on the roof of the next building were a man and woman dancing—in tights and leotards! He could hear the melancholy strains of a torchy love song coming from inside their apartment.

The woman was reed thin, dressed in salmon leotards; juxtaposed against the pink and peach sunset, she seemed to blend into the horizon like one of the ribbons of wispy clouds. Effortlessly, the man hoisted her on his shoulder and spun her around as she stretched out her arms. Suddenly, he stopped, the dance was over, and the woman was facing Gaston. She saw him watching them.

Gaston burst into applause. *"Bravo! Magnifique!"*

The man gracefully lowered the woman to the ground and they both took lavish, theatrical bows. When Gaston's applause continued, they broke into laughter.

"Come down and join us!" the man called to Gaston.

"I shouldn't intrude," Gaston said, hoping they would insist.

"It's much too hot for dancing," the woman said and then went off to a corner and in a moment returned with a ladder. She leaned the ladder against the wall. "A friend of ours used to live in your apartment and we did this all the time. It's safe!" She laughed as Gaston scrutinized the makeshift stairway.

"All right, but if anything happens, my demise will be on your head!" Gaston teased and swung his legs over the balcony railing and onto the ladder.

"I'm Gaston Dubois," he said, shaking their hands once he was on safe ground.

"Tommy Brand and Sylvia Dubrovnik. Glad to know you. We didn't know the apartment had been rented. When did you move in?" Tommy asked.

"Almost a month ago."

"No kidding! I usually pride myself on being the neighborhood busybody," Sylvia said as she smoothed her sweaty blond hair behind her ears. She was not an attractive woman, Gaston thought, with her angular face, thin lips, and pale gray eyes, but her bone structure would handle makeup well. As he followed them inside their apartment he realized that her beauty was in the way she moved her body. Just bending over to pick up a towel, she used muscles that most women didn't even know they had. Her carriage and movements went beyond grace—Sylvia was an artist.

While she opened a chilled bottle of cheap white wine and arranged an odd assortment of saltines, wheat wafers, American cheese slices, and a tub of peanut butter, Tommy excused himself to take a shower.

Sylvia talked nonstop for nearly twenty minutes, asking Gaston every question about himself, where he came from, his aspirations, his job or lack of it, and barely stopped long enough to allow him to answer.

Tommy came walking back into the room wearing only a pair of white Bermuda shorts and a towel around his neck. He opened a cold bottle of beer and wolfed down most of the crackers, which he smeared with a generous portion of peanut butter.

"Sylvia is the resident fixer-upper. Doesn't matter who you are or what it is, she has the answer for everything," he said, taking a big gulp of beer. Gaston noted the sarcasm in his voice and the grudging look he gave her.

Sylvia returned his look with one of even greater rancor. "Don't pay any attention to him. He got kicked out of his apartment—a lover's spat—and being the prideful person he is, he doesn't accept my generosity very well."

"Call a spade a spade. It's charity and I've never had to ask for it before."

"Well, it won't be long. As soon as we get those parts in the play—"

Gaston was fascinated and interrupted. "The theater? Are you on Broadway?"

Tommy's face instantly lit up. "None other. But I'm trying not to get too carried away. Sylvia always makes it sound as if we have the parts in the bag. There's a new musical opening in the fall and we've been auditioning for the past month. The only parts left are second and third lead. The pressure is on."

Gaston sipped his wine thoughtfully. "I'm in the same position. My auditions haven't gotten me very far either." He looked up at them, eyes filled with conviction. "If someone would just give me the chance, I could make a success of it!"

Sylvia caught his enthusiasm. "I know you could too!"

"You in the theater?" Tommy asked.

"He designs clothes," Sylvia piped in.

"No kidding!" Tommy picked up the bottle opener and pried the cap off his second beer.

As he did, Tommy's eyes inspected Gaston more closely, as if he hadn't seen him before; the scrutiny made Gaston uncomfortable. Then it hit him. Tommy was a homosexual. The tension between Sylvia and Tommy made sense now.

"My mother owns Maison Dubois in Paris," Gaston said, feeling Tommy's eyes roving down his legs like a pair of hands. He wanted to let Tommy know he was not the least bit interested. It wasn't the first time Gaston's looks had gotten him into this situation.

Sylvia's eyes grew wide. "You don't mean *the* Dubois? Tommy, did you hear that? We have a celebrity among us!" She sidled up to him. "Why, you're a notorious bastard—bachelor, I mean."

Gaston winced at her blunder but he was aware that his background had been fodder for more than one columnist over the years. Nevertheless, she had saved him from an uneasy situation. Gaston was smiling when he turned toward her.

"I do seem to surround myself with women," he said seductively.

Tommy instantly backed off, impressed with Gaston's tact.

"If you're so famous, what's the problem?" Tommy asked.

"I think Sylvia is the only person in New York who has ever heard of me. The bankers must not read *Women's Wear Daily*," Gaston joked. "Without money, I can't open my own shop. I don't know how to do anything else but design and make clothes."

Tommy sipped his beer thoughtfully. "You can't borrow from your family?"

Gaston shook his head. "That's how my mother plans to lure me back to Paris. I have to do this on my own."

Sylvia looked wistfully at Gaston. "There must be something we can do. After all, we're neighbors and neighbors should help each other out."

"Here we go again!" Tommy said, rolling his eyes heavenward. "What did I tell you? Fixer-upper."

"I don't know any bankers . . ." Sylvia was thoughtful for a moment and then suddenly clapped her hands. "But we do know someone in the garment industry, don't we, Tommy?" She turned on him with intense eyes, daring him to back down from the challenge.

"Never!"

"Oh, come on! It's not for you, but for Gaston."

"What *are* you talking about?"

"We can't get your shop opened," Sylvia said, "but we can get you an ''in'' with some of the people in the garment district. Tommy's uncle, Abe Goldberg, is a big manufacturer there."

"Goldberg. Goldberg? I'm not familiar with his designs," Gaston said.

"Shit. My uncle Abe doesn't design clothes . . . he steals the designs and then slaps pieces of material together and charges outrageous prices. It would make you sick. *He* would make you sick."

"Cut it out, Tommy!" Sylvia turned back to Gaston. "It's not as bad as all that. Abe Goldberg is a big wheel on Seventh Avenue. Tommy hates him because he tried to get his father to boot him out of the family because he wanted to be a dancer."

"And a few other things," Tommy said, his contempt slipping momentarily into his eyes and voice.

Sylvia ignored him. "It's not much, but it would be a start. It wouldn't be so bad to work for Abe Goldberg. What could it hurt?"

Two days later Gaston stood in Abe Goldberg's office surrounded by stacks of material swatches tossed helter-skelter on three imitation leather chairs and sketches that had no apparent order or style to them. It was difficult to decipher which ones had been accepted and which rejected.

The secretary was a harried, middle-aged woman who seemed at a loss over what to do with Gaston, and rather than think about it any longer, she finally told him to wait in Mr. Goldberg's office—a move clearly taken to remove him from her sight. Her irreverence for Mr. Goldberg's authority should have been a clue to the man who might be his future employer.

As Gaston looked around the office he realized that a month away from the fashion world had seemed like a death sentence. No wonder he'd been so depressed. Not once in his entire life could he remember a day that he wasn't surrounded by and immersed in the world of fashion. He missed the chatter of the vendeuses and mannequins, and the bustle of fitters as they raced between dressing rooms. He needed to see the bright-colored silks, pastel velveteens, and sheerest organzas every day to jolt his mind and set his creativity to spinning. He hadn't sketched since the day he'd told his mother he was leaving Paris. He was a designer, first, last, and always. He promised himself as he stood in Abe Goldberg's office that he would never allow himself to be away from fashion again.

Gaston spied a sketch that looked a bit too familiar and had just retrieved the drawing from the pile on Abe's desk when the door slammed behind him.

"Are you another of my nephew's faggot friends, or just a plain thief?"

Gaston spun around and faced the man whose crassness he found appalling.

"It looks as if you are the thief, Mr. Goldberg, not I!"

Abe Goldberg's deep-set brown eyes examined Gaston as if he were looking for flawed stitches. Gaston did not flinch but used the time to assess his assessor. Gaston picked up the sketch and held it in the air.

"This is *my* design from this coming fall collection. But I'm afraid you are behind the times. These clothes are fitted too loosely, they are laughed at in Paris."

"Who the fuck are you?" Abe Goldberg demanded, going around to his desk, shoving a stack of wool samples to the edge of his desk, and planting his wide girth in a red plastic swivel chair.

"I am Gaston Dubois and I designed this ensemble for Maison Dubois of Paris. I want to know how the hell you got it!"

Abe Goldberg's smile was sly. "I got my ways."

"I think I should inform my mother that her security needs improving."

"Perhaps you should," Abe said, biting off the end of his cigar and spitting it into the wastebasket. "So tell me why the son of one of the world's best couturiers is standing in Abe Goldberg's office on Seventh Avenue wanting a penny-ante job?"

"My mother and I don't see eye-to-eye."

"That's understandable. I never got along with my old man, either. But that doesn't explain why you came to me."

"I can't get a loan to open my own business. I live next door to Sylvia Dubrovnik, Tommy's dancing partner. He said maybe you could use me." He paused. "I need a job."

Abe peered at Gaston. "Ambitious too. I like that. I'm afraid I'm the only ambitious person in my whole damn family. Despite what Tommy tells you, I admire the kid. He's got guts to go after what he wants alone. I just don't happen to like the company he keeps. If ya know what I mean."

"I do."

"If Paris thinks your clothes stink, you tell me why I should hire you."

Gaston was unsure how to answer. He opted for the truth. "Because American women do want my clothes. They lead more active and independent lives than European women. I can design pretty clothes for American women, but I like to see women in comfortable clothes. I think they are sexier that way."

Abe jammed his cigar in his mouth and chewed intently on it, then swirled his chair around to face the window. Gaston wondered what he was doing since the dirty venetian blinds were closed.

A full five minutes passed before Abe spoke again.

"I got this gut feeling that even if I do hire you, you won't stay longer than necessary. You got big plans, doncha, son?" he asked, turning around to face Gaston again.

"Yes."

"I got some plans of my own. I run a pretty big business here in New York and I got a lot of things . . . money, control, power. What I don't have is respect. People around town respect those things I just mentioned, but they don't respect me. I'm gonna hire you, son, because you're gonna give me the kind of respect I want."

"I don't understand."

Abe leaned forward, his small eyes fiercely intent. "I'm gonna pick your brain. I want to know everything about couture, real couture. Next year at this time, I want to put on my own show and I want New York to sit up and take notice. No stolen Diors or Balenciagas. I want class stuff, the best designs and the best-made American dresses money can buy. And I want my name on the label."

"I would be a fool to do that."

"Come on, son. This is America. I'm an old man; dreams are supposed to come true here. You'll be paid handsomely, but for one solid year, you can't go anywhere, work for anyone but me. You got plenty of insurance in this deal. There isn't a seamstress on the entire Eastern seaboard that can do one-tenth the handwork your little gals in Paris do. I only want this one shot. I couldn't produce a couture line twice a year—hell, once a year—like you were used to doing in France. I just want to do it once. I want every one of those assholes at *Vogue* and *WWD* and *Bazaar* to eat every stinkin', rotten word they've ever written about me."

"I could get well paid anywhere and not have to give so much. There has to be more for me."

Abe's smile was appreciative. "If you're smart—and at this point I have every indication you are—you'll take this time to learn how we do things in America. I'll be your mentor. I'll connect you with every textile man from Bangor to Raleigh. I'll tell you where to buy your machinery and how much to pay for it. I can tell you which unions to use and which ones to avoid. When the year is up I can help you get financed and at the best rates. You'll need lawyers, accountants, bookkeepers, and managers. I know the best. In this year you can make a niche for yourself. Together, we can set New York on its ear." Abe chewed on his cigar again. "After all, that's why you're here, isn't it?"

Cécile Thorpe raced across two-inch-thick white carpet on high-heeled satin mules, flung herself across the white brocade bed, and lunged at the ringing telephone.

"Hello?" she said, out of breath, pulling the tie of her magenta and azure dressing gown around her waist.

The operator informed her it was a transatlantic call from Paris. Cécile knew instantly it was Renée.

"How wonderful to hear your voice!" Cécile said. "I wish Gaston had moved to New York years ago. Think of all the calls I'd have gotten!"

"Cécile, please be serious! Have you seen him yet?"

"No. The party is tonight. I just sent an invitation to the address you gave me. He left a message with my housekeeper to expect him and that he would bring someone."

"A girl?"

"Yes."

"Who?"

"I have no idea. Quit acting like a mother hen. He's a grown man."

"I know, but I worry. I shouldn't have been so hard on him. There's no telling what he might do. Loneliness can drive people to decisions they shouldn't make. I wish you knew more about this girl."

"No wonder he left Paris."

"I never questioned his girlfriends in Paris," Renée retorted defensively. "Oh, I just wish he would come home. I miss him so much."

"I know you do," Cécile said, checking the clock. "Look, I have to get dressed. My guests are due here any moment."

"Tell him I called and that I love him and miss him."

"I will. Goodbye, Renée."

"*Au revoir.*" Renée hung up and the line went dead.

Cécile replaced the receiver. "Mothers! God spare us all!" she moaned.

Gaston received the invitation to Alvin Thorpe's birthday party, but did not reply because he was busy on the sketches for Abe's line of fall coats, and because he did not know anyone he would feel comfortable escorting. The secretaries at Abe's and the two salaried models he'd met had emptied the full content of their brains within the first five minutes of conversation with him. Gaston knew about Cécile's parties—he'd heard his mother discuss them for years. Cécile Thorpe was not only a Dubois client but as close to being "family" as a friend could be.

On the ninth day he realized his delay was caused by the fact that he wanted to go to the party, but he wanted to make an impression. Gaston was not at an impressive point in his life.

At eleven o'clock at night it was 98 degrees in his apartment and the only breezes in Greenwich Village were those made by cars passing on Bleecker Street. Gaston sat dressed only in boxer shorts on his balcony, drinking a beer he'd poured over ice cubes thinking it a disgusting thing to drink, when Sylvia appeared on the roof below.

She was dressed in a thin cotton nightgown through which passed an orange neon light from the liquor-store sign one block over, creating a delightful silhouette. Gaston smiled.

"*Bonsoir!*" he called to her.

She jerked her head up and saw him. "Gaston!" She waved. "Isn't this ghastly weather? I couldn't sleep and thought it would be cooler out here."

"Would you like a beer?"

She came over to the now permanently standing ladder. "Sure. Bring one down. I've got some pretzels and dip."

In moments Gaston was scrambling down the ladder and handed her the beer.

She looked at his shorts. "Dressing formal, I see."

He laughed. "I'd completely forgotten. You should take it as a compliment, for it shows how comfortable I feel with you."

Sylvia glanced away and when she looked back at him there was a gleam in her eyes he hadn't seen before.

Gaston felt hot and not from the weather. "Where's Tommy?"

"Out."

Gaston knew Tommy had a new lover and Sylvia had mentioned it would only be days before Tommy moved out permanently. In the past week he hadn't slept in his cot in the living room but once.

Gaston sipped his beer and let his eyes linger over Sylvia. She and Tommy had gotten their dancing parts on Broadway, and though the play didn't open for weeks, Sylvia was thrilled with her triumph.

Gaston looked at Sylvia. She had been overly good to him since his arrival. He wanted to do something for her—thank her for being his friend.

"Sylvia, how'd you like to go to a party?"

"What kind of party?"

"A very fancy party on Fifth Avenue with lots of exciting people. Think of it. Sylvia Dubrovnik sipping champagne, eating caviar and oysters with Porfirio Rubirosa."

"The Dominican Republic playboy?"

"The same. Not to mention Kitty Carlisle, Adlai Stevenson, and William Burroughs. You could get lucky and see Joe DiMaggio and Marilyn Monroe."

"I think you're teasing me. I don't belong with those people."

"Oh, yes you do! That's what I want to show you. In fact, you're better than they are because you have great talent. I know it. You keep calling it 'just hard work,' but I've seen you practicing with Tommy both here and at the theater. Someday you're going to be the one they give parties for."

Sylvia burst into laughter that quickly turned to tears. Her voice was thick with emotion. "I want it, Gaston! I want all of that world and more! I want to be the greatest dancer ever. I've lived for nothing else. I want New York to notice me!" She clutched his arm so tightly, her nails dug into his skin.

"I believe you! Then you'll go."

"No."

"Why not?"

"I can't. I don't have the right clothes."

Exasperatedly, Gaston ran his hand through his sweaty hair. "Shit!"

"You picked *that* up pretty quick!"

Gaston shook his head. "Be quiet! Stand up!"

Sylvia stood and he turned her around, lifted her chin to the light, then lowered it. He lifted the hem of her nightgown and looked at her legs and feet. He stood back and scratched his head. "Something very young in sand and turquoise. And short to show off your legs. But we have to do something with your face."

"What's the matter with my face?" she asked angrily.

"It's perfect, but I'll do your makeup and dye your hair."

"My hair!" she screamed. "No dice, buddy. You keep away from my hair."

"Trust me," he said, coming closer and putting his arms around her slim waist. "I'm going to make you a legend in one night."

Sylvia peered into his alarmingly sensual eyes, thinking he looked like a buccaneer with no shirt and his chest covered in a glowing film of perspiration. "Save your amorous overtures for someone else, Gaston," she said and he laughed.

He held her for a long moment and she realized he was *not* making an advance at all. "Just who are you doing this for? You or me?"

Ambition curved Gaston's lips upward. "Both."

Gaston did not phone Cécile Thorpe's home until Sylvia's dinner dress was finished. He spoke to the maid and informed her he would be bringing someone. The afternoon of the party, Gaston dashed home, his tuxedo in one hand and an assortment of cosmetics in the other. Gaston had been up past midnight the night before giving Sylvia's dirty-blond hair a wealth of honey-, beige-, and champagne-colored highlights. Her vividly spoken objections died when she viewed the glorious results.

Thus, when it came time to apply her makeup and create the chic "doe-eyed" look by flicking up the ends of her eyeliner, Sylvia placed herself willingly in Gaston's hands. But it wasn't until she saw the dress he'd created just for her that she truly recognized his talents.

The short evening dress with strapless lace corselet in sand beige and a swathed silk skirt in turquoise not only fitted her body like a second skin, it exemplified her personality. In Gaston's dress, Sylvia felt like the woman she had always known she would be—the person she was striving to become.

As she looked at herself in the mirror, noting the matching lace sling-back shoes and wondering how he did *that*, she almost hated Gaston for showing her this world that was not *quite* hers. She adored the feel of real silk and admired the precision cut of the dress, but it was knowing that no one could ever wear this dress, because it was uniquely hers, that caused her jitters. More than ever she was anxious to conquer New York, and when she did, she vowed all her clothes would be made like this.

When she turned to Gaston, who looked inhumanly handsome, her eyes were glowing with the intoxication of the moment.

"I knew it would be so," he said, his eyes merry but still critical of his work.

"You look . . . the best!" she replied excitedly.

He took her hand and kissed it. "It's time," he said and opened the door.

After embracing and the customary introductions, Cécile said: "I think New York agrees with you, Gaston. You look marvelous. The way your mother talked I expected an emaciated, brooding artiste."

"You've talked with Maman?"

"Yes, just today, in fact. She sends her love," Cécile said and then looked at Sylvia. "I adore your dress. Where on earth did you find it? I have to fly to Paris for dresses like that!"

Sylvia's eyes went to Gaston and he smiled mischievously.

"I should have guessed!" she exclaimed. "I hope he didn't charge you as much as he does me."

"Cécile," Gaston said. "Sylvia is a dancer in a new Broadway musical."

"How wonderful. Sylvia, there are some people here I think you should meet. Perhaps you've heard of them. Marge and Gower Champion."

"Here? Right now?" Sylvia was incredulous. "I'd love it!"

"Excuse us, Gaston," Cécile said and ushered Sylvia toward the terrace doors, relishing the role of "patron."

In the first hours of Cécile's party, Gaston realized that as much as he needed these people, he needed the noisy, coarse world of Abe Goldberg more. At this point in his life he needed knowledge of the way "things got done" and to rub shoulders with the purveyors of the American mass market. Some innate sense told him that learning to battle it out on the streets with the street people would be all-important to him in the years to come.

He and his mother had often fought over his focus on the young working women and Renée's inability to see couture beyond the society ladies she'd dealt with for two decades. Already he was seeing the division of two camps. One believed clothes should have a strong shape and look as if they could walk across the room alone. Dior, Balmain, Fath, and his mother believed in that credo. He thought clothes should have no existence apart from the body.

Gaston sipped the dry champagne, and critically scanned the room, making an accounting of how many votes he would take and how many would go to his mother.

Chapter Twenty-nine

Native New Yorkers have never sold all their worldly goods and arrived in a foreign place with nothing but romantic ideals to feed them. They never go through the periods of disillusionment that others do. Native New Yorkers know from the moment they are born that their city is at once the best and the worst the world has to offer. To a native New Yorker, haughtiness is a birthright.

Kate Millgrew was a native New Yorker. Daughter of G. W. and Eloise Millgrew, of the railroad and banking Millgrews; recent graduate of the National Academy of Design on East Eighty-ninth Street—a noted center of conservatism in the arts; and now employed as a sixth-grade art instructor at St. Vincent's Private School, Kate Millgrew was living the life her parents had planned out for her. She hated that life and hated herself for not doing something about her problems. At twenty-one years of age Kate had nothing to be haughty about.

In fact, she had just finished her third glass of champagne at Cécile and Alvin Thorpe's party, wishing she had the courage to tell her parents that she wanted to leave her pink floral bedroom on the twelfth floor of a plush Park Avenue building, quit her job, and live her own life, when her eyes fell on the most beautiful man she'd ever seen.

He was looking at her *feet*, of all things! Kate took another glass of champagne and placed her lips on the edge of the glass so as not to smear the precisely drawn edges of her coral lipstick. Surreptitiously, her blue eyes stole another peek at him.

She watched as he lit a cigarette for a woman and whispered something to her which caused her to blush and giggle. He was so at ease in his body and his good looks. For the first time in her life, Kate Millgrew wanted a man sexually.

Gaston watched the blue-eyed brunette expertly drape herself over the gray suede sofa. The five-inch-wide tiers of her slim-cut scarlet chiffon dress fell into place like the petals of a rose. Good stuff, but not Parisian. She took out a cigarette and lowered her dusky shadowed eyelids while a man lit the end. She tilted her head, gave him the compensatory smile, and looked boldly at Gaston.

He couldn't decide if it was the perfectly arranged chignon, the meticulously applied makeup, or the constrictive manner in which she held her body, but something about her made Gaston want to walk over to her and douse her with his drink; perhaps then she would be more human. He chuckled to himself, thinking how she would look if he purposely "rearranged" her façade. He imagined cold champagne running down her bodice, the chiffon clinging to her breasts. He shook his head and dispelled the image before it went any further.

There was something about the imperious woman that set his teeth on edge. She had to be the epitome of haughtiness. It was understandable, though, since she was undoubtedly the most beautiful woman in the room. He'd always had a weakness for velvety blue eyes like hers, and past experience had taught him to be wary of such women. Gaston did not have time for emotionally expensive involvements. Of all the people at the party, she was the one woman he intended not to meet.

Kate Millgrew's hand was shaking as she put her cigarette out in the chunky onyx ashtray. Several friends stopped for a moment to speak with her and then they moved on. When she looked back, the man who had been watching her was gone. Just then, Daphne Henderson sat next to her.

Daphne and Kate had graduated from high school together, and like most of the girls in their crowd, Daphne was conveniently married to the customary Harvard law graduate, was furnishing her first home in Scarsdale, and frantically spending her father's money on clothes, the theater and posh, "in" restaurants in the city.

"Doesn't Cécile always do things with panache?" Daphne asked in her usually affected, breathless manner.

"Yes," Kate replied, peering over Daphne's shoulder for another look at "the man."

Daphne turned and followed her gaze. She turned back. "Isn't he just gorgeous? Muffy and I have been talking about him since he breezed in here with the Russian princess."

"What princess?"

"Well, maybe not a princess. But her name is Sylvia Dubrovnik and they say she's a descendant of Russian royalty. Isn't it exciting to be here when a 'discovery' is made?" She angled herself on the sofa to have a clearer view of Gaston. He was kissing Sylvia on the cheek and put his arm around her tiny waist. "They're lovers," Daphne said matter-of-factly.

"How can you tell?"

"I'm a married woman, Kate," she said, exasperation circling her words.

Kate watched him, her heart sinking. She had wanted to meet him, speak to him, touch him, despite the cold brutal looks he'd given her.

"I wonder who he is?"

"Gaston Dubois. I thought you knew," Daphne said. "Word is he just moved to New York. His mother owns Maison Dubois in Paris, and Deborah told me he designed the princess's dress. He's a real lady's man," she said appreciatively. " 'Experience' is his middle name."

Kate nervously lit another cigarette. "Honestly, Daphne, I just wondered who he was. I wasn't asking for his life history," she said huffily, thinking she could still feel his eyes on her breasts.

Eddie Duchin's music filled the room as the guests began to depart. Alvin and Sylvia were discussing Russian czarist art when Cécile implored Gaston to remain.

"How is it going, really?" she asked.

"Just fine. No complaints."

"Are you and Sylvia . . . ?" Cécile began as she spread a spoonful of Beluga caviar on a circle of rye bread.

"Just friends. We help each other out."

"I see. And your work?"

"I have a job."

"Really? With whom?"

"Abe Goldberg."

Cécile choked on her caviar, losing every bit of decorum she'd spent fifty years attaining. "That bastard of the fashion industry? That son of a bitch who blatantly steals from your mother and Lanvin? You can't be serious!"

"I am quite serious, Cécile."

"No wonder your mother worries about you so much. She was right to check up on you."

"Check up on me?"

"Gaston, this has gone too far. If I'd only known . . . I talked with your mother several times about this and now I think it's imperative."

"What is?"

"That you go back to Paris. Abe Goldberg will ruin you. Renée told me she regretted not giving you money. This is worse than she ever would have imagined. When she hears this . . ."

Frustration and anger rocked through Gaston. How dare his mother enlist Cécile's aid to force him back to Paris. He was proud of what he'd accomplished. He was more determined than ever to succeed. But the thing that tore at his gut most was the realization that his mother didn't trust him—or his talent. They were an ocean apart and were still butting heads.

"The next time you talk to Maman, tell her I will do this on my own. I don't want her to help. Cécile, I love my mother but she has to let me go," he hissed through clenched teeth.

Gaston stalked across the room, grabbed Sylvia's arm, and dragged her out the door.

Four months after Cécile Thorpe's party, Sylvia Dubrovnik was a star with new offers pouring in by the week.

Kate Millgrew found the courage to move out of her parents' home and on to California where she free-lanced as a set designer for Paramount Studios.

Gaston sketched hundreds of designs for Abe Goldberg, only to have most of them rejected. What he didn't know was that Abe kept his very best designs locked in a safe-deposit box at the New York First City Bank.

When the Thanksgiving holidays arrived, Gaston declined Cécile's invitation to dinner, and climbed down the ladder to the roof of Sylvia's apartment. They had spent the entire morning at the Macy's parade, a spectacle he wouldn't have believed if he hadn't been there.

He tapped on the door and she motioned him to come in. She finished basting the turkey and put it back in the oven.

"I'm starving," she said. "How about you?"

He put the cranberry sauce on the counter—his contribution to the dinner—and put his arms around her waist. "Famished." He kissed her passionately, and when she eased away, he whacked her lightly on the rump.

"What was that for?"

"I don't know, I just felt like it." He laughed. He lifted the lid on the mashed potatoes. "Do we have time for . . ." He inclined his head toward the bedroom.

"No, we don't. Besides, I have something I want to talk to you about."

"I must be losing my touch," he said, grabbing her again. "Where's the passion—the romance," he joked.

"Gaston . . . I'm trying to be serious."

"So am I."

Sylvia shot him a warning glance and continued about her cooking while he set the table.

They had become lovers shortly after Cécile's party, more out of need on both their parts than anything else. Sylvia's fame came quickly, and there were times when Gaston helped keep at bay that "sinking feeling" she often had. She leaned on him as a real friend and more than once she made it clear that she was not in love with him. There were times he fantasized that she was, only because he wondered what it would be like to have someone really love him. She told him that the adoration of her audience was the only love she needed and perhaps that was true for her. She certainly did whatever she wanted to do and never thought of the consequences. It was her lack of forethought that made her the generous person she was but it was also the cause of her unconscious selfishness at times too. Sylvia would be a hard woman to live with because her life and career were self-oriented. She took scrupulous care of her body and she worked exhausting hours on her craft. Dance came first—a man would come second or even third in her life. Sylvia was his friend and frequent bed partner, but that was all. He kept hoping that someday there would be more for him.

Sylvia handed Gaston a mug of eggnog. "Here's to your first American Thanksgiving," she said.

"Thank you." He sipped it and found he liked the freshly grated nutmeg. "Now, what is it you wanted to talk about?"

Sylvia sat across her junk-shop dining table from him. "Guess who I had lunch with yesterday?"

"Mary Parkman Peabody."

"Good try, but not close enough. Lucia Chase."

"I'm impressed. What does the cofounder of the American Ballet Theater want with you?"

"She asked me to become a permanent member of the troupe."

"My God! That's fantastic! You took it, of course."

"No, I didn't."

Gaston was incredulous. "I thought that's what you wanted!"

She leaned closer, her eyes deadly serious. "I do, but not just yet. She said something else that I found even more intriguing. Right now there's talk about a new production that's being scored by Rodgers and Hammerstein and choreographed by Hermes Pan. If I could get the lead in that play, which is a meaty one, I'd be able to go anywhere. I'm only nineteen years old and something tells me that the place for me is not in classical ballet. I'm a very good dancer, Gaston, but I'm not prima ballerina material. Unfortunately, I like being center stage."

"So I noticed," he said glumly.

"If I stayed on Broadway, I could have it all."

Gaston nodded. "I commend you for knowing yourself so well. I think that's what I like about you best. You paint no illusions."

She smiled broadly. "I take that as a compliment. But I didn't bring all this up to toot my own horn. Gaston, I want you to go with me."

"Pardon?"

"I did some very fast but accurate checking. This is going to be an enormous production with tons of costumes. What would you think of designing for the theater?"

"I don't know . . . I . . ."

"You'd be another Erté!"

Gaston's mind whirled with the possibilities. It would be an unbelievable undertaking. He couldn't quit Abe's, so if he did the theater designs he would have to work at night. Sylvia was smarter than he'd given her credit for. They both needed visibility and she was going after it like a steamroller. If he got the job and the play was a success, there would be nothing to stop him. He didn't care how exhausted he got or how much sleep he would lose, he would do it.

"What are your chances of getting that part?"

Her smile radiated confidence. "My source tells me I'm their first choice."

"What do I need to do?" he asked eagerly.

"The play is set in New York and on a tropical island. I play a businesswoman who gets stranded in the tropics and falls in love. You can go crazy with bright colors and fabulous skirts and headpieces for the native dance sequences. And sophisticated city chic for the New York scenes. I really think you'd make the show. Several of the background scenes will be abstract. It'll be a whole new realm for you. Make up a few sample sketches for me to show the producers when they call."

Gaston's excitement was growing by the moment. "I'll work on them this weekend."

For the rest of the afternoon, despite the snow squall that blew in from the Midwest and the aroma of turkey and pumpkin pie wafting through Sylvia's apartment, Gaston found he could only think of steamy tropical nights filled with the fragrance of jasmine and gardenia.

The radiator in Gaston's closet-sized office belched for the third time and released a thin thread of steam. It was only eleven o'clock and already he'd gone through two pots of coffee. His hands jittered from too much caffeine but his condition was becoming a necessary evil. It had taken three weeks for Sylvia to get a firm contract for the play but not once did she ever believe the part was not hers. Her conviction drove Gaston to create some of the best designs of his life. He'd forgotten what sleep was like, but Sylvia made certain he ate properly and she was always there with encouragement—usually in the form of outright harassment. She had enough determination for both of them.

Twice Abe commented on his "pasty face" and wondered if he was having "woman trouble." Gaston quickly relieved Abe's fears that he was hitting the bottle or nursing a broken heart.

This morning was Gaston's most nerve-wracking day to date, for Sylvia had taken his designs to the producers. She told him she would call at noon. He didn't think he would last that long. With the holidays almost upon him, Gaston's work load had lessened. There were no more orders to get out, and he would take a one-week break before the mad rush for the spring shows in February.

Gaston had not told Abe but he was nearly finished with all his designs and had already begun constructing toiles, and three ensembles were completely finished. In October, Gaston had taken it upon himself to find one cutter, one fitter, and one seamstress he could teach. He hired all three free-lance from Ritter Brothers. After his first three weeks with them, Gaston came to the firm conclusion that there had to be some genetic differences in French and American seamstresses to account for the fact that the latter could not re-create so much as the first stitch. He examined the differences in bone structure of the hands, thinking that was it. His American workers were just as intelligent, even more so, in some cases. But the generations of whispered secrets that make haute couture the fascinating world that it is were not in the American repertoire. Gaston did the best he could.

The result was the most exquisite clothing made in America, but *he* could tell the difference. His greatest realization was that America consisted of an enormous number of interesting women who could not afford haute couture, but who were discerning. They wanted what Gaston Dubois could give them and he was more determined than ever to open his boutique.

A jangling telephone brought Gaston quickly to his feet. He glanced at the clock. It was 12:15.

"Gaston! You did it! They loved your designs. You have to get down here right away. And get this . . . *Tropical Holiday* will star Sylvia Dubrovnik and Tommy Brand!"

"Tommy?! I didn't know he was even being considered. That's terrific!"

"He didn't tell me, either. He said he wanted it to be a surprise. He beat out over four hundred dancers. Won't it be great? All three of us working on the same project. Anyway, they want some publicity photos this afternoon. Can you get away?"

"I think so . . . I'll see you in half an hour. And Sylvia . . . thanks!"

"Forget it. Didn't I tell you we'd set this town on its ear?"

"Yes, and I never doubted you for a moment."

Renée Dubois opened the *Paris Journal* and found herself staring into the smiling face of her son. He stood between two people she'd never seen before. She read the caption. "Broadway's newest star." Quickly she scanned the column below and discovered that her son was designing costumes for the theater, which was a welcome relief from being Abe Goldberg's lackey, and that this was the girl he'd escorted to Cécile's party and had been seeing ever since. She didn't know who Tommy Brand was, but she intended to find out.

She looked at the photo again. She wanted to be as angry with Gaston as he was with her, but she couldn't. She was angry at herself for thinking she could make him come back to Paris. She'd been wrong to withhold money from him, but now she realized that he didn't need it. It was no wonder Gaston did not phone her and when his letters came they were usually terse notes stating only essential facts about his well-being. She should be grateful, she supposed. At least he hadn't cut her off completely. His letters to Juliette were more intimate, but there had been a change there too.

She wanted to see him, to tell him how proud she was of his newest success. She wanted to hold him and tell him she loved him; whether he wanted to hear it or not. She picked up the telephone to call him and glanced at the photograph once again. Something in his eyes told her he didn't want to hear from her. This was the time in his life when he had to find his own way and she sensed that her absence was part of that growth and helped to sustain his drive.

"The theater," she mumbled to herself.

Gaston's dreams were lofty, indeed, and he should have them, she thought. When she folded the newspaper and placed it in the bottom drawer of her desk, her eyes misted with tears. As much as it pained her she would not force her presence on him, for she wanted him to have his dream.

Chapter Thirty

On March 1, 1952, less than ten months after he arrived in America, Gaston Dubois awoke praying that he could give Abe Goldberg the dream the old man had spent forty-three years scratching, stealing, wrestling, and yearning for.

The ballroom at the Roosevelt Hotel was packed with every fashion journalist from Topeka to Newark. There were the syndicated columnists from *Vogue*, *Harper's Bazaar*, and *Women's Wear Daily*. *Mademoiselle*, *Glamour*, and *Modern Bride* had also sent representatives. But there were no international journalists and not a single celebrity. There was none of the elaborate security he'd known at the showings in Paris. Abe Goldberg's show required no special passes or press cards with photos and signatures because no one believed there would be anything worth stealing. Abe Goldberg was a Seventh Avenue shyster who, it was rumored, had hired a French designer, but everyone knew that if he was any good, he would have been in Paris. These people were here for one reason and one reason only—to hang Abe Goldberg by the balls for having the audacity to pit himself against the couture world.

When Gaston peeked out from behind the curtain he saw smirks instead of smiles, heard whispered aspersions and sensed preconceived judgment against them. When he turned and faced the model talking to him, Gaston already felt defeated.

"Should I wear the opera-length gloves pulled up or pushed down with the shantung dustcoat?"

"Pushed down," he said, noting the unexpected sparkle in the girl's eyes.

"I've never seen clothes like this, Mr. Dubois. They're heaven!"

Gaston watched as she rushed away and retrieved her fringed umbrella from the dresser. She stood in line with the other models awaiting his signal.

His nerves were strung like piano wire from the endless nights, the coffee, and Dexedrine. But it was all worth it. This wasn't Abe's show anymore, it was his. If only he could pull this off. . . .

The curtain rose to a smattering of applause.

All through the show Gaston kept watching the faces of the journalists and critics for a sign. But when the curtain fell, he couldn't tell what the reaction of his audience was, for although they gave him a great deal of applause, they vacated their seats in record time. Not a single person remained to congratulate him.

Backstage, he, Abe, and the models stood gaping at each other, wondering what could have been so wrong.

"Let's get drunk," Abe suggested as he lumbered down the hall toward the Roosevelt bar.

"I want to get this stuff packed and back to the shop. Then I'll join you."

"That's okay, I won't be good company for at least three hours," Abe said with a wilting smile, and turned away.

Gaston carefully hung his precious designs on padded hangers, wrapped each in plyfilm, and marked them. Boxes of shoes, belts, scarves, and costume jewelry were catalogued and put in the van parked in the alley. Gaston did not rush himself, relishing these moments of solitude and lack of pressure. Oddly, he felt a tremendous sense of release now that it was over. That was something to be said for failure, he thought. He had done his best and of that, he was proud.

Abe and Gaston had dinner together and talked about the upcoming Yankee season, the stock market, and the weather. Not once did they mention the show. Gaston went home that night after consuming the largest steak on the Eastern seaboard and fell into an exhausted sleep.

The next morning Abe stalked into Gaston's office chewing on his customary Havana cigar and tossed a stack of newspapers in his lap.

"The sons of bitches and the assholes gave Abe Goldberg respect."

Gaston's jaw dropped. "Are you serious?" he asked excitedly, scrambling through the papers to the fashion columns. He saw the pictures and read the captions.

"The wrapped bottle-jersey blouse, tapered blue and green velvet pants, and lilac cummerbund were this reporter's favorite."

"Balenciaga's influence was seen in the charcoal shantung spring suit with collarless yoke, loose white gilet, and coolie hat, but there was an individuality that made it a success."

"The easy, livable look, so important to the American woman, while still giving enormous attention to details, makes the entire Goldberg collection a triumph."

"You're off the hook, son," Abe said, grinning broadly.

"My year isn't up yet."

"You mean you want to stay?"

"I have two months left to pick *your* brain," he answered, taking out a pad and pen. "Tell me about these textile men in Bangor."

Grant Morgan sat with Michael Segelman, his promotions director, and Milton Greene from *Look* magazine, the playwright Arthur Miller and his wife, and John Jessup, the editor of *Life*. Grant was in New York to oversee the preliminary background layouts for his new movie, *Serendipity Song*.

With a schedule that packed twenty-four hours of work into sixteen, he felt derelict in spending these hours watching a Broadway musical when he had his own musical to worry about, but Arthur had insisted.

He hated opening nights. The curtain was five minutes late in rising and there was no telling if *Tropical Holiday* would be worth his valuable time. As much as he despised the profession, theater critics did serve their purpose.

When the curtain rose, Grant's applause was weak.

* * *

Gaston watched from the wings as the chorus girls kicked back their red satin detachable skirts and gyrated across the stage in the most seductive calypso number he'd ever witnessed. From the applause after the first and second acts, there was no doubt in his mind they had a hit. But then, he told himself, he'd known it the minute he read the script. He also knew Sylvia and Tommy would go a long time before they had to worry about their next meal.

No matter what anyone ever said, Gaston knew he'd take the pressure of success over the pressures of failure any day.

Sylvia spun across the stage, her deep lavender silk skirt spinning high to reveal her shapely legs. She landed in Tommy's strong arms and froze her position as the music swelled to a heart-stopping crescendo and abruptly ended.

In a flash the audience was on its feet, their applause shaking the rafters of the Fontaine Theater. Gaston was clapping so hard his hands hurt and the muscles in his arms got stiff.

Grant Morgan was the first man to jump to his feet and yell "Bravo!" It had been a long time since he'd been immersed enough in a play to lose himself. Not once during the entire performance did he think about the money he needed for his new movie, the problems he was having with casting, costumes. . . .

He looked again at the star, Sylvia. There was something about her that intrigued him but he couldn't put his finger on it. It wasn't her dancing or singing, or her unusual striking looks. It was . . . the color of her dress.

The oddest shade of purple, it was, and upon closer inspection he could see it was a multicolored fabric that ran from lavender to purple to deepest violet. Grant was fascinated with the color; it reminded him of something.

Finally, after the applause died down and everyone was scrambling for the exits, Grant sat back in his seat, took out his playbill, and scanned the credits. *Costumes . . . Gaston Dubois.* Grant leaned back, thinking fate was about to clamp its intrusive tentacles around his life once again.

"Michael, tomorrow morning I want you to contact the costume designer, Gaston Dubois, and offer him a contract with

Monument Studios for *Serendipity Song*. Explain he'll be designing for Doris Day. Pay him whatever it takes. It's my hunch he'll have a lot of offers after tonight. I want Monument's to be the one he takes.''

Chapter Thirty-one

Grant watched Gaston walk toward the backlot New York street setting where the crew was about to shoot an outdoor sequence. It seemed incredible that Renée's son had been working for him for over two months and they had barely spoken.

There was so much Grant wanted to say and couldn't because Gaston did not know about him, or at least that's what he assumed. Gaston had never asked to see him after that initial meeting when he first came to California, and Grant had not detected any recognition in Gaston's manner.

Grant went back to his desk and tried to shut his mind to everything but his work. It was no use. For two months now, he'd been reliving every moment, every word he ever shared with Renée. He thought he'd buried her, the sight and feel of her, beneath the cornerstone of the Monument Studios building, erected in 1934, seven months after his marriage to Darma Logan. But since the night at the Fontaine Theater, Renée had become a part of his life again, and every time he looked at Gaston he was cruelly reminded of the debacle he'd made of his life.

Grant's inexplicable antagonism toward Gaston grew every day. He couldn't come within shouting distance of the young man without wanting to strangle him, as if that could end his dreams of Renée. Just to test Gaston's ambition and fortitude, he'd placed impossible demands on him, thinking he would quit and go away. For years Grant had been called a tyrant by his critics, but this was the first time he believed he truly earned the label. Ever since Gaston's arrival at Monument Studios, Grant was being forced to face many fears, ghosts, and demons from his past.

Grant was forty-eight years old and suddenly all the ambitions he'd exulted in during his youth and middle years had lost their luster. The studio could and did run itself, and though he worked twelve-hour days, it was not necessary. He pretended he was needed. He was not.

Grant had given his life to the movies, to preserve ideals on celluloid film and to make himself rich. He had married a woman he didn't love, and it wasn't until three years after the marriage and Darma's first encounter with the county "drunk ward" that he realized she had never loved him either. She was a spoiled, rich, little girl, accustomed to getting her way. Grant was just another toy, and once she'd finally landed him, she moved on to other "toys." There wasn't a movie star, producer, or director who had not laid Grant Morgan's wife. Grant had joked to Michael Segelman, his only trusted friend, that half his profits from his movies went to keeping Darma's liaisons out of the newspapers. Her alcoholism and drug addiction were not so easily concealed. Even Louella Parsons and Hedda Hopper, both personal friends of Grant's, could not avoid Darma's public tantrums and abasements.

While there were many movie stars and studio heads who would have sought a divorce when faced with such a disastrous marriage, curiously Grant Morgan was caught in a web of his own making. He touted himself as a venerator of the "art" of filmmaking, and had been guilty of smugness and pomposity in the thirties and forties, openly criticizing the big studios for their commercialism and banal movies. It was no wonder that from the lowliest secretary at M-G-M to Jack L. Warner, there was not a soul in Hollywood that didn't like seeing Grant Morgan stewing in his own juices.

The biggest loser in the tragedy of Grant's life was Darma. James Logan had given his daughter everything except a sense of herself. Grant pitied her and felt responsible for her. For the past three years, she had been confined to their estate in Beverly

Hills, but the two private nurses, the maid, and housekeeper could no longer care for the wasted woman. Eight months ago Grant had placed Darma in a sanatorium and was told that because she'd never been able to quit the booze or cocaine, there was not much of Darma Logan Morgan left. The slurred speech, the lapses in memory, and lack of coordination were not signs that Darma was drunk, but that she was dying.

It seemed incredible to Grant that she could have gone downhill so quickly. Just a year ago the doctors had told him there "was slight damage to the liver," but that if she got off liquor she could lead a normal life. Just last week he was informed that her kidneys had completely failed and she'd suffered a mild heart attack. She wouldn't last out the night. That was four days ago and she was still hanging on. Grant knew that his nightly visits would not last much longer.

Grant spun his chair around to face the window and pushed back his hair. His sandy hair was still thick, though slightly gray, and errantly fell on his forehead. He gazed at the two men arguing outside Soundstage 21. It was his director, Bob Zimmermann, and Gaston Dubois.

"She looks like a sow!" Bob Zimmermann growled at Gaston.

"Doris Day couldn't look bad if she was covered in tar! You don't like the costume because she makes your girlfriend look like shit. Maybe you should cast your girlfriend as the lead, but then no one would come to the movie, would they?" Gaston retorted angrily.

Grant walked up just in time to hear the tail end of the argument. His nerves were rankled as it was and he was just waiting for Gaston to push him over the edge.

"Bob!" Grant yelled.

Bob Zimmermann whirled around to face his producer. His bald head gleamed in the bright California sun. His face was beet red. Grant had never seen him this angry. "Grant! Will you tell this fucking fairy to get off my back?"

Gaston's back tensed as he clutched his fist. "I'm *not* queer!"

"All designers are queer, especially ones who hang around with Tommy Brand!"

Gaston nearly slammed his fist into Bob Zimmermann's face when Grant lunged at him and pulled his arms behind his back.

"Knock it off, Gaston! Jesus Christ! You're both acting like children."

Gaston scuffled for a minute with Grant and finally broke free. He glared at the director and then at the producer. "You don't pay me enough to put up with his bullshit."

Grant's voice was cool when he spoke to Bob. "Go back to the set. I'll meet you inside." He waited until Bob left, then turned to Gaston. "Suppose I hear your side first."

"What difference does it make? You're just going to side with Bob anyway," Gaston said.

"Try me."

"Zimmermann's girlfriend is putting pressure on him. She wants Doris's part and knows she can't get it, so she's making trouble for everyone. Today is just her latest trick. I don't have time for this pettiness and neither do you, I would imagine."

Grant knew what Gaston said was true and it goaded him all the more. Zimmermann would have to get rid of the girl—at least on his set.

"I'll handle it, Gaston. You just make sure those costumes for the embassy scene are finished on time."

"They will be," Gaston said, as Grant turned and walked onto the soundstage.

Gaston trudged down to the wardrobe rooms. He was beginning to hate Hollywood. He hadn't had a moment's peace since he'd arrived. Half the town thought he was homosexual and the other half thought he was banging every woman within one hundred miles. The papers were full of it. First there had been the stories about his affair with Amanda Sommers.

It had happened suddenly, that first day on the studio lot. It was late, after ten o'clock, and except for the few lights burning in the executive offices, everyone had gone. With no secretary to announce her, she had barged in the door. He was working on designs he'd begun in New York.

She was one of the most beautiful women he'd ever seen. Her radiant auburn hair was piled on top of her head and her blue green eyes flashed merrily at him. She had a sense of humor that he was to greatly appreciate later.

"My God, but you're gorgeous!" she exclaimed. "If I'd have known, I would have been here sooner," she said, eyeing him appreciatively.

"I could say the same about you," he replied good-naturedly.

"We've never had a costume designer like you, of course, most of them were women. I think I'll like you much better!" She stuck out her hand. "Amanda Sommers."

"Gaston Dubois," he replied, and for a moment he thought he caught that imperceptible flicker of recognition he sometimes saw whenever he mentioned his name. Gaston had to laugh to himself for she was practically licking her lips as she made no effort to conceal her appraising eyes. Before he had a chance to say anything else, Amanda tossed her gloves and purse on his desk, came around to where he stood, and put her arms around his neck.

Amanda's rapacious lips covered Gaston's. Her hands massaged his back with a sensuality that caused his body to take over where his brain had been. He didn't know how or when she had stripped off his shirt and unzipped his slacks and let them fall, he could only feel her hands, fingers, mouth, and tongue everywhere. Every nerve ending in his body was electrified and he was not fool enough to make her stop.

She pushed him into his desk chair where she mounted him and in seconds was moaning with her own orgasm. When he exploded inside her, he was completely out of breath and drenched with sweat.

He looked at her, ran his fingers over her smooth, unlined skin, and smiled.

She smiled back at him. "How does it feel to have screwed a woman older than your mother?"

He looked at her more closely. She wasn't a day over thirty and hardly the forty-three his mother was. "Impossible," he said, stunned.

"I met your mother once when Grant and I first went to Paris back in '31. I was there the first day he fell in love with her."

Gaston pushed her off his lap, thinking she was some kind of banshee, depleting him of his energy and then hitting him with lies about his mother.

"I don't believe you."

"There aren't many who know about it. Just Grant, me, your mother, and Grant's wife. That's why Darma is so looney tunes. Grant never loved Darma and she knows your mother is the reason."

"This is utter nonsense. Another Hollywood tale." Gaston stood and yanked on his pants. "I think you're the one who's crazy. You come in here, practically rape me, a stranger, and then start malicious gossip about my family. You better go."

She proceeded to repair her makeup. "Don't get in such a dander. You're in Hollywood now and, believe me, you'll need all the friends you can get. That's why I'm here. I want to be your friend."

In the following weeks, Gaston could not accept the idea that his mother and Grant had been lovers. It was simply too outlandish a story. But he did notice that Grant watched him more than he realized. Every time he passed by Grant's office, he always saw a man's shadow behind the venetian blinds. And at the commissary, though they were tables apart, he'd often look up to see Grant's head turning away. It was curious behavior.

Gaston knew it was time to rely on himself, however. Trusting Amanda Sommers had been Gaston's first mistake. He was soon to learn that *nobody* in Hollywood, especially Amanda, did anything without a motive. Amanda's career was at an all-time low, even though she looked magnificent—thanks to face lifts and a rigorous personal regimen. But she was yesterday's news in her career. With Gaston as her escort, Amanda found herself mentioned in all the columns, her photograph was in *Variety* again, and she was heading back to the top. Gaston was getting nothing out of it except exhaustion, and he dumped her—but Amanda had the last word.

The press had a field day with Amanda's story of their breakup. She told them she'd been dumped all right—for another man— Tommy Brand.

But Amanda's story backfired on her. In less than a week of the story coming out in print, Gaston found himself besieged with eager young starlets, all too willing to fill his bed, and "cure" his sexual problems.

Gaston decided Hollywood was a planet unto its own. And the rulers of this universe were the studio heads.

Serendipity Song's original settings were to be New York and Hollywood. For the first two months of working on the film, Gaston never heard mention of location shooting.

The "Hollywood Party" scene was changed to one with a

Western theme complete with cowboy boots and chaps. Gaston tossed his designs for Los Angeles sundresses, halter tops, and cuffed short shorts into the wastebasket and prepared himself for long nights ahead.

Days and nights became one endless roll of time. Gaston took the phone off the hook, kept the coffeepot going, and took Dexedrine to stay awake. He was smoking over four packs of Lucky Strikes a day. He didn't eat or sleep. He finished the designs and they were good.

When he walked into Grant's office he was unaware of his bloodshot eyes and the six pounds he'd lost.

"You look like shit," Grant said, noticing how Gaston's hands shook as he took out a cigarette. "Must be all those girls I've been reading about."

Gaston glared at him, wondering what there was about Grant he didn't like. He should be grateful to the man for giving him this job. Of course, he could never be certain if it had been his talent—or that his mother truly had been Grant's lover. His mother loomed over his success now as she always had. Perhaps that was why he pushed himself so hard trying to break away from the stigma.

"I finished the Western costumes."

"That's why I asked you in here, Gaston. There's been another change. We're moving the shoot to Mexico. There'll be a fiesta scene instead of the Western number. I've arranged for you to have lunch with Bob Zimmermann today to discuss the details."

Gaston nearly exploded, but controlled his temper. "How long do I have?"

"Two weeks, but you can take three if necessary."

"Two weeks! I can't get them done that fast!"

Grant's jaw tightened and Gaston could see the vein in his temple pulsate. "I don't care how you do it—hire twenty more dressmakers if you have to—but I want *your* designs and I want good ones. I've got the best script to hit Hollywood in five years and I'm going to make a musical to end all musicals. I hired you because you're the best. Give me Oscar-winning costumes, Gaston, and nothing less. When we go to Mexico, I want you to go along and supervise. I do not intend to leave anything to chance."

Gaston said nothing, put his useless sketches in his valise, and turned to walk out the door. His face was red with anger. He despised men who could play with people as if they had no other life, but it was a fact of life that was magnified to its greatest intensity in Hollywood.

"And Gaston, take care of yourself, would ya? You do me no good lying in a hospital bed."

When Gaston looked back at him, Grant's smile was genuinely concerned. He was more baffled by Grant than ever before.

It took eight months to complete the filming of *Serendipity Song*. Shortly after the decision to shoot in Mexico, Darma Logan died in a private sanatorium from renal failure. Shooting was canceled for a week, during which the funeral and memorial services were held. The funeral was extravagant, but only Grant's closest friends attended the wake at his home in Beverly Hills; therefore, Gaston was more than surprised when Grant personally asked Gaston to follow him to the house. It was a mystery that was soon to be solved.

When the last guest had departed, Grant ushered Gaston into his study.

Gaston accepted a glass holding three fingers of brandy. The ice cubes rattled loudly.

"You need to do something about those shakes of yours," Grant said, gesturing at Gaston's hands. Grant poured himself an equally strong drink, downed it quickly, and poured another. "Darma always loved this house," he said, looking around at the walls of books. " 'Course she was never here very much. It's not a happy house, no children. . . . When you were growing up, was yours a happy house, Gaston?"

"Yes, for the most part it was. Especially when Karl was alive."

Grant had almost finished his drink. "Karl? Tell me about him."

Gaston wondered what purpose there was in the questioning but he continued. "Karl was my stepfather. He was very good to me, taught me a lot of things . . . and he loved me and my sister very much."

"Your sister?"

"Juliette. She was the strangest little girl. Ugly as sin, but now she's almost grown and quite beautiful. She has fabulous blond hair and the most unusual blue eyes." Gaston stared into Grant's level gaze. "That's funny . . ."

"What is?"

"I just noticed . . . your eyes . . . are almost the same color as Juliette's."

Grant's expression didn't change. "That is unusual," he said, rising for another drink. "How old did you say she was?"

"She was seventeen in January."

Grant poured another Scotch. "I wish I'd had children. They make a difference . . . especially later in life."

Gaston watched him, puzzled. "Tell me, why did you ask me here?"

"I like your directness." He seated himself. "One reason is to apologize for being so harsh on you during this film. I don't want you to take it personally. I push everybody, but on every movie I make, I always feel as if my back is to the wall. Which could be the reason I've won so many Oscars. I have a lot of confidence in you. I knew Renée Dubois's son could be nothing but a genius."

Gaston bristled at his words. "So, it was my mother's influence that got me this job. Did she pay you or only have to sleep with you to buy me this favor?"

In seconds Grant was on his feet and slapped Gaston across the face.

"You don't ever talk about Renée like that. I don't give a shit who you are!"

"Fine time to be gallant, Mr. Morgan."

"Your mother is the finest woman on earth. I haven't spoken to her in over twenty years."

"Guess responsibility is too much for you, huh?"

"What are you talking about?"

"My sister—I wonder how she'll take it when she finds out she's a bastard—just like me."

Suddenly, Gaston felt as if he couldn't breathe. He wanted to get as far away from Grant and Monument Studios as possible. At that moment he wanted to obliterate Grant—and his mother— from his life.

Grant watched him leave, shaken and equally angry. Why hadn't Renée told him about Juliette? Why had he been so foolish as not to make contact before this? Gaston had been his only link to Renée and now he'd blown that too.

He wondered how much longer he could go on pretending his make-believe movies were his life.

Chapter Thirty-two

Gaston turned the prescription bottle upside down. His tranquilizers were completely gone—which seemed impossible since he'd just had them refilled two weeks ago. He looked at the clock. It was three minutes past midnight. He would never get to sleep without something. Luckily, the drugstore stayed open all night. Wearing an undershirt, dungarees, and trenchcoat, Gaston left his apartment.

Kate Millgrew scrounged through her purse and the pockets of every jacket and coat she owned for money. It was late, she had forgotten to cash her last paycheck at the bank, and she was out of cigarettes.

"Eureka!" she cried when she found five dollars in one of her beaded evening bags. What a waste it had been shipping those out here from New York. In her two years of independence, Kate had not once used an evening bag or gown. Free-lance set designers were lucky to find steady employment and pay rent on meagerly furnished apartments. Despite the drawbacks, Kate had never been this happy.

Once she had learned that in Hollywood the race went to the strongest and fittest, she set out to be the very best. She was talented, but in time she found she was not stellar. She kept looking for her niche, but she had not found it.

Now that *Murder at Midnight* had "wrapped," Kate was again pounding on studio doors for another assignment. Paramount had nothing and neither did M-G-M. She wasn't discouraged, though. There was still Twentieth Century and Monument Studios. In the meantime she needed those cigarettes.

It was pouring rain when she ventured out, but the drugstore was only nine blocks from her apartment.

Kate paid her bill, pulled the collar of her raincoat up around her ears, and made a mad dash out of the drugstore, smack into Gaston Dubois. The paper bag ripped with the impact of their bodies. She cursed aloud and looked down at the carton of cigarettes being soaked by the rain.

"Now look what you did!" she groaned.

"You ran into me, lady," he said, bending down to help.

She shoved his hand out of the way. "Never mind, I'll do it myself," she said, glaring at him.

She could tell he hadn't shaved in days, and rainwater had matted his hair to his head. He looked like a skid-row wino in one of those old George Raft movies she saw on television. But there was something oddly familiar about him.

"Don't I know you from somewhere?"

"That should be my line," he said gruffly, handing her the cigarettes.

She looked more closely at him. She could never mistake those violet eyes. "You were at Cécile Thorpe's party two years ago." She studied him up and down. "What happened to you?"

"What kind of question is that?"

"I thought you were the handsomest man I'd ever seen."

"And now I'm not?"

Kate laughed. "I didn't mean it like that . . ." she said, thinking that his eyes could mesmerize anyone no matter what the rest of him looked like. She had been in Los Angeles for two years now and she would have had to be dead not to know about Gaston Dubois. Since the release of *Serendipity Song* there were already whispers of an Oscar nomination for his costumes; every studio in town was after the man who put Edith Head and Jean Louis to shame, and to date he'd turned them all down. In an interview for the *Los Angeles Times* he'd stated that he was about to open a boutique, *Gaston*, to be located off Wilshire Boulevard on Rodeo Drive near Carroll and Co. Everyone connected with the movies thought he was crazy. Kate thought his idea was a stroke of genius.

Gaston was feverishly trying to place this washed-out looking young woman at Cécile's party. He knew everyone who'd been there, but the memory was a blur.

Kate thrust her hand at him. "Kate Millgrew."

"Gaston Dubois." His violet eyes peered at her. "I can't for the life of me remember meeting you that evening."

"We didn't . . . not formally, anyway. But you did spend a great deal of time staring at me. You really made me nervous."

Gaston's face lit with recognition. "The haughty girl in the flower-petal dress!" He looked across the street. "Can I buy you a cup of coffee?"

Kate smiled. "I'd love it!"

Kate devoured two glazed doughnuts and three cups of coffee while Gaston talked. She told him a little about her work and how she got to Hollywood, but it was evident he wanted a listener and she was happy to oblige.

Gaston Dubois was a very lonely man, she discovered. He told her he didn't have friends in Los Angeles as he had had in New York. She questioned him about all the parties he attended which were reported in the newspapers.

"I don't go anymore. I can walk into a room full of people and everyone is your friend only as long as your success sustains itself. Those people are not friends," he said as a shadow fell over his face.

Kate instinctively knew Gaston felt he'd told her too much. Quickly he switched the topic to his new shop.

"I've got just about everything lined up, though I still need to find a store retailer."

"What for?" Kate asked.

"I know how to set up a French boutique, but American women buy differently. I need to combine the two somehow . . . and yet I want it to be ultra chic."

"I don't see what problems you could have. After all, *you* are the boutique. It should be like your designs—dashing, young, carefree, and stylish."

Gaston nearly blushed at the compliment. It was the first time since coming to Hollywood that he'd met someone who genuinely believed what she said. He was intrigued.

Kate was munching on her doughnut. "Even I could set up your boutique for you. I know enough about scene settings." Suddenly she stopped chewing and looked at him. "Gaston, I'm serious. I need the work and I know I'd do a damn good job. What have you got to lose?"

Gaston was unsure. He had intended to hire a professional, not an out-of-work set designer, but something told him to risk the gamble. He scribbled his address on a paper napkin. "Meet me at my place tomorrow at eleven and I'll show you the location I've rented. Then we'll see just how good you are."

Kate smiled back at him. "I think I like you, Gaston, especially when you don't look so gorgeous."

"I was thinking the same thing about you, Kate."

One should never trust first or second impressions, Kate thought to herself as she inspected the installation of the loft railing and curved staircase. Gaston was *not* beautiful on the outside or the inside and she had just about had it with him.

She slammed the construction blueprints down on the carton of lighting fixtures and stalked back to his office. The sound of hammers, electric drills, and saws filled her ears. She had a splitting headache.

He was gulping a glass of water when she barged in. "When are you going to get off those things?"

"When you get off my back! Besides, a mild tranquilizer never hurt anyone."

"Why don't you try sleeping instead?"

"I'd love to, but in case you don't read *Variety*, I have just signed a contract to do the costumes for *The Eyewitness*. The preliminary sketches are due on Monday, and to top it all off, you keep changing your goddamn mind about the boutique every five minutes! So help me, if you've come in here with something that is going to cause those very patient men out there to walk off the job, you can walk right along with them."

Kate was dumbfounded. "All my ideas have been improvements!"

Gaston's frustration seeped through his words. "True. But please, try to think of them *before* construction!"

"I can see we are not in a good mood, so I won't bother you."

"No, 'we' are not! And I do have other things on my mind."

Kate carefully shut the door without a sound, knowing Gaston would read all the sarcasm into the gesture she'd meant. Kate watched as leaded-glass panes were inserted into the front door and checked the padded peach satin walls in the main showroom. It was going to be the most lush boutique Los Angeles had ever seen. Despite her differences with Gaston, this was the most challenging and exciting project she'd ever done. The three years of searching for her niche had paid off. She couldn't imagine anything more rewarding than what she was doing.

She looked down at her plans. She would go ahead with her idea of French cradle telephones in every dressing room without Gaston's approval. She had decided to upholster the dressing room walls in cream satin and use a different cheval mirror in each room rather than all mirrored rooms. She wanted to take out the last two dressing rooms and combine them into one large completely mirrored room. Thus for ball gowns, bridal gowns, and party dresses there would be more room to maneuver. Kate believed that, besides the initial overall impact of the store when the customer walked in, the dressing rooms were most important. Here was where the customer would be spending most of her time. Even if she intended to buy only a blouse, she would always be seeing herself juxtaposed against a luxurious setting. The customers' mental images would help sell clothes. This was the "illusion" she constantly referred to in her plans.

Kate was not unaware of the pressures on Gaston. The boutique was costing twice what he'd planned, and to pay for it, he'd had to accept Monument's offer to do another movie. Gaston complained daily about Grant Morgan, "the ogre," and his demands. *Serendipity Song* had been nominated for ten Oscars; Gaston's was the first to be announced. She knew he wanted the award if only because it would kick off the boutique, but she sensed there was another reason for his need of it—something she knew nothing about.

Despite the construction delays, it appeared that the boutique would open on schedule the day before the Academy Awards.

The party at Romanoff's after the Academy Awards was more star-studded than the skies over the Hollywood Hills. Samuel Goldwyn, Leland Hayward, Jack Warner, and Darryl Zanuck all stopped by Grant Morgan's table to congratulate him on his "sweep." Gaston sat next to Doris Day, who eyed his Oscar appreciatively. Marilyn Monroe gushed over Gaston's accomplishment and said she would visit his boutique soon. Susan Hayward and Claudette Colbert reiterated what Marilyn said.

Gaston finished off his Scotch and soda and ordered another. Michael Segelman leaned over to him.

"That's your fifth drink, don't you think you should take it easy?"

Gaston peered at Grant Morgan's "henchman." "You sound like Kate."

"Maybe you should listen to her," Michael whispered in punitive tones.

Gaston had no use for Segelman, especially tonight when he'd never been so positive about everything in his life—especially his shop.

The opening of *Gaston* the night before had been a stroke of genius. With tensions high over the Academy Awards, everyone in Hollywood grabbed the opportunity to go to a free, highly publicized bash. Forty-two cases of Moët and Chandon were consumed before ten o'clock and the waiters dressed in peach satin waistcoats and cream pants to match the boutique's color theme went scrambling for extra champagne. Kate had nixed Gaston's idea of an hors d'oeuvre table and instead placed strategic buckets of fresh strawberries with stems intact everywhere. The turnout was twice what either of them had expected. Over three hundred of Hollywood's most noted, wealthy, and powerful attended.

Gaston now looked at the Oscar sitting at his elbow. As studio heads, agents, and movie stars offered their congratulations, Gaston knew he deserved none of it. This award should have been given to Jean Larousse, the man who had nurtured Gaston's talent from childhood and who had taught Gaston how to make women love themselves.

Gaston knew that women inherently hated their bodies—a ridiculous notion, but still, a fact. He wanted to make them all beautiful. Someday, he would open another boutique, and then another, but for now, this was his beginning. Gaston had wanted this award desperately, thinking it would in some way repay Jean for all he'd done.

Curiously, Gaston did not feel successful. The Oscar coupled with the fabulous opening of *Gaston*, was not enough; he felt that something was lacking. He had done it all on his own and had never had to call upon his mother for help. He liked his independence and this feeling that he was not responsible to anyone except himself, he told himself. Why, then, did he feel as if there were something missing?

He and Grant Morgan were not getting along any better than they had on *Serendipity Song* and that inexplicable tension between them seemed to grow like a cancer. He worked torturous hours to keep up with deadlines, but nothing pleased Grant. Gaston wished he could let Grant's criticisms roll off his back but he couldn't. He latched onto them and carried them around like barnacles.

Kate sided against him, saying he was at fault, charging that he deliberately kept crews waiting while he altered a perfect costume. Gaston didn't listen to Kate's bitching about anything anymore, especially not about the pills he took to get himself up nor the pills he took to catch some much needed sleep. She was the nagging fishwife type, and as soon as the boutique was in full swing, he would not need her any longer. Perhaps then he would get some peace and quiet. The more he thought about it, he realized that it would be good for Kate to get away from him too. He had pushed her a great deal and it was obvious to him that they would never be able to work together.

Gaston yawned. Sleepy? He couldn't get sleepy tonight! He still had a speech to give, and everyone said this thing would go on till dawn. Surreptitiously, he slipped a tiny pill out of his coat pocket and swallowed it.

Kate waited impatiently by the radio, listening for the Oscar results. She was more certain than he about his chances. Perhaps that was why he hadn't wanted to escort her to the ceremony: he was afraid of losing. It didn't matter now. She had desperately wanted to go, but she never pressed it with him. He was unbelievably edgy these days, and she knew why. Gaston was becoming addicted to the pills he took. She didn't know what they were specifically, only that he had changed into someone she didn't know and didn't *want* to know.

When they first began working on the boutique together she

had enjoyed being with him, watching his dream become reality. In the beginning, all their ideas jibed. Sometimes they would even have the identical idea at precisely the same moment. She had loved working late at night at his apartment, sketching the interiors while he cooked cheese omelettes. They were perfectly in tune with each other. She would fall asleep on the floor, and at some point he would have moved her to the couch, for when she awoke in the morning, he would be sitting next to her with a cup of hot coffee and marvelous pastries he'd found at a nearby bakery.

His voice was light then, with none of the tension and anxiety it held now. His eyes used to dance with the fire of ambition tempered with a labor of love. She fell in love with him.

It was during the initial construction phases when the first walls were going up and their emotions were high and their illusions still intact that they became lovers.

Kate had left early wanting a hot bath to soothe her aching muscles and told Gaston she would come by in the morning for coffee before they drove over to the construction site. She had just stepped out of the shower when the doorbell rang. She grabbed her favorite chenille robe, wrapped her sopping hair in a towel, and asked through the door, "Who is it?"

"Gaston," he said.

Kate unlocked the door, expecting him to remind her of some chore she'd forgotten, and found herself staring at the largest bouquet of yellow roses and gypsophila she'd ever seen.

"What's this for?"

Gaston walked in and put the flowers on the table. When he turned to her his eyes were filled with a sincerity that she had never seen before. He took her in his arms and kissed her passionately. "I need you, Kate."

An unaccustomed warmth spread throughout her body. She put her arms around his neck and kissed him back. She was surprised at her own aggressiveness for she found she couldn't hold back. She kissed his cheeks, his chin, and throat. She held him tighter and leaned her body into his. She could feel his hands as they untied the belt of her robe and rested on her hips.

At no point did Kate think about the fact that she was a virgin, nor did she remember those horrid tales her mother told her about "the first time." All Kate knew was that she wanted Gaston.

When they walked into the bedroom, he did not stop kissing her and he kept one hand on her breast, teasing her nipple until it was hard. By the time she was on the bed, Kate thought her entire body was on fire.

"I love you, Gaston," she said during the one moment when her breathing did not threaten to cease functioning.

As he eased himself inside her, he said: "I love you."

His penetrations were slow at first and then quickened and increased the flames inside her. Kate had stifled her moans but when she climaxed nothing could stop the scream of pleasure that roller-coastered out of her mouth. Seconds later, Gaston exploded with his own orgasm. When Kate opened her eyes and looked up at him, he was smiling at her.

"You really do love me."

"Yes, really."

"Good," he said, taking her in his arms and rolling to one side. He locked his legs around hers. "That's the way it should be."

For three weeks, Kate celebrated the end of her virginity by making love to Gaston in his car, on the couch, in his bed, in her bed, and even on top of cardboard cartons of building material. She was an insatiable wanton and she was in ecstasy. Gaston teased her that she was "only after his body," but they both knew theirs was a special love.

Kate did not think about all the women Gaston had been involved with, including the notorious Amanda Sommers, or that Kate herself had been referred to in the gossip column as "Gaston Dubois's newest clothes hanger," or worse: "Gaston's girl," when they didn't refer to her by name. Kate didn't care, because she knew he loved her.

As the weeks passed and the boutique took shape and the bills rolled in, Gaston took out a second loan. Then a third. It was difficult to convince conservative bankers, even the Hollywood variety, that luxury would insure profits. They still thought they were bankrolling a movie and that "props" did not a "hit" make. Gaston became frustrated and looked elsewhere for the money. The contract with Monument for *The Eyewitness* came at precisely the time when he placed the order for the Italian marble columns and floors.

Instead of having dinner with Kate, playing gin rummy, or

making love to Kate, Gaston worked. The work on the boutique, the designs for his first line of sportswear, the dozen evening gowns, and now the costumes for Monument created tremendous pressure. Gaston abandoned food and sleep and began taking pills again. His nerves were taut and his disposition abominable.

Kate tried day after day to reason with him to no avail. He made enemies of everyone he worked with and the only thing that saved him from being kicked out of Hollywood altogether was that his clothes and costumes were incomparable.

Gaston purposely fed the gossips himself, letting wisps of information about the boutique and his *prêt-à-porter* line seep out to the public. Keeping the bulk of his genius a secret, he wanted only to spark interest. What he created was a blazing fire. As the weeks passed and Gaston was pestered by the press for more details, he wallowed in the limelight he'd created for himself. Like a falling ax, he cut Kate out of his life. Except for the time she put in on the job, they did not see each other.

Initial shock turned to hurt and then to anger over the rejection. Kate was numb with pain for weeks, but Gaston saw none of it. He had become self-centered and egotistical.

Kate blamed herself for being naïve and believing in him. She blamed the pills he took for the alteration in his behavior, but in the end, she blamed herself for not being strong enough to get the hell out.

Kate had always been a hopeful person and her memory perversely reminded her of the beautiful love they had briefly shared. Convincing herself this nightmare would pass, she made excuses to see him. She invited him to lunch, but he never showed; she offered to work late, only to have him leave early; she thoroughly humiliated herself. Gaston waved her away as if she were a bothersome insect.

Hedda Hopper reported that Gaston Dubois had resumed his affair with Amanda Sommers. Louella Parsons stated that he was seen with two starlets, one blond, one "very brunette." Stories about his association with Tommy Brand resurfaced. Kate telephoned his apartment but never found him in.

Months later, Kate finally realized that Gaston had real problems and she could not help him. The night before the Academy Awards she made her decision to leave Hollywood. She wondered if it was the right thing to do. Once before she'd been strong when she left her parents and came to California. Now she was going back, but this time she didn't feel strong at all.

Gaston awoke with a terrible hangover. Success had its drawbacks, he thought as he fixed himself a double Alka Seltzer and turned on the shower.

Gaston raced through his shower, called Kate but got no answer, finished shaving, and mixed a cup of instant coffee. Just as he reached the door, he turned back, and dialed Kate's number again. Nine, ten. . . . He slammed the receiver down, grabbed the tie he'd left over the back of the sofa, and cursed as he dashed to his car.

When he walked through the leaded-glass door to *Gaston* his headache vanished and his smile reappeared. He greeted the salesgirls and went to his office. His secretary handed him a list of his appointments and told him the head fitter requested a meeting at three, to which he agreed.

"Mary, let me know when Miss Millgrew comes in," he said and signed the papers she'd handed him.

"She called earlier and said she wouldn't be in today."

He frowned. "She can't be ill, because I called and she wasn't home. Never mind, I'll handle it."

Mary went back to her desk as Gaston closed the door.

Gaston checked on a shipment of silk, the sequins and bugle beads he'd ordered two months prior, and placed a call to New York to Abe Goldberg.

"Hello, Frenchie!" Abe said. "You're hot stuff this morning! The *Times* is splattered with your pictures. You must be on top of the world."

Ironically, he felt the opposite. "I feel rotten. Must have been too much party last night."

"I can imagine."

"Abe, I got the first shipments you sent: the slacks, blouses, shorts, and jumpsuits. How long do you think it'll be for the skirts?"

"Isn't mass production a kick?" Abe laughed, but getting no like response he quickly said: "They should arrive tomorrow."

"Good," he said impatiently. "We may have to set up production out here."

Abe gasped. "That would cost a fortune! Just hold your goddamn pants on! I got that order out in three weeks. I don't do that for nobody, especially this quality! What the hell do you want, Gaston?"

"Miracles."

"Go talk to God, I haven't got the time!"

"Abe, I'm sorry. It's just been hectic and I'm running as fast as I can and it still doesn't seem like enough."

"Yeah, I can understand that. And losing Kate hasn't helped either, I guess."

Gaston's brain was fuzzy but he knew he'd heard Abe correctly. The old man must be senile, he thought. It was a shame. "Where would you get an idea like that?"

Abe stuttered a moment. "I read it in the *Tribune*. One of their reporters was at Idlewild when she flew in on the red-eye. She was pretty terse with him but he got the story that she was back in New York for good. The item was right next to you and Oscar."

Gaston was unbelieving and he had to find the truth. "Abe, I gotta go. I'll be looking for those skirts." He hung up.

It wasn't possible! Kate would never leave him and *Gaston*. She'd told him it was partly her dream, too, because now she'd found her career. Why would she walk out on him like that?

He raced to her office, burst through the door, and found the room devoid of everything except a desk and chair. Her antique inkwell and feather pen were gone as were her pictures of her parents and the snapshot of the two of them at Malibu. He opened the drawers. Her makeup kit, hairbrush, and stash of Hershey Bars were also missing.

He snapped on the intercom. "Mary, I'm going out for an hour. I'll call you for messages," he said and rushed to his car.

On the way to Kate's apartment, he knew it was true. She was not going to be there. And what had he expected? He'd got what he wanted—he'd spent the past five months driving her away. Gaston Dubois had been kissed with success again.

He pulled up to Kate's apartment and slowly mounted the steps. The rooms were empty. It was as if she'd never existed. He slammed his fist on the iron railing and felt instantly weak.

He sat on the steps looking at the dandelions growing in the cement cracks. He needed her more than anything and that had scared him to death. He had always been dependent on his mother, and he'd pushed her away too. He liked being free, doing things on his own, didn't he? This sinking feeling in his stomach made no sense to him. He would miss her, but it wasn't the end of the world. There had been some good times, but she had become too possessive. He'd tried to explain it to her but he could see now she hadn't understood. He could find another assistant by five o'clock today and things would go just as smoothly as before.

He rose, thinking of the shipment of English woolens that was due, the seamstress he was to interview. Gaston knew that being in his boutique, wearing his creations, and being fitted by Gaston himself was as close to heaven as a Beverly Hills wife could get. He smiled. Yes, his boutique was his sanctuary and he did not need anything else or anyone.

Chapter Thirty-three

Of the hundred-plus film festivals held around the world each year, it was the glamorous private parties that made Cannes the most celebrated of them all. The long days of screenings would always be there, but Cannes was more than a trade show. The casinos were perpetually packed to overflowing, and the prostitutes were often dressed more tastefully than the movie stars or the wives of the world's wealthiest producers. For the film industry, Cannes was a glittering working holiday in black tie. But Grant Morgan was not thinking about parties or movies when he flew to France that May of 1954.

The thirty-two-hour-long appearance he put in at Cannes was torturous for him: all he wanted was to see Renée. He rented a fire-engine red Fiat convertible and headed north to Paris.

The sign was new, encompassing three buildings, and he particularly liked the new gray and white striped awnings over the entrances. Grant sat in the car, tired, hair windblown, and feeling much in need of a bath, but he didn't care. He had waited a lifetime to see her. As he approached the door, he suddenly felt unsure.

What if she hated him so much she wouldn't speak to him? What if she were in love with someone else? He'd read stories about her and Greek shipping magnates, princes, and shahs. He had never believed any of it. He knew he was being overly romantic about the situation, denying her any other life except what existed in his memory.

He knew about Karl and the glory she'd brought her family during the war, but he expected that of her. Those stories were fact . . . the gossip was fiction. He knew his Renée.

Renée didn't pay any attention to the bright red Fiat parked in the no-parking zone in front of her store, but Pierre did.

"Can you believe the audacity of these people? I just paved the alleyway in back for parking!"

Renée shrugged her shoulders and went inside.

From the moment she opened the door she knew something was not right. She looked around and saw her vendeuses busily chatting with their customers. Beneath the glittering crystal chandelier a mannequin piroutted in a tailored black and white linen walking suit. Everything seemed normal, but as Renée walked through the showroom, chills coursed down her back and sent out a warning.

Then, suddenly, *she knew*. She hadn't seen him but she could feel him watching her. She spun around and there, next to a display of lynx, ermine, and fox stoles, stood Grant.

His sandy hair was shot with a multitude of gray but it was still thick, and as an errant lock fell on his forehead, he pushed it away with that familiar gesture she remembered. His deeply tanned face was marked with lines. But it was his eyes, the dark deep blue of her daughter's, that she remembered the most and when they smiled at her she ran into his arms.

She said nothing as she reveled in the feel of him, the pressure of his arms around her, the touch of his lips on her head, and the smell that was uniquely Grant. She closed her eyes, opened them and found this was not a dream.

She had been running in perpetual circles all her life, screaming into the wind only to have her cries flung back at her unheard. Until this moment nothing had made any sense. *He was back*. The world had been made right again.

"I was afraid you wouldn't see me," he said.

"I wasn't sure you would come."

"We were both fools."

"I know."

With his arm around her shoulders they walked out of Maison Dubois, leaving a dumbfounded Pierre staring after them. Grant opened the door and helped her into the car, and as he started the ignition, she knew where they were going.

The sun filtered through the skylight and fell on Renée while she slept. Grant looked down at her thinking how beautiful she was. Though time had etched fine lines around her eyes and throat, he thought it remarkable that French women always carried their age better than American women. He ran his hand down her thigh and back again. She moaned.

"What are you doing?" she asked groggily.

He pressed his finger into the side of her hip. "Testing."

"For what?"

"To see if you're done." He chuckled and raised himself on his elbows and kissed her lips.

"Am I?"

"To perfection."

Suddenly Renée burst into tears, and pulled him to her. "This time—"

"Don't worry. I'm not leaving without you. And if you won't come with me, then I won't leave. It's as simple as that."

"If it's so simple, why didn't we do it before? Why did we waste so much time?"

"Only the young can afford to waste time. We thought we were being smart. I'm not young anymore, but I've gotten damn smart."

"What about your movies? The studio . . . your employees. . . ?"

"What about them?" he said gruffly, momentarily feeling guilty over his abandoning everything he'd spent a quarter of a century building. "I've got accomplished people running the show. There are cables and phones, you know." He turned to her, the acid of lonely nights stinging his insides. "Or maybe you don't know."

"It works both ways," she said bitterly as she sat up and pulled the sheet to cover her breasts.

"I know this isn't easy for either one of us. But the way I look at it is that we have two choices. We can go on blaming each other for not making moves when we should have, or we can forgive each other. I know you can't forget what's happened, that's idiocy to think so, but we can go on from here. We can build, can't we?''

She looked at him. He was right. It was time to end the blaming—especially of herself. They had both earned this chance at happiness. She'd been a fool twice before and she was not about to make it three.

He placed his finger under her chin and tilted her face to him. "I can read your answer in your eyes."

Her smile was playful. "Am I so transparent? Are you telling me I no longer have any mystery? And that I hold no excitement?"

"Precisely," he said, pulling her into his arms and then giving her a light whack on the rump. "We'll be like those stodgy old married couples we saw in the restaurant who don't talk to each other. We'll sit in our rockers in front of the fire to warm our bones."

Her hand reached between his legs. "To warm what?" she asked as her lips quickly sought his mouth.

Grant's hand went to her breast and massaged it slowly. He leaned her back on the bed and kissed her cheeks and eyes. "I love you. I've always loved you." As he moved over her once again he said: "There will never be another man in your life but me. Say it."

"There is no one but you . . . there never was."

"Tilt your head down so that I can't see your face, only the hat. That's right. Now put your hands on your waist." The photographer snapped another round of film as Juliette thrust her flat abdomen forward to show the white pearl buttons on the skirt of the black Molyneux afternoon dress. The lights were unusually hot today, she thought, or maybe it was the thick, loosely tied white ascot at her throat. She moistened her lips and raised her left eyebrow and brazenly stared straight into the camera.

"*Magnifique!*"

The camera stopped clicking.

Juliette whipped the black horsehair hat off her head and called for the wardrobe mistress. The steel-boned corselette that had reduced her waist to nineteen and half inches had cut off her circulation and she was sweating like a racehorse. Her size-eight feet throbbed inside the size-seven shoes she wore, but she loved every minute of it.

"These were perfect," André said.

André Faverges was France's Richard Avedon. He had been a painter before becoming a photographer and his intense interest in contemporary art movements was reflected in his work. He emphasized sharpness and geometrical precision. His hard-edged, strong images rocked the fashion world in the early fifties at precisely the time when Juliette began modeling. They worked well together and both had become famous. He made her into a timeless, memorable woman who had no past, no future, only now. He played up her fresh-air looks and juxtaposed them against the rarefied fashion-world atmosphere. Though she was always well-groomed, with perfect nail color and coiffure, he might one day photograph her slouched carelessly on a chair and the next play the model game of stiffly posed studio shots. All were minor works of avant-garde art.

Juliette stated she would not have a career without him.

André knew it was his emotional involvement with her that made her pictures unique. It was a facet of his work he intended to keep secret.

André had just changed film when the door opened. "Monsieur Dumain! I was not expecting you!"

"I know. I thought I would see for myself what I was paying four hundred francs an hour for," he said, eyeing Juliette appreciatively.

Juliette dropped her gaze and pretended to give instruction to the wardrobe mistress. Monsieur Guillaume Dumain was France's newest addition to the publishing world. It was for the main fashion layout of his third issue of *Modern French Woman* that Juliette had been hired. She had heard about Guillaume Dumain from other models who had worked for him.

They had told her he was, unequivocally, the handsomest man on earth. She must remember to set her girlfriends straight—he was the handsomest man in *the universe!* He was in his late forties, unless he carried his age better than she could judge. His raven black hair showed no gray and did not look dyed. He was tall, athletically built, and she could tell he took great pains to keep in shape. But of all his handsome features, it was his dark brown eyes that fascinated her most. They smoldered and beckoned to her, promising an excitement she could only guess at.

For the first time in her life, she felt powerless . . . and, unbelievably, she found it intoxicating.

She did not flinch under his stares, but turned and walked off the platform and into her dressing room. She could feel his eyes on her like the hot breath of a panther stalking his prey. Through the closed louvered doors she heard M. Dumain ask André pointed and personal questions about her. Juliette smiled and realized she wasn't quite so powerless after all.

Monsieur Guillaume Dumain, otherwise know as the Marquis de Dumain, dropped his royal heritage at the age of twenty-three when he entered the business world. Crowns, he discovered, had their place, but behind the ticker tape in his walnut-paneled office overlooking the Seine, he needed brains and guts more. For the past twenty-five years he had lived a fast-paced life traveling the world over in search of the "right deal." Guillaume Dumain had found a lot of "right deals" so that at forty-seven he owned an empire with assets of over a billion dollars. He and J. Paul Getty were two of the world's richest men. Guillaume Dumain married only once, when he was twenty, and three years after the marriage his socialite wife left him for an older, wealthy man. At twenty-three, Guillaume gave up poverty and wives.

He dated the most beautiful women in the world, used them like short-term investments, and then "rolled them over." He treated them well, but always with a curious detachment for which he would become infamous. During the thirties in Paris and the forties in the United States, Guillaume protected his reputation, built his fortune, and became a philanthropist. Not until he reached his late forties did he fear anything. Suddenly he realized that his life was entering a final phase. He'd always wanted to publish a magazine and *Modern French Woman* was the culmination of two years' work. It was exciting work, it kept his name in the public eye, but best of all, it provided him with what he needed most: very young mistresses.

When Juliette arrived at André's studio the following morning, a white wicker basket filled with a profusion of summer blooms awaited her. There was no card, but she guessed it was Guillaume. At two o'clock, when she normally broke for a lunch of crisp vegetables and a thick slice of dark bread, a messenger arrived and handed her a card.

"Will you be my guest for dinner at Lasserre?" It was signed G.D.

Juliette was so excited she could not concentrate for the remainder of the afternoon. André finally ordered her to leave. When she raced out the door wondering what she would possibly wear that would make her look older, she could hear André cursing all the way down the hall.

Désirée sat on the pink ruffled day bed, thinking her cousin was acting quite strange.

Juliette's hair was set in neat rows of blond bobby-pin curls and she had smeared her face with an apricot masque. She held up two dresses, both different shades of red, and then tossed them on the chaise, shaking her head. "Too outré."

"What?" Désirée asked but Juliette paid no attention.

"Black net or fuchsia silk? White is too virginal."

"Why don't you ask your mother!" Désirée offered innocently.

Juliette pouted at her thirteen-year-old cousin. "Mother is not to know where I'm going. She said she was working late. I hope she does."

Désirée's eyes were huge with appreciation for the risk Juliette was taking. Her curiosity was about to explode. "Juliette, do you have a new boyfriend?"

Juliette swirled the full yellow silk skirt around her slender legs. "A man, Désirée. An older man!"

"Why would you want to go out with an old man?"

"Not an 'old man,' silly, an older man. There's a difference. Older men are sophisticated and worldly. I can learn a lot from someone with experience. Young men are too interested in their careers, always thinking about themselves and where they are going."

"Like Gaston?"

"Precisely. He's never been interested in what his girlfriends really think or feel. He doesn't have time. I want someone who will pamper me—like Papa used to do."

Désirée looked at the poster of James Dean hanging on the wall. "I still think I'd like a movie star."

Juliette shrugged her shoulders exasperatedly. "You're just a child with childish dreams. I'm a woman," she said, looking in the mirror. "It's different. I have needs. . . ." She turned and looked at Désirée intently. "This man I'm seeing is everything I want. He's even rich and powerful. So, even if Maman did know, I'm sure she would approve. But just in case she doesn't—this will be our secret. Promise?"

Désirée nodded earnestly. "Promise."

Guillaume Dumain called for Juliette in a silver Mercedes-Benz at eight o'clock and talked about her work for the magazine on the way to Lasserre. It was a warm summer night and Juliette was glad she'd selected the hand-painted voile off-the-shoulder dress. He chose the open-air dining area so they could see the stars. Guillaume was the perfect gentleman throughout their marvelous dinner. Juliette's head was spinning with excitement. He complimented her and teased her playfully. He was affectionate without being burdensome about it. He was just about the most marvelous man she'd known since her father died.

Juliette promised to meet him for lunch the next day.

After one week of hour-long lunches and two clandestine dinners, Juliette was certain she was in love. When she mentioned this momentous occurrence to André, his face turned to stone and he began fidgeting with his camera lens.

"Didn't you hear what I said?"

"Of course I did!" he bellowed and turned away from her.

She dodged the enormous umbrella lights and stood next to him. "I thought we were friends. I thought you'd be happy for me."

When he turned to her his green eyes were hard and oddly sad. "I think he's wrong for you."

"What are you talking about?"

"Dumain is the cause of half the French female population losing their virginity. He hates women, Juliette."

"You're wrong! He's not like that at all!"

"Listen, little girl. I'm ten years older than you are and I know what I'm talking about. If you don't believe me, ask your mother."

"What does she have to do with it?"

"I read somewhere she was his mistress. Like mother like daughter. . . ." he said bitterly.

Juliette reeled back and slapped him across the face. Both of them stared at each other. Juliette wondered how their emotions could have run away from them like that. André had never acted so hatefully, and to make up lies about her mother . . .

Furiously she turned away from him and stalked out the door. It was obvious André needed time to cool down. And so did she.

Chapter Thirty-four

Renée wondered offhandedly how Grant felt about being in Karl's house. She watched as he looked at the multitude of family photographs, all framed in silver, sitting atop the piano. Suddenly she felt very nervous, for the time had come to tell him about Juliette.

"Grant, there's something we have to discuss. Something very important to both our lives. And once you hear it, maybe you won't be so anxious to marry me."

"I know about my daughter," Grant said casually.

Renée almost gasped with shock. "How?"

"Gaston told me about her and I put two and two together. That was almost a year ago." He looked at her and knew what she was thinking. "Before you say anything, hear me out. I came to Paris to find you, not my daughter. I love you, and you have to know that in your heart."

She saw the earnestness in his eyes and knew he was telling the truth.

"I've thought about this a long time. You had a life with Karl, not with me, and you owed allegiance to him. I don't feel cheated for not knowing about Juliette. I feel, well, wonderful! After all, I'm becoming a father fairly late in life, even if she is grown-up. The only thing I worry about is that she won't accept me."

Renée felt crushed. How could she do this to him? He wanted to shout his news to the world and she was going to have to deny him this joy.

She took his hand and kissed it, wondering which was worse, to break his heart or her daughter's. "There's something you don't understand. Juliette can never know you're her real father. It would kill her. She adored Karl—in fact, she uses him for a model in choosing her men. The boys she has dated have all looked like him in one way or another. Nobody could replace him in her eyes."

Grant was stunned as he saw his dreams explode around him. When he put his arms around Renée he was trembling, but common sense told him she was right. "God! How I wish it didn't have to be this way. I'd like her to be proud of me and want me for her father."

"So would I. And she will love you, I know it. Perhaps we aren't looking at this correctly. As her stepfather, you can be more of a friend to her and that's what she really needs now. You'll know you are her father and that's most important."

Juliette was still in a rage when she walked into the salon and found her mother in the arms of a stranger. He was kissing her—hungrily. After hearing André's accusations about her mother and Guillaume, the scene shocked and appalled Juliette.

"Mother! What is going on?"

Renée turned around and smiled. She rose and hugged her daughter. "Juliette, I want you to meet Grant Morgan."

Stiffly, Juliette shook his hand. Grant tried to smile but he was in awe at seeing his own flesh and blood. He couldn't help thinking how much she looked like the pictures he'd seen of his mother when she was young.

"It's a pleasure," he said.

Juliette retracted her hand instantly, not knowing what to make of the situation. She'd seen her mother go out to dinner with men, she'd even accompanied her to parties; but never had she witnessed her mother kissing anyone other than Karl. Oddly, she hadn't thought of her mother having sexual urges like she had. It was one thing for her to kiss boys on the front door step or after too much wine, to let them fondle her breasts until they were panting so heavily they could barely speak. She liked the power she had over them at those times, but always she'd stopped them when she felt their hands try to dip into her panties. Instinctively, she knew she would lose her control and that would be disastrous. Surely, her mother didn't feel like that. Juliette decided she didn't like this Grant Morgan for the simple fact that he came between her mother and her memory of her father.

Juliette sat on the fauteuil chair across the coffee table from them.

"Grant is an old friend of mine," Renée began. "He's a movie producer and head of the studio where Gaston works. He's been telling me about your brother." Juliette said nothing. Renée continued. "Grant and I have known each other for a long time."

"How long?"

"Over twenty years," Renée replied, not liking the cold look in her daughter's eyes as she scrutinized every hair on Grant's head. Something was not right.

"Mother, do you know Guillaume Dumain?"

"I've heard of him. He has a notorious reputation."

"But you've never met him?"

"Not that I recall. Perhaps at a party. . . ."

"André said that you and he were lovers," Juliette said, looking pointedly at Grant.

Renée bristled; this wasn't like Juliette. But it wasn't the time to scold her either. Something was happening and Renée felt as if the situation were already out of hand. "That's not true."

"André said he read about it."

"There are many things printed about me that aren't true. In fact, I don't think I've ever been correctly quoted once. Juliette, why are you acting like this and why such an interest in a man I don't even know?"

Juliette was quiet, as if she hadn't heard her mother. She kept staring at Grant, assessing him.

Suddenly it dawned on Renée as she looked at Grant and then back at Juliette. Not until this past year had Juliette fully matured, and with maturity, her physical makeup had altered just enough so that today she was Grant's mirror image. It was all

Renée could do to stifle her own gasp of surprise. She had been foolish to think that she could keep the truth from her daughter.

Juliette's blue eyes were at once fire and ice. Her thoughts were tumbling over themselves so fast even she did not realize what she was saying or what was happening.

"You look very familiar to me, Mr. Morgan. You have known my mother for a long time. Have you always been lovers or is that a recent occurrence?"

"Juliette!" Renée exclaimed.

"No, let her go on," Grant said, his eyes bearing down on his daughter.

"You were lovers a long time ago, weren't you?" Now her eyes were filling with tears, her voice was cold and lifeless. Her pain rose in a blaze of fury as she bolted to her feet. "How many more lovers do you have, Mother? How many more bastards? My God . . ."

Juliette raced into the hall and out the door. Renée dashed down the steps and called after her, but it was too late. Her daughter was lost to her.

Renée found Juliette's address book and telephoned all her friends. No one had heard from her. She left a message at the model agency to have Juliette contact home if they heard from her. André's answering service took only her name and number.

Renée sought comfort in Grant's arms. "I did it for Karl, really. He never knew. He wanted children more than anyone on earth and deserved them more than anyone. To hear Juliette talk he is almost a god, and the thing is, she's not far wrong. I never wanted to hurt either of them. I just wish we could find her so I could tell her that."

"We will. Paris isn't that big. Maybe she just needs to be alone for a while. I don't believe for one minute that we've lost her. She loves you. You'll see I'm right."

It was a night filled with phone calls; none met with success. Pierre offered to come over, but Renée explained that Grant was with her. Pierre contacted friends both on the police force and private investigators to see what they could come up with. At midnight, it seemed as if Juliette had indeed vanished.

Renée tossed and turned all night and not even Grant's presence could calm her.

At 5:30 A.M. the telephone rang. The operator announced it was London.

Renée bolted up in the bed. Of course! Juliette had gone to Céleste's!

"Renée, chérie." Céleste's voice was disturbed and low.

"Aunt Céleste! What is it?"

"I need you to come to London. Herbert has died."

Renée was in shock. "That's impossible! You said in your last letter the doctor gave him a clean bill of health."

"The doctor was wrong. It was a heart attack shortly before midnight. I need you." Céleste was crying.

"I'll be there today. I'm bringing someone with me."

"Who?"

"Grant. He's with me now."

"I'm surprised he'll still speak to me."

"Grant holds no grudges. But I'll let him tell you that himself. We'll be there as soon as possible."

Renée knew this was not the time to bring up Juliette's running away.

"Thank you, Renée. You don't know how much I need you now."

"You were always there for me . . . so many times. That's what families are for."

At eight o'clock Grant and Renée raced through the airline terminal to the Air France counter to buy tickets for the next flight to London.

One concourse over, at the Pan Am counter, Juliette requested a window seat on the flight that would take herself, André Faverges, two wardrobe mistresses, four models, and a layout coordinator to Saint Bart's Island in the Caribbean. Only Juliette was aware that Guillaume Dumain would follow the next day on his private plane.

When she had gone directly to his office after the confrontation with her mother, he'd been more than sympathetic. He soothed her frazzled nerves, took her to a lavish restaurant for dinner, and when they went back to his penthouse, he showed her into the powder blue guest room and quietly shut the door. Juliette had never felt so protected in all her life. She had been right about

Guillaume. He reminded her of Karl, she thought with a pang, and she would not trust anyone else.

It was Pierre who discovered Juliette's whereabouts the day the family flew back from London. Renée sent cables to the villa where the modeling group was staying, but she never received an answer. The agency informed Renée they were to be in Saint Bart's for two weeks and then would go to Eleuthera, then to Paradise Island. The shoot was to take over three weeks. The girl on the other end of the phone stated that she was surprised Juliette was on the trip because she was slated to do work in Paris for the next three weeks.

"Monsieur Dumain must have changed his mind about her."

"Dumain? What does he have to do with my daughter's schedule?"

"He owns the magazine. He can do anything he wants," the girl said indignantly.

Renée instantly redoubled her efforts to contact her daughter, but as the days passed, there was no word.

Céleste, who had flown back to Paris with Renée and Grant, was worried more about her niece than she was her grandniece. "Give Juliette some credit! And some time. She will come back to you, but in the meantime you need to do something about your own life!"

"Look at you! I should be consoling you and here you are, trying to cheer me up."

Céleste's look was stern. "You finally have the man you've always wanted. It's plain to see he isn't going to leave you, but he will if you keep letting obstacles stand in your way. Your daughter is on the other side of the world for the next few weeks so you certainly can't stand over her shoulder anymore. I think it's time you got on with it."

Because there had been no engagement or advance publicity, because the bride and groom were celebrities, and because Céleste's good friend Lady Sara Covington made it her business to spread the joyous news, the marriage of Grant Morgan and Renée Dubois made the international papers.

Since neither her son nor her daughter were present, Renée's joy was dimmed. Grant fully understood and did not insist on the lavish wedding he thought she deserved. Instead, they both agreed that a honeymoon in a remote place was called for.

Villefranche was like a plunge into the mysterious past. Located on the west side of Cap Ferrat, its days were warm and the nights cooled by Mediterranean breezes. They occupied a small suite in the Hotel Welcome where from their balcony they could overlook the old port and the bay beyond. They walked down rue Obscure, a few steps from the waterfront, where heavy beams supported houses that bridged the street in medieval times, creating a dark tunnel that had to be lit even at noon.

They made love in the mornings, slept in the afternoons, and ate at marvelously quaint hideaways at night. Renée had waited all her life for Grant but rather than feeling cheated she reveled in the climax of the anticipation. He still had that uncanny ability to make her forget everything except him and the moment they shared. Because they traveled without fanfare, they were not bothered by reporters and they faded into anonymity with only the fact that they were so obviously on their honeymoon to draw attention to themselves.

For the first time, Renée knew what it was like to give completely of herself. She found she wasn't afraid to tell him she was anxious about Juliette and felt impotent to help her. From the things Grant told her about Gaston, she thought she understood him better. Grant tried to make her realize that her children were grown and there were mistakes they would have to make themselves, for which they would have to find their own solutions. She tried to heed his advice but it was not easy. She had never been good at letting go.

Grant rented a sailboat and they left before dawn to explore the fishing villages that dotted the Côte d'Azur. They stopped for huge bowls of bouillabaisse, spent hours lingering over a bottle of wine at a seaside bar, and through it all, Renée had to keep reminding herself they were truly married and that their happiness would never end.

Juliette opened the louvered shutters and looked down at the young brunette waiting in the convertible below. Lisette was only fifteen, though she had lied to the agency, telling them she was seventeen so she could get this job. Lisette was large-breasted for a model, but on her, negligees had never looked so good. Juliette closed the shutter and turned back to Guillaume, who was packing his Louis Vuitton suitcase.

"Don't lie to me, Guillaume. You aren't flying back to Paris on business. Unless you consider Lisette your business!" she accused.

He flashed her a menacing look that made her shrink back.

"I do the dictating! You understand? If I tell you I'm going to Paris then I am."

Juliette knew it was foolhardy but she couldn't stop. "A month ago you couldn't wait to be with *me*. You told me I was everything you ever wanted. You said you loved me!"

"I did. But that was then and this is now," he said, slinging half a dozen silk ties on top of neatly folded shirts.

"I believed you," she said to herself as she sank numbly into a rattan chair. "I believed you loved me."

He walked over to her and took her chin in his fingers. "I love you to pieces. But I love Lisette too. Now it's her turn. She understands that, why can't you?"

Gentian blue eyes slowly looked up. Gone was the innocence and softness that entranced men like Guillaume Dumain. Juliette knew that he'd been the one to relieve her of her artlessness and that she would never be the same. They were chilling eyes that riveted through to his soul. For a split second, Juliette knew she had touched him. "I understand perfectly, Guillaume. Now please go."

From the dazed look on his face she could tell he was not prepared for her response. He expected pleading, more accusations, and protestations of love. Suddenly they both realized that *she* had left *him*.

Blithely he shrugged his shoulders. "When you get back to Paris . . ."

"I won't be working for you."

"Why not?"

"That's *my* affair," she said, looking back at the louvered window. "Yours is waiting for you in the car." Rigidly, she rose, went to the door, and opened it for him.

When he reached the door, he paused for a moment as if to say something, or merely to look at her one last time; she wasn't sure. She turned her head and he left. She slammed the door and threw the double-bolt lock.

Juliette burst into sobs, clutched her stomach, and sank to the floor. It had all been an illusion, just like the world she created in her photographs. Guillaume had not loved her, even cared for her. He had lusted after her and that was all.

How could she have been so stupid as to fall for it? It was the oldest game in the world. These were modern times. Surely she had more brains than her great-aunt Céleste or . . . her mother.

Juliette's mind traveled back to her last encounter with her mother. The pain of her mother's betrayal was still there, but it was not as intense as it had been a month ago. She could thank Guillaume for that. Not that he had eased her mind, but he had taught her a difficult lesson—one whose pain was just as great.

She thought about the man who was her father. When she had seen them together they were kissing. She could tell from the way they looked at each other that they loved each other. Now they were married. The Nassau papers had carried the UP wire photograph of Grant and her mother on the steps of the Ile Saint-Louis home where the informal ceremony was held. The photograph was not clear, but they had been smiling at each other, not at the camera. Pangs of jealousy shot through her.

Juliette couldn't think of anyone but Karl. She remembered the happy times they'd shared. Only Karl had made her feel beautiful and loved. Her mother was proud of her work and of the person she was, she knew, but she had always gone to Karl with her problems.

She had to accept the fact that he was dead. Sometimes she thought she was a bit daffy needing him the way she did, even after his death. In those first weeks, it had been Guillaume's resemblance to Karl that had blinded her to his real motives.

As she sat on the clay-tiled floor of the villa on Saint Bart's Island, Juliette realized she hadn't loved Guillaume at all. What she wanted was not a lover, but a father. It was a curious revelation, she thought, since she'd been running away from the one person who was exactly that.

"What an idiot you are, Juliette!"

She'd been blind. All these weeks she'd put her mother through the pain of not knowing *exactly* where she was. Juliette had avoided the calls, torn up the cables. She'd even told the front desk manager at the hotel to inform anyone calling for her that she'd checked out. At the time she'd told herself she wanted to be truly alone with Guillaume.

She had been running away from the truth.

Quickly, she telephoned the airlines and booked the next charter plane to Miami. Juliette wanted to go home.

Chapter Thirty-five

Virginie Ruille signed the papers that would give her controlling interest in the Banco Milano and the First Federal Bank of Brazil, and which would purchase outright the assets and liabilities of the National Bank of Rome.

The photographers from *Time* and *Paris Look* recorded the occasion on film and nearly a dozen financial columnists barraged her with questions that she fielded like the international banking magnate she was. Virginie had spent her life building Crédit de Paris into the worldwide network it now was. She should have been thrilled with her accomplishment. In reality, she was moderately pleased. She wanted more for her family business, for she knew that power, once gained, must multiply continuously or it is lost. Virginie had lost only twice and did not intend to lose again. Once had been Edouard, the second time was Antoine Junot.

Emile stood off to her left, a placid smile belying the saturnine thoughts lurking in his eyes. Virginie quickly looked back at the cameras, unable to abide his presence.

Emile had no real power and was not an overt threat to her. She had given him few responsibilities in exchange for the meaningless title he coveted. She used him to her advantage and benefited from the few talents he did have.

Now forty-five, Emile had become an excellent public speaker. She kept him occupied traveling around the world, speaking at public functions that would promote the bank and their interests, both financial and political; and which would keep him out of her sight. Emile especially loved the assignments, since once he gave his stock speech, nothing was required of him except that he enjoy the bounties of the country in which he was being entertained. He'd found margaritas, flautas, and tacos in Mexico; pasta with clams in Rome; and the most exciting women on the beaches in Rio. Emile denied himself nothing when it came to food, liquor, and women.

Virginie kept close but discreet watch on Emile, making certain he did not cause her "problems" as he had in the past with his perversities. Her reputation was sacred to her and often she warned him that she could not afford an international scandal.

Virginie glanced over the heads of the reporters to the back of the room where Henri stood. Tall, like his grandfather, Henri had matured into a handsome young man. He still had Lady Jane's cornflower blue eyes and blond hair, but they were tempered now by Edouard's strong bone structure. As he watched her, his eyes snapped with excitement. He had looked forward to this day as much as she. Finally, he gave her the signal.

"Gentlemen," Henri said before the reporters had finished their questioning, "I'm afraid that will be all for today. Unfortunately, we have a very tight schedule. Thank you for coming."

Henri opened the boardroom doors and shook hands with the journalists as they filed out the door, making a point to say something personal to every man. It was a technique he had learned from his grandmother.

Virginie watched him proudly. Henri was everything she had ever wanted in a grandson and more.

Virginie turned toward Emile. "You can go now. Henri and I have things we need to discuss."

Emile's dark raisin eyes flickered in his bloated face. "Glad to oblige, Mother," he said caustically. As he lumbered out of the room, Virginie wondered how his heart managed to pump blood through that much fat.

Clearly, Henri had as little time for his uncle as Virginie did, for he seemed completely unaware of Emile's presence.

"I have the portfolios on those properties you asked me about," he said.

"Good." She took the files from him and briefly flipped through them.

Henri watched her face, knowing he would find no clues there to her thoughts. Only when she was furious with Lucienne or Emile would she allow her rage to show in the slightest tinge of blush on her throat. She was a perfectly controlled woman. He knew she wasn't going to like what she read in his reports.

"Your suggestion is?" she asked.

"That we curtail our expansion for now. We have bought five insolvent banks in the past eight years. The one in Bangladesh is causing us more problems than we had anticipated. I trust your judgment but I'm worried about stretching our assets this thin."

The tiniest grin of satisfaction flitted over her lips. She was not one to lavish praise. "I agree."

Henri played her game. He'd worked seven weeks on these reports only to hear her say "I agree," but from her that was praise enough. For years she had tested his knowledge, talent, and drive. He no longer had to prove himself. Henri knew he was the heir apparent to the Ruille fortunes and he found he enjoyed the crown. He was just as anxious as his grandmother to increase their wealth and their power. He had never lost in the banking world, but because he was young, he knew there was still that chance to fail. Henri vowed he never would. The restrictions he imposed on himself were, at times, just as great as Virginie's demands. He did not resent her hard ways with him, rather he thanked her. He was well aware that great wealth was a responsibility not to be taken lightly. He had to beware of his enemies and those that would like to see him collapse, as well as be alert to forces, even in his own family, that could cause the end of the Ruilles. Virginie did not view matters in quite the same way. She believed she held some kind of mystical power over Emile and Lucienne, but he was wary of them both.

"What about the bank in Riyadh?" Henri now mentioned his pet project. Since he was sixteen he'd investigated Saudi Arabia. More than any other spot on earth he wanted a branch there.

Virginie's gaze was level. "The bank there was terribly mismanaged. I don't see any hope of buying it."

Henri's hopes died. Once Virginie passed sentence, debate ceased.

"Instead"—she paused dramatically, increasing the tension—"we will build our own branch!"

Henri's face lit up. "But how? You just said—"

"These are things experience teaches, Henri. We may be expanding rapidly, but it is my belief that we would be better to sell all our other branches rather than delay in Riyadh. I have obtained a charter. It will take a few years to establish ourselves in Saudi, but I believe it is an imperative move. Someday, that bank alone could carry the rest of the conglomerate."

Though Henri was happy to hear his grandmother's decision, he also criticized her lack of vision and hesitation in waiting to make the move to Riyadh. He believed they would have been better off building in Saudi than buying these bothersome managerial problems in Rome, Rio, and Milan. Henri was not stupid, however; he knew the only reason Virginie was interested in them was because they were located in the same cities as branches of Maison Dubois.

Henri despised the Dubois family himself, but not to the extent that his grandmother did. He was sick of having his bastard half-brother's fame and disgusting lifestyle shoved down his throat every time he picked up a newspaper or went to a society party. In recent years, Gaston's fame in Hollywood had become like a monkey on his back—taunting and jeering at him. Henri hated it. He hated the idea that he had a brother somewhere he'd never met; one who flaunted his bastardy to the press like a medal of honor. Henri despised Gaston for being born at all, especially on the same day as he was. Gaston's flamboyant lifestyle, his women and drugs, were all too much like his father. Henri tried to be everything—except like his father. He did not drink or gamble and he was selective about his bed partners.

Henri believed, as his grandmother did, that Renée Dubois was responsible for Antoine Junot's death and probably for his father's too. The latter he was not so certain about since his aunt Lucienne stated she was convinced Edouard had committed suicide. Henri understood revenge. He would like to see all the Duboises crumble, but unlike his grandmother, he was not willing to make bad business decisions for the sake of revenge.

"I'm sorry I had to delay your dream a bit, Henri, but these other banks were a more pressing matter."

Henri couldn't help himself. "I don't agree."

"Really? And why not?"

"If Renée Dubois did not have outstanding loans with these banks, you would not have been so keen on acquiring them, would you?"

Virginie laughed airily. "I'm not that much of a fool. If you had looked closely you would have found that these banks were in trouble before she took out her loans. I checked the dates. They each made the mistake of thinking a celebrity clientele would win them new investors. They were wrong. A bad banker can ruin himself in one afternoon without even trying. I bought these banks because their problems were not insolvable and we can make money with them. The fact that Renée is indebted to them was luck." She paused reflectively, and when she looked at him, Henri was stunned by the ferocity in her old eyes. "I have *never* questioned luck."

Henri treaded softly with his next question. "Are you going to call her notes?"

"I don't think so. Right now, I could hurt her very badly, but it would not ruin her. According to the papers, she and her new husband are in the south of France somewhere. It seems the entire family made the news this past week. Juliette's affair with Guillaume Dumain is over—a fact that must be comforting to her mother, although Juliette has not come out of hiding to give an interview. Gaston was picked up for drunk driving in Los Angeles and spent four days in jail before anyone bailed him out." Virginie chuckled malevolently. "Renée's children must be a source of comfort to her."

Virginie went to the window and looked out. "I know the web I'm spinning, Henri, and it's too soon to pull the cord. I will know when the time is right. Trust me."

Henri nodded. For now, he would.

Book Five

1958

Chapter Thirty-six

In the late fifties, haute couture hit its zenith. Never before had there been the competition, the demand, and the quality in fashion. Security was at an all-time high. Employees were subject to intensive scrutiny before being hired. The spring and fall shows were conducted like top-secret affairs of state. Even the top designers in Paris kept a wary eye on the newcomers in Milan, Rome, and London. It seemed the entire fashion world was paranoid.

The models were more beautiful than ever and twice as thin. They lived on raw meat, cocaine, and dexies. The photographers expected them not only to pose perfectly dressed, made up, and coiffed but also to keep their poses while atop moving trains and boats. They were expected not to "melt" in steamy jungles; to ride camels, elephants, and exotic llamas; and never, ever to complain. The public reaction was for MORE.

Riding the crest of the modeling world was Juliette Heilmann. Always disciplined about her body, health, and face, her professionalism won her many accolades in the fashion world. Every magazine in Europe and America wanted her. *Harper's Bazaar* needed a long-legged blonde to pose in bikinis. They hired Juliette. She was photographed in chiffon caftans on Italian verandas, in white duck slacks and coral silk blouses atop mountains in Peru, and clad solely in Harry Winston's million-dollar diamond neck collar, three-inch bracelets, and sapphire tiara, her blacked out silhouette was juxtaposed against a blazing orange African sunset.

To millions of fans, Juliette lived a fantasy.

In the years following her flight to Saint Bart's Island, Juliette had lived out her own fantasy. In Grant, she had found the father she needed. He never tried to replace Karl's memory, only make new memories for her. She had everything she wanted. She was happy—almost.

There was something missing in her life, but she didn't know what. She had many escorts to parties. Many men wanted her, but she could never get close to any of them. Perhaps it was because she knew they wanted only her looks. She remembered how Gaston had treated her when they were children. He loved her for herself. So did Grant and Pierre, as had Karl and Jean when they were alive. She couldn't think of any man she felt comfortable around. Except for André, the photographer who had made her famous. Juliette thought perhaps she was asking too much out of life. She had money, fame, a family that loved her. It should be enough.

"More to the left, Juliette. That's it. Wonderful! Give me those fabulous blue eyes. A little more hip. Flash some thigh. Great!" André's camera clicked a hundred times as she moved easily from side to side in a diaphanous silk dinner dress.

"That's it." He smiled.

"What a day. I'm melting."

"You shouldn't be. I can see right through that thing."

"Really?" She quickly checked her breasts. The nipples did show. She looked up with a tantalizing smile.

André turned away and started packing up his gear. "I suppose you've got a hot date with that duke tonight, huh?"

"Baron," she corrected.

"Sorry."

"No, I don't. What made you think that?"

"I can't pick up the papers without reading something about your love life."

She stopped pulling the pins out of her hair and looked at him. She had worked with André for years. He'd never talked about anything but work. True, he'd encouraged her to go for some really outlandish stunts in his pictures, decisions they'd made over late coffee at a café. But he'd never mentioned other men in her life. Nor women in his life. In fact, she was under the impression he and Regina, the dark-haired temptress from Vouline's agency, were close. She would have bet money they were nearly engaged.

It was almost an unwritten code between them that they would never get personal, though she didn't know why. She'd worked with lots of photographers, but none of them made her look as good as André could. There was a special rapport between them. He made everything easy for her.

"If you wanted to know about my love life, why didn't you ask, André?"

"Huh? Well, I guess I never thought about it."

"Just what would you like to know?" she asked, walking toward him. She noticed that he suddenly seemed all thumbs. He actually dropped his camera.

He looked at her, his brown eyes sincere and warm. "I make good spaghetti. Would you like to try some?"

"Tonight?"

"Tonight."

His apartment was filled with huge, down-filled sofas that he'd had covered in off-white canvas. There were mounds of fat pillows in bright pastel cottons everywhere around a glass-topped coffee table. The kitchenette was small but workable and it was lacquered in a deep, sensual plum. He told her he'd refinished the wood floors himself. There were no drapes on the wall of glass that overlooked Paris.

While he started the sauce, Juliette made a salad. They talked of everything they'd never said. Juliette thought time had never passed quite so quickly.

While she cleared the table, he washed the dishes. She dropped a knife. They both bent to pick it up. Their faces were inches apart. In all these years, André had seen her nearly naked, in and out of every kind of dress, and not once had he ever made a pass.

He kissed her, tenderly, gently, as if he were afraid to let himself go. Her arms crept around his neck and she pulled him closer. His tongue probed her mouth. Juliette's heart was slamming against her chest and she felt breathless.

"André . . . we shouldn't be doing this."

"Why not?"

"Because . . . of Regina."

André's shoulders snapped back. "Regina? What are you talking about?"

"You're going to marry her, aren't you?"

"No. How did you get that idea?"

"Regina, probably. She's told all the models that you two were serious. She has for years."

"Is that why you've always been so distant with me? Never talking about anything but your damn career. I thought you were some kind of ice maiden."

"Thanks a lot."

"You really mean this, don't you? You really thought Regina and I . . ."

"Yes."

"The only one I've ever wanted was you. Couldn't you tell?"

"No."

"I've been in love with you since you were sixteen."

"André . . . I—"

"Oh, shut up," he said, clamping his mouth down on hers. With strong arms he picked her up and carried her to his bedroom. He laid her gently on the bed and kissed her hungrily. Just as he rose to snap off the light, Juliette opened her eyes and looked around.

Everywhere, on the walls, the ceiling, were pictures of herself staring back at her.

"My God! What is this?"

André knelt one knee on the bed as he hastily stripped off his shirt. "Sanctuary." He smiled.

Juliette opened her arms as he nuzzled his face in the crook of her neck. Never had she felt so at peace.

"I'm going to ask Aunt Renée for a job."

"Désirée! You're only sixteen. Your studies will decline if you work after school."

"Don't worry, Maman. I'll still be valedictorian."

Annette sighed. "That's not what I'm worried about. I'm

afraid you'll overtax yourself. You know what all this work has done to your father."

"Don't I."

"I don't understand you, Désirée."

"It's very simple. I want to be a part of Maison Dubois. It's Papa's whole world."

"Not his entire world. You and I . . ."

"Have always come second. I don't like it any more than you do."

"So what is this? If you can't beat them, join them?"

Désirée's lavender eyes flashed. "Why not?"

Annette looked at her daughter thoughtfully. "You're sure this is what you want?"

"Yes."

"I know you think I've been strict with you, early curfews, inspecting the boys who call for dates. But whenever it's been something you're very sure about, then I've agreed. Haven't I?"

"Yes."

"I think you want this job for more than simply an opportunity to be with your father."

"That's a big part of it. But you're right. I want to be part of this empire Papa and Aunt Renée have created. I see Juliette becoming more famous all the time with her modeling. Gaston has taken America by storm. Well, I want to be somebody too. I think it would be exciting to feel the kind of power Papa has. To be a part of everything that Maison Dubois is."

"It will take a long time to learn everything, Désirée."

"I've got the rest of my life."

When Désirée came to Renée armed with a list of her academic honors and asked for a position in the company, Renée was stunned.

"You're just as stubborn as Juliette and Gaston! Why don't you enjoy these years? Go to parties, have some fun. You don't need to be working."

"Aunt Renée, you were my age when you started Maison Dubois. Maybe I have the same needs as you."

Renée looked affectionately at her beautiful niece. There was a hunger in her eyes she'd once seen in her own. "Chérie, those were hard days for your papa and me. I had no choice. We had to eat."

"I think that even if you hadn't been poor and hungry you would have created Maison Dubois. It was your dream. You can't deny that."

"You're right." Renée felt as if she were looking at herself. Désirée's ambition was very much the same as hers had been, but there was no such thing as pain, revenge, death, or heartbreak to cloud her perceptions.

"And if I don't give you a job?"

"I'd go out and start my own shop," Désirée said firmly.

There was no confusion to Désirée's simple thinking. A sudden pang for the loss of her youth jabbed at Renée. Perhaps Désirée would help fill the void left by Juliette and Gaston.

"All right. The job is yours. But it won't be easy. If you're going to do this, you'll do it my way. At no time will your job interfere with your studies. Agreed?"

"Yes," Désirée said eagerly.

"Good. Then you'll have six months with purchasing, six months with design, and the last six months with your father. If you want to know about Maison Dubois, you'll have to know everything—from the way we make buttonholes to the way the boutiques are managed. After your graduation from school, your father and I will meet and decide where you are qualified to do the most good. That's the way it is in any large company. Once you've proved yourself then you can request what *you* want to do."

"I swear, Aunt Renée, you won't regret this!"

"I think you're right. I don't think I will."

Chapter Thirty-seven

Gaston awoke in time to see two women, one dressed in red chiffon, one in black leather, walk out the door. He tried to focus his eyes, but couldn't. He rolled onto his back and stared at the ceiling. He saw the image of a naked man lying on rumpled black satin sheets. There were two empty Scotch bottles on the pillow next to him.

Suddenly he couldn't see anything anymore and tried to focus on the mirrored ceiling again. He wasn't quite certain when he'd had it installed. Was it last year or last week? He wondered why his friends had left. Or even if they were his friends. A wave of dizziness washed over him as he tried to sit up. He fell back on the bed. Now he remembered . . . they were hookers . . . and expensive ones too.

He was falling asleep again. He couldn't remember how much coke they'd done, but he did remember complaining about a headache.

"Tension," the blond girl had said, and she gave him some pills. He took them, and when the headache didn't go away, he took some of his own.

He pushed the empty bottles to the floor and hugged the pillow against his chest. Why was it there was no one here? He shouldn't be alone. He hated being alone.

"Kate?" he yelled and opened his eyes long enough to see the phone. He scooted over the bed and picked up the receiver. "Where's she? Oh, yesh." He tried to dial but his fingers wouldn't stay in the holes long enough.

"Kate?" he said into the phone. Tears ran down his cheeks.

He forced himself to concentrate. "Find Kate . . ." he told himself. Finally he managed to dial.

Gaston could hear the phone ringing. Then the ringing stopped. "Kate?"

"No, sir. Miss Millgrew is in the bath right now. May I take a message?" a woman's voice said.

"You get Kate. Huwry. Tell her it'sh me."

"One moment."

Gaston watched the man in the ceiling blur into a flesh-colored blob against black satin.

"Who is this?" Kate's voice was indignant.

"Kate? Need you . . ."

"Gaston?" She gasped. "What is it? What's the matter with you?"

"Gotta shleep, Kate. Tell you . . . that . . ."

Alarm rang through the lines. "Gaston! What did you take? How many pills, Gaston?"

"Dunno."

"I'm hanging up now. I'm going to call the rescue squad. Are you at home?"

"Dunt hang up. Come home to me, Kate."

"Goddamn you, Gaston!" she screamed. "Are you at home?"

"Yeah."

"I'm on my way!" Kate yelled as she slammed down the receiver and jerked it back up again. "He better not die on me!" She dialed the operator. "Get me Cedars of Lebanon's emergency room in Los Angeles. It's a matter of life and death!"

The call rang through immediately and Kate relayed the pertinent information. Then she rang the airport and booked a flight on the next plane to Los Angeles.

Kate hailed a cab outside the LAX terminal and sped off to Cedars of Lebanon Hospital.

She looked out the window as the palm trees streamed past.

She remembered the day after the Oscars when she arrived in New York. Gaston had phoned her mother's house.

"I want an explanation," he demanded.

Three thousand miles between them and she could still feel his magnetism.

"I'm sick of your pills and bed full of starlets. I wanted out and I got out."

"Bitch."

"Bastard!"

She hung up on him—then and a thousand times more. Their verbal harangues were lengthy and upsetting. Finally Kate realized she was upsetting the entire household. She leased an apartment of her own.

She had an unlisted number, but Gaston was relentless. He tracked her down. This time he was strictly business.

"I'm ready to open a branch of my shop in New York. I want you to design the interiors. I want it similar to LA but more city sophisticate."

"Forget it, Gaston. We're poison to each other."

He kept after her, upping the salary every time until she decided that if he wanted to play the fool, then let him.

The silver, glass, and black Art Deco décor of *Gaston New York* was touted as the city's smartest atmosphere in which to shop. In the first month the boutique doubled the gross sales of the LA store.

Gaston asked Kate to manage the store for him at a ridiculously high salary. She was stunned. But if going bankrupt was his way of assuaging his guilt, then fine with her. She signed the contract he offered, and that day bought a diamond and coral pin to go with the mink jacket she'd bought the month before.

Kate spent the next three years running Gaston's shop, talking to him long distance, reading about his love life, and wishing she'd never met him. She was utterly in love with him and there was nothing for her to do about it except go on.

Over the years, Gaston turned to her more and more for advice. His calls at night and on weekends increased. When she discovered from her maid that he called when she was out on a date, inevitably she would read later that the same day he'd have pulled some crazy stunt at a Hollywood party, or that some blond bimbo was his newest girl. Gaston was out of control. And Kate couldn't stop him. She wondered if he was doing these things to spite her or hurt himself. She didn't care. Until the day he came to her and told her he loved her and needed her, she knew she couldn't expose herself to him. She was too vulnerable and he wasn't ready.

Kate pushed open the hospital room door, placed her luggage on the chair, and went to his bed. He opened his eyes.

"You look like shit," she said, smiling.

"You've gotten a gutter mouth," he replied.

"Comes from being in the business world."

His smile faded as he looked at her. Incredulously, his eyes filled with tears. "You're the most beautiful thing I've ever seen," he said and reached up and pulled her down to him. He held her to his chest. "What a mess I've made of everything, Kate."

She was crying when she looked at him. "Yes, you really have."

"Why do you put up with me?"

"I don't know. But I'm not going to anymore."

"What does that mean?"

"It's make-or-break time for us, Gaston. I'll give you one year to get your act straightened out. If you can't . . . then it's over. You won't see me again."

"I will make it. I don't want to live like this. I never wanted to live like this. I've become somebody I don't even know."

"We'll start with no more pills . . . or women . . . or inhuman work loads. Is it a deal?"

He squeezed her hand, his eyes filled with the determined fire she'd seen that first time at Cécile's party. "It's a deal."

Kate leaned over and kissed him. It was the first time she'd felt his lips in over four years. It could have been a lifetime.

Reluctantly, he let her go. "I want to go on a trip, Kate, and I want you to come with me."

"Where are we going?"

"Home . . . to Paris."

Book Six

1965–1972

Chapter Thirty-eight

Kate was still the most beautiful woman Gaston had ever known and now, in her seventh month of pregnancy, she was twice as beautiful. When the call came from Renée to their New York apartment informing them of Céleste's death, Kate had not hesitated about making the trip. Gaston loved her more every day and it seemed impossible to him that something this wonderful could be happening to him.

They had come a long way together since that day in the hospital when he'd been certain his life was over. As he looked back on it now, he wondered how everything had gone haywire without his realizing it. He still worked hard, but he was not driven any longer, trying to prove something to himself that was pointless. His boutiques were successful and he'd managed to open three new branches with less stress than when he'd opened his first. Having Kate by his side made all the difference. She was just as involved in the business as he was and yet she made certain he did not run himself into the ground.

It had been hell getting off the pills and booze for good, but not half as painful as the loneliness he'd felt when Kate had left. It was a life he never wanted to go back to.

He leaned down to his wife, who was sitting next to Juliette in the shade, several feet from where the priest had just said his prayers over Céleste's grave. "It's getting too hot out here for you. I'll walk you to the limo and then we'll go on to the house."

Kate nodded and turned to Juliette. "Will you and the twins ride with us?"

Juliette's eyes scanned the crowd. "I thought surely André would be here by now. He said his plane would be here in time for the burial. Maybe I should stay here a while just in case he comes late. I don't want to miss him."

Kate smiled. "I should think not. How long has he been gone?"

"Almost five weeks. I think it's the longest five weeks of my life. The children miss him terribly. Michelle had nightmares for the first two weeks he was gone. And Louis, he just sulks all day. It's been difficult trying to explain Aunt Céleste's death to them. Louis is convinced that André is dead too. Even Maman can't get through to him, though she and Grant have tried."

Kate reached out and took her hand. "I know André feels very strongly about his photojournalism, but hopefully he won't have to go back to Vietnam."

"It's pretty tough fighting a global political situation. And you know . . . I'm not so sure I should."

Gaston's pride for her shone in his face. "I hope he knows what he's got."

"He does."

Just then they heard a commotion in the crowd slightly beyond them. One by one people pointed at Juliette and smiled. "She's over there," someone said.

Juliette straightened and scanned the crowd. She sensed his presence before she saw him and then, suddenly, there he was; tired, unshaven, still wearing fatigues and looking as if he'd stepped from another world. Juliette nearly leapt into his arms. André held his wife while she buried her head in his neck and cried.

"It's all right. I'm home and I won't be going anywhere for a long time."

"Thank God," she whispered and kissed his beautiful, sweet face.

* * *

Of the three hundred friends that attended the funeral services at the church, nearly all followed to the cemetery and almost one hundred came to the Ile Saint-Louis residence afterward.

Pierre, Annette, and Désirée followed in their limousine. Pierre was in a trance, as he had been the past three days since Céleste's death. He thought of nothing except the days when there'd been little food and no coal—and Céleste's loving arms. Now she was gone. The pain was excruciating.

"Pierre, chéri, is there anything I can do?"

"No."

"Maybe if you talked . . ." Annette pleaded, knowing it wasn't good to shut himself away at times like this. But he always had . . . always.

"Annette, please . . . don't badger me."

"I was only—"

He leaned forward. "Where's Renée?"

"In the car ahead."

"I don't see her."

Just then, Désirée sensed the tension building between her parents. "It's all right, Papa. She's here. We're all here with you."

He patted Désirée's hand as he fought back tears.

Annette looked at him. He was back there in the past reliving those days when he and Renée had built that inner sanctum they would not share with anyone. There had been a time when Annette would have felt rejected, but now she knew Pierre better and, unbelievably, she loved him more.

Désirée had become a part of Maison Dubois, and Annette had done the same. True, her job was secretarial in nature, but she was with Pierre. She had a better understanding of the incredible demands on his time. She respected him more and he, in turn, found he had more time to be with her. Because she was there, he often asked her to accompany him to lunch with buyers and clients. When they were alone, they had more to talk about. He asked her opinion about his decisions. Though she believed her suggestions were not profound, she realized after a time that he often considered them seriously.

Finally they were working as a team.

Céleste's death was one of those times when Pierre's moodiness, his need for solitude, intruded upon their well-constructed world. It was a painful time for Annette, for it reminded her of all those years she'd waited and needed Pierre and he'd been too busy or too preoccupied to think of her. But those days were fewer now, and wisely, Annette knew this period of mourning would pass.

Désirée looked at her parents, both in their own private worlds. She saw the familiar pain of rejection in her mother's eyes, and vowed never to be like her. She would never allow herself to love a man that much, to put a man at the center of her life.

Désirée was smarter than her mother, she thought. She would marry herself to her career. She would be independent.

It wasn't easy following in her father's footsteps, living up to Gaston's fame and Juliette's beauty. But Désirée wanted it all, just as much as they and maybe more.

She knew she could get it all, too, if they would just quit treating her as a child. They were much too protective of her. She needed a chance to prove herself. The Dubois family was a tough lot, but she loved them, and she knew they loved her. She wanted to prove she was worthy of the name—and the love.

For the first time she was going to have to do battle with them. She knew she must get her way. Désirée knew the fight would be worth it.

The clock chimed twelve as the moon edged out from behind a cloud, illuminating the tiny balcony outside the French doors. Désirée started up the stairs when she heard muffled voices coming from the library.

"What about Désirée?" Pierre asked.

"You can't be serious?" Renée exclaimed. "She's a child and only beginning to learn the company. Do you have any idea how important London is to us right now? The entire fashion world is focused on London. Why, it's almost as if Paris never existed."

"Désirée has done a damn good job for us. And you couldn't find anyone else as loyal."

"I know. It's just—"

Suddenly the library doors flew open. Désirée stood before them, determination blazing in her eyes.

"My father thinks I could handle London, why don't you?" she demanded of Renée.

"I think you're much too impatient, to put it bluntly. Your

ambition sometimes gets in the way of your better judgment. I'm wondering if this isn't one of those times. London is multifaceted. There's retail clothing, retail linens, and linen manufacturing. You'll have wholesalers, manufacturers, and retailers to deal with. It's a very large order for one person."

"So, what better way to prove myself? It'll be a miniversion of the whole corporation. Look at it this way, if I do well in London, I'd have no trouble taking on more responsibility later on. I know I'm ready for it. I want this assignment."

"I know you do. But the timing—"

"Is that what you told Gaston when he wanted to go out on his own? Or Juliette?" Désirée knew she shouldn't have said that, but she felt the need to push all the buttons she could.

Renée looked from Pierre to Désirée. It was a big risk she was taking. She wondered if Désirée had the stamina to handle such a load.

Désirée had done everything to prove herself. Renée had two other managers in mind, both male, both competent, and both Londoners who understood the workers and the public better than she and Pierre together. She had been deadly serious when she stated that London was important, and she wondered if Désirée understood that she would be commanding the hub of their entire operation at this point. Outside of the perfume and cosmetics line, the linen company was supporting Maison Dubois. Their young designers in London were the ones with their fingers on the pulse of what was happening in fashion. It was the London boutique that fed the other stores across Europe. Most of all, Renée wondered if Désirée was aware of the power she would wield. Désirée's command in London during the current revolution in the fashion world was vital to their survival. It was not an easy decision.

Désirée was adamant. "Name one time I have let you down." She paused. "You see? You can't. The only thing you have against me is the fact that I'm only twenty-three. Look at all you had accomplished by then! What makes you think I'm not made of the same stuff, Aunt Renée?"

Renée wasn't sure if it was Désirée's argument or the late hour that wore her down. "All right. Your father will take you to London and spend the first two weeks with you. He will continue his monthly trips to check on things, just as he did with Céleste.

Once a quarter, I will inspect everything. In the morning the three of us will go over the details and make the rest of the arrangements."

Désirée's eyes were bright with the fire of triumph and anticipation. "You'll never regret this, Aunt Renée. I'll make you proud of me and the London operations."

Renée stood and hugged Désirée, thinking for a split second that it was much too heavy a burden for a young girl. She continually wished for Désirée the thing she'd wanted Juliette to have, the thing she'd never had: carefree youth devoid of responsibility. As she watched Désirée walk out the door, she wondered why the Duboises always chose the hardest roads.

Chapter Thirty-nine

Virginie handed Lucienne her personal check for ten thousand francs. "That should be adequate," she said coldly.

"Only for a week. Everything has gotten frightfully expensive these days," Lucienne said, goading her mother.

"You will be home for the holidays," Virginie stated.

"Only if you've taken care of that little matter I told you about."

An imperceptible tensing of Virginie's jaw told Lucienne she'd hit the bull's-eye.

"If you're referring to the photographs of you and your latest lover . . ."

"Yes." Lucienne sneered. She adored playing this game. "She *is* lovely, isn't she? All that blond hair . . . a natural blonde too. Did you catch that in the picture, Mother?"

"You disgust me, Lucienne."

"I'll need more money next week. The house in Saint Moritz needs a new roof. The servants are asking for raises. It's amazing how much it costs for the necessities of life."

"I hardly consider a case of Moët and Chandon every week, caviar, Bélon oysters, and imported mussels as 'staples.' Furs and jewels are not 'clothes' and your trips to the Aegean to sunbathe are extravagances. Let me put it this way, Lucienne.

Curtail the expenses or find out the hard way how the other half lives."

Lucienne stood and leaned over her mother's withered face. "You listen to me, old woman. I'm calling the shots now. I know as well as you what your investors would think if they knew Virginie Ruille's daughter was a lesbian. They'd pull their money out of your bank so fast no one could stop the landslide. You can't afford any scandal—especially not the nasty kind I could dish out."

"You're pathetic."

"I'm winning . . . and you don't like it."

"Just look at you, Lucienne. Fifty years old, two face lifts, and you still look used up."

"I am used up. But I can go on playing this game forever."

"Why would you want to?"

"It amuses me," she said as she picked up the check and shoved it into her Hermès bag. She stood and smoothed her newest Courrèges miniskirt. "I'll see you next week."

Virginie watched her daughter leave, thinking that not once in her life had she ever exhibited a single trait that would lead Virginie to believe they were of the same blood.

As she neared the end of her life, Virginie wanted nothing more than to see her children happy, but that was an impossibility. Renée Dubois had robbed them all of future peace.

Virginie, now in her eighty-first year, hated Renée more than she did the night Edouard died or the day Renée coldly refused to save Antoine Junot from the Nazis.

Virginie had waited a long time for her revenge. She enjoyed and savored every year of anticipation. The time of waiting was over, for Virginie was nearly at her goal.

In the middle of the decade of the sixties, the Ruille fortunes were massive. The largest single contributor had been the investments Virginie made during the war. Unbeknownst to her grandson, she had kept over half the money in America, buying oil leases in Texas and Louisiana. She invested in mining in Brazil and Argentina. She backed a diamond mine in Johannesburg and gold mines scattered from Alaska to Peru and back to Africa. She opened banks in Dallas, Miami, Atlanta, and Chicago; all under the auspices of United States Investments, Inc. No one knew the extent of her power and wealth, and she preferred it that way.

She would never allow anyone, not even Henri, to come that close to her. She had never trusted anyone and the philosophy had worked well. Confidences and shared intimacies were for the masses, not for someone like Virginie Ruille.

When Renée Dubois announced to the public that she was opening a chain of fifteen *prêt-à-porter* stores in the United States, Virginie made certain that her representatives approached Renée's managers about the financing they would need. With careful investigation and three discreet bribes, Virginie's managers were able to offer a better deal than any other American bank. American Dubois Incorporated borrowed over two million dollars for their boutiques and invested eight million of their own monies. It was Renée's largest corporate move to date and she was financially stretched to the limit.

Virginie couldn't have been more thrilled.

Henri had finished his negotiations for new branches in Tokyo, Zurich, and Brussels, which were major outlets for Maison Dubois.

Of the thirty-seven banks Virginie ruled throughout the world, thirteen of them held loans made out to Dubois Incorporated. The European sector loans tallied to a meager one and a half million dollars, since most of the loans were nearly paid off. However, once this was coupled with the half million in Tokyo, three hundred thousand in Zurich, two hundred thousand in Brussels, and a whopping two million in America, the total sum came to over four and a half million dollars.

Should someone call the notes simultaneously, Renée Dubois would be finished.

To make the gesture plausible, Virginie had called in a story to *Paris Journal* about a management reorganization within the Dubois corporation. The reporter there owed her a favor and she decided it was time to collect.

This single story was meant only to set the gossips twittering. It would be followed by another and another. Virginie was in no hurry. She had waited a long time for this day. She wanted to enjoy it.

Chapter Forty

Cap Camarat, southwest of Saint-Tropez, was succumbing to the inevitable horde of bikini-clad tourists and foreign money. For the most part it was Parisians who had purchased homes here and who occupied them during the August holidays. The jet age was changing many things and the Côte d'Azur was one of them. Polynesian-themed nightclubs sprouted like thatch-roofed mushrooms along the sandy beaches, and motorbikes disturbed the nocturnal serenity. For seven years, Grant and Renée had brought the twins here during the summer holidays, but now, as he watched the erection of another hamburger stand on the corner where M. Andelot used to sell his *fruits de mer*, Grant conceded that it was time for them to search out a new retreat.

"Grant," Renée said, "the children would like to drive over to Saint-Raphaël for lunch. Louis wants to look for some new fish for his aquarium and I promised Michelle some new sandals. Honestly, sometimes I think Juliette doesn't pay any attention to what that child has to wear."

"Maybe she's growing too fast for Juliette to keep up."

As if on cue the twins came bursting into the room. "Do you think we'll find some angelfish?" Louis asked Grant as they headed out the door.

"I'm sure we could find sharks if we tried hard enough," Grant said and closed the door behind them.

The ivory telephone did not start ringing until Grant had started the engine on his brand-new Porsche. It, like all his cars, was red.

Pierre came out of the bathroom and flipped a navy silk tie around his neck. "Where do you want to go for lunch?"

"I don't care," Annette called from inside the walk-in closet at their suite at the Pierre Hotel in New York City.

Since Désirée had moved to London, Annette had found herself completely alone. She began insisting Pierre take her on his business trips. Even if it was a one-day jaunt to Milan, Annette convinced him she should go. Pierre found he liked the companionship, and as the months passed, even had her sit in on some of his meetings. He had forgotten how intelligent Annette was. The rediscovery was fascinating for him, and Annette had never been so happy.

"I feel like something exotic," Pierre said, buttoning his vest and adjusting his lapis lazuli cuff links. "Maybe East Indian. . . ?"

"All that curry? I don't think my stomach can handle spicy food."

"How about Japanese?"

"That sounds fine," Annette called.

"What are you doing in there?" Pierre asked, walking over to the closet. "Annette?"

Clad in a low-cut negligee, Annette approached him. She wore her hair down around her shoulders in soft curls, and even at this distance he could smell her perfume. It was a special fragrance Renée had mixed exclusively for Annette. Pierre was convinced that on no other woman would it exude quite the same effect. Her smile was seductive and her eyes smoky with desire. The pastel peach silk was transparent and he could see the suntan lines left from the bikini she'd worn last week during their stay at Martha's Vineyard. Pierre's reaction nearly overpowered him, but he was not as surprised as he should have been. This was only another in a long line of pleasant discoveries he'd made on this trip.

Annette had made a hit with his American managers and investors. Their wives adored her, and barraged her with questions about fashion that she answered with a keen sense of awareness he hadn't known she possessed. She conversed skillfully about French and American politics, and with an honest subtlety, she plugged Maison Dubois every chance she got. Annette had turned out to be the best promotions director he ever had.

"Well, where do you think we should have lunch?" she asked, standing next to him, her tiny frame leaning into him.

Pierre almost couldn't catch his breath to answer. He picked her up in his arms. She was still light as a feather after twenty-six years of marriage. "In bed," he replied huskily as he devoured her mouth.

"I was thinking the same thing," she said as he laid her on the bed.

Annette leaned over and called the front desk. "This is suite 401. Hold all our calls for the rest of the afternoon."

When she hung up Pierre was completely naked. Annette could only remember once before when he'd undressed *that* fast.

The desk clerk at the Pierre informed the overseas operator that he would take a message for suite 401, but he would not ring through to the room. The Pierre's reputation for abiding by their guests' wishes was one of tradition.

Désirée Dubois frantically watched the minutes tick away on her quartz desk clock. It was as if she were waiting for the world to explode.

How could she have been this stupid? And stupidity was all it was too.

Two days ago when the call came from the Paris accounting department, she had stuck the memo on the stack of all her calls to return. Her secretary Martha's idea of "urgent" had never carried any weight, and after three years at the London office, she'd learned to deal with matters one at a time. The call to Dallas never went through; the connection was bad due to hurricane winds in the area. When she called Milan, the manager there, a new employee with Maison Dubois, stated that they were having a misunderstanding with the bank about their loan, but that she felt she could handle it. The woman told Désirée it was "simply a late payment."

Yesterday morning there were calls from Zurich, Brussels, Mexico City, and Rome. Désirée had been at the linen company from seven in the morning until noon when she left to visit the mills in Manchester regarding the new prints Renée was coordinating for an extended bed and bath line. Désirée did not arrive back in London until eleven at night. She did not call the office all that day. Knowing she was slated for a noon meeting with the store managers of the retail lingerie and linen shops and the Chelsea boutique, she arrived at the office at seven forty-five. She was exhausted and still had a headache from the previous day.

The telephone was already ringing when she opened the door. There were calls from every branch store in the United States, each of which had telephoned Paris first, and were then referred to her. Milan called again, as did Rome, Zurich, and Mexico City. The story was the same: the loans were being called on every branch of Maison Dubois.

Désirée thought this was some kind of nightmare. It was impossible for that many different banks scattered all over the world to do the same thing at the same time for no reason.

At 9:45 she had her reason. Howard Simcox, Céleste's stepson and now retired from Renée's employ as the accountant for the linen company, arrived. He was carrying copies of the London *Times*, *The Wall Street Journal*, and *Paris Journal*.

He tossed the papers on her desk. "It's a good thing I like to keep an eye on things," he said. "Somebody doesn't like you at all."

Désirée scanned the stories. *Nepotism causes financial woes for MD* read one of the headlines. *Fashion, females, and finances: a bad corporate mix* blared across the top of page nine in the *Times*. *Empires or Empresses?*

Désirée was in shock. She read them once and then again, not believing what was happening. "We've had bad publicity for the past two years, but it didn't mean much. It was mostly gossip, but this is slander!"

Howard looked at her. "The headlines read that way, but the articles are pure fact. It's a tricky piece of work, but there is nothing there that isn't true. In fact, the one in *The Wall Street Journal* is practically a history of the demise of haute couture. I went over them with a fine-tooth comb. Somebody wanted to stir up some trouble."

"I just wish I knew who and why. The phone has been ringing off the hook. My father is in Cape Cod and Aunt Renée is in the south of France with the twins. Juliette is on an airplane to Hawaii to meet André who is on his way back from Saigon . . . again. She'll be gone for three weeks doing an assignment for *Harper's Bazaar* on Maui. God only knows why Gaston doesn't answer in Los Angeles.''

Howard held up his hands. ''I haven't got any advice except keep trying to contact Renée. I don't know what else to tell you.''

Désirée canceled her lunch meeting and continued calling New York and Cap Camarat. Her stomach churned with acid from too much coffee and too many cigarettes. She talked with every branch, many times keeping one on hold while she compared stories. Her head pounded.

At 2 P.M. there was still no word from New York and she left another message at the Pierre Hotel.

By 6 P.M. she was emotionally exhausted and physically drained. A handful of aspirin and two straight Scotches didn't help.

She read the articles again and realized that this was not an attack on her personally, but on all women trying to break into the corporate world. The thing that bothered her most was that they had been moving along rather well. Sales were off in some areas, but with their new ad campaigns for their ''wet look'' designs she was certain they would have a fabulous rebound.

She wanted desperately to handle this crisis without calling on anyone, but it seemed as the hours passed that everything was out of control. Blessed with a cool temperament, she was doubly perplexed by the magnitude of this chaos. It was like an avalanche and she was powerless to stop it. For Désirée Dubois, it was a new experience. She had always known what to do, how to do it best and do it with expedience. Confusion was not in her repertoire.

Désirée kept her calculator rolling as she tallied up the number of loans being called and their amount. It was insanity! This last total came to over four million dollars! Still the phone kept ringing.

When Désirée picked up the receiver at 8:55, her voice was hoarse and she could barely see from the blinding headache. It was Pierre.

''Papa!'' she cried. She wanted to burst into the tears she

needed to shed just to release tension. Instead, she pulled herself together and calmly explained what had happened, leaving out nothing including the headline stories.

"We'll be on the next plane. Keep trying to get Renée."

Désirée continued for the following thirty minutes. Renée was out of breath when she picked up the receiver.

"Désirée! Chérie! What a wonderful day we've had. We drove all the way to Cannes, went out on a boat with friends, and even slipped the children into a casino. We were just walking in the door—"

"Aunt Renée, something has happened."

"It's not your father . . . or Juliette? It's not—"

"It's business."

"Tell me."

Désirée explained everything at length, and answered all of Renée's questions as specifically as she could.

"We'll drive back immediately. You fly to Paris on a charter plane. Don't discuss this with anyone."

"I won't. I'll see you in the morning."

Renée hung up the phone and turned to Grant, who had been listening to the conversation. A worried frown tracked his brow.

"What is it?" he asked.

"Virginie Ruille."

The core of the Dubois family sat in Pierre's office high above Paris. Désirée stood at the window, her face ashen. She had dreamed of commanding this office someday. Some diabolical twist of fate had intervened in a matter of three days and was about to rob her of all her work, plans, and dreams. She was angry and unbelievably frustrated. If she were a man she would go out and get drunk and probably get into a fist fight. Instead, she stood here, impotent, while other people decided her future. She wished she were dead—no, she thought, she was too angry to die. She wanted to get even, but she didn't know who to blame.

"I've made calls to half of Europe and can only come up with a million and a half from private individuals," Pierre said.

Renée shook her head knowing that was only a fraction of what they needed. "What about the public sector?"

"No bank will touch us. They're all convinced this is the

beginning of the end of haute couture," Pierre said, his voice strained and angry. "It's all this London crap. Can't they see that bell bottoms and industrial zippers are only a fad? It's the fad that is dying, not fashion!"

Renée stood resolutely. "I'll be damned if I'm going to let my business sink into oblivion. We've got to find a way!"

"How do you intend to save it, Renée?" Grant asked calmly. Despairingly, she slumped back onto the sofa. "I don't know."

"Well, I do."

Every head in the room turned to him.

"Désirée, go to Renée's office and book me on a flight to New York, then connect me through to Los Angeles on a nonstop if you can. But get me there as fast as possible."

Désirée was dubious, but she did as she was asked.

"What are you going to do?" Pierre asked.

"I think we are all agreed that drastic measures are called for. The way I see it, you'll need over four million to cover the loans and to make certain that nothing else goes awry. The only place I know to find money like that is Hollywood."

Renée's hand flew to her mouth. She knew what he was thinking and it wasn't right. He'd given over twenty years of his life to Monument Studios . . . and twice he'd abandoned her in order to keep it alive. She knew what this gesture meant.

"Grant, you can't . . . not the studio."

"I can collect a pretty penny for it. I just hope I can do it in the time allotted."

Pierre was flabbergasted. "We can't ask you—"

"You didn't ask. I'm offering." He walked over to Renée and placed his hand on her cheek. "In the past few years I've found that there is nothing more important than my life with you, my daughter, and my grandchildren. I think the timing is perfect. Just this past week I've been seriously considering retirement. Perhaps this is a sign that I'm supposed to slow down. I've earned a vacation. It's important for us to keep Maison Dubois alive. It's Pierre's livelihood and the future for Désirée and the twins. I suppose Gaston will always have his boutiques to provide for Kate and Amie, but what if they have more children . . . and someday Désirée will have children. I'm thinking about all of them. Monument Studios was my dream, but now we can use it to keep the family going. And I want to tell you, that's more important to me than any movie ever was."

Renée was nearly overcome with emotion. "You are a special man, indeed, Monsieur Morgan."

He chuckled. "Yeah? Just don't forget it," he teased and kissed her.

Just then Désirée came back into the room. "I've got you booked for a flight that leaves in an hour and a half."

Grant kissed Renée. "I'll run home pack a few things, grab a cab from there. I'll call when I make New York and again when I'm in LA."

"Will you stay with Gaston and Kate?"

"Yes. Call them and tell them I'm coming." Grant went over and shook Pierre's hand. "Don't worry."

"Good luck." Pierre's face was hopeful again.

Désirée followed Grant out and went to her office. Renée started to leave, too, but Pierre stopped her.

"Renée, I waited until Désirée was gone before I brought this up. We have another problem."

"What?"

"It's Désirée. Our investors are concerned about the bad publicity we've been getting. They don't hold anything against her, but if I want the money, I have to 'do' something about her. Her profile has been too high."

"You mean they actually believe this smear campaign in the paper?"

"I'm afraid so."

"Well, I won't do it."

"Are you crazy? We have to have the money! I've . . . already agreed to their terms."

"You want to get rid of your own daughter?"

"Not forever. Just until all this blows over. I haven't told Désirée or Annette that we think Virginie is behind all this. After all, we have no proof."

"And we'll never find it, either. . . . Pierre, surely we could do something else to assuage the investors. Maybe place Guillaume over Désirée. That way she could stay in London. All her work wouldn't be for nothing."

"He's a good manager. That might work. Yes . . ."

Renée pressed the intercom. "Send Désirée in here."

Désirée walked in. Renée's heart went out to her niece. She looked exhausted and emotionally frazzled. And it was no wonder. For days she'd handled a monstrous situation. Renée doubted she could have done as well when she'd been that young.

"Do you think Uncle Grant will get the money, Aunt Renée?"

"Yes, I do. But there's something else I have to discuss with you. I'll come right to the point. Our investors feel that the time has come for a change in our management. Maison Dubois is going to have a difficult time battling this bad publicity even if we do save her."

"Our name is impeccable," Désirée countered.

"It only takes one bad apple, as the saying goes—"

"What are you really trying to tell me?" Désirée asked, intensely probing Renée's eyes.

"I'm placing Guillaume de Pont as head of the London offices."

"You're firing me?" She scanned her father's implacable face. This wasn't happening to her. The two people in the world she loved and admired most were now her enemies. She felt as if the earth were swallowing her up.

"No! That's not what I'm saying at all, Désirée."

"What then?"

"Just until we get everything back on track, I feel it advisable to lower your profile just a bit. I want to keep you in London."

"But not in control, right? You want some corporate man to tell me what to do and when to do it. Is that it? And what if the investors wanted me sent to Calcutta? Would you do that, too, Aunt Renée?"

"Désirée, you're blowing this all out of proportion."

"No, I'm not. I've done a damn good job for you in London and you both know it. . . ." She looked at her father. Why wasn't he saying anything? Her father wouldn't do this to her . . . not to his only child . . . He'd fought against Renée years ago to give her the London branch in the first place. No, her father was on her side. It was her aunt she was battling now. For the first time she realized that the press had been right when they'd said Renée had nerves of steel, a will of iron. Renée didn't care who she hurt just as long as Maison Dubois survived.

Renée watched as Désirée's defenses turned to anger. She'd seen that look in Gaston's eyes just before he'd left her. Renée was instantly shaken. Suddenly she wanted to take Désirée in her arms. She wanted to explain about this diabolical vise she'd been placed in. She wanted to tell her how Virginie was turning the screws. But she could tell from Désirée's eyes it was too late.

"Désirée, it's not the end of the world."

Coolly, Désirée faced her. "You're right. It's not. But it is the end of my association with Maison Dubois. I want to thank you for the education you've given me, Aunt Renée. It was invaluable."

Désirée spun on her heel and dashed out the door before she burst into tears. She had her pride and never . . . never would she let her aunt see her pain.

Four days after Gaston, Kate, and two-year-old Amie met Grant at LAX, he was still no closer to selling Monument Studios. Hard-luck stories traveled fast in show business and there were still enough of the old guard around to relish the downfall of "maverick Grant Morgan." Because of his hands-off policy of recent years, his managers had turned out three flops in a row. Grant was beginning to believe that no matter how he played the game, his way or theirs, he was never going to win. The studio should have brought over ten million dollars, but because of the circumstances, Grant was asking six million and he hadn't gotten the first offer. He reduced the price to five million, thinking surely someone would jump on it.

Grant contacted every backer he'd ever worked with and was turned down cold. On his fifth day in Los Angeles he had precisely twenty-four hours left when Gaston came home and said, "I've brought someone to see you."

Michael Segelman stepped through the door. "I understand you have a movie studio you want to dump."

Stunned and relieved, Grant's smile filled his face. He took Michael's hand and pumped it up and down. "Can't think of anyone I'd rather dump it on! But where did you come up with this kind of money!"

"That's the bad part. I haven't."

Grant's enthusiasm faded. "I don't understand."

Gaston broke in. "Michael and I want to buy the studio together. I was able to come up with almost a million."

"I've got about two million. That's a chunk. I think I've hit up every relative I've got on the East Coast. I'm still working on it."

"Together you have three million between you?"

"Yes," Gaston answered.

"Sold!"

Michael was incredulous. "The studio is worth ten times that!"

"I'll float you for the last two million. But I need three million in twenty-four hours. How good is your family's credit?"

"Excellent!" Michael's face was that of a man who'd just had his every wish granted. "I'm dumbstruck, Grant! This is very generous of you."

"Generous, hell! You have no idea how it turned my gut knowing I was going to have to sell out to one of these bastards. I know my baby is in good hands with you."

"Shall I call Mother with the good news or do you want to?" Gaston asked.

"We both will, son."

Henri Ruille walked into Virginie's office and handed her three thick files, all marked "Dubois." "That's the last of them. They were all paid with cashier's checks. So much for bringing Renée Dubois to her knees," he said, sarcasm ripping through his voice.

The faintest blush sprouted on Virginie's crepey neck. Her emerald eyes leapt with a fire he'd never seen before, but when she spoke her voice was alarmingly calm. "I suppose you could do better?"

"I knew all along what you were up to, buying those branches. It didn't take a genius to see that it would never work. Renée Dubois has too many friends, which is something you have always refused to acknowledge, and this time it cost you. You never had a chance."

"You're so clever and quite free with criticism."

"I would never say these things to you if I did not have a plan of my own in mind."

Virginie's eyebrow raised as curiosity flickered in her eyes. "Tell me."

Henri withdrew his gold pocket watch, one which had belonged to Claude Ruille. "I think not. Wouldn't you rather enjoy the intrigue as it unfolds?"

"It's possible."

"Good. I'm late. I have an appointment with a young lady."

Virginie turned back to the reports on her desk. "I'm not interested in your *amours*."

"You should be. Her name is Désirée Dubois."

The taxi pulled into Orly Airport. Désirée handed her tickets to the porter and followed him into the terminal. She was glad she only had a few minutes to make the flight. She hated hanging around in airports.

She sat in first class, buckled her seat belt, and turned to the stewardess.

"As soon as we're airborne, I'll have a double Scotch."

"Yes, ma'am."

Two rows back, hiding behind a copy of the London *Times*, was Henri Ruille. He waited until the plane was in the air and Désirée had her drink before he made his move.

She was looking out the window when he walked down the aisle and leaned over to her.

"Hello, Désirée."

She looked up. She recognized him immediately. He was in his early forties, and she had to admit his photographs did not do him justice. He had fascinating eyes fringed with long blond lashes. His thick blond hair surrounded a deeply tanned face. He was broad-shouldered, and though he was dressed in a gray silk three-piece suit, his well-muscled physique showed.

"It's been years, Henri," she said as he sat next to her. "I must have been only nineteen at the DeMeyers' party when I saw you last."

"Really? I thought you were older."

"I thought you were younger."

He smiled at her. For years she'd heard her father speak of the Ruilles as if they were from another planet. She'd seen them all at balls, parties, charity functions that both families attended. They had many friends in common, but always the Duboises had kept their distance from any and all Ruilles. When she'd been a little girl her imagination had transformed the Ruilles into monsters with laser eyes that could destroy. As she looked at Henri, she didn't think he looked formidable at all. He looked . . . sad somehow.

He glanced at her empty glass. "Can I get you another?"

"Please," she said as she watched him signal the stewardess and order her drink. She took the glass and nearly downed the straight Scotch in one gulp.

"Hadn't you better ease up on that stuff?"

"It's been a rough week." She sighed heavily.

"So I read in the newspapers."

"Ah ha! So that's why you're sitting here. My aunt told me you Ruilles love to gloat. Well, go ahead. And then go away. I want to be left alone."

He signaled to the stewardess for another drink. "I don't believe you. From what I've observed over the years, you Duboises are never alone. You really stick together."

"Until now." Désirée had never been so depressed. And to make matters worse here was her supposedly lifelong enemy buying her drinks—letting her cry on his shoulder. With the third Scotch, her emotions came tumbling out.

"You're right. I don't want to be alone. I don't understand any of this. I always believed our family was one. I never thought of them as cousins, aunts, uncles, mothers, and daughters. We were always in and out of each other's houses, each other's lives. We stuck together, helped one another, loved one another."

She turned liquid lavender eyes on Henri. There was something indescribable there, something he knew nothing about. Was it vulnerability?

"You're from a big family. You know what I'm talking about, don't you?"

He paused, peering into her eyes as if he were searching for something. Abruptly, he leaned his head back on the headrest. "No, I'm afraid I don't."

Désirée looked out the window. They were flying over the English Channel now. In the reflection of the window, Désirée saw an image of Renée's face.

How she'd wanted to make Renée proud of her. She'd worked hard, as hard as anyone. And this was her repayment. It was clear Renée thought more of her investors than she did her own family. All these years, Désirée had been duped into believing family was an unbreakable bond.

This time Désirée signaled for another drink.

Henri's eyebrow raised in surprise. "You really know how to celebrate."

"Celebrate?"

"Sure. Maison Dubois weathered the crisis. Your corporation is intact, isn't it? It seems to me everything should be wonderful."

"Wonnerful," Désirée mumbled as the stewardess announced they would be landing.

Four Scotches had done their work, for Henri had to help Désirée buckle her seat belt. When the plane landed, he kindly offered to drive her to her apartment.

"No thanksh. I'll get a cab. . . ." She teetered on unsteady legs.

"Allow me," he said graciously and hailed the cab for her. "What's your address?"

"What?" She climbed in, thinking how fuzzy his face had become in that short plane trip. She leaned forward, trying to focus, but his face grew dim. Désirée fell onto the backseat.

Calmly, Henri pushed her over, got inside the cab, and gave the driver his own address. He smiled, thinking his grandmother had never gotten this close to a Dubois. He intended to get even closer.

Chapter Forty-one

"Minis, midis, maxis! Every time I think I have it all figured out, somebody starts a hemline war!"

Renée patted Pierre's hand sympathetically. "That's what makes fashion so exciting."

He peered at her over the top of his bifocals. "Exciting, yes. Ulcers, no!"

"These are all the reports from sales and accounting?"

"Yes," Pierre replied, "and they couldn't be more dismal."

"You said that six months ago and look at what's happened." She leaned back in her chair. "In 1968 when I was in Cannes and found those counterfeit scarves with my label on them, you told me it was a fluke. Here it is four years later and we're seeing what I think is going to be a real threat. Look at these figures. In 1969 we lost four million lire in our Milan and Rome stores. In 1970 sales were down 200,000 francs and the losses spanned to Switzerland and included the London boutique. In 1971, the losses in the United States reached 150,000 dollars, and this year it's nearly double that!"

"Overall, we're still making more money than we ever did. However, I agree that something has to be done about this counterfeiting, but what?" Pierre asked.

"Grant's contacted the best private detectives he could get. I want to concentrate most of their work in the States, since that's where most of the counterfeit shipments are going. Two detectives will work Europe, but just the cities that have posted the largest losses."

"How much is this costing us, Renée?"

"I was hoping you wouldn't ask. Two thousand dollars a man each month . . . but they pay expenses!"

"Whew! That's over twelve thousand dollars a month. I hope they *are* worth it!"

"If we do our part, they will be. We need to stir up some controversy over this thing. See if Kate can help us. She knows some of those consumer advocate people in America. I can get some newspaper and magazine coverage here and in London. The police aren't any help since label counterfeiting is only a misdemeanor. When the public gets angry enough, that's when we'll see the action. Possibly some legislation that will work in our favor."

"Until then we have to rely on our own wits—and finances!"

"Right! That's why I want you to find me the best attorney money can buy. I want to find out where this junk is coming from and stop it. At this point it's just a trickle. Ten years from now, we could drown."

Désirée looked up from her desk in time to see a bright red sun fall behind Big Ben. She rubbed her eyes and rolled her neck, trying to loosen the tension in her neck.

The last of the Christmas orders had been shipped a month ago, but it felt like yesterday. Retailers were having record sales and HD Exporters was no exception.

As a major importer/exporter of Asian goods, HD Exporters was cashing in this holiday season on the sudden but welcome demand for anything Oriental. Brass-backed porcelain ashtrays ran from twelve to thirty dollars while huge white porcelain greyhounds ran five hundred dollars. Cloisonné bracelets and earrings were the rage on the Riviera. From clothing to leather tobacco jars and hand-painted china and ginger jars to rattan chairs, HD Exporters supplied large retailers and mail-order cataloguers by the hundreds. In the past two years, their garment factory in Taiwan had quadrupled their output and Désirée had found buyers for their entire line of silk kimonos, lavishly detailed Chinese robes, and loungewear.

She had worked hard to make her company successful but she never felt the same kind of satisfaction she had known when she worked with her father and aunt.

She glanced at the gold clock, pressed the intercom button, and summoned her secretary.

"Penny, if you have those letters finished you can go. I'll lock up soon."

"There was another call from your mother, and Mr. Ruille's secretary said to change from the Dorchester to the Sheraton Park Tower. She said you would understand."

"I do. Is that all?"

"Yes. Have a nice weekend."

"You, too, Penny."

She knew the call from her mother was about her plans for the holidays. She didn't want to go to Paris, for her visits were still too strained. She forced herself to be civil to her father, but she'd never understood his not coming to her defense. Anger was an unfamiliar emotion, and not knowing how to handle it made her keep her distance. She tolerated her mother, for she meant well, and not being involved in Maison Dubois until recently as promotions director, Annette was not responsible for the schism between Désirée and Pierre.

Désirée no longer respected her father or her aunt Renée. When the choice had been loyalty to Désirée or loyalty to the company, the company came first.

In many ways she felt she was fortunate to have gotten out when she did. It saved her from more heartache in the future.

Tonight she didn't want to think about the past. Tonight she would be with Henri. It had been two and a half weeks since he'd been to London and she had counted the days like a child waiting for St. Nicholas.

She'd been to Vidal Sassoon's for a cut and blow dry and a quick application of "Candy Apple Red" nail lacquer before her lunch meeting at the Waterside Inn. Before returning to the office she went to Harvey Nichols and purchased an expensive lavender cashmere sweater dress that nearly matched her eyes.

She wanted to look perfect tonight, for she was convinced Henri was going to propose. She had no evidence to support her hopes other than a certain inflection to his voice when they had spoken on the telephone. In the past six months Henri's visits to London had become more frequent and more lengthy. Most importantly, the only business Henri conducted was Désirée.

Checking the time, she grabbed her full-length lynx from the closet and turned off the lights. Just as she closed the door she glanced out the window and saw fat white snowflakes tumbling down. The city lights sparkled at her, promising a night of romance.

His nose was ice cold as he snuggled his face into her neck. "God! I thought I would never get here!" He kissed her lips but she was trembling so much they both burst into laughter.

"We could go inside," she said, kissing his cheek.

"*You're* the one who wanted the romantic walk in the snow!"

"But if we hadn't gone to the gardens, we would have missed the carolers and the musicians."

"You know what? You're crazy. I've never met anyone who gets so worked up about Christmas."

"And why not? It only comes once a year."

"I always wanted to just get through it. Having all the family around—it's such a tense time."

"Henri, not all families are like yours."

He put his arms around her. His eyes sparkled in the lamplight. "I suppose your ways are better."

"I always had more fun." She giggled and slipped out of his arms. She bent over a pile of snow and made a snowball.

"Don't you dare," he said, grabbing her hand. The snowball fell as he put her arms around his neck and kissed her.

Désirée reveled in the kiss. It was unlike Henri to kiss her in public. His watchword had always been "propriety." Maybe she was making her mark on him. Maybe he *was* changing.

"God, Désirée. You don't know what you do to me."

"Wanna see more?" she teased.

"I'm all yours."

"Truly?" she asked, her voice suddenly serious.

"Yes, Désirée, truly."

She thought her heart would burst. It was the closest Henri had come to admitting his feelings for her. She wanted to believe he loved her. She felt that he did, but he'd never said it in so many words. She wondered what there was about men who were afraid to say anything. Sometimes she thought it was because of their age difference, but he denied it.

Arm in arm they walked to the hotel. They peered into each other's eyes as they rode the elevator to the eighth floor where he'd reserved a room. As usual, Henri had room service provide them with her Scotch and a dozen roses. This time they were red. He had never given her red roses before. She hoped it was a sign. Désirée was looking for signs everywhere.

Henri had barely locked the suite door when he took her coat and began peeling off her dress. He kissed her with those tiny weightless kisses that sent chills down her back and made her forget everything but him. She unbuttoned his jacket, dropped it on the floor, and had just moved her hands beneath his shirt to his bare chest when, suddenly, he stopped her.

"What? What's wrong?" she asked breathlessly.

"Nothing is wrong. I—I just . . ."

His blue eyes delved into her. She felt as if he were probing her soul. For a fraction of a second she saw that vulnerability in his eyes she'd seen only once or twice before. In that second, she saw that this was not the Henri who pushed her to run his import business, nor the "older experienced man" she'd sought for advice. This was not the corporate genius or the tax expert. And, as always, the sudden revealing flash that kept her hopes high, fed her dreams, and made her love him—vanished. He had reverted to type again.

"What is it, Henri? What do you want to say to me?"

"It—it was nothing."

Désirée's frustration was at an all-time high. They couldn't go on like this forever. There was a wall between them, one he'd erected and she couldn't tear down. But some inner sense told her that he *wanted* her to confront him.

Henri often confided things to her, but there was always that invisible boundary he would never cross, one that would lead to total commitment. It was one she was ready to make.

"I love you, Henri."

He just looked at her, his face expressionless. She pressed on.

"I think about you all the time. I dream about you at night. For four years I've lied to you that there were other men I dated. There's never been anyone but you, Henri. I've pretended that I was the only one in your life, and I've tried to ignore the pictures of you in the society pages with other women. But I can't help how I feel, Henri."

"You—you shouldn't be saying all this."

"Why not? I must sound foolish. Does that bother you? I'm not afraid anymore, Henri."

Suddenly, before she could say another word, he took her face in his hands and brought her lips to his. He kissed her as he'd never kissed her before—gentle, yet slowly devouring her with his lips and tongue.

He pulled her body into his, crushing her ribs with his hands so that Désirée thought she could barely breathe. She couldn't tell where she began and he ended. His moan was like a whimper and then, just as suddenly as the kiss had begun, it ended.

He turned away from her.

"Henri. Didn't you hear what I said?"

"Yes." He didn't look at her.

"I've never told anyone I loved them, Henri. Only you."

Still he kept his back turned. "You know how silly you get at this time of year. Perhaps it's just this romantic Christmas mood you're in. You just got a bit carried away is all."

"What?" she nearly screamed at him. "I've never thought anything out so thoroughly in all my life. I'm sick of this emotional tug-of-war you play with me. One minute I'm on the moon, the next I've crash-landed. You've told me that you were 'fond of' me, that I 'mean a lot' to you. But you've never said you love me, Henri. I don't believe you come all the way to London to get laid!"

"No, this isn't a weekend fling."

"Then what the hell is it? Because I need to know—tonight."

"I thought we could spend some time together."

" 'Time together'? Four years is enough 'time together.' "

Rejection and anger vied for top billing inside Désirée. At that moment she felt that if she'd had a gun she would be tempted to use it. She had to get away from him. She started to gather her things. What was the matter with him? When would he ever get the guts to say what he felt? And why the hell wasn't he stopping her?

She picked up her lynx. She was surprised at the look of shock on his face.

"You can't be leaving!" he stammered.

"Why not?"

"I have dinner reserva—"

"Damn!" She raced to the door, then turned. "If I ever have a transplant and need a heart, I hope I get yours."

"Why do you say that?"

"Because it's never been used!"

Henri Ruille rode in a taxi down the Champs-Elysée still hearing the reverberating sound of that slamming door.

For three days he had remained in his hotel room thinking about the words she had said, the things he had not said, and knowing the end of their relationship had been his fault. He could have stopped her; he could have told her what he really felt. He could have given her the ring he'd bought for her almost three years ago; the same ruby and diamond ring he carried in his pocket every time he went to London to see her. But, as always, he was too frightened.

He was more than frightened, he was terrified. The mere consideration of stating his feelings to Désirée caused him to break out in a sweat. He knew he needed Désirée and, yet, he was incapable of telling her. He wanted nothing except to be with her. She made him laugh at life and not take himself so seriously. She had a lot of love to give and she'd been giving of herself since the first day they met. Désirée Dubois meant the world to Henri Ruille. When he was with her, it was impossible for him to imagine anyone connected with her being as vicious as he'd been brought up to believe. When Désirée spoke of Renée it was with pride, admiration, and pain. Désirée loved her family in a way that was foreign to Henri. He tried to understand it but couldn't.

No one had ever told Henri that he was loved until Désirée. He knew she would have said it long ago, but he'd held her back by his aloofness. He didn't want to act and react the way he did, but he knew nothing else.

He studied his past, his relationships, and in the Sheraton Park Tower Hotel, he realized that there was only one person to blame for the shambles his life had become—his grandmother.

Virginie had taught him to hate Renée Dubois, and above all to avoid trust and love.

The taxi pulled to a halt in front of the Crédit de Paris

building. Henri paid the driver and used his key to unlock the door. He signed the security book and noticed that his grandmother had left only moments earlier. The security officer unlocked the inner metal doors and bid him good evening. Henri checked his watch. It was 9:37.

Henri glanced at the memos on his desk, noticed the poinsettia the office girls had purchased for him, and flipped the calendar to today's date: December 23, 1972.

Paris. December 23, 1972. 10:06 P.M.

Juliette spread out the skirt of her red and green plaid maternity dress and placed the nuts, crackers, and an empty bowl in her lap. "I suppose we should be cleaning up, but I wanted to get this last batch of cookies finished before we went to sleep."

Renée smiled at her daughter. "I don't know what there is about Christmas that seems to infest everyone with insomnia. But I'm just as much a victim as anyone."

"Except for André," Juliette said.

"He was out with the twins all day. He has to be exhausted. Did you see all those gifts they came back with?"

"Yes," Juliette replied and surreptitiously glanced at her mother. Though she was trying to be cheerful, the tight set to her jaw and furrows in her forehead gave her away. "You're worried about Grant, aren't you?"

"Does it show?"

"Only to those who know and love you."

"He was supposed to fly back yesterday from New York, but he called and said he'd discovered something about the counterfeiting that couldn't wait. He even talked Gaston into bringing the family to New York two days early so Gaston could help him."

"It sounds serious."

"I don't like it, either. I know Grant and Pierre have been adamant about this counterfeiting thing, but I want everyone here for Christmas. It'll be our first holiday together in years. I was so looking forward to seeing Kate and Amie."

"I'm looking forward to seeing you get the STYLE award the

day after Christmas. It's about time you got some recognition for your work."

"I'm flattered I was even considered, but just knowing that you and André are happy, and Gaston and Kate are together, is all the lifetime award I ever wanted."

Juliette wanted so badly to break the news about Kate's pregnancy, a secret she had vowed not to tell, when the ringing telephone saved her from betraying her brother.

It was New York.

"Why, Grant? Why must I come to New York?" Renée was asking. "There must be some mistake! Grant! What kind of men have you hired? Are you certain? It's not gossip?" Renée paused. "I don't believe any of it! Yes, I'll catch the next plane out. I love you too. Tell Gaston I'll have Juliette call his apartment with my flight number."

Renée slammed down the receiver. "Damn!" She rifled through the papers on her desk and made three quick calls. In less than fifteen minutes she was booked on a flight to New York.

New York. December 24. 6:32 A.M.

Gaston hung up the phone and poured himself another cup of coffee. He turned to Grant. "Juliette said Renée was on a one P.M. flight. She'll get into Kennedy at four this afternoon."

"I hated telling her," Grant said.

"Does she believe you?"

"No."

"I didn't think she would. *I* don't believe it. Something tells me there is more here than what is on this detective's report."

"The facts don't lie. We've been to the retailers, seen the goods, contacted the warehouser, and established a direct link to HD Imports. HD Imports is run by Désirée Dubois and bankrolled by Henri Ruille. That guy has no mind of his own except what Virginie programs into it," Grant said. "Everything has been checked and double-checked."

"I guess I'm reluctant to believe that anyone in our family is capable of something like this."

"I hope you're right," Grant said.

London. December 24. 8:00 A.M.

Désirée rolled over and buried her swollen face in the pillow. She had cried for five days straight and still there seemed to be no end to it. Her life was a shambles. She had lost Henri for good. He had not called her at work or at home. Twice when there had been a knock at the door, she had fully expected it to be him. She wondered if he'd ever cared about her at all or if there was some perversity in her character that made her love him. Désirée had never been this miserable in her life.

It was Christmas and she should be with the ones she loved.

She looked at the ceramic Christmas tree she kept in her bedroom window that her decorator convinced her would "work" with her contemporary white, beige, and chrome décor. Now, as she looked around her room, she hated it. This was not Désirée Dubois. This was someone she didn't know and someone she didn't want to be any longer.

There was no smell of almond cookies coming from the kitchen. There was no fir tree in her living room decorated with thirty-year-old pinecones and newly frosted cookies. There was no fire in her fireplace because she'd filled it with crystal votive candles that would "meld with her décor."

She had lied to herself for too long and look at the mess she'd made with her life. She hadn't been truly happy since she left home. She had wanted to get even with her father and her aunt for what they'd done, but the revenge had been demeaning and, in the end, she had become the untrustworthy person she'd been wrongfully accused of years ago. There was no victory in trying to destroy the family she loved and there was no sense in denying that love to herself anymore.

Désirée couldn't stand it any longer. They may not want or need her, but *she* needed her family. She wished it could be like it once was when she would talk about clothes and model gossip with Juliette, and play with the twins. She wanted to see Gaston, Kate, and Amie. She wanted to hug her mother and kiss her father—and she wanted to beg Renée's forgiveness.

Whether they were ashamed of her or not, Désirée *had* to go home.

She placed a call to her parents' house in Paris.

Pierre had fallen asleep only an hour before, worried as he was about Renée's sudden and unexplained trip to New York. He had to clear his throat to speak. "Hello."

Tears were streaming down Désirée's cheeks when she heard his voice. "Papa?"

"Désirée?"

"Papa, I want to come home."

Boston. December 24. 4:06 P.M.

Renée buckled her seat belt and braced for the landing. A nightmare of a snowstorm had closed Kennedy and LaGuardia. The Pan Am flight 404 had been rerouted to Boston where the landing strips were clear. The captain had announced the alternative flight schedule to the passengers at three o'clock. Renée asked the stewardess to send a wire for her to Maeve Dunning. Upon hearing the Broadway actress's name, she was quick to consent.

The Pan Am jet circled Boston for nearly forty-five minutes before landing was cleared through the tower. Renée collected her bags and immediately placed a call to Maeve Dunning. Her wealthy client was only too happy to offer sanctuary from the storm.

"I'll take a taxi from the airport to your house."

Maeve was her usual gushy theatrical self, but her heart was twenty-four carat. "The house is all yours. We closed for the holidays last night after the second performance. I'm taking some friends to Connecticut to my farm. Are you sure you wouldn't like to join us?"

"Not this time, but I'll take a rain check. I would like to borrow your car. It's very important I get to New York."

"No problem at all. We're taking the train."

Her second call was to Gaston's New York apartment.

"Thank God you are all right!" Grant said, relieved to hear her voice. "The weather here is terrible. I swear nothing is moving."

"It's snowing here, but it isn't that bad . . . yet. I've contacted Maeve Dunning. She's lending me her car."

"Are you sure you'll be all right?"
"I'm fine. I'll see you tonight. I love you," she said.
"I love you too," he replied and hung up.

Paris. December 24. 10:24 A.M.

Henri Ruille felt as if his insides had been torn out. Repeatedly he tried to convince himself this was a temporary situation. As he'd always done in the past, he would bury himself in work and his problems would fade.

Henri had been sitting at his desk since six-thirty and he had done nothing save doodle Désirée's name on his notepad like some love-struck adolescent. He could think of nothing but Désirée and his fear of reaching out for the one thing he wanted.

All his life he had wanted a woman to love him and have children, lots of children—maybe four or five. He had plenty of money and could provide for a large family. He wanted there to be more to his life than what he had. He was forty-five years old and all he had to show for those years was his work.

Virginie would tell him to look at things logically. Hadn't she told him once that his children were the branches of the bank they had founded? He was responsible for hundreds of jobs, which meant people and families that relied on the Ruilles for their livelihood. When he thought of his work in that respect, he did feel great satisfaction.

He looked down at the file on his desk. They were opening a branch in Amsterdam next month and there was a great deal of work to do. He flipped through the papers and noticed that a copy of the central audit was missing. Assuming it was in Virginie's office, he started down the hall.

Hospital-neat, there was nothing atop Virginie's desk save her gold ink-pen set and a leather calendar book. Henri knew she kept current papers locked in the top right desk drawer. He went to the wall where the early Picasso hung and moved the painting to the left. There, taped to the wall, was the desk key.

Virginie was unaware that Henri knew about the key, or her eccentricities when it came to such matters. He really didn't care. All he needed was the audit in order to finish his work, but when he inserted the key in the top right desk drawer, it didn't fit. He tried it in the center drawer and nothing happened.

He tried the key in another drawer, then another. When he reached the bottom left drawer, the key inserted easily and clicked the lock open. Suddenly Henri knew he would not find the Amsterdam audit in this drawer.

Cautiously, he pulled the drawer out. It was filled with documents. Some were bonds she'd bought over half a century ago that now were worth a fortune. There was a deed to an Italian villa in Claude's name. There were yellowed newspaper clippings, and as he unfolded them, he saw that they were all of Renée Dubois.

Henri's search became more bizarre with every piece of paper he picked up. The hairs on the back of his neck bristled. There was the newspaper announcement of Gaston's birth, and beside it Virginie had written "the whore's bastard" and then circled it in red pencil.

There was a canceled personal check to a Dr. de Lemare, the famous psychiatrist; on the back she'd printed Emile's name. Henri lifted out a folio filled with private detectives' reports describing payoffs to police and newsmen over Emile's "affairs." It wasn't until he read the last report that he realized what Emile was capable of—and it made him sick. For the first time he realized that the "gossip" about his aunt Suzanne had been the truth.

At the bottom of the drawer he found snapshots, some over twenty years old and some recent. As he flipped through them, he saw that these were not ordinary family photographs. They were all of Lucienne and they were beyond incriminating; they were perverse. Henri's hands shook as he realized his aunt was a lesbian. The last of his childhood idealisms shattered into a thousand pieces as he tossed the snapshots in the drawer.

He covered his face with his hands, thinking that perhaps this was a nightmare, but when he looked up he knew this was reality and what his grandmother had presented to him as real for forty-five years had been the fantasy.

Henri left the drawer open with documents, snapshots, and detectives' reports still in disarray. The fury inside him mounted.

Virginie had molded, programmed, and fashioned him into the heartless person Désirée had accused him of being. He was not a man, but a caricature of a man. He knew what he wanted, he'd always known what he wanted, but Virginie had twisted him since the day he was born, so that as her automaton, he would want only what she wanted. She had used him just like she did everyone. He'd believed her when she said he was special, but that, too, had been a lie. She allowed no one to really know her and she'd taught him to do the same. The only thing he feared any longer was living without Désirée. She was the only person who truly loved him.

For the first time, Henri Ruille understood his father. At some point, Edouard must have come to this same realization about Virginie. Lucienne told Henri once that Edouard fought with Virginie over Renée Dubois that last night. When Virginie threatened to cut him off with no money, Edouard had killed himself.

Henri understood everything now, but most of all, he knew he was stronger than his father. He was not going to commit suicide. He was going to make Virginie pay for what she had done to Edouard, to Lucienne, to Emile, and mostly for what she had done to him.

New York City. December 24. 10:03 P.M.

The snow tires on Maeve's Cadillac were no match for the snow-packed icy streets of New York. It had taken Renée much longer to drive to New York than she'd expected. Nothing had gone right for her since the day before. Her mind was in a thousand places and she'd left her purse with her wallet and her makeup at Maeve's house. Fortunately, Maeve had stuck some American currency in her coat pocket as she was walking out the door. By now, she was certain Grant was worried about her, but she was only a few miles from Gaston's Fifth Avenue apartment. The snow was coming down so heavily it was like trying to see through a wool blanket. The windshield wipers were on high speed and still it was difficult for Renée to see the traffic lights.

It was well past nine-thirty and the last of the stores had just closed for the night. Restaurants and bars were packed to the rafters with last minute, late-night shoppers who sought refuge from the cold. Now that the sun had set and the temperature dropped, the streets were rapidly freezing over. Automobile headlights, traffic lights, and Christmas lights mingled with the snow to create one giant blurry scene.

At the stoplight Renée's thoughts wandered to Désirée and Pierre. Now that she was here in New York, she knew the detective's findings were accurate. Désirée had been wrongly blamed four years ago, and she and Pierre should have defended her more forcefully. Instead, they had taken the easy way out. It was not Désirée's fault she'd turned to Henri Ruille, but Pierre's and Renée's. Somehow, Renée knew she must find a way to bring her niece back to her.

Just then the car behind her began blowing his horn, startling her out of her reverie. She jumped and hit the accelerator. Park Avenue had been recently plowed and the traffic moved a bit faster. The light at Park Avenue and East Seventy-seventh was green and she kept going. Just as she sped through the light at Park and East Seventy-sixth, it turned yellow but she made it.

The light at the next corner was already red, but was turning yellow as she approached and when she reached the intersection it was green.

The white 1972 Buick Le Sabre speeding down East Seventy-fifth to the corner of Park Avenue did not slow down when the light turned yellow, but rather increased its speed as the light turned red.

The white car running the red light and the white fluffy snow blended into one another, but Renée saw the headlights on her left side as they headed straight for her. Her only hope of avoiding a collision was to get out of its way. She depressed the accelerator at precisely the same moment as the Buick Le Sabre hit the back end of the Cadillac.

The Cadillac went into a tailspin and tires squealed on the ice, sounding like a screaming woman. Headlights spun into a whirlpool of white light as the Buick Le Sabre sped across Park Avenue, past Madison and then to Fifth. It did not stop to regret the havoc it had created.

The Cadillac whirled across the street and smashed headlong into a twenty-foot lightpost.

The steering wheel crushed itself into Renée's chest and broken wedges of glass shot in every direction. Blood spurted over white leather seats as the horn blared.

The snow continued falling on this picture-postcard holiday night.

Chapter Forty-two

Paris. December 24. 6:20 P.M.

Henri counted the rings. Fifteen . . . sixteen. Désirée was not home at her London flat. He couldn't understand it. She had planned a large cocktail party for that night and it was due to begin at seven. He knew the caterer would have answered, even if Désirée had stepped out for a moment. Something was drastically wrong.

Henri placed a call to Désirée's assistant, Penny.

It was answered on the first ring.

"Merry Christmas to you, sir." Penny's voice was unusually strained.

"Merry Christmas to you. I was wondering if you knew anything about Miss Dubois. She doesn't seem to be answering her telephone this evening."

"I should guess not. . . ." Penny said hesitatingly.

"What are you talking about?"

"I'm not . . . supposed to say anything to you until after the holidays. Those were her instructions."

"Say anything about what?"

"Her resignation."

"Her what?"

"She had me type it up today. It's the only thing left on her desk. She cleared it out this morning."

He should have been prepared for this, but he wasn't. He should have known when she walked out, she meant out of his life—totally. He felt his insides ripping. He had to get her back. He had to tell her that he loved her.

"Penny, that still doesn't explain why she isn't at home tonight."

"I'm sorry, sir. I don't know why I thought you'd know."

"Know what?"

"She's left London. Gone home to Paris."

"Thank you, Penny."

"Merry Christmas again, sir."

New York City. December 24. 10:31 P.M.

Renée could hear sirens screaming inside her head. Or were they outside of her? She thought at one point she'd heard carols being sung by an enormous choir.

Why was it so difficult for her to breathe? She felt as if she were choking on her own vomit. No, it wasn't vomit, it was blood. She was being moved onto a bed, but it was rolling. It was warm now and not so cold.

She could hear people shouting orders all around her, but still everything was white. She couldn't tell if it was snowing, but then, it must have been because these people were covered with white snow. She coughed and choked again.

She couldn't see anything and she could not feel her body at all. She could hear voices and they said she was dying. She didn't want to die.

She heard them talking about cutting her throat. It was then she knew that the Nazis had come for her again. She was going to die and this time she knew she would not escape. She forced herself to open her eyes, but only managed a small slit. She strained her eyes and finally was able to see the man who loomed over her with a silver knife in his hand.

Was he going to cut off her ears like the Nazis in Paris? She wanted to fight him but she couldn't. She had to have help. Suddenly she saw Karl. Was he going to help her? Or was he there to welcome her to the other side?

Paris. December 24. 5:45 P.M.

Désirée stepped off the London-to-Paris shuttle hoping she could find the right words to say to her father . . . and later to Renée. Would he still hate her for leaving Paris? Would her mother ever forgive her for shunning her and rejecting all her efforts to reestablish bonds between them?

How could she ever forgive herself for the time she'd wasted? Valuable time. She had been presumptuous to think that she could go all her life without needing anyone. She had been such a fool. It would require a lot of love for them to take her back. She was afraid there wasn't that much love in the whole world.

The terminal was a sea of bustling bodies carrying extravagantly wrapped packages, suitcases, and duffel bags.

Then she saw them. Annette stood next to Pierre, her eyes filled with tears and a huge smile on her lips. Pierre seemed not as tall to her, and older than she remembered. His hair was completely white now, but his eyes still blazed with amethyst fire. They were joyful eyes and she could wait no longer to feel his arms around her.

"Papa!" she cried, bursting into tears.

"It's all right now, chérie," he said, stroking her hair. "You're home now and that's all that matters."

New York City. December 25. 6:42 A.M.

Grant followed the nurse out of Renée's intensive-care room to the nurses' station.

"The call was just put through. I'm sorry it took so long. I suppose with it being Christmas and all . . ." she said apologetically.

"Pierre?" Grant spoke into the receiver.

Possessing only a sketchy summary of the incident from the nurse, Pierre asked: "My God, Grant, how did it happen?"

"An automobile accident. The police here say it was a hit-and-run. Renée is in intensive care. They did a tracheotomy last night, but she's still having problems."

"Juliette is on another phone making flight reservations. We're all coming. I insisted that only I go, but Juliette and Annette were adamant."

"I don't blame them. Some Christmas, huh?"

"Grant . . . I have some good news."

"Tell me. I could use some about now."

"Désirée has come home. For good. She's left London."

Grant paused, wondering about the timing. Had Désirée known about their discovery? Did she think she could fool her father and her aunt or not? Grant was too tired, too worried about Renée, and too weary of it all to think about his niece's motives. "Will she want to fly to New York?"

"Yes. In fact, she's the one who is most insistent. It's like a miracle to me."

"It *is* curious. I know Renée will be glad to see her."

"What do the doctors say?"

"The worst is over, but they're keeping a close watch. I'll stay here and Gaston will pick you up at Kennedy."

"See you soon."

Paris. December 25. 9:00 A.M.

Henri walked into his grandmother's lavishly decorated house. The seventy-six-year-old butler took his hat, coat, and gloves. He wondered how Virginie had managed to keep the man in her employ for so many years. How had she manipulated him? Was there some scandal in his past that she used against him and now kept concealed in her desk drawer?

Virginie was all smiles when she greeted him. "Welcome, chéri! You're prompt as always. Emile has just made champagne cocktails. I thought them a bit strong for brunch, but he insisted, and since it was Christmas, I let him have his way."

"How generous of you," he said with sarcasm singeing his words.

Virginie's head cocked to the side momentarily, but when he smiled at her she again let her guard drop. It was the holidays. She did not tolerate unpleasantness on the holidays.

Lucienne sucked deeply on a gold-tipped Russian cigarette, exhaled, and smiled at him. She rose, smoothed the taffeta skirt of her Oleg Cassini dress, and placed a perfunctory kiss on his cheeks. She peered at him and he could tell instantly that she suspected something.

"You should take better care of yourself, Henri. You look like hell."

He accepted the drink from Emile and raised his glass.

"I want to toast you all for perpetuating the longest on-going illusion of all time."

Emile said nothing, only stared blankly at his nephew. Henri knew his brain was capable of no more. Virginie was shocked but covered her surprise. Only Lucienne seemed to know what he meant and what was about to happen. She made no attempt to hide the victorious glint in her eye. She sat on the sofa, folded her arms across her chest, and smiled as she waited for the performance to commence.

"Henri," Virginie said imperiously, "if this is about some disagreement we've had concerning business . . ."

"This is about life, Grandmother, but this time it is you who are going to be the pupil and I the teacher."

"You cannot speak to me like that, Henri," she said, clutching at the vestiges of her power.

"I can speak to you any way I choose. I'm not afraid of you, Grandmother. You can't hurt me or try to destroy me the way you have Lucienne and Emile." He held up his hand to stop her when she tried to speak. "I think I know how it must have been for my father with you. He was struggling to get out of your web, but you held him too tight. The only way he could save himself was to die. I pity him, but I understand him. Well, I don't have to die. All I have to do is walk away and that's just what I intend to do."

"Henri, you aren't making any sense at all!"

"I think this is the only time in my life I've made sense." He paused. "I went to your office and found a certain key that unlocked a drawer that contained all the answers I've been looking for."

Virginie's face was noticeably ashen, and trembling, she sought the support of the chair behind her as she continued to stare at her grandson . . . the heir to her empire.

"I know about Lucienne and the fact that she never loved Antoine. Ho! How you must have loved perpetuating that fairy tale for me. And Emile and the string of dead whores he's left across the continent."

"Whores aren't people."

"Is that how you justify his murders? Is that how you justified all these years that Renée Dubois was your enemy—*my* enemy? Because you labeled her a whore and she bore my father's son? My half brother?" He walked closer to her. "Or was it because my father loved her—and not you!"

Henri's fury raged white-hot in his eyes. He placed his hands on the side of her chair and leaned his face into hers so that he could stare all the way to her soul. It was just as he thought. She had none.

"I pity you, old woman. You have nothing left now, because there was nothing to begin with. You taught me never to trust and never to love anyone except you and the business, but I found out too late that neither of you gives anything back."

Virginie refused to answer and regarded him as one regards an errant child. She would let him have his say, then she would punish him.

Henri continued. "But then I got lucky. I found Désirée and she does have a heart and a soul and, until four days ago, she was willing to give me all of it. Can you believe that? A no-good, cruel, unloving . . . Ruille. . . . She was going to love me! It's incredible, isn't it? No one has ever told me they loved me except for Désirée. Do you know that, old woman? You never did. It took me four damned years to realize you are the reason I can't love her. It's such a simple thing to do. Why couldn't you do that?"

Henri was shaking. He wanted to take his hands and wrap them around her throat and choke the life out of her. But he knew it would do no good because she'd never been alive.

He had to get away from this house and the lunatics that lived here. He turned away from her and started for the door.

"Henri, come back here and apologize!" Virginie demanded, knowing he would return if she commanded him.

"I'm leaving, Grandmother!"

"No you aren't! You have no place to go. You just said so."

Suddenly he stopped and whirled around to face her for the last time. "Yes I do. I don't know a whole lot about love, but I do know that it can't be turned off and on like water. Désirée loved me four days ago. If she's willing to take me back, I'll make it worth her while. Because I do love her, I just have to find a way to show her."

Henri did not wait for the butler to bring his coat, but raced out the door and to his car. In less than two minutes, he'd put the château behind him.

Chapter Forty-three

New York. December 29.

Désirée took a deep breath as she grabbed the metal handle of her aunt's hospital-room door. She was thankful that Renée was not in danger any longer. Désirée had been to the hospital four times before, but always in the company of her parents. This time, Renée had specifically requested she come alone. She knew from the furtive looks Gaston had given her and the disappointment in Grant's eyes that they knew about the counterfeiting.

It was time for her to come face-to-face with her sin. She thought she could handle just about anything, but now she wasn't so sure.

She opened the door.

"Don't hang back," Renée said as she stood near the safety of the exit.

"I know why you want to see me."

Renée smiled, but winced at the pain from the deep gash in her cheek and the bruises around her left eye. "What makes you think you are so smart? Come," she said, patting the edge of the bed. "Sit next to me."

Désirée thought the lump in her throat would choke her before she got the first words out. "Can I ask you something?"

"Of course."

"Does Papa know?"

"No. Just myself, Gaston, and Grant."

"Thank God! I don't want him to know what a fool I was. I hated you for pushing me out of Maison Dubois like you did. I was so full of anger and spitefulness. I wanted to get even with you and make you hurt like I was hurting. I met Henri on my way back to London. I needed a job and he conveniently had one ready for me to step into. He always kept a low profile and no one other than my assistant knew that Henri was connected to the firm in any way. He was always talking about the necessity for discretion. I guess that's why no one in our family traced me to the Ruilles—until now. Anyway, I worked for him for over a year before the counterfeiting came into play. Henri told me his grandmother was putting up the money for the productions in Taiwan. I remember the night we went out and celebrated this great idea of hers. All Henri could think about was the money we would make. I wanted to prove I could run an enterprise just like Maison Dubois on my own. I wanted Papa to be proud of me, not ashamed."

Désirée burst into tears and couldn't go on. Renée put her arms around her niece and rocked her back and forth, just as she'd done with Pierre when he was a boy.

"I don't blame you, Désirée, you have to know that."

Désirée pulled back and searched Renée's eyes. "I betrayed you! How could you forgive that?"

"No, *I* betrayed you. I should never have let you go. When we had to borrow the money from the investors in Europe we were forced to agree to get rid of you. They were frightened of the bad publicity, afraid couture was at an end and that they would lose all their money. The only reason they lent us the million and a half was because of friendship. We felt we owed them for their loyalty. What we didn't realize was that we had a loyalty to our own first. And that was you. You have had to take the brunt of all this. You have been ostracized from your family and *that* is what is unforgivable. Désirée, chérie, I wanted you here so that I could beg your forgiveness, not the other way around."

"Aunt Renée, I've always wanted to be like you and now you make me feel more unworthy than ever."

"Don't ever say that, Désirée," Renée scolded. "You are a Dubois, you are family." She held her niece's face in her hands as she peered into lavender eyes. Dubois eyes. "I've always known you would be all right, Désirée. I never worried about you."

"Why is that?"

"Because deep down you knew that loving is the most important thing in life. Money and power are useless in the end—they pay bad returns."

Désirée squeezed Renée's hand. "I'm glad you and Papa were good teachers."

"So am I, chérie."

Epilogue

Henri Ruille juggled four pieces of burgundy luggage but managed to make it to an empty telephone at Kennedy Airport. He inserted a coin, checked the number on the piece of paper he'd kept clamped between his teeth, and dialed the number. It was ringing. He'd never been so nervous in his entire life.

A child answered the telephone. He could hear what sounded like a party going on in the background. People were laughing and talking. The child enunciated every syllable as precisely as she could.

"Dubois residence."

"Hello!" Henri said cheerfully. "To whom am I speaking?"

"This is Amie."

"Amie, I'm a friend of Désirée's. Is she there?"

"Yes," she said politely and dropped the receiver on the floor as she screamed Désirée's name.

When Désirée answered the phone, he thought his heart had stopped.

"Hello?"

Her voice had never sounded so sweet and never had he known it was possible to miss anyone quite as much as he'd missed her.

"Désirée?"

She gasped. "Henri? Is that you?"

"I love you, Désirée. I flew here to tell you that."

"You—you flew here? In New York? You're in New York?"

"Are you happy about that? Tell me, God, tell me you are happy about that."

"Why?" she asked skeptically. "Did your grandmother send you here to spy on me?"

"I have no further dealings with Virginie Ruille. I came here to be with you . . . if you'll have me."

Désirée was laughing and crying while she gave him the address. "Just get in the first taxi you see and come to me!"

Virginie Ruille sat in her library. The walls held only the finest grade moroccon leather-bound books. There were no unsightly paper jackets to destroy the "look." She sat in the same chair Louis XV had occupied when he ruled France. She replaced her Haviland china cup on its twenty-four-carat gold-banded saucer and glanced at the note Lucienne had sent.

She would not be in Paris for the New Year for she was sailing for the Orient with her friends, the Krakis. Virginie knew about the tightly knit Greek shipping family whose eldest daughter had proclaimed to the press that she was a lesbian. Virginie thought it disgusting and indiscreet of Lucienne to spend so much of her time with them over the past few years. Other than stating she would see her mother sometime in the late summer, there was nothing else on the card. Lucienne made it clear she did not need Virginie any longer—not even for money.

Virginie had miscalculated when it came to Lucienne, for her daughter had proven herself more a Ruille than any of the males in the family. Virginie had discovered the secret Swiss bank account Lucienne had kept for the past twenty years and the fact that all her residences were paid for—in full. All those times Lucienne had come begging to her for money and Virginie had relented, her daughter had neatly tucked the money away. And by declaring herself a lesbian, Lucienne had denied Virginie the one thing she had demanded of her daughter—grandchildren.

Emile had left the house drunk on Christmas Day and she had not heard from him since. He had not bothered to call her nor had he felt obligated to reply to her direct request for his presence for New Year's Eve dinner.

Virginie's New Year's Eve dinner had always been a tradition, more revered in the Ruille household than Christmas. There had been a time when her friends and family filled every chair in the house and three cooks were hired to prepare the vast amounts of food.

Virginie looked at her calendar. The dinner would have been yesterday, but there were no family, no children, no grandchildren, and no friends. She was one of the most powerful women in Europe and she had passed New Year's Eve—alone.

She looked out the leaded-glass window at the bare tree branches. From the deep recesses of the house she heard voices as the butler answered the door. The butler tapped his arthritic fingers on the library door.

"Come in."

He handed her a large brown mailing envelope, with a return address marked "R. Dubois."

"A special-delivery messenger brought it."

Virginie used the sterling silver letter opener to slit the flap. She withdrew a color photograph of the Dubois family.

Juliette and André stood on the far left with the twins, Michelle and Louis, in front of them. On the far right were Gaston, Kate, and Amie. Next to Pierre and Annette in the middle back row stood Désirée, her smile the broadest as she looked up into Henri's eyes.

Virginie's hands were trembling as she looked at the center of the photograph—at the woman with the bruised face and a patch over her cheek. She was holding her husband's hand and he was looking at her and not at the camera.

Virginie held the portrait up to the light and scrutinized the face of the woman in the center. It was still there in those flashing lavender eyes . . . that look of challenge and defiance she'd seen that day in her gardens.

Her fingers wanted to tear at those lavender eyes, but all she could do was rip the photograph to shreds and let the pieces fall around her. And when she looked down at the floor, they were all still looking up at her—taunting her.

Virginie pulled her sweater around her shoulders and looked out at the snow. When she leaned her head back against the chair, a lone tear trickled down her withered cheek.

It was her first tear.

THE IRRESISTIBLE NATIONWIDE BESTSELLER

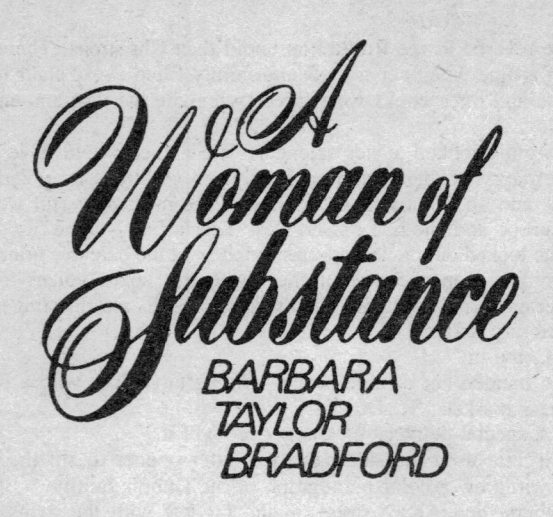

A Woman of Substance
BARBARA TAYLOR BRADFORD

Set against the sweep of 20th-century history, it tells the compelling story of Emma Harte, who rises from servant girl to become an international corporate power and one of the richest women in the world.

"A long, satisfying novel of money and power, passion and revenge." *Los Angeles Times*

"A wonderfully entertaining novel."

The Denver Post

49163-X/$4.50US/$5.95Can

An AVON Paperback

Buy these books at your local bookstore or use this coupon for ordering:

Avon Books, Dept BP, Box 767, Rte 2, Dresden, TN 38225
Please send me the book(s) I have checked above. I am enclosing $_____
(please add $1.00 to cover postage and handling for each book ordered to a maximum of three dollars). *Send check or money order*—no cash or C.O.D.'s please. Prices and numbers are subject to change without notice. Please allow six to eight weeks for delivery.

Name _____
Address _____
City _____ State/Zip _____

WOS 6/86